into the tide

Cottonwood Cove ~ Book 1

laura pavlov

Into the Tide
Cottonwood Cove, Book 1
Copyright © 2023 by Laura Pavlov
All rights reserved.

Laura Pavlov
https://www.laurapavlov.com

Cover Design: Emily Wittig Designs

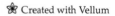 Created with Vellum

To anyone who has ever felt like they weren't enough…remember
that YOU ARE!
Be brave.
Be confident.
Be fearless…
BE UNAPOLOGETICALLY YOU.
Because you are enough.
xo ~ Laura

one

. . .

Hugh

I'D PLANTED my ass on a stool at the bar at Reynolds', the restaurant I'd opened a few months back. Business was booming, and between opening this place and running my parents' pub and diner for them, I was existing on very little sleep. I hadn't expected business to be as busy as it had been since the day we'd opened the doors. We were understaffed at the moment, and I needed help.

The door swung open, and sunlight flooded the space, highlighting the marble bar top and the rustic wood flooring. My two best friends, Travis and Brax, walked in, letting the door fall closed behind them.

"Hey, sorry we're late. I've got sandwiches." Travis held up a bag and walked toward me.

"Thanks for picking those up." I pushed to my feet and made my way around the bar to grab us each a drink. "You guys want a beer?"

"Hell, yeah." Brax pulled up a bar stool and sat down. The guy was always down for a good time.

"Nah. I've got to go back to work, so I'll just stick to water for now. Those fuckers on the site can't figure out how to hammer a nail unless I'm standing right over them," Travis grumped.

I laughed and handed them their drinks, grabbing a Coke for myself. Travis was a contractor and was responsible for the majority of the new construction in town. He'd worked on this restaurant for months, and the dude never let up. But he was a grumpy motherfucker, and most people pissed him off. Lucky for me and Brax, we'd been his best friends since preschool, so we usually got a pass.

"Are you sure you aren't just micromanaging them again?" I raised a brow and unwrapped my sandwich.

"Right. You're a bit of a dick when it comes to work. Are you sure this isn't you being a control freak?" Brax asked, over a mouthful of food.

Brax owned the largest real estate company in Cottonwood Cove, and he was about as relaxed as you get when it comes to running a business. These two were night and day with how serious they took things, and I fell somewhere in between.

"Pfft... please. I have no choice when every time I look over, they're fucking around." He shook his head before narrowing his gaze at me. "You look tired. I'm sure you're ready for Lila to start helping out." Travis's little sister was going to be home for a few months, and she'd agreed to come work with me at the restaurant.

"Yeah. You're giving me Trav-vibes over here, and I can't deal with two damn control freaks in my life." Brax reached for his beer.

"Yeah, I'm fucking drowning, man. The timing couldn't be better with her coming on board, even if it's just temporary." I took a bite of my turkey on rye and shrugged.

Travis studied me. "This place is a huge undertaking, and you're still trying to run Burgers and Brews and Garrity's. You can't be in three places at once, brother. And you're talking about expanding to the city? You need to figure out how to manage all this shit. Lila's brilliant, so hopefully she can help you get things figured out and running smoothly over the next few months."

He was right. I'd taken over our family restaurants when my father retired, and since opening my own place, I was stretched too thin.

"I can't believe I'm going to say this, but I actually agree. And you know it kills me to agree with this one," Brax said, as he flicked his thumb at Travis. "But you need help, or you're going to burn out."

"Agreed. And you know I don't like people in my business, but I obviously trust Snow," I said, after I finished chewing, referencing the nickname I'd always called Lila.

My siblings were all busy with their own careers, and my youngest sister, Georgia, was taking summer school classes and would be graduating from college in December. I sure as hell wasn't going to burden any of them with my shit.

"Yeah, I think she'll help out a lot, and then you can figure out if you need to bring on more people full time when she leaves. She'll definitely get your ass organized." Travis reached for his chips and tore open the bag.

"Aside from work, you look like you're wound awfully tight, so I'm guessing you haven't been laid in a bit either." Brax barked out a laugh. The dude was too loud for his own good. And, of course, the asshole found it hilarious that I was in a bit of a rut in that department. I hadn't been out in two months, and I slept every free minute that I had, but it still wasn't enough.

"Thanks for pointing that out, dickhead."

"You're a lover, man, so you're always moodier when you aren't getting female attention. No shame in needing a release, brother."

"Oh, for fuck's sake—he gets laid plenty. That's hardly been a problem for him." Travis rolled his eyes.

"Hey, maybe I'm tired of the game. I'm getting older. And

not all of us are so lucky to marry our fucking high school sweetheart," I said, shooting Travis a look.

He nodded over a mouthful of food and reached for his water. "Cry me a river. I'm not Hugh fucking Reynolds, Cottonwood Cove's biggest player."

"Don't be humble, you broody bastard. It doesn't suit you," I said.

"Please. This fucker doesn't have a humble bone in his body." Brax smirked. "Still not sure why Shay agreed to marry you and carry your moody-ass spawn... but I wouldn't look a gift horse in the mouth."

"You and me both, brother," Travis said.

"She's the best. Don't fuck it up." I reached for my glass and took a sip. They'd just found out recently that Shay was pregnant, and he was still processing the fact that he was going to be a father soon. "Anyway, Snow was in here last night with Delilah, Sloane, and Rina. Are you still pissed about her being back here?"

Travis's shoulders stiffened at the mention of his little sister's decision to come back home for a few months. I wouldn't bring up the fact that my dick had also stiffened at the sight of her last night. She'd always been gorgeous and sweet, but hell, when she left Cottonwood Cove four years ago, I'd looked at her more like a kid. But Lila fucking James wasn't a kid anymore. She'd just graduated from college and returned home. I'd always called her Snow for as long as I could remember, because the girl had watched *Snow White* more times than any one kid should, and her dark hair and all that sweetness made it an easy nickname to hold on to.

Travis loved the shit out of his wife, Shay, but anyone that knew him well knew that his kryptonite was Lila. They'd been through a shit ton at a young age, and he'd been looking out for her our entire lives. The number of dudes the three of us had threatened on her behalf over the years was countless.

And when she'd left for Northwestern in Chicago on a full cross-country scholarship, he'd been proud as hell. But I knew that it was tough for him having her so far away, as it had always been the two of them against the world.

"She's refusing to stay with me and Shay because she says we're newlyweds and are expecting our first baby, so she thinks we deserve some kind of bullshit privacy. My dad is a fucking train wreck, but that doesn't stop Lila from wanting to fix him. She's too fucking loyal. Too fucking stubborn. And too fucking good to be dealing with his shit. I'm sure it's a big adjustment, as she's been racing and competing for so long, and now that part of her life is over. And as much as I want her to come back home, I don't want her to get sucked into my dad's bullshit. She deserves better. She deserves more." He shook his head.

"Fuck, Trav. You've got to chill out. She's a grown-ass woman. I say this because I also ran into her last night when I stopped by to have a beer with this fucker," Brax said, raising a brow at me as if I didn't remember. "She was just leaving, and damn, your baby sister has grown up into a fine woman." He whistled, knowing it would get under Travis's skin. We'd seen her over the years since she'd gone away to school, and we'd always given him a hard time about how pretty she was.

"Fuck you. Don't be looking at Lila like that. She's still young. Far from a grown woman." Travis shot Brax a warning look. "She got offered a job at that big, fancy company she interned with this past year. She's so damn smart. They agreed to hold the position for her until the beginning of September so she could come home for a while and make sure Dad's okay. The man isn't going to change, so I don't know why she's insisting on putting her life on hold."

I understood his need to protect her, because I had two sisters that my brothers and I were protective over. But this was different. My siblings and I had two parents who worried about all of us plenty. But Travis was all Lila had unless you counted their father, who had checked out years ago.

"Let her come back for a little bit, spend some time with you and Shay. Maybe your dad will clean up his act while she's here, and then she'll head back to Chicago. She said the job is waiting for her, so let her take a few months and just relax."

"Jeez, man. I agree. The girl has worked her ass off. When we were younger, I can't remember a time that I saw her when she wasn't out on a run or training. It took her to college, where she spent four years going to class and racing. Let her have a break." Brax shook his head, and I chuckled because the dude was rarely logical, but this was the wisest thing he'd said in a while.

"She seems happy to be home. She's probably exhausted," I said.

"That's true. But I don't like her living at Dad's house. He runs with some shitty people, per usual. I don't want her around all that, you know?" Travis balled up the paper that had been wrapped around his sandwich and set it on the bar.

I understood his concern. We'd always looked out for her. There was a few years between us in age, and, at times, I knew she resented the way Travis, Brax, and I treated her like she was a little kid. And if I were being honest, I didn't particularly like the idea of her staying at her father's house either.

"You know I've got the casita at my place, so I'll offer it to her when she comes in this week to talk about the job and what she'll be doing. Georgia plans on moving in there after she graduates, but that won't be until after Snow heads back to Chicago." Georgia was my baby sister, the youngest of us Reynolds kids. We were close, and she had already called dibs on the private guest suite, after I bought the run-down cabin two years ago and completely renovated it.

He was nodding around a mouthful of food. His shoulders had completely relaxed.

"Thanks, brother. I owe you one for this."

"Should I be offended that you didn't ask me to hire her? We can always use an extra hand at the office, and I'll bet there'd be a lot of dudes in Cottonwood Cove buying homes if Lila was working there," Brax said as he waggled his brows mischievously.

"Fuck you, asshole. Not a chance. Hugh would never cross that line, but *you* think with your dick too much."

I barked out a laugh when Brax gaped as if he'd just been slapped in the face.

"Hugh thinks with his dick, too. Just ask Tory Hopkins. She drunk-cried to me last week about the way you rocked her world and then left her high and dry." Brax finished off the last pull from his beer.

I shook my head. "You asshole. Why are you even talking to her about that? We dated in high school, and, if you recall, I found her under the bleachers giving Tony Randall a blowie. So, she can spin that shit however she wants, but I didn't leave her high and dry. I left her with Tony's dick in her mouth. It's not my problem that she still misses mine all these years later."

"And this is exactly why neither of you fuckers are allowed near Lila. But at least I know this one is loyal as hell, and he'd never make that mistake. You, on the other hand... I'm not sure you wouldn't cross that line."

"Fuck off. Have I ever crossed the line?" Brax held up his hands as if he were completely offended.

"You did fuck my high school girlfriend," Travis reminded him.

"You were on a break!" Brax shouted. "And no offense, but everyone fucked Donna. She was a busy girl."

"Hugh didn't, and if you'll recall... *neither did I.*" Travis tried to hide his smile. It was an ongoing joke between the three of us. Donna had strung him along for a year and a half, which was a lifetime for a teenage boy. She'd claimed she was saving herself for marriage. And then she'd dumped him and proceeded to get busy with everyone he knew.

But not me.

I wasn't that guy.

I loved women, and I enjoyed sex. I dated plenty, but I preferred to keep things casual. Hadn't found any reason not to yet. And I respected bro code and took that shit seriously.

Brax did, too. He just talked a big game.

"All right, I need to get back to the office." He grabbed his wrapper and dropped it in the bag before pushing to his feet and clapping me on the shoulder. "Thanks for helping out Lila."

"Of course. You know I'd do anything for her."

He saluted me and Brax before making his way out the door.

"I guess I better get back and make sure everyone's working. We're busier than usual," Brax said. "So, you sure you can handle having Lila working here?"

His tone was all tease, but I knew what he was insinuating.

"Of course. I've known her my entire life, and she's Travis's sister. No problem. Some of us can control our dicks." I raised a brow and gave him a hard look. I'd always looked at Lila like a little sister. And sure—I wasn't blind—she was fucking gorgeous now.

But unlike Brax, I knew when someone was off limits.

And I didn't appreciate the way he was talking about her.

"Yeah, yeah, yeah. But damn, she looks good, man. And she's smart and has her shit together. It might not be as easy as you think, brother." He smirked before clapping me on the shoulder. "But I'll be here to talk some sense into you when you waver."

"Never going to happen. Get to work, jackass."

He raised his hand over his head and walked out the door.

I chuckled about the fact that Brax was worried. I'd never had a problem controlling myself around women. I wasn't that guy.

This would be a piece of cake.

two

. . .

Lila

"HEY, GIRLS," I said, as I sat down at the table across from my three best friends I'd grown up with. We were finally old enough to drink at Garrity's bar, and last night we went to Reynolds', so we were proudly flaunting the fact that we were all twenty-two now and could hit any bar in town. We hadn't gone to the same colleges, but we'd stayed in touch and remained just as close over the years.

"I can't believe we're getting together two days in a row," Sloane said as she pointed to the mug of beer they'd gotten me. "Drink up, girl. We all walked here, so we're good to go."

The place was fairly quiet, nothing like the crowd over at Reynolds' last night. It was an older group here, all locals, most of whom had stopped me on my way in to say hello. I'd hugged each one and answered the four hundred rapid-fire questions they'd asked me.

J.R., an older man I'd known my entire life, came waltzing over to our table. The man had a personality bigger than life, and I'd always loved seeing him. He rarely said the right thing, offended most people he spoke to without realizing it, and everyone in town loved him for it.

"Well, looky here. If these aren't the four best-looking

heifers I've ever seen," he said, slapping his hand down on our table. He was tall with gray hair and a gray beard and had been the town Santa Claus at the winter festival every year for as long as I could remember.

Del groaned. "J.R., did you really just call us cows?"

"I called you heifers. It's the ultimate compliment you can pay a woman," he said, raising a brow at her before winking at me when I smiled at him. I think he enjoyed ruffling people's feathers.

"Who told you that? I'm guessing it was a highly intoxicated man." Rina chuckled.

"There is not a woman on the planet who finds being called a cow the ultimate compliment. Lucky for you, we're not easily offended," Sloane said, and she blew him a kiss because we adored the goofy guy.

"Well, good. Because you're my favorites, and I'm happy to see this one back home." He flicked his thumb at me. "Take care, ladies. My wife looks all huffy over there. I think she's getting jealous, so I need to get back."

We waved goodbye and laughed some more about the heifer comment when he walked away. Seventies music piped through the speakers, and I bopped my head to "Y.M.C.A." when the beat started. Garrity's smelled like garlic and butter at all times. They had a limited menu of appetizers and a full bar.

"We've got lots of catching up to do." Rina held up her glass and waited for us all to follow. "Cheers to being reunited and to Lila finally being at home for longer than a half a second."

I smiled and tapped my glass with theirs. "It was hard to get away with all the training, racing, and classes. I've basically just been surviving these last four years."

I also had no money for things like plane tickets home and travel beyond where my races took me. My friends never had to worry about that kind of stuff, and I tried not to complain about the fact that I did. My dad had come out to visit me two times over the four years I'd been at school to celebrate Christmas with me, and Travis usually came at least twice a year to visit and see my races. He'd offered to fly me home a few times, but he always preferred to come to me. I knew he thought that he was protecting me from our father by keeping me away.

But I did not need protecting from my own dad.

Next to Travis, my father was the only family I really had, unless you counted grandparents who lived across the country and had never been very involved in our lives.

"I'm so glad I got to be there to see you win nationals," Del beamed.

Delilah McCallister was the best friend I'd ever had. She, Sloane, Rina, Travis, Shay, Hugh, and Brax had all been at that finish line, cheering for me at nationals. I'd wished my dad could have been there, but I knew better than to push Travis about it. They didn't get along, and they hadn't for a very long time.

I knew when to pick my battles.

My father had watched me on TV, as had most of the people in Cottonwood Cove. I'd felt pretty damn good to have their support when I was so far away.

"Me, too. I can't tell you how much it meant to me that you were all there."

"We wouldn't miss seeing you fly down that final stretch for anything in the world." Sloane smiled before taking a long pull from her beer.

"I was on FaceTime with Parker, screaming as you came around that final corner, so he could watch, too," Rina said, referring to her boyfriend whom she now lived with.

"Tell her what you did." Sloane used her hand to cover her mouth, and I looked between them trying to figure out what I was missing.

"Sloane Carpenter! You promised you wouldn't tell

anyone." Rina was laughing now and shaking her head. "So maybe I got so excited I peed my pants. That was such a close race. You caught her right before you both crossed the finish line."

Now all four of us were laughing, and I reached for her hand. "I think I peed my pants when I basically had to throw my body across the finish line."

"So, if we're being completely honest... I actually shit my pants last week in the car when I left Cottonwood Cove Café. I swear Mrs. Runither put something in her mac and cheese because that shit *runneth* right through me. No pun intended." Sloane shrugged as if this were just common small talk.

The table erupted in laughter. Damn, I'd missed my girls. Missed being home.

"Did she grill you about your sex life?" Delilah asked once she composed herself. "That woman has no shame. It's really gotten out of control."

Loretta Runither had been born and raised in Cottonwood Cove. She was in her mid-sixties, but it was impossible to tell her age because she was always getting work done. Her brows hadn't moved since the day I'd met her as a little kid, and her lips were extremely plumped and overlined in her signature tangerine lip color.

"Oh, yes. She straight up asked me how many dudes I've been with. I mean, she didn't say dudes. She said, 'You kids are so different these days. I'm guessing you got your cherry popped in college?' Like, excuse me, but who the hell asks someone that? She's got some weird obsession with everyone's virginity. And how does she know I'm not a virgin? I'm offended both ways—one, that she is basically slut-shaming me and two, that she thinks she can ask a woman something so personal. I'm offended for all the feminists on the planet and all the virgins—*no offense, Lila.*"

My mouth fell open, and I leaned forward to whisper. "Keep your voice down. And I'm not totally a virgin, but thank you for pointing that out. You're no better than Mrs. Runither."

Sloane's hand hit her chest. "*No. You. Didn't*. A. We're best friends. We're allowed to ask this shit about one another. B. You *are* a virgin. You have not had sex, and that, by definition, makes you a virgin."

"Well, she's rounded second base, or is it third base?" Rina asked.

"Oh, God. Please stop." I shook my head and reached for my beer. "I'm not against having sex. It's not like I'm holding out for marriage or anything. I just haven't felt it with anyone, you know?"

"You do not need to explain yourself to us or to Mrs. Runither," Delilah said, over her laughter. "You'll know when it's right. There's no hurry. Plus, I didn't think Jeremy was the right guy for you."

"Damn, he was easy on the eyes, though. Think of the little running superstar babies you would have had with that guy." Sloane held up her hand and ordered us another round. I glanced around the bar for Hugh, but I figured he was working at Reynolds' tonight. Marcy Stevens had worked here for years, and I assumed she was sort of head honcho over here now.

"Jeremy is such a great guy, and I really tried to make that work, but I just didn't feel the attraction. It was more of a friendship. Maybe something's wrong with me." I shrugged. Being a twenty-two-year-old virgin hadn't been the plan, but trust didn't come easy for me. And the few guys I'd dated just didn't feel right. It hadn't been the way I'd imagined it should be. Unless I was just broken, which was a possibility. Hell, no one would be surprised if that were true. I'd sure tried hard to prove to everyone that I wasn't, but at the end of the day, the best grades, a national collegiate title—none of that changed the way most people here looked at me.

The sad look in their eyes when they spoke of my mother.

Her life taken way too soon. The empathy about the poor little girl growing up without a mama.

The daughter of a drunk.

The gossip mill in Cottonwood Cove had been rampant about the visits my father had received from Child Protective Services at our home over the years.

Apparently, Travis and I were supposed to end up being deadbeats.

And we'd both done pretty damn well if you asked me.

Aside from this pesky V-card that I was somewhat desperate to lose at this point.

"Nothing is wrong with you," Delilah insisted. The girl had always been my biggest cheerleader. My ride or die. The girl who would keep your secret if her life depended on it.

"I think the pressure of losing your virginity is too built up now. You need to have a fling your first time. No pressure. No expectations. You're looking at every guy like they have to be a future husband. Just look at them and know they have a dick, and that's all that really matters at this point." Sloane laughed so hard, we all gaped at her.

"That's quite possibly the worst advice I've ever heard," Delilah said as Marcy set down a basket of garlic bread and chicken fingers, and we all dove in.

"Agreed. But, I do think there's something to what she's saying." Rina placed some food on her plate and thought over her next words before she spoke. "Maybe you don't have to look at them as *just a penis*. However, the fling idea isn't a bad idea. No expectations. I think you felt all kinds of pressure with Jeremy because he was all in, and you thought if you did the deed, you'd have to stay with the guy. No, you need a one and done, and then it's behind you."

"You guys, I'm not afraid of sex," I said over my laughter. "I wasn't looking at Jeremy like he needed to be husband material. Hell, the guy would make the best husband. He's loyal and kind and honest and sweet. I just felt nothing when

I kissed him, and I hate saying that. I tried for a few months, hoping it was just nerves or something, but it wasn't. And him being a teammate made it even more awkward. I was actually more attracted to that guy I made out with my junior year, Carmine."

"The one with the tattoos and the cigarette breath?" Rina asked as she fanned her face.

"Yep. The one you guys pushed on me when you came to visit, and we all went out. I mean, I couldn't stand his personality, but he had those dangerous vibes, and at least I felt something when I kissed him."

"Damn, I bet he had a big schlong. He kind of radiated that big-dick energy." Sloane reached for the beer Marcy had just set down and took a sip.

"You can't tell the size of a man's penis by his attitude," Rina said, shaking her head and smiling. "No freaking way."

"I disagree. There are a few men who just have it. You just know they're packing, right?"

"Name one." Delilah raised a brow and crossed her arms over her chest as if the whole conversation was absurd. Which it was, but I loved every second of it.

"Hugh Reynolds. My God, have you seen the hands on that man? I'll bet women tear at that long hair when they're in the throes of passion with that sexy god."

Rina spewed beer across the table and started coughing profusely. I patted her on the back, but we were all laughing so hard, it was challenging to be of help to her.

"I'm not even going to argue with that one. Sorry, Lila. I know he's your brother's best friend, but there's no way she's wrong about him." Rina wiped her mouth with a napkin before cleaning up the beer on the table and leaning in close to whisper. "You know how he dated Kara Whooters for a short time?"

"Yes." I raised a brow, wondering where this was going.

"She said he gave her three orgasms in one night. *Three.* Ummm, have any of you ever experienced that?"

"Holy shitballs. Boomer needs to up his game." Sloane rubbed her hands together.

"Well, I don't know how to even respond to this breaking news. But I do have a meeting with him tomorrow about the job he offered me." I shrugged.

"That's who you should have sex with," Sloane said too loudly, and we all looked around to make sure no one was listening, and I shot her a warning look. "What? It could be a job perk. He's experienced and obviously a great lover. The man just knows how to please his women. I swear I orgasmed when he asked me how my beer was last night. That voice. Those hands. That freaking *hot Jesus hair*. I am here for all of it."

"Does Boomer know that you've put this much thought into the way Hugh Reynolds pleases his women?" Delilah asked, because Sloane and Boomer had been dating since high school.

"Please. Boomer doesn't worry about that. Not with all the sex we're having since we moved in together. But there's no shame in looking, as long as you don't touch, right? And you could make this happen while you're here."

"What if you made a list of all the things you want to do while you're home? You know, like a bucket list. You have this other life out in Chicago where you're this superstar runner and a big-time businesswoman, but you're here for a few months. You can do all the things you want while you're sort of on this break from your regular life. Like girls gone wild on spring break in Miami Beach, this is summer break in Cottonwood Cove, Lila-style. Find a guy to have a fling with and knock it right off the list," Rina said as she smiled at Sloane, and they nodded like this was a genius plan.

"For God's sake, you two. It's not a grocery list; it's her

virginity. It's not something you check off a list." Delilah was always the voice of reason.

"You lost your V-card to Scotty Manchester. He had chronic tuna breath. I think that was something you checked off a list," Rina said with a smirk.

"You know, some people think that his tuna breath is because ole Scotty-boy likes to head down south more than your average man." Sloane waggled her brows before holding up her hand for another round.

"I assure you, that is not the reason for Scotty's tuna breath." Delilah raised a brow, and we all lost it again. I polished off my beer around a fit of laughter. It felt good to be here with them, having a great time just like we always did. I didn't have to worry about practice the next day, or racing, or midterms or finals. I didn't have to worry about making sure I secured a job for my future. I felt like just a normal person for the first time in my life, if I were being honest with myself. I wasn't driving toward some epic dream or trying to accomplish something that everyone thought would be impossible.

Unless you counted losing my virginity, which had apparently become the impossible dream.

I'd planned to lose it a few different times, but it just hadn't happened.

We spent the rest of the night carrying on like fools, drinking far too much, and I slept at Del's place. She lived with her sister, Jory, and we'd tiptoed in way too late. But it felt like old times, having sleepovers and laughing with my friends.

It was exactly what I needed.

———

The next morning, my head pounded as I walked to Reynolds' Bar and Grill. I'd hurried home and taken a quick shower and pulled myself together. I hadn't ever been hungover because I'd always been too busy to allow myself to feel like crap the next day. I had always been very consistent about my work ethic, so I was embracing my inner rebel as I pulled open the door.

"Bear?" I called out, because I didn't see anyone in the bar area. I'd called him that since we were kids. He'd called me Snow, and I'd called him Pooh Bear, but he'd insisted I drop the Pooh when we got older. I still laughed when I thought about the way he'd tried to gently ask me to just use Bear because he didn't want to hurt my feelings.

Hugh Reynolds was a huge man with a big personality, who women had chased for as long as I could remember—but to me, he'd just been Bear. Charming and protective and kind. Sure, I'd gotten mad at him and Trav and Brax more times than I could count for running off any boy who tried to talk to me when I was in high school. I probably had those three to blame for my current situation, although they hadn't followed me out to college, so I guess that was on me.

He came around the corner, carrying a large box in his big arms. I couldn't help but zone in on his hands now that Sloane had mentioned them.

My God, those were some giant hands.

He set the box on the bar and reached up for the brim of his navy baseball cap, spinning it around in one quick movement. The man managed to make turning a cap around on his head look like the sexiest thing I'd ever seen.

"There she is. I heard you were out getting into trouble at Garrity's last night." He smirked.

Dark, thick hair that stopped at his shoulders and sage-green eyes framed by long, black lashes. He had more facial hair now than he did a few years ago when I left for school, and it worked for him. I'd always known Hugh was beautiful, but it was more than just physical. He was smart and loyal and funny, and people had always been drawn to him.

I'd been more of a sit-back-and-observe kind of gal, and I'd admired the way he owned every room he entered.

"The gossip mill is still rampant in Cottonwood Cove, I see." I raised a brow and moved toward him as he wrapped his arms around me.

He smelled like leather and cedar and sexy man.

Was that a thing?

No one had ever smelled sexy to me, but it didn't surprise me that Hugh did.

And I probably reeked of day-after tequila and nachos.

He pulled back and smiled. "Come on. Take a seat and fill me in. What can I get you to drink? I heard you're a tequila girl now."

He made his way around the bar, and I sat on the stool and dropped my purse onto the marble bar top.

"Please don't say that word," I said as I rubbed my temples. "A water would be great. How do you know what I was drinking?"

"I stopped by to help close down Garrity's last night, and Marcy said you all had just left and that you were having a good time. I think that's good for you, Snow. You deserve to cut loose for once in your life." He slid the water toward me and then unbuttoned the cuffs of his white button up and rolled them up a few times, exposing the inked muscle on his forearms as he leaned forward. His veins bulged against his tanned skin, and the move was so sexy that I squeezed my thighs together in response.

Hello, hormones.

What the hell was that about?

The man shows me his forearms and my body finally reacts for the first time ever?

It must be the remnants of tequila left over in my body.

I'm guessing booze and sexy boys go together—maybe that's where I'd gone wrong.

All work and no play had landed me with a college degree and no life experience.

"I think you're right about that, Bear. Time to live a little, huh?"

"I think that's a good thing. I still can't get over seeing you win that national title," he said, as the corners of his mouth twitched, and he smiled. Had I ever paid this much attention to a man's movements before?

"I still can't believe you all came for my final race." I shrugged.

"Damn straight. I followed your career pretty closely. Looking up all your results online and watching you kick ass over the years," he said. "It's amazing. You deserve it all. How do you feel being back here?"

"Aside from my brother having a temper tantrum about it, it feels really good to be home."

"He's worried about you being pulled into your dad's mess. It's fair, right?"

God. Why did Hugh have to be so logical?

"My dad's not perfect, but he's human. We're all flawed, aren't we? I don't know why Trav can't ever give him a pass."

Hugh's tongue dipped out, sliding along his bottom lip, and he tucked his hair behind his ear. I sucked in a breath and had the sudden desire to run my fingers through his hair.

"You still want to save the world, huh, Snow?"

"I'd be fine just saving my father."

He studied me for a long minute before he nodded. "I get that. So, you'll spend the summer here and then head back to that big-time job you've got waiting for you."

Travis was so determined for me to leave. But I liked being home. I'd missed it.

"That's the plan. Thanks for offering me a job. So, when can I start?"

"Of course. I mean, you're slightly overqualified, but I

could use the help. Maybe you can figure out how to get things running smoother because I'm fucking tired."

"There's nowhere else I'd rather be." Why was my voice all husky and breathy?

Thank you, hangover, for making me sound like a cat in heat.

He smiled. "Well, good. Because I need you, Snow."

Oh, yeah. This man definitely gave a woman three orgasms in one night.

No doubt about it.

"Good. Because I'm all yours."

What? Did that sound as inappropriate aloud as it sounded in my head?

I'd been home for two days, and my dad seemed happy to have me here.

I had a job and a sexy-as-sin boss.

Obviously, nothing could ever happen with him.

It was Hugh Reynolds, for God's sake.

But that didn't mean I wouldn't enjoy spending my working hours with him.

Things were looking up in Cottonwood Cove.

three

. . .

Hugh

"HOW'S IT GOING IN HERE?" I asked, as I came around
the corner and paused in my office doorway. Lila had been
working here for a week, and she'd already eased my work-
load tremendously. She was a numbers girl. So, she was going
through all the books to see where I needed to increase and
decrease my spending. I was more of a people guy. I enjoyed
the customers and the employees. The creative part. The
books, the money—I'd never been great at that end of the
business.

"You can definitely afford to bring on more help and cut
back your hours. It's Sunday, and you should have at least
one day off a week." She raised a brow, and her dark gaze
locked with mine, and I swear my dick responded like she
was directly looking at him. Her long, brown hair fell in
waves down her shoulders, and a speckle of freckles was scat-
tered around her nose. I didn't know when Lila James grew
into the sexiest woman I'd ever seen, but she had. And that
did not sit well with me. She was Travis's little sister for
starters. Completely off limits. She wasn't sticking around for
long. And I'd never been great at the relationship game
anyway. I was selfish. I worked a lot, and when I wasn't

working, I liked to do what I wanted to do. Take out the boat in the summers and ski in the winters.

So, I kept my attachments light and drama free. Dinner with a gorgeous woman, followed by a round of good sex— that was more my style. Looking at Lila as anything more than a friend would be an asshole move. She was innocent and sweet and far too smart for my dumb ass. It was just an attraction, nothing more. I prided myself on self-control, so I'd rein it in.

Starting right now.

"Well, *you're* here on a Sunday. I told you to take the day off." I moved inside and sat in the chair across from her.

"I just wanted to finish going through this month's expenses and get you all caught up. Dad had a church meeting and a dinner afterward, so he's busy today." She turned away from the large monitor on my desk and set the calculator aside before leaning back in my desk chair.

I internally called bullshit on Tate James.

The man was definitely not at church today. He had a massive drinking and prescription drug problem, and everyone here knew it. Travis had all but cut ties with the man, but Lila was a different story. A bleeding heart who'd always seen the best in people.

I admired it, but I didn't agree with it.

I wasn't as cut and dry as Travis was, but I also knew when to walk away from people. Tate was a train wreck and always had been. He'd fucked up more times than any man should be allowed to. He'd always pull his shit together for a short time and then go off the rails again. It was a pattern that repeated itself over and over for as long as I'd known them, which had been most of my life.

Things had gotten worse when Lila left for college. Travis tried to protect her and keep her away, but Tate had recently been hospitalized twice for liver disease amongst other health issues, likely due to his lifestyle, and he'd said what he needed to say to get Lila back here for the summer.

"Yeah? How's he doing? You've been staying there for a week. Is everything okay?" I asked. I'd offered her my casita, but she'd wanted to be close to her father, and she'd also said something about not needing any handouts. She was too proud for her own damn good.

"He's doing well, Bear. I know no one thinks he is, but I haven't seen him take a sip of alcohol since I've been home, and I went through all his meds, and he's only taking the medication that he was prescribed from the hospital." Tate's drug of choice had always been prescriptions since he'd hurt his back years ago when his kids were young, so she was clearly worried that he'd have a slipup now. Lila wasn't willing to admit that he'd never really stayed clean long enough to even call it a slipup. "I think getting sick so much and finding out his liver isn't in great shape really scared him. It was the wake-up call he needed." She smiled like she couldn't contain her pride, and my chest squeezed.

His wake-up call should have been leaving his young kids in a car while he was bar hopping all those years ago, or the fact that he'd neglected his young daughter so badly that she'd ended up hospitalized for two weeks with pneumonia when she was only seven years old. Tate had been too far gone to spend his days with her in the hospital, but her brother had been there every day. CPS had been notified by the hospital that there were signs of neglect, which was the reason Travis and Lila had been put into the system and were separated from one another for a brief time. Lila just never wanted to see any of it, while Travis couldn't forget a single detail.

I grazed my hand over the scruff peppering my chin. I wouldn't take this moment from her, even if I knew it wasn't what she hoped it was. "Well, that's great that he's taking care of himself. So how about you come with me to Sunday dinner with the family? I'm heading over there, and everyone's home, which doesn't happen often, and they'd love to see you."

She bit down on her plump bottom lip and thought it over. "Are you sure? I don't want to intrude."

"Are you kidding? They all watched you race at nationals. You were blowing up the family group chat. They'd love to see you. My mom keeps asking when you're going to come by. Come on. You'll eat a good dinner, and everyone will fawn all over you. Let's go."

"I always did love your mama's cooking. Remember when she spent an entire Saturday teaching me how to cook when I was maybe fifteen years old, and I'd complained about eating mac and cheese every day?" She laughed, but I didn't find it funny. The lack of care that she and Travis received from their father most of their lives wasn't something I could pretend didn't happen. The way my best friend had been forced to grow up so quickly, doing everything he could to protect Lila. She pushed to her feet and came around the desk, and I followed her toward the door.

"I do remember that, because Trav and I got to sample all the dishes you guys made. It was not a bad deal for us," I said, as my hand found her lower back. We made our way through the restaurant, and I guided her toward the exit. The place was going off, per usual, but between Danielle, who'd been waitressing for me since we opened the doors here, and Kline, who was my lead bartender, they had it handled. They'd agreed to close up on Sundays for me. I still came in for a few hours, but it would be nice to go to dinner and not have to come back here and close up at least one night a week.

I held up my hand to Kline to let him know I was leaving as we walked by the bar.

"Have a good night, boss. You taking Lila with you?" he said as he leaned over the bar to speak to us.

"Yep. Family dinner tonight," I said, watching as his gaze moved to Lila, and he literally perused her body with no shame at all.

The fucker.

Stick to pouring cocktails, dickhead.

Kline was a great employee, but would I want him dating my sisters? Hell, no.

Lila was included in that mix. I'd always felt protective over her.

"Damn. I was going to see if you wanted to grab a drink with me after work tonight, Lila." He waggled his brows at her, and I fought the urge to pull him over the bar and shove the bottle he was holding up his ass.

"Hey, how about you get back to the customers and stop harassing the employees?" I growled, catching Kline completely off guard.

"Sorry, brother. Just offering a pretty lady a drink. I meant no offense." He held up his hands and raised a brow as if he were confused by my reaction.

I should feel like a dick, but I didn't.

"You're fine. He's overreacting, as usual." Lila shot me a look and then turned back to Kline. "How about tomorrow night?"

What the fuck?

Kline smiled. "Yeah, sure. That would be great."

"We're going to be late. Let's go." I placed my hand on her elbow and led her toward the door.

"You leaving?" Brandy asked. She'd been our hostess here for the last few months, and the girl was nosy as fuck for a seventeen-year-old who should be more interested in what her friends were doing than what I was doing. I wasn't in the mood for the inquisition that always came when I saw her, so I tried to make a fast dash out the door.

"Yes. Family dinner. Kline's locking up."

"Are you going to family dinner, as well, Lila?" she asked

when we were one step out the door.

"Yes. I am." Lila paused to look at her with confusion. "Why do you ask?"

"I just, well, I know you've been gone for a while. And I just didn't know you were still so friendly with the family."

What the fuck was happening here? Between Kline and Brandy, I was getting agitated, which was not the norm for me.

"She's always been a family friend. No explanation needed." I shot her a warning look that basically said to step the fuck off, and her eyes widened.

I pushed open the door, and we made our way outside, and I led her to my truck. I loved the weather this time of year. It was warmer in the day but cooler at night down by the water. Reynolds' was only a block from the cove, so the ocean breeze swirled around us.

I tugged open the door, climbing in, and I reached for the seat belt and pulled it across her body.

"What are you doing, Bear? I can buckle my own seat belt." She shook her head and chuckled.

"Old habits die hard, Snow," I said as I clamped it into the metal bracket beside her before shutting her door and making my way to the driver's side.

Lila fell forward and started laughing once I pulled out of the parking lot. Her hands were on her knees, and she finally looked up at me.

"What's so fucking funny?" I asked, still irritated that my own damn employees harassed us on our way out the door.

"Well, first off," she said, sitting back upright. "I'm a grown woman, and I don't need you buckling my seat belt or biting off Kline's head for asking me to have a drink."

"He's a fucking player, Snow. I don't want you getting mixed up in that."

"You do know I've been living on my own for the last four

years, right? I am very capable of deciding what and *who* I want."

Now it was my turn to shoot her a look. "Is that right? And you think you want Kline fucking Barley?"

"I'm not saying that I do. I'm just saying that I can speak for myself. And since when do you hate the guy so much? He's your head bartender."

"I don't hate Kline. He's a great fucking bartender. I just don't like him for you."

"The last thing I need you doing is deciding who you like or don't like for me. Same with Travis and Brax. I'm not a kid anymore."

I nodded. "I know. I just want you to tread carefully with Kline. He's a good employee, and if he hurt you, I'd be forced to fire him and then I'd have to kill him. And that just gets messy."

Her head fell back in laughter again, and she glanced over and smiled at me. "Shall we talk about the girl who is barely old enough to have a driver's license and wants to claw my eyes out every time I'm around you?"

"Fucking Brandy. Her dad is Coach Benson, and he was my baseball coach. He called in a favor to get her the job, but she's a nosy little thing, right?"

"Umm… nosy isn't exactly what I would use to describe her. I'd say she's developed quite the crush on you, Bear." She covered her mouth with her hand to muffle her laughter. "You always had a way with the ladies, and that obviously hasn't changed. The long hair, the scruff, it only adds to the appeal."

My dick strained against my zipper, and I adjusted myself as slyly as I could. For whatever reason, getting praise from Lila, and the way her gaze scanned over me before quickly turning away, had the big guy standing at attention.

"You like the hair and the scruff, Snow?" I said, and a pink hue climbed her neck and covered her cheek.

I shouldn't have said it. I was playing with fucking fire.

"Doesn't everyone?" she purred.

Damn. I was going to need a cold-ass shower tonight.

"I'm not sure about that. So, what's your story? Your brother said you were dating some guy who was on your cross-country team. Jeremy? Is that still a thing?" We turned the corner, as my parents lived just a few blocks away from downtown, and I pulled into the driveway of the ranch house where I'd grown up.

"Nope. I'm single and ready to mingle," she said and nervously waved her hands around as she laughed.

"You're fucking cute as hell, Snow." I roughed a hand over her hair after I turned off the engine. "But be on guard with my brother. God knows Finn will be hitting on you if you let him. Cage is too uptight to try it when he's with Gracie."

"Stop worrying, *Dad.*" She smirked as we both climbed out of the truck. "I can handle myself. I'm so excited to see Gracie. I haven't seen her in a long time. Cage is still doing the single-dad thing?"

"He is. And he's damn good at it. We all help when we can. She's the fucking cutest kid on the planet." I reached for the knob and held the front door open, and she stepped inside.

"Wow, they've done some renovations," she said, spinning around to take it all in.

"Yeah, you know my mom and her house decorating skills. She's always making changes and redoing things." I closed the door, and the chatter coming from the kitchen was loud, per usual.

"Hello?" I shouted, my hand grazing Lila's. I glanced over to see she looked a little nervous, and my finger wrapped around her pinky instinctually, to comfort her.

"You good?" I leaned down, my forehead almost touching hers as I assessed her.

"Of course. I just haven't seen everyone in a while. I hope I'm not underdressed." She shrugged.

"You're perfect." As the words left my mouth, I saw a blur in my peripheral, and my baby sister, Georgia, came charging toward me like a fast-moving train. My hand moved from Lila's as I braced for impact. Georgia was a firecracker at all times, and we'd always been close. She wrapped her arms around me and hugged me tight. "Thank God, you're here. There are all sorts of *'what are your plans for the future'* talks going on, and I can't handle it. And, oh my gosh, is that Lila?" My sister squealed and shoved away from me before barreling into the woman beside me. They'd grown up together, being in the same grade their entire lives.

"Hi, Georgia. It's so good to see you." They held hands after they broke away from their hug and beamed at one another.

"Look at you. You were always gorgeous, but holy shit-balls, you have blossomed, my friend," my sister said over a fit of giggles. I glanced down at her trademark Doc Martens, jean shorts, and a tank top that hung off her shoulder, which I was certain my mother had already nagged her about.

"Well, thank you. You're looking stunning yourself. I see you kept your hipster style. You may need to give me some fashion tips while I'm home, because I need to freshen things up," Lila said, her voice teasing.

She didn't need to freshen up anything.

She was fucking gorgeous.

"Okay, let's let Lila breathe, all right?" I said, wrapping an arm around my baby sister and placing a hand on the small of Lila's back, leading them into the kitchen.

The whole room erupted when we walked in, and everyone took turns hugging Lila and welcoming her into the fold. That was my family. And I wouldn't change a damn thing.

These were my people.

We fought hard, and we loved harder.

"Uncle Hughey. Hugs." Gracie moved in front of me. The little nugget was too cute for her own good. She held up her hands, waiting for me to scoop her up like I always did. Hell, I used to hold her in the palm of one hand when she was a baby. Now she was four years old and the smartest little girl on the planet.

I lifted her into the air, settling her neck against my scruff and tickling her. She clapped her hands and broke out into a fit of giggles. I pulled her close to me, and her little head settled on my shoulder as I turned toward Lila.

"Do you remember Lila? She's Uncle Trav's sister," I said.

"Hi, Gracie. I haven't seen you in a long time. You're so big now, and you're so pretty."

"You're pretty." My niece reached her arms out for Lila, who scooped her right up. Everyone laughed and gawked at me because Gracie always wanted me, no matter who we were with, and these fuckers were green with envy.

"I see how it is, Gracie girl. You're jumping ship on Uncle Hughey?" I grasped my heart like I was wounded, and she laughed some more before turning her attention back to Lila and petting her hair and smiling at her like she was the most beautiful thing she'd ever seen.

Trust me, I understood it.

Gracie wasn't the only one gaping at my best friend's little sister.

four

. . .

Lila

TO SAY THAT THE REYNOLDS' house was like something out of a movie, would be an understatement. They were better than a movie. Five rock star children with huge personalities and parents who were just as amazing.

We were seated at the enormous farmhouse table they'd had since I was a kid. There was food and drinks and laughter. Everyone talked at the same time, but somehow, they were all able to keep up. It had always been this way when we were growing up.

This was the family everyone wanted to be born into.

The Kennedys of Cottonwood Cove.

They were all gorgeous and smart and funny.

Confident and cool.

And I'd be lying if I didn't admit that I'd daydreamed more than once when I was a kid about what it would be like to have a family like this.

Cage was the oldest, and he'd always been a bit broodier than the rest. A little more serious than his siblings. He'd been raising Gracie on his own since he'd had a one-night stand with some supermodel in Los Angeles, where he'd been attending vet school. The woman didn't want to keep the baby, and Cage agreed to raise her on his own. He'd moved back to Cottonwood Cove to have the support of his family, and it was easy to see how much they all adored his little girl.

Chocolate eyes the size of saucers and two little light brown buns on top of her head that were bursting with curls. She was adorable, and I didn't miss the way she'd moved onto Hugh's lap when we sat down to eat.

Finn was next in line, and he'd been working as an actor since he'd graduated from college. He'd been the star of a soap opera the last few years, but apparently, he'd been cast in some upcoming Netflix production that was being filmed at the old Scott Ranch not far from Cottonwood Cove. Everyone in town was thrilled about it, and having a local guy who'd grown up here starring in it, made it even more amazing. It sounded kind of like a twist on my favorite show, *Yellowstone*, and his family was talking about this being his breakout role.

"Yeah, I'm not holding my breath. We'll see how it goes. Sometimes they don't make it the whole way through production, so I'm taking it one day at a time." Finn shrugged and then winked at me, which earned him a growl from Hugh. The table erupted in laughter as they were always giving one another a hard time.

"It was a wink. Take it down a notch, big guy," Finn said with a smirk on his face.

"Yeah. It always starts with a wink." Hugh forked a carrot and held it up for Gracie to take a bite. My ovaries nearly exploded at the sight of this big bear of a man holding this little angel on his lap and feeding her like it was nothing out of the norm.

"Georgia, would you please do something about your shirt? You know how I feel about bras hanging out at the table," Alana said, which made everyone chuckle again.

"It's not even really a bra, Mom," Georgia groaned. "It's more of a fashion statement. I mean, when you're the president of the Itty-Bitty Titty Committee, you don't need the support. But a little black lace can add a little something-something to a white tank top, you know?"

"What's a titty?" Gracie tipped her head back to look at Hugh, and Cage hissed something under his breath.

"Ah, fabulous question. What is a titty, Georgia?" Hugh asked, with a wicked grin on his face.

"Can we please not say titty around my daughter?" Cage grumped.

"Why? More than half of the people at this table have them," Brinkley said over her laughter. She was the second youngest in the family. Hugh was the middle child, and he appeared to be close to every single one of his siblings. They'd always been a tight family.

Brinkley was a sports journalist, who lived in San Francisco, which was a two-hour drive from here.

"Do I have a titty?" Gracie asked in the sweetest voice, still looking up at Hugh like he set the sun. Alana gasped. Her husband, Bradford, barked out a laugh, Cage rubbed his temples as if he were exhausted by the conversation, and Finn's fist came down on the table as he laughed so hard it made everyone else do the same.

"This is all Aunt Georgia's fault, isn't it? She and her fashion bra trend has caused quite the commotion." Hugh tried to hide his grin and stroked the little girl's hair away from her face.

"Will you get me a bra, too, Uncle Hughey?" Gracie asked, placing one hand on his cheek.

"There's a lot I'd do for you, sweet girl, but I pray to God that bra shopping is not one of them."

Even Cage laughed now before raising a brow and looking at his daughter. "Okay, that's enough about that."

"Daddy doesn't like titties?" she asked, and even I couldn't hold it in any longer. Laughter bellowed around the room, and Alana covered her face with both hands, but it was easy to see her head shaking with muffled laughter, even if she was trying to hide it.

"I assure you, your daddy does not have a problem with titties." Georgia took a sip from her wine glass and smirked.

"I have to agree with that one," Brinkley said, agreeing with her younger sister.

"Girls. That's enough." Alana shook her head and dabbed at her eyes as she pulled herself together.

Hugh looked over at me. "Welcome to Sunday dinner, where nothing is off limits."

I loved every second of it. The banter and the arguing and the love. It was impossible to miss.

"So, Lila, how long are you going to be here for?" Bradford asked me. "I hear you're helping out Hugh quite a bit down at the restaurant. We're grateful for that because he's working way too much."

"I'm planning to stay through the summer. I'll head back to Chicago around the first of September."

"Are you still running?" he asked. "I know there was some talk about you training for the Olympics."

I nodded. I'd been approached by several coaches, and a lot of people thought I would want to continue racing after college, but I didn't. I'd achieved what I'd set out to do, and it was time to walk away. "Nope. I was more than ready to be done. I want to start living a normal life, I guess."

Hugh glanced over, and my gaze locked with his. There was so much empathy there, it comforted me. Not many people understood how much time and energy went into training at the collegiate level. The pressure. The expectations. The discipline and the determination it took to get there.

I was exhausted.

"I think that's wonderful. You've been working hard your entire life. It's time to just... live, right?" Alana asked, her green eyes that matched Hugh's sparkled as she looked at me.

"I think so, yes."

"Well, Lila, you know if you want to start living, I'm your girl. I live that YOLO life, and I have zero regrets," Georgia said, her blonde hair falling around her shoulders.

"What's a YOLO life?" Bradford asked, and I didn't miss the way he looked at his youngest child with absolute adoration.

"It means *you only live once*, and if most of us lived our lives the way Georgie does, we wouldn't have jobs or roofs over our heads." Brinkley raised a brow at her sister. They looked nothing alike. Hugh and Brinkley looked more like their father with their dark coloring, and Finn and Cage had lighter brown hair while Georgia was the blondest of all the Reynolds kids, just like her mother.

"Hey, jobs and roofs are overrated if you ask me. Life is short; you need to enjoy it. Everything always works out, so *carpe diem, bitches*," Georgia sang out.

"What's bitches?" Gracie asked.

"Do not repeat that word, Gracie. For God's sake, Georgie, can you not control yourself around a kid and watch what you say?" Cage hissed at his sister. "And for the record, *you* don't have to worry because your parents support you. Not everyone has that luxury. The real world is not all sunshine and rainbows."

Georgia groaned. "The real world is what you make it. I choose to start my days with positivity and joy. So, you and your attitude can suck it, Cage. Our parents supported you, too, and then you went off to be a big fancy doctor, so I'd hardly say life has been unfair to you."

"First off, I'm a veterinarian in Cottonwood Cove, which means I'm dealing with crazy animal people in this town, and there's nothing fancy about that. But yes, I had a plan when I was in school. You need to figure out what you want to do. You graduate in six months."

My eyes were bouncing between them, and I was completely fascinated.

Hugh barked out a laugh. "All right... let's call a truce. She doesn't have to have it all figured out tonight."

"Agreed. And she does have parents who have a pretty good track record at raising capable children," Bradford said, raising a brow at his oldest son.

Cage nodded. "I love you, Georgie. I just worry about you. You know I want the best for you."

"Daddy loves Aunt Georgie," Gracie said, and she clapped her hands together.

Hugh leaned down and kissed the top of her head.

"I love you, too, but you worry too much." Georgia seemed completely unfazed.

This family even argued without anyone getting offended. It had always been this way.

Drama in my house growing up usually led to physical fights with my father and brother, police visits, arrests, worry, and sleepless nights.

This was refreshing.

"So, Lila, I'm doing this article on a retired professional football player, and he was saying that the toughest part about walking away from his sport is that he'll miss the high of game day. He said it's tough when so much of your identity is wrapped up in what you did in your sport versus who you are. Was it hard for you to walk away?"

I thought it over. "I think my situation is a little different."

Hugh's gaze locked with mine, and he studied me. "How so?"

"Well, I started running as sort of a way to escape, I think. After losing my mom, and all that happened with my dad when I was young, I just sort of needed something to..." I paused and shook my head. "Take me away, I guess. And it was the first thing I felt like I was good at, so I knew it was my ticket to go to school and have a future. I figured that out at a young age."

The table was quiet, and I wondered if I'd shared too much.

"You won the California state championship all four years in high school, and you were the first female in the state of California to accomplish that, so I'd say good is an under-statement," Hugh said, catching me off guard that he'd remembered those specific stats. "And then you went on to be the collegiate national champ. You've more than proven yourself."

"Thank you. But I guess I don't feel like I need to prove anything anymore. I don't need to set a record or win a race to get me to the next place I want to go. I've been so busy looking forward, I haven't enjoyed just being where I'm at. I don't miss racing because I never loved race days, to be honest. I love running, and I still do, and it feels good that I can just do it for myself now. For the first time in my life, it's just for me."

"I think that's amazing, Lila. And I'm sure glad you're back home for a while. I've missed that sweet face of yours," Alana said, her eyes wet with emotion. "And who knows, maybe you'll end up wanting to stay."

Hugh shot his mother a look, and I knew what he was saying without even speaking the words. Travis didn't want anyone giving me any reason to stay. He thought my dad would bring me down, and he was so determined that I deserved more than this place that we all called home. My brother had spent his entire life protecting me, and I didn't need protecting anymore.

He'd been in battle so long that he didn't know how to stop.

"Well, all I know is that it feels good to be here now. And thank you for having me tonight. I don't think there's anyone that has a better Sunday dinner than the Reynolds family," I said, and everyone chuckled.

"We'd be so pleased if you'd join us every Sunday while you're home," Alana said, and Hugh chuckled.

"I hope you keep coming and that you aren't running for the hills after the infamous black lace bra strap showing," Georgia said with a dramatic gasp. "And my big brother trying to boss me around."

"Daddy is a boss!" Gracie shouted over her giggles.

"You got that right, baby girl," Cage said.

"But remember who the real boss is," Hugh whispered, loud enough for us all to hear.

"Uncle Hughey is the real boss, Daddy," Gracie sang out as Hugh blew a raspberry on her neck, and she fell back in laughter.

"Damn straight!" Hugh shouted.

"Hey, I thought I was the boss." Finn feigned offense, being the natural actor that he was.

"I've gots me a lot of bosses." Gracie shrugged.

The rest of the night was more banter and laughter and way too much food.

I said my goodbyes to everyone, and Hugh insisted on driving me home. I offered to walk as I'd left my car at home this morning. I preferred to walk most places, and I enjoyed it, but he was never going to agree to that, and I didn't fight it.

"Thanks for inviting me tonight. Your family is just as amazing as I remembered. I can't imagine how much fun it must have been growing up with all of your siblings."

Hugh turned down the street and headed toward my father's house.

"Yeah, it was a lot of fun, but we all have our moments. Both good and bad, just like everyone else. You know Trav just wants what's best for you, right? He always has."

"I know. But it doesn't mean that I can't come home and

be happy, too. I grew up here, just like he did. We have the same father. I think I'm capable of handling myself. He's so hell-bent on keeping me away, and I just wish he realized I'm not a little kid anymore."

My eyes narrowed as I saw a tall man standing on our front porch with his hands flailing around, and I could hear the shouting from inside the truck. His left hand reared back and made contact with the person he was blocking with his big body, and I saw my father fall forward. I reached for the handle just as Hugh pulled to the curb, not even certain the car had come to a full stop. I was out and running toward my father.

"Hey! Leave him alone!" I shouted as I approached him. His arm was lifted again, and I knew he was going to hit my father who was sprawled out on the ground and not fighting back. I reached for his hand, but it swung back too quickly and nailed me right in the cheek with a force I hadn't been prepared for. Everything was a blur when I stumbled to the ground, and Hugh came out of nowhere, diving through the air and tackling the guy who'd just hit me. I crawled over to my father to see if he was okay, and he just sat up, laughing as blood poured from his nose. Two men stood in the doorway, holding beers in their hands and watching Hugh punch the guy in the face as he shouted at him.

"Don't you ever fucking put your hands on her again, do you hear me?" I jumped up and raced over to him, reaching for his arm that he held above the man who was bleeding and begging him to stop.

"That's enough," I said, and my voice broke on a sob.

Flashbacks of a childhood filled with ups and downs flooded my head.

Reminders of why running had always been such an escape for me.

What was happening? My father had been fine when I'd left earlier.

"Damn, Lila girl. I'd have knocked him out myself if I would have known he put his hands on you," my father's words slurred.

He was drunk or high; I wasn't quite sure which.

In my lifetime, I was more familiar with this version of my dad than the sober one. But I hadn't seen him drunk or high since I'd returned home, and I'd hoped that him having all these health issues would mean he was trying to get better.

It wasn't my first time being wrong, nor would it most likely be my last.

But I'd never stop trying.

Because beneath all that sickness and addiction was a great man. I may be the only one that still knew it, but that didn't matter to me.

If you had one person in your corner, there was still hope. And everyone deserved that, didn't they?

"Lila James. Look at you," Bradley purred from our doorway, looking like the creep he'd always been. He was the friend dad used to get into the most trouble with. I couldn't stand the man.

Hugh pushed to stand and lifted the guy on the ground to his feet with him. "You're lucky I don't call the cops. Apologize to her, and then get the fuck out of here and don't come back."

"I'm sorry. I didn't see you behind me," he sputtered and spit blood on the grass. "You owe me twenty bucks, Tate. You will pay me." He stormed out of our yard and down the street.

"You all right?" Hugh asked as he stalked toward me, almost predatory. His large hand grazed my cheek, and he held up his phone and turned on the flashlight before cursing under his breath. "Come on. You're not staying here."

"What? I live here."

"Not anymore. You have two choices. You pack your bags and go to Travis and Shay's, or you stay in my casita. That's it. What's it going to be?" His green gaze was hard, and he turned to glare at my father when Dad pushed to his feet and started apologizing.

"I'll stay with you. Please don't call Travis right now. He'll be furious, and I'll talk to him tomorrow. I promise."

Hugh nodded. "Let's go pack up your shit."

He stormed past my father and shoved Bradley and Pat out of the way. There were two more guys I'd never seen sprawled out on the couch, with beer cans covering the coffee table.

"Party's over, boys. Leave." Hugh pointed toward the door and then raised an eyebrow at me and tilted his head toward the hallway leading to my room. I hurried inside and swiped at the tears rolling down my cheeks. Travis would hate our father even more now. He didn't understand that this was a disease, and he was doing his best to beat it.

That was why I was here.

But nothing was going to get resolved tonight. Dad was drunk. His friends were creepy as hell, and I didn't want to be here, anyway.

And I knew Hugh well enough to know that he wasn't going to leave without me, so I tossed a bunch of clothes in my bag and grabbed my toiletries, as well.

When I came out of the room, wheeling my suitcase behind me, my father sat on the floor of the living room with a bottle of vodka in his hand, and he tipped his head back and took a long pull. Bradley was still there, of course, laughing his ass off just like he always did when Dad fell off the wagon.

I often wondered if that term even made sense anymore. Because in all honesty, my father had been off the wagon more than he'd ever been on it.

I hated that so much for him.

But it didn't mean that it had to be his reality for the rest of his life.

"I'm sorry, Lila girl. I love you. I just had a slip." Dad tried to push to his feet and fell back on the floor as Bradley's laughter filled the small space around us.

Hugh stepped in front of me and took my bags, blocking my line of sight to my dad. "Truck. Now. I'll be right there."

I did what he said because I was too tired to fight him.

My cheek throbbed with pain as I climbed into his truck.

But nothing compared to the way my heart ached.

five

$\bullet$ $\bullet$ $\bullet$

Hugh

SHE WAS quiet on the drive to my house, and I didn't miss the way she kept swiping the tears from her cheeks, trying to hide her sadness. And don't even get me fucking started about the bruise on her face from that piece of shit who'd backhanded her. It didn't matter whether he knew she was there or not. They were a bunch of sloppy drunk fuckers, and she had no business being around them.

I pulled into the garage and turned off the truck before looking over at her. "You all right?"

"Yeah, of course. You didn't need to bring me here. I would have been fine there." Her voice wobbled.

"Not a chance in hell that I was leaving you there." I turned on the interior light and leaned forward to inspect her face. I gently grazed her cheekbone with my thumb, and her eyes locked with mine. "Jesus, it's pretty swollen and bruised. Let's get you inside and get some ice on it."

I jumped out of the truck and grabbed her bags, and she followed me inside. I flipped on a couple of lights and left her bags by the door as I made my way into the kitchen.

"Wow. This is so nice. When you bought the place, it needed a lot of work, right?" she asked, as she paused at the kitchen island. I filled a baggie with ice and wrapped a towel around it before gently placing it against her cheek. Her hand came over mine to hold in place, and for whatever reason, I didn't let go. I didn't want to.

"I've got it," she whispered, lifting her hand just enough for mine to pull away.

She cringed a little, and I couldn't stop myself from reaching out to stroke her hair. She'd been hit and needed comfort, and I wanted to give it to her.

"Yep, I pretty much renovated every square inch of this place with the help of your brother and his guys," I said, and she leaned into my touch, closing her eyes. Lavender and honey flooded my senses. "You'll be all right. Just give it a minute, and it won't feel that cold. It'll start numbing up."

And damn it if my body wasn't reacting. I'd never been big on stroking a woman's hair or being overly affectionate, but somehow, it didn't bother me with Lila.

Her eyes opened, and I saw the sadness there. The heartache this girl had experienced with her father wasn't something any kid should have to deal with. "Thanks for being there for me."

"Always. You know that."

"Are you sure you don't mind me staying in your casita tonight?"

"Listen, Lila, the place is yours for as long as you're home. If you don't want to stay here over the next few months, you'll have to stay with Trav and Shay." I pulled my hand away from her hair and stepped back. I needed to put some space between us. I couldn't think straight when she was looking at me like that. All sweet and sexy. "You know Travis isn't going to be okay with you staying at your dad's now. And I don't disagree after what I just witnessed."

"I can take care of myself," she said, squaring her shoulders and pulling the ice away from her face.

"That's not the issue. No one doubts that you're a strong

woman, but you shouldn't have to take care of yourself when you're at home. You should feel safe, and there is no fucking way that place is safe for you when your father is drinking or drugging or whatever the hell he's doing."

Her face hardened. "It was a slip."

"Come on, Snow. You're smarter than that. I haven't seen him sober in years. Why do you think Travis tried so hard to keep you away?"

Her dark brown eyes welled with tears, and my chest squeezed, causing me to step forward. Closer.

"That's because he doesn't have anyone to help him. Travis is too angry. That's why I'm here." She shrugged as two tears streaked down her pretty face. One moved over the large bump, which had now turned a dark shade of purple on her cheek. I leaned forward and gently swiped them both away.

"You can't fix someone who doesn't want to be fixed."

"He does, Bear. I know he does." Her words broke on a sob, and I moved closer, wanting to pull her into my arms, but she set the ice on the island and held up both hands. "Think about the way your family was tonight. Is it so wrong that I want that for my family? That I want Travis to stop hating our father, and I want Dad to care enough about his life to take care of himself? Why is it so bad to want that?"

Her shoulders quaked, and the tears started falling down her cheeks, and I couldn't stop myself. I rushed her, pulling her into my arms and wrapping her up.

"It's not wrong. I understand why you want that. You're good and strong and kind, Lila. And your father is lucky to have you. But you need to protect yourself while you're here, all right?"

Her head tipped back, and she looked up at me. Dark brown eyes wet with emotion and pain. "You're not going to tell me he's not worth my time like everyone else does?"

"Not if you agree to stay here and be cautious. But we

have to tell Travis what happened, because when he finds out, he'll be pissed we kept it from him."

"All right." She nodded. "We can tell him if you promise to support me. I just need someone on my side, you know?"

I wrapped my arms back around her and kissed the top of her head. "You've got me, Snow."

We stood in the kitchen, me holding her for what felt like hours.

And I was in no hurry to let her go.

———

Lila and I had eventually called Travis and told him her version of what happened, leaving out some of the details. I'd told him she would stay with me, and that was the only thing that kept him from coming over here and dragging her to his place. He'd been enraged that his sister had been knocked down. She'd failed to mention that she'd also been hit in the face, but I didn't throw her under the bus because she'd looked at me with those pleading eyes, so I'd let it go. For now.

I'd knocked the shit out of the asshole who'd hurt her, and I'd threatened both Bradley and Tate to stay the fuck away from her when Lila was in her room packing. I knew Travis would be coming to the restaurant to see her, and he wouldn't miss the swollen bruise on her cheek, but at least he'd be calmer by today.

The casita had a door to the interior of my house, as well as its own entrance on the outside. It was basically a bedroom en suite with its own bathroom and walk-in closet. The exterior door just offered a bit more privacy if someone wanted to come and go without entering the house. I'd told her to come on over in the morning and help herself to breakfast as we'd be sharing my kitchen. What I hadn't expected was to see Lila in a pair of tiny running shorts and a tank top, standing in my kitchen looking like a fucking goddess. Her tan legs were on full display, feminine muscles running down her thighs as I took her in from behind like a fucking creeper. Her ass was small and round—perfectly peach shaped, and her arms were slim with just enough muscle to make it obvious she was fit. Her body was a work of art. No doubt about it.

I cleared my throat to let her know I was there before I spent another second checking her out.

She whipped her head over her shoulder and smiled. Her cheeks were flushed, her hair pulled away from her makeup free face, and a dark, long ponytail ran down her back. Her cheek was still swollen and discolored, but somehow, it looked sexy as hell on her this morning.

"Hey, I hope it's okay I took you up on breakfast. I just went for a run, and I was starving, so I thought I'd make us both some bacon and eggs." Her gaze scanned my body, moving slowly down my chest and stomach, and her eyes widened, which caused me to look down to see what she was gaping at.

Nothing like a little morning wood to scare the shit out of your best friend's little sister.

I'd completely forgotten that I had on nothing but a pair of joggers, and they left nothing to the imagination when your dick was rock-hard.

And mine was.

I chuckled because there wasn't much else I could do in this situation.

"Sorry about that. It's a morning thing." I smirked.

It's actually a Lila thing.

She shook her head as if she hadn't realized she was staring and turned back to the stove. "Oh, no. I hadn't noticed. I mean, of course, I noticed, because it would be impossible not to, but I wasn't staring. Oh my gooooooood," she groaned.

"There's no shame in looking, Snow." I shouldn't have said it, but I liked seeing her all worked up.

A pink hue ran up the back of her neck, and I adjusted myself because this shit was getting painful. "Do I have time to grab a quick shower?"

"Yeah, yeah, of course." She waved a hand over her head, and when I got to the doorway of my bedroom, I heard her shout. "I'd make it a cold one, Bear!"

I laughed my ass off as I stood under the freezing cold water. I was not proud when I gripped my dick and leaned my forehead against the wall and thought of the way Lila had just looked at me. All innocent and sexy. Curious and wanting.

Her body in those little running shorts and tank top.

The way I could see the outline of her perfect tits through the fabric.

How badly I wanted to touch her.

Taste her.

It didn't take long to find my release, and I made a silent promise to myself that this would be the last time I allowed myself to fantasize about her. She was going to be staying with me. I needed to pull my shit together.

Maybe I just needed to get laid.

By someone other than Lila James, of course.

I'd make that my mission this weekend. I was probably just horny because it had been a while.

I slipped on a pair of jeans and a T-shirt and made my way out to the kitchen.

She'd just plated some eggs and bacon and toast, and damn if my stomach wasn't rumbling.

"This looks amazing. I'm usually lucky to grab a piece of toast before I get out of here," I said, moving to the fridge to pour us each a glass of juice.

"I'll replace the groceries when I go to the store after work today," she said, as we both sat down at the same time.

"Don't be silly. We can share. Hell, if you're willing to cook for me, I'd be happy to keep the fridge stocked."

She smiled. "I'll cook and shop, too. It's the least I can do for you letting me stay here."

I forked some eggs and groaned when I took a bite. Damn, she was a good cook. "Is there anything you're not good at?"

She took a bite of toast and thought it over. "There are several things I'm not good at. That's what I was thinking about on my run today. You know how Georgia lives that YOLO life? That might be something I should try."

"What do you mean?" I devoured a piece of crispy bacon.

"I've been talking to Delilah, Sloane, and Rina about it, too. They think I should do sort of a bucket list while I'm home." She raised a brow at me. "You know, things I haven't done before that I'd like to start trying."

What the hell was she talking about?

"What types of things do you want to do while you're here? Maybe I can help? Because if you keep cooking like this, I'm never going to let you leave."

She smiled and reached for her glass, taking her time with the fresh-squeezed juice. I watched the way her slender neck moved as she swallowed, and I had the sudden urge to kiss her there. To lick the sweat right from her body.

"Well, Bear, if you must know. Two nights ago, I got drunk for the first time. I'd never allowed myself to do anything so frivolous in the past, so that was a first."

"Getting drunk is overrated. But everyone needs to experience it at least once in their life, I guess." I chuckled. "So you've already got one checked off the list. What's next?"

"Well, the most important thing is to get my dad into a program while I'm here. I've been researching this for a while, and I've talked to him about it. He's open to it. We've tried everything else. Fighting, crying, more drama than anyone needs in one lifetime, and that hasn't worked. So, it's time to try something new. A Hail Mary of sorts, and I found a place on the outskirts of town that has really great success stories."

I nodded. I didn't want her to get hurt, but Tate James had yet to show any desire to get better. But I wouldn't say that. I wouldn't take that from her. Because if I were in her shoes, I'd do whatever it took for anyone in my family. So, I understood her need to keep trying. Travis was far past believing that his father could change, but it didn't mean that she had to be.

"All right. Sounds like you've got a plan for that one. What else do you have on this list, Snow?" I took a long pull from my glass.

"I'd like to lose my V-card while I'm home." She shrugged, and orange juice sputtered from my mouth all over the table. Did she just bring up her virginity so casually, as if she were discussing the weather and not the fact that she'd never had sex? That no man had ever had the pleasure of rocking her fucking world? Her head fell back in laughter before she looked at me as I tried to clean up my mess. "Have you never met a virgin, Hugh?"

"What? No. Of course, I have. I just—I didn't know." I cleared my throat, trying to think of the right thing to say.

"You didn't know I was a virgin?" She chuckled. "I mean, it's not something I advertise. That's why I've been avoiding Mrs. Runither. The woman can sniff out a virgin as fast as she can spot a manwhore."

"I hope you aren't looking at me because you think I'm either one of those," I teased, trying hard to change the tone of my voice.

Did it just get really fucking hot in here?

"I don't know, Bear. Are you a virgin, or are you a manwhore?"

"Well, I lost my virginity when I was sixteen, so that's out. I suppose I've had some years where I could possibly have been considered a bit of a manwhore—mainly through college. But I've never lied to anyone about who I am or what

I wanted. And lately, that shit has gotten less appealing to me. So, honestly, I don't think I'm either."

She watched me with complete fascination. "Obviously, you're very experienced. Maybe you could teach me a thing or two."

"I don't take things that I don't deserve, Lila. And I don't know that this should be something you put on a bucket list."

And I'll be a motherfucker if my dick wasn't hard as a rock again. Hell, I'd just gotten off less than twenty minutes ago, and here I was, talking virgins and whores with the hottest girl I'd ever laid eyes on, and my dick thought it was time to party.

"Why not?"

"Because. It shouldn't be something you just check off a list. It should be special. It should happen organically." I shrugged, hoping I was making sense, even if my voice was gruffer than usual.

Thoughts of Lila James coming apart beneath me flooded my head.

"Did it happen organically for you?" She raised a brow, her voice teasing. "At the age of sixteen, did you find yourself a loving soulmate and share that special moment surrounded by candlelight and romantic love songs?"

"Fine, smart-ass. It wasn't organic. It was with Eileen Johnson, who was two years older than me, and she climbed me like a fucking spider monkey." I barked out a laugh. "But, you're different."

"How so?" She rolled her eyes, assuming what I was going to say was going to annoy her.

"You're special. Always have been."

"So are you, Hugh. But that doesn't mean it has to be this big deal. At this point, I'd just like to get the deed done, you know?"

Was she trying to kill me?

"Hello?" a voice shouted, startling me from my fucking

raging erection about Lila James's untouched pussy. I was a bastard for fantasizing about my best friend's virgin sister while staring at the bacon and eggs she'd just made me.

"Hey, Trav," Lila called out, before waggling her brows at me mischievously. She knew what she was doing, and she was enjoying herself.

"What the fuck happened to your face?" Travis barked, moving close to his sister and placing his hand beneath her chin, turning her cheek so he could inspect it.

"I told you that I fell last night," she said, looking away, because he looked like he wanted to kill someone.

"You didn't mention that you got hit in the face on your way to the ground. I thought you tripped. Did Dad do this?"

"Of course not," she said, her voice angry now. "It was an accident. Some guy was there arguing with him. I got in the way. But Hugh hit him enough times that he won't be walking straight for days, so you can calm your ass down." He reached for a piece of bacon on her plate and took a bite.

"Well, thank God someone was thinking clearly." He held up his fist, and I bumped mine against his.

"No problem, brother. She's going to stay in the casita. That's the deal. And she's willing to cook, so I'm not complaining."

"Good. Whatever it takes to get you out of there."

Lila studied her brother and glanced over at me before speaking. "I've been looking into some programs for Dad, Travis. I've agreed to stay here at Hugh's, but I'm not going to give up on Dad. You get that, right?"

He nodded and shook his head. "I think I know you well enough to know that." He reached for a piece of toast. "Damn, don't tell Shay that this is the best breakfast I've had in months. I love her, but she can't cook for shit."

Lila and I both laughed. I'd had Shay's cooking, and he wasn't wrong.

"I won't say a word."

"You want to come over tonight, and I'll pick up takeout?" Travis asked Lila.

"Del's meeting me at Cottonwood Cafe when I get off work tonight. We're having dinner," Lila said. "How about tomorrow night?"

"Yeah, sure. Shay's starting to show, so I'm sure she'll want to talk babies with you. But it's good for you to spend time with friends while you're here, so I'm glad you're doing that. What else do you want to do while you're home aside from saving a man well past being saved?" Travis asked as he studied his sister. I loved the dude like a brother, but he could be an asshole when he wanted to be.

Lila squared her shoulders and sighed. "I'd like to just be a normal person, if that's all right with you, Trav? Go on some dates... have some fun. You know... things you've always done."

"There's no sense getting attached to anyone when you're leaving at the end of the summer. And the casual thing isn't really your style, is it?" he asked, and she pushed to her feet and got him a fork, as if she knew he wanted to dive into her eggs next. He smiled and did exactly that once she returned to her chair and handed him the utensil.

"I don't know what my thing is because I've been too busy chasing one goal after the next my entire life. How about you just let me live and stay out of my business while I'm home?"

"You're my little sister. Of course, I'll always be in your business." He chuckled. "Have some fun with your friends while you're home, but there's no one worth your time here. That fucker, Kline, was asking me about you yesterday when I ran into him at the gas station. I told him to fuck off, and I'm telling you, he's not a guy you should be hanging out with."

"Oh, really? Why? Because he's not a freaking saint? News flash: Neither are you. So, stop judging everyone else so harshly. I'm an adult. Back the hell off, Trav." Lila pushed to her feet and walked to the sink to rinse her plate before her phone rang, and she waved at us and walked out of the kitchen after answering the call. She pulled the door closed behind her as she went into the casita.

"She's acting insane. Thank God she's staying with you, buddy. You're the only person I trust with my sister. Hell, the way Brax keeps talking about her means I need to watch that fucker now, too."

I chuckled. "I got you, brother."

That was a promise I intended to keep.

No matter how tough it was, I'd keep my promise to him and look out for his sister.

six

. . .

Lila

"LILA JAMES, I heard you were back in town," Mrs. Runither said when Del and I checked in at the hostess stand. I cringed because I knew it was coming. Her face was completely frozen, and her lips mimicked those of a puffer fish. I wanted to reach out and poke them, just to see if they were firm or filled with air. "I bet you two have so much to talk about with this one going through men faster than a rooster can count to ten."

Since when did roosters start counting? The woman made no sense, but she was always so confident that most people just went along with it.

The place was fairly quiet, but it was a Monday night. Cottonwood Cove would start getting busy with tourists here in the next week or two. The town surrounded a gorgeous cove on the coast, and we were only a two-hour drive from San Francisco, but we lived in this quiet, peaceful pocket that I'd always loved. We had water sports in the summer and skiing in the winter.

"Thank you for that, Mrs. Runither. I've had three boyfriends in the last six years, so I'm guessing that means roosters count fairly slow," Delilah said, with a little bite to her tone. This woman had pretty much slut-shamed everyone in town over the years, which was saying a lot, considering she'd been rumored to be cheating on poor Mr. Runither many times with tourists who'd come through town.

"Well, of course, dear. You've got to test the waters," she purred, as she led us to the back of the restaurant to my favorite booth. It's where Dad and I always sat when we'd come here.

We both slid into opposite sides of the booth. "And you're looking quite lovely, Lila."

Here it comes.

Wait for it.

"Thank you." I turned my attention to my menu, hoping that would be her cue to walk away.

"I see your breasts have filled out. I mean they're still barely a handful, but they look a bit fuller. I bet the fellas don't mind that one bit. Mr. Runither loves my ladies." She glanced down at her ample cleavage that was always on display. It looked more like someone's ass than someone's boobs, with the way they were shoved together with what looked like a butt crack between them.

"I'm sure he does," Delilah said over her laughter as she glanced over at me with a wicked smile on her face.

"Yes." Mrs. Runither leaned over the table, and her big girls nearly spilled right into the dish holding the sweetener.

And, oh my, is that her nipple?

Yep, right out in the open.

At a place that serves food.

She glanced down and tucked herself back in. "Anyway. Have you dipped into the erection pond? That's code for have you taken the pussy cat out for a ride and popped that cherry. You know what I mean, Lila James?"

Well, no matter how much you prepared for it, you were just never quite ready when it happened. And the fact that she had several different ways of asking was even more alarming.

"I do just fine, Mrs. Runither. Don't you worry about me."

"Oh, I don't worry about you. I wish I could be a virgin again." She leaned forward and held her hand up to cover one side of her mouth as she whisper-shouted. "Have you heard that they can do a surgery that makes you a virgin all over again? It's just a couple stitches. A few nips and tucks down south, I think. I don't know why, but my doctor doesn't believe I'm an ideal candidate. Not with my pushing sixty and how active I am... *in the bedroom.* If you ever need any tips on how to close the deal, you just let me know, Lila."

My mouth gaped open. "Um. Thank you."

Delilah raised an eyebrow as if she were done with the conversation, and Mrs. Runither waved at us before hurrying away to greet some customers who'd just walked in.

"Remind me again why we come here?" my best friend asked, and she didn't hide her irritation.

"Because it's not crowded, and we can talk," I said with a chuckle. "Plus, it's almost like a Cottonwood Cove rite of passage to be grilled by the old sexpot."

"Perhaps it's not crowded because the owner has a crazy-ass obsession with the customers' sex lives. I mean, she just used *popped that cherry, erection pond,* and *take the pussy cat out for a ride* all in one sentence. This is not normal. You know that, right?" She shook her head, just as our server, Jenna, approached and took our orders after we made a little small talk.

"Well, at least it's interesting. I swear, my virginity is really a topic of conversation back here in Cottonwood Cove. No one seemed to care about it in Chicago." I paused when Jenna set our drinks down before hurrying off.

"I still can't believe you told Hugh you were going to put it on your bucket list," she said, as her head tipped back in laughter. "So, who are you considering for the deflowering?" She smirked.

"Well, there's Kline, and that would be easy because he seems more than willing. But then I'd have to work with him, and if I didn't like it, that could be super awkward."

"True. But he is hot, and he's funny. He's got those tats that give him a little edge." She smiled.

"Good point. I'm supposed to have a drink with him tonight, so I can feel things out. See if there's an attraction. Maybe we can all go out next weekend, and I can check out my options."

"Yes. I'm going out with Quincy again Friday night, so let's get the girls together for Saturday night."

"Deal." I shot a quick text to Sloane and Rina in our group chat, and they immediately sent back thumbs-up emojis and a few eggplant emojis, as well, because those were Sloane's favorite.

"So, how is it living with Hugh? Oh my gosh, I can't even imagine seeing him in the morning. What was he wearing this morning when you had breakfast with him?"

I was laughing so hard I barely pulled myself together when Jenna set down our grilled cheese sandwiches and french fries. Once she walked away and was out of earshot, I bit off the tip of a fry and turned to Delilah. "I've lived there all of one day. And yes, he wore joggers this morning."

She fanned her face. "No shirt?"

"Nope."

"Baseball cap?"

"Yep. Turned backward."

"My God. I've seen him at the beach, and that man is chiseled perfection. Why not add him to the list?" she asked.

"I kind of joked about it, but he was definitely not interested. I'm clearly not his type, and Travis would lose his shit. So that's out."

"Travis is such a cockblocking bastard sometimes." She

shook her head and reached for her sandwich. "You are definitely Hugh's type."

"How do you know?"

"I just do. I think you're kind of everyone's type. You're gorgeous and smart and funny." She shrugged.

"Says my bestie."

"Trust me, Lila. He'd go for it if it wasn't for Travis. Just feel things out. Maybe you could have a fling and keep it between the two of you. And me, of course. You've got to let me know how good it is. Although, your first time is never all that fabulous, but I'm sure he'd make it amazing."

I reached for my drink. Was it hot in here?

"Okay, that's enough sex talk for one night. What else can we put on the list?"

"Hmmm... you could tell off Drew Compton. Remember how she made out with Dougy during senior prom? That girl was a bitch back then, and nothing has changed."

Dougy and I had only dated for three months when we went to prom, and I'd found him in the bathroom making out with Drew, which had been completely mortifying at the time.

"Well, that was on Dougy. He was my date, not Drew."

"Yes. And Drew was with Robert. They'd dated for three years, and she made out with his best friend at a party. Shady lady, that's all I have to say."

I laughed again. "Damn, I've missed you, Del."

"Me, too. Can we just have you tell her off for me? I can't stand the girl."

"Fine. I'll add it to the list."

"Let's go to that biker bar while you're home. Flirt with some of those hairy, handsome beasts."

"Ahhh... Sloane will be so happy. Remember how many times she tried to get us to go there?"

"That'll be a good one to check off. What else?"

"The top of the list is helping my dad. I found a place that has inpatient care, and I'm going to go check it out next weekend."

"Aren't those programs expensive?" she asked.

"Yep. But I'll cross that bridge when I get to it. I've got a plan, and I've been messaging with the woman over there."

"You're a good human, Lila James. The best I know," she said, biting off the corner of her grilled cheese.

"Takes one to know one."

We finished up our dinner and walked over to Reynolds', where Quincy was picking up Del, and I'd agreed to have one drink with Kline.

My phone vibrated after I hugged her goodbye, and I looked down to see a text from Hugh.

BEAR

> What time will you be home? I shouldn't be too long, so let me know if you need a ride.

I chewed on my thumbnail.

> Just got to Reynolds' to meet Kline for a quick drink, and then I'll be home. Are you here?

I knew that he wasn't, but curiosity was getting the best of me.

BEAR

> Brax talked me into a double date, but I'm tired and not feeling it, and this dinner is moving fucking slow.

Why did that make me smile?

> Are you always the heartbreaker, Bear?

BEAR

> Not trying to break any hearts. Just not feeling it.

You're preaching to the choir. Story of my life. I'll see you in a bit. xx

BEAR

Call me if you need a ride, and be careful with Kline, all right?

<eye roll emoji> <eye roll emoji>

I dropped my phone into my purse and pulled open the door. Brandy was smiling, but when her gaze locked with mine, she frowned.

"Hey," I said as I stepped closer. "Can I talk to you?"

She squared her shoulders. "Sure."

"Do we have a problem?"

Her jaw dropped as if she were shocked that I'd noticed. "I, um. No. I. I'm sorry. I guess I felt a little threatened by you, that's all."

"That's silly. I'm not here to do anything to hurt you. I'm just here to help out for the summer."

"I guess I have this little crush on the boss, and he seems to be giving all his attention to you, not that he ever gave me any." She frowned dramatically, which made me laugh, and it also showed her age.

I chuckled. "How old are you?"

"I just turned seventeen."

"Well, he certainly can't be giving you any attention because that would get him into trouble, seeing as he's a grown man. Hugh and I grew up together, so we're just good friends. But even if I weren't here, he wouldn't be any different to you, Brandy. He's not that guy."

She let out this long, dramatic whine, stomped her foot, and then shrugged. "I guess you're right. What do you think of Lionel, the new busboy? We go to school together, but he's always been so shy."

I fought back my urge to laugh at how quickly she rebounded from being upset. Lionel had just started working here at the same time I did, and he seemed like a really nice kid. "I think he's good-looking and very nice. Maybe you should try to talk to him since he's pretty shy. I was always a little shy myself, and I wasn't very confident with boys, so if someone made the first move, it was easier for me."

She tapped her fingers along the wood of the hostess stand and tipped her head to the side. "Really? I can't imagine you ever feeling insecure because you're so pretty. Seems like every guy in the room is always staring at you."

That made me laugh. "I don't think we've been in many rooms together, then, and don't look now, but Lionel keeps glancing over here. I think you should go talk to him. I'll cover things here until you get back."

She beamed up at me and extended her hand. "Thanks, Lila. Can we start over?"

"Absolutely. Now, go get your flirt game on and talk to that cute boy."

"You don't have to stay up here. I'm already off the clock. Danielle is finishing up the last table of the night. I was just hanging around to try to talk to Lionel."

She hurried off, and I smiled as I made my way to the bar. Kline was wiping down the bar top, and he looked up and raised a brow.

"I thought you were blowing me off," he said, his voice all tease.

"No. I was having dinner with Del, and I told you I'd stop by on my way home." I pulled out a bar stool and sat down.

"What are you drinking? It's on me."

"Thank you. A glass of chardonnay would be great."

"You got it." He moved to grab a glass, and I chewed on the back of my thumbnail as I pulled my phone out of my purse and glanced down to see if I had any new texts.

I didn't.

Why did that disappoint me?

He pushed the glass in front of me and raised his glass, which looked to be some sort of hard liquor straight up. "Cheers to you being back in town, Lila James."

"I will drink to that," I said, tapping my glass to his.

He studied me as he took a long pull and emptied the dark liquid in one gulp before setting the glass down on the bar and rubbing his hands together. "Damn. I'm happy you're here. But I've got to ask, what's the deal with Hugh?"

"The deal? I don't think there is one." I took a sip and set my glass down. I wasn't in the mood for a drink, and I was ready to head home, but I didn't want to flake on him.

"The dude nearly took my head off when I spoke to you. Is he just being a protective friend, or is there something there?" he asked.

I chuckled. "He's always been protective. That's all it is."

"All right. You want me to give you a ride home? Are you staying with your dad?"

"No. I'm staying in Hugh's guest casita for now. And you know he lives really close, so I'll be fine walking. But thanks for the offer."

"I see." His tongue swiped out to wet his bottom lip, and it seemed very deliberate.

I waited to swoon. Wanted there to be butterflies. But there was nothing.

He was good-looking and appeared to have a good personality.

So, once again, I was the problem.

I chuckled. "What do you see?"

"Probably the prettiest fucking girl I've ever laid eyes on."

"Very smooth," I said, raising a brow as I took another sip.

"How about I take you to dinner this week? Just you and me. And not here. We can go somewhere else. I think we're both off on Tuesday."

"Sure. That sounds fun."

"Damn, you're cute even when you're not even trying," he purred before running a hand through his blond, wavy hair. This man had swagger, and I'm sure plenty of women swooned over him, so maybe it would just take me some time.

"Thank you." I shrugged as he turned back and started wiping everything down. We made some more small talk, and I actually laughed a few times, so maybe I was being too quick to put him in the friend zone.

He surprised me by offering to walk me home as Hugh's house was on the way to his place. He said he would leave his car at Reynolds' since he'd had a couple of drinks.

And he didn't go for the kiss when we got to the door. He hugged me and walked backward as he waited for me to get inside.

Maybe he did have potential.

seven

. . .

Hugh

AFTER THE WORLD'S most painful date, I pulled down my street. Lila had texted me that Kline had walked her home, and she didn't need a ride. I didn't like the idea of her hanging out with him, and it didn't make a whole lot of sense. Kline wasn't a bad guy, but he was a player. And he definitely wasn't good enough for Lila.

Turning off my truck, my phone vibrated on the dashboard, and I reached for it.

CAGE

Stella Jacobs brought her pig, Princess Lowanda, into the office today and asked if I could give the pig Botox because she thinks she's looking too wrinkly. I cannot make this shit up.

GEORGIA

Hey, a girl's got to do what a girl's got to do. #nojudgment

FINN

My agent suggested for me to consider Botox. But if the pig can't get it, I'm going to put my foot down.

BRINKLEY

I'd like to inject Botox into my boss's ball sack because he's a misogynistic pig.

CAGE

Remind me never to cross you.

FINN

Didn't Brinks write on your face with a Sharpie because you wouldn't give her a ride to the movies to meet that horndog, Scotty Peters?

GEORGIA

That was me, Finny! And Scotty Peters was hot. <fire emoji>

BRINKLEY

I just ran into him last time I was home, and he didn't look good.

FINN

He got veneers from Dr. Anderson, who isn't even a dentist. He's a dental hygienist. How he is getting away with this shit, is beyond me. So that's what you get when you go for the too-good-to-be-true deal.

CAGE

So… You're welcome, Georgie. I saved you the embarrassment of dating a dude whose teeth are too big for his mouth.

BRINKLEY

And he was an odd shade of orange. Like he spray-tanned so many times I think he's permanently stained.

GEORGIA

Like tangerine? Cantaloupe?

BRINKLEY

He didn't look like a fruit. More like the color of an overcooked sweet potato.

FINN

Damn, I'm hungry now. Where's Hugh?

CAGE

He got sucked into going on a double date with Brax.

BRINKLEY

Good. He needs to get back out there. He's acting like an old man.

GEORGIA

I wish he'd date Lila James. Damn, they would make such pretty babies.

CAGE

Um... I'm fairly certain Travis would kill him long before they could procreate.

BRINKLEY

But, yes... those would be some pretty babies.

I'm home. No one is acting like an old man or making any babies with his best friend's sister. I'm leaving all the procreating to you guys. But thanks for thinking of me, Georgie. I say, give Princess Lowanda the Botox. And, Brinks, if you need me to come to the city and kick someone's ass, you just say the word.

BRINKLEY

And this is why Hugh is my favorite today.

FINN

Because he's a brute? I'm a lover, not a fighter. Sorry, Brinks.

GEORGIA

Love you, guys. Going to meet some friends for a drink. I'll text you tomorrow.

CAGE

Gracie keeps coming out of her room after I've put her to bed. Remind me to thank Mom for letting her eat an extra piece of cake tonight. Got to go deal with a fucking sugar meltdown.

A slew of heart emojis came through, and I tucked my phone back into my pocket and climbed out of the truck. I saw the light on in the casita when I'd pulled into the garage, and I strode into the house, making my way to her room.

I knocked lightly on the door to the casita.

"It's open," she called out.

When I stepped into the room, it smelled like lavender and honey—and Lila.

There was a candle burning on the dresser. Did she have a candle that smelled just like her?

I chuckled because the room looked much nicer than the

way I'd had it. She'd added her own bedding that was a lot more girly than the brown down comforter I'd had in here. I'd told her to make the place her own, and she'd definitely done that.

But it wasn't the white and pink bedding that had me gaping; it was the beautiful woman wearing a pair of tiny white pajama shorts and a little tank top lying on her stomach on the bed, legs bent at her knees, writing in a notebook. Her hair was tied up in a knot on top of her head, and she wore no makeup and looked fucking stunning. She hurried to sit and pulled the notebook onto her lap and patted the bed beside her for me to sit.

"Hey. How did the date end?" she asked, as she bit down on her bottom lip and waggled her brows playfully. I sat beside her, and she nearly tumbled into my lap when the mattress dipped down with my weight. We both chuckled, and I helped her straighten before kicking off my boots. We both moved to sit with our backs against the headboard.

"Exactly how it started. With Brax pulling his typical shit by offering me up and then begging me to go because he wanted to take out Carly, and she would only go if she brought Brenna."

"Brenna Wilson? She was in your grade, right? A cheerleader?"

"Yep. And she and Carly proceeded to take about fifteen shots of tequila, and Brax joined right in. So, I got stuck driving their drunk asses home and paying the bill because Brax miraculously forgot his wallet. The fucker."

Lila was laughing hysterically, and she turned to look at me. "Did you go for the kiss?"

"What are we, girlfriends?" I teased.

"We're roommates, and we're friends. So, spill it."

"Well, let's see. Brenna vomited before she got in my truck, then again after she got out of my truck, and once more on her doorstep when I helped her to the front door. She went for the kiss, and I shut that shit down." I shrugged. "How about you? How'd it go with Kline?"

"It was fine. Thankfully, he didn't go for the kiss, because I wouldn't have wanted him to, you know? But he's nice, and we're going to dinner in a few days, so we'll see."

Why was I relieved that she hadn't hooked up with him?

It didn't matter the reason, really.

I wanted the best for Lila, and it sure as shit wasn't Kline Barley.

"What are you working on?" I asked, glancing down at her notebook.

A pink hue covered her cheeks, and she turned to sit on her heels and face me. I couldn't look down because I wondered if she was wearing panties beneath those tiny shorts, and I didn't want to stare.

This was Lila fucking James.

What the hell was wrong with me?

"Well, I told you I was making a list. I don't want to call it a bucket list because that sounds like I'm dying. So... I need to come up with a name."

"It's all the things you want to do while you're home, right?" I asked, trying to block out the memory of her telling me she wanted to lose her virginity. That had shocked the shit out of me. The thought of someone touching her bothered me. But I liked that she'd shared something so personal with me at the same time.

"Yes. Like things I want to accomplish or check off, you know? Things I haven't made time for before." She beamed at me like this was the most exciting thing in the world.

"Like a rainy-day list," I said.

"Exactly. But it's not a rainy day."

"How about a Snow Day list?" I laughed because it wasn't even fucking June yet, but it was a good play on words with her nickname.

"Yes! A Snow Day list. I love it." She pulled out a Sharpie and wrote the new name on the cover of her notebook.

"So, what do you have so far?" I asked, crossing my legs at the ankles.

"Really? You want to know?" Her tongue peeked out, and my dick jumped to attention. The fucker hadn't done anything when Brenna Wilson gripped him under the table tonight, and I had to pry her hand away as she hiccupped a good forty times in a row and then broke out into a fit of giggles. That shit was not happening. She kept leaning in to talk to me, and her breath smelled like pickles and pina coladas, and if I never smelled either again, I'd be a happy fucking camper.

I cleared my throat and shifted enough to make sure she wouldn't notice my raging boner beneath my zipper. "I do."

"Bear. You can't be talking about this with Travis. This is for me. It's none of his business."

"Hey, didn't you just say we're roommates and friends? You can tell me anything. Obviously, if someone is bothering you or if you're in danger, I wouldn't keep that from Trav. But he doesn't need to know what's on your list." So why the fuck did I want to know what was on it so badly?

"Okay. You promise?" She held her pinky out to me, and I remembered her teaching me all about pinky promises when we were young. I'd tried doing it with my brothers who had a slightly different strategy when it came to making you keep your promises when we were young, which was basically that if you broke your word, you were going to get your head stuck in a toilet while Finn flushed rapidly and Cage held you still. They both gaped at me and laughed their asses off when I'd held up my finger. I'd given it one final shot with my sister, Brinkley, who told me she didn't trust a pinky promise and that I'd need to put it in writing, swearing I wouldn't tell our parents that she broke the front window if she agreed to give me her ice cream for a week. Apparently,

Georgia had broken a few pinky promises with Brink when she was in her tattling stage, so the Reynolds kids all required a bit more than just a pinky promise when they were making a deal.

But not Lila James.

She'd always been different.

I rolled my eyes and tucked my hair behind my ear before offering her my pinky. She held it there, and I didn't miss the way her chest rose and fell rapidly as I moved closer.

"What am I promising, Lila?" I asked. My voice was all tease, but it came out huskier than I'd expected.

"Repeat after me. I, Hugh 'Bear' Reynolds, do so solemnly pinky swear that I won't tell a soul what's on your Snow Day list. I also swear that I won't breathe a word of this to Travis, that overbearing, brut of a brother of yours."

I barked out a laugh and repeated the ridiculous words while our fingers stayed joined for much longer than necessary. My gaze zeroed in on her plump lips, and her dark eyes locked with mine. Something caused me to look down, and I noticed her nipples were poking against her thin, white tank top, and I nearly came undone right there. I quickly pulled my hand away when my dick twitched and reminded me that I was sitting on a bed with my best friend's little sister who was hot as hell and talking about her untouched pussy.

I'm human, after all, and that was all I heard every time she talked about this fucking list.

I leaned back against the headboard. "All right. Let's hear it."

"Number one is to get my dad into a program. I've got an appointment to go look at the place next weekend."

"That's a solid start," I said, and she smiled. She dropped from sitting on her heels to sitting on her ass and crossing her legs in front of her. Jesus. If she wasn't wearing panties, I would have a straight shot of her—

Stop thinking with your dick, asshole.

I stared at her face, making a conscious decision not to let my gaze move below her neck.

"Number two is the biggy. Lose this pesky V-card so it can stop being a topic. You know, Mrs. Runither straight up asked me if I was still a virgin in the middle of her restaurant, as if there was some sort of neon sign on my forehead that said no man wanted to sleep with me. It's humiliating that the whole town seems to know my business."

I pushed to my feet and flipped the switch to turn on the ceiling fan because I was suddenly sweating like a rabid animal.

"Fuck Mrs. Runither. That woman is insane. Did I ever tell you about her coming to the restaurant a few months ago with a hotel key?" I said, dropping back down to sit on the bed. We needed more furniture in here. There should be a chair for visitors. And maybe a second ceiling fan.

"No," she said over a fit of laughter, her eyes were wide as they danced with excitement. "What did she do with the key?"

"She slipped it into my hand and told me that Mr. Runither was going on a hunting trip, and she had a room at that little hotel downtown, if I'd like to join her." I shook my head. The woman was old enough to be my mother.

Lila fell back on the bed in a fit of laughter, and there was something about the sound of her laugh that had always felt like home to me. It was genuine and real, just like her.

She sat back up. "Stooooop. You're serious?"

"I'm fucking serious."

"What did you do?" she asked, and she watched me like this was the most sinister thing she'd ever heard.

"Well, I went to the hotel, of course. Rocked her fucking world." I kept my voice even because it was just too easy to mess with her.

"You didn't?" she said on a gasp.

"You're right. Of course, I didn't. What the fuck do you

think of me?" I dove forward and tipped her back as I tickled her, and she laughed hysterically. "Do you think I'm desperate, Snow?"

She stopped laughing, and her hand came up as she ran her fingers over my scruff. "I don't think you're desperate, Bear. I think any woman would be lucky to be with you."

"Repeat after me," I said, reaching for her pinky finger. "I, Lila 'Snow' James, know that Hugh Reynolds would never jump in the sack with old Mrs. Runither."

As she repeated the words while laughing her ass off, I tugged her hand up and bit her pinky finger just enough to make her squeal as she writhed beneath me.

My phone vibrated in my back pocket, pulling me from my daze as I jumped back and moved to my feet. *What the fuck was I doing?*

I pulled out my phone to see a text from Travis.

"It's your brother. He's asking how things went with Kline." I cleared my throat, trying to pretend that I didn't like what had just happened. That I didn't like the feel of her soft body beneath mine or the way she ran her fingers along my beard.

"Tell him that I'm still out, and he should mind his own business because I'm an adult. Why don't you tell him that?" She sat up, clearly aggravated that he was texting me.

I typed a quick text back to Travis, letting him know that she was home, and I was just saying goodnight to her, and everything seemed to go fine with Kline. I tucked my phone back into my pocket.

"You can't be mad at the guy for caring. Read me the rest of your list now that you've admitted you were wrong to believe I'd mess with a married woman who was old enough to be my mother. And, for the record, I still don't think your virginity belongs on a goddam list." I crossed my arms over my chest. I wasn't going to sit on that bed again because I needed to put some space there.

"Says the guy who's not a virgin." She smirked. "Number three is to tell off Drew Compton for making out with Dougy, my prom date, senior year. I don't really feel strongly about that one. It's more for Del because she despises her. I don't care much for Drew or Dougy, so at this point, I'm fine with what happened back then."

How the fuck does a guy lucky enough to take Lila to a dance end up making out with Drew Compton? That girl had taken her shot with me too many times to count. I was pretty good at reading people and had always known she was trouble.

"I'd be fine to see you tell her off. I'm not a fan. She cheats on her poor boyfriend all the time at the bar. And Dougy's an asshole for doing that to you. I can't believe you never told me that. I would have been all too happy to punch him in the face on your behalf."

"Exactly why I didn't tell you or my brother. I think Brax probably heard about it because his little brother was good friends with Dougy. But he was the one I didn't have to worry about as much as you two."

She was right. Brax was a bit more rational where Lila was concerned. He'd always thought we were a little over the top, especially the older she got.

"That doesn't surprise me. What's next?"

"Number four is to go to a biker bar and flirt with a hot bad boy," she purred, and fuck me if she didn't look sexy as hell when she was talking about it. "Number five was to get drunk, but I've done that now, and I'm not in a hurry to do it again. I still put it on the list because it's nice to have one to check off." She chuckled and reached for her water bottle and took a sip. "Number six is to skinny dip out at Cottonwood Cove because it seems like a rite of passage for anyone who grew up here, but somehow, I've never done it. Have you?"

"Does a bear shit in the woods? Of course, I've done it. Obviously, I grew up a few blocks from the cove and live even closer to it now. The tide comes in late at night, and that's the perfect time for a dip. Hell, I still walk there some nights on my own when it's hot as hell out and jump in to cool off."

"Naked?" Her eyes perused my body from my face all the way down to my toes, and I didn't mind it one bit.

"It's the only way to skinny dip, Snow. That's an easy one. Those are all fairly easy, and they definitely should not be on the same list as your virginity." Why was I so focused on that? It was none of my fucking business.

"Will you go with me one night and stand guard while I strip down and run into the tide so I won't have to drag the girls there? Sloane will not be able to do it on a night she isn't washing her hair, Rina hates the water, and Del still believes that old wives' tale that there's a creature in the cove after dark." She laughed.

I ran a hand through my hair and studied her as I thought about it.

"Or I could ask Kline to go with me," she said, raising a brow when I didn't answer quick enough.

"I'll go with you. Do not ask any random dudes to take you down to the water to skinny dip, nor should you be telling them that you want to lose your virginity. Got it?"

"Got it, Bear."

"So, that's it?" I asked because she looked like she had something else on the list, but her hand was covering the bottom of the notebook.

"Well, I had just added this one before you walked in, but it seems stupid to put it on there before I check off number two." She shrugged.

"What is it?"

"Del told me that showering with a man is pretty amazing. So, I thought I'd add it to the list," she said, before quickly looking away. I moved closer and placed my large hand beneath her chin, turning her face to look at mine.

"Have you never been touched, Lila?"

"I have. Of course, I have. I've dated a few guys. I mean I haven't done *a lot*, and obviously, I've never had sex, and when I talked about showering with Jeremy once, he said he didn't feel comfortable showering with me before we had sex, so we just never did it."

I'd never been more turned on in my life, watching this gorgeous woman who was embarrassed that she hadn't done much and had no clue how fucking sexy it was that she was curious and wanting to explore all of these things that most people took for granted. Hell, I was one of them. I didn't think much about any of this shit because I'd been having sex for so long.

"You've got time, Snow. And Jeremy is a dickhead for saying that. You don't have to have sex with someone to shower with them."

"Have you showered with a lot of women?" she asked, her eyes searching mine as I held my hand beneath her chin.

"I've showered with one or two. I never much cared for it because it felt too intimate. But it certainly didn't have anything to do with whether or not I'd had sex with them. It was more about feeling close enough to want to share that with someone."

"I think it would be even sexier to take a bath with someone. Have you ever done that?" she asked, biting down on that juicy bottom lip.

"I have not. I'm not a big bath guy." I chuckled. "You always were a bath girl, weren't you? I remember Travis used to bang on the bathroom door because you'd be in there for so long."

My voice was gruff, and I knew I was messing with fire talking about this shit with her.

"I'll always pick a bath over a shower. It's just more relaxing, you know? That was what I most looked forward to after every race."

I glanced over at the door leading to her bathroom. "I know there's just a shower in there, but you know you're welcome to use my tub in my bathroom any time, right?"

"Ahhh… I might take you up on that. I'm a little sore after my run this morning."

I ran my thumb over her cheek before stepping back and walking toward the door.

"Any time."

"Thanks, Bear. And I'm definitely adding that to the list."

Bathing with a man.

Fuck me.

I needed to get out of here before I did something I couldn't take back.

Took something I didn't deserve.

I wasn't that man.

"Goodnight, Snow."

She stared down at her notebook, writing quickly, but she glanced up and smiled.

"Goodnight. Thanks for helping me. I can't wait to start checking things off the list." She laughed, and I shook my head, tugging the door open.

The first thing on my list tonight…

A cold fucking shower and a date with my right hand.

I'd never cross the line with my best friend's little sister in real life, but in fantasy…

I was going to let myself enjoy every dirty thought I had about Lila James.

eight

· · ·

Lila

HUGH and I had fallen into a rhythm over the last week. I handled the books at all three locations, and I had taken over the scheduling for him, as well. We'd come up with a plan to increase staffing at each location, but the focus was mostly on Reynolds' as it was the busiest by far. He was running a few interviews today, and my hope was that this would lighten his load. The man was burning the candle at both ends, and I knew he'd eventually burn out if he didn't get things under control. I liked helping him organize his businesses. The financials had been super easy to input on QuickBooks, and I showed him how to categorize everything. He'd been doing a lot of it by hand, and he wasn't keeping up. Now things were up-to-date and running smoothly.

I'd jumped behind the bar last night with Joseph, another bartender, as Kline had been off both yesterday and today, and I'd helped manage the rush while Hugh was busy in the kitchen helping the servers. I'd loved working behind the bar. I'd picked things up quickly, and it had been a lot of fun. Del, Sloane, and Rina had come by for a drink, and they'd been thrilled to find me behind the bar. We had plans to go to the biker bar this weekend after I toured Havenwood, the facility that I was looking at for my dad.

Things were falling into place for me, and I was happy. It felt good to just enjoy each day as it arrived. I was running in the mornings and going as far as I felt like going, as there was no set workout that I had to complete. Hugh and I ate breakfast together every morning, and then we'd head to work and usually end up eating dinner together and heading home at the same time.

I leaned back in my chair as my phone rang, and I saw my father's face on the screen.

"Hey, Dad," I said, holding the phone up as he was FaceTiming me.

"Hi, sweetheart. I wanted you to know that I went to work today at the auto shop, and I'm home now and going to make a little dinner and watch some TV." He was sitting on the couch, and I quickly assessed that he was sober.

He'd been doing these check-ins ever since I moved into Hugh's house on the days that I didn't make it over to see him. I appreciated that he was trying because none of this would work if he didn't.

"That's great, Dad. I'm proud of you. One day at a time, right?" I encouraged.

He nodded. "One day at a time, sweetheart."

"I have that appointment this weekend, so I'll get all the information and bring that over to you."

He stared at the phone screen for a long moment before speaking. "Sounds good. You know, sometimes, you take my breath away because you look so much like your mother. I miss her every day."

A lump formed in my throat. "Me, too, Dad. And it's okay to miss her. Just don't try to numb those feelings away, okay? Missing someone you love is part of grieving. It sucks, and it isn't fair that she's gone—but she would want us to live a good life, wouldn't she?"

"You're right. Of course, you got your smarts from her, too." He chuckled. "God, she would be so proud of you and Travis. I'm going to make you guys proud this time. I promise I will."

"You don't need to promise anything, Dad. You just need to do this for you right now. Wouldn't it feel so good to not be a slave to this addiction after all these years? To just wake up and not have to battle it every day? I know it's easier said than done, but I'm here to support you every step of the way."

"I'm so glad you're home. These last few years without my sunshine around have been tough, even though I have loved watching you accomplish so much. I'm just—well, I'm just happiest when you're close by."

"Me, too," I said, blinking a few times because my eyes were welling with emotion.

"All right. I'm going to go heat up that lasagna you made for me. I swear, you froze enough meals to feed me for three months."

"Eating well is important, too." I shrugged. My father had gotten very thin, and I knew he didn't bother preparing healthy meals for himself because he hadn't done it when we were growing up.

We said our goodbyes, and I leaned back in the chair just as the door swung open and a sexy-as-sin Hugh Reynolds stood in the doorway, leaning against the doorjamb. He wore a wrinkled white button up and some cargo pants. His wavy hair stopped at his shoulders and was a disheveled mess, yet he managed to be the best-looking man I'd ever laid eyes on.

"Take a break. Travis is here picking up food for Shay, and someone else is asking for you." He smirked, and I squeezed my thighs together because there was just something about the way those sage-green eyes looked at me lately.

"Who?" I asked as I pushed to my feet because I was glad my brother was here. I'd gone by to see him and Shay last night, but I'd spent the whole time talking to her and barely asked how he was doing.

Hugh smiled. "It's Coach Lewis, and he just got back in town."

I ran past Hugh and sprinted down the hallway and up the stairs to the restaurant, hearing him laugh behind me. Hugh's office was in the basement, but I couldn't wait to see Coach Lewis. He'd been out of town since I'd been back home. My high school coach was like a second father to me in a lot of ways.

Travis was standing at the bar talking to him, and I lunged at the older man.

"There she is," he said as he wrapped his arms around me.

"I thought you weren't getting back until next week?"

"Yeah, well, Brenda got homesick for the dogs, and Coach Callaway hasn't been pushing the practices the way I do," he said with a chuckle. Coach Callaway was his assistant coach, and the man was a big softy, so that didn't surprise me. Coach Lewis's wife, Brenda, was one of my favorite people in Cottonwood Cove, and I'd always loved them both dearly.

"Well, I'm glad you came back early."

"Me, too. And standing here looking at a collegiate national champion. Do you know how impressive that is, girl?" he teased.

"I tell her that all the time," Travis said, beaming down at me like he always did when he wasn't being a domineering, stubborn ass.

"Yeah, yeah, yeah. I'm just happy to see you."

"How's working at Reynolds'? This place has been the hottest restaurant in town since it opened, and it doesn't look like it's letting up any time soon from what I can tell. That's why I thought I'd come and hit Hugh up at the same time I came to see the superstar."

"What can I do for you?" Hugh asked as his chest grazed my back, and cedar and mint flooded my senses, per usual.

"Well, I was going to see if you and Lila would stop by our booth at the Cottonwood Fair," Coach Lewis said. "We rented a large space this year to have all the families come out and kick off the season. I know you're catering for the fair, but I was hoping you'd cut me a deal on providing some appetizers for our booth," he said.

"I think we could probably donate the food, pending my new chief financial officer doesn't have a problem with it," Hugh teased. The man was ridiculously generous, and I loved that about him, but I was also a numbers person, and there were areas he could tighten things up. Charity was not one of them. There was always room to give back to your community.

"I think we could make that work." I chuckled.

"Thanks. But I don't mind paying for the cost of the food," Coach Lewis said, and Hugh shook his head as if it weren't up for discussion. The older man smiled and nodded before turning his attention to me. "And, of course, the main reason I stopped by is to see if you would come speak to the kids about your journey to being the most decorated runner in the state of California to date, then going off to one of the best universities in the country to get your degree and win a collegiate national title at the same time." He shook his head and smiled.

The man had always been a huge support to me. He'd pushed me when I'd needed it, and he'd believed in me when I didn't believe in myself.

"Of course. I'd be honored to speak to them." I sighed. I'd missed… this. Being home and seeing people that had been a part of my life for such a long time. I'd been so busy these last few years that I'd forgotten how much I missed home.

"And you sure look good, Lila James. You look… happy. I'm really glad you're home."

"Just for the summer. She's got a big job waiting for her back in Chicago come September. This is just temporary,"

Travis said, and it was maybe the hundredth time I'd heard him explain that to anyone and everyone who I'd spoken to around him.

"Well, there are big jobs here, too. You know, if you ever want to be a coach, the kids sure would love it. Having the famed Lila James out there teaching them her secrets, I'd be willing to pass the torch to you any day." He winked.

Travis's eyes doubled in size. "I mean, she could go help out until she leaves, but it wouldn't be long term. She's got big things to get back to."

I felt Hugh's shoulders stiffen from behind me as if even he thought my brother was being a bit much about it. Coach Lewis looked between Travis and me. "I don't think this is a girl you ever need to worry about, Travis. She's worked hard her whole life. I think she's earned the right to choose her own path, don't you?"

"Hell, yeah. It's just not going to be here. She's got so many more opportunities in Chicago."

"Oh my gosh," I groaned. "You're acting like one of those obnoxious, overbearing parents, Trav. People are going to start calling you *Karen*."

"What the hell does that mean?"

"Dude. You could stop reminding everyone that she's leaving. We all know. But this town is good enough for everyone you're talking to, so it might start to rub people the wrong way if you keep insisting that she needs to get the hell out of here," Hugh said, and he chuckled, but I could tell he was frustrated with Travis, too. We'd been spending a lot of time together, and I was getting pretty good at reading him. And it was nice to have someone on my side when it came to my brother.

"Whatever. Call me Travis, call me Karen, call me fucking overbearing. I want the best for you. End of story. And does Coach Lewis know that you're going out with that jackass Kline tonight?"

"I don't know anything about a date, but it's not really my business, is it?" Coach Lewis said, also appearing annoyed with my brother.

I groaned at the change in topic. "Of course, you don't know anything about it. You just got here. And I'm not dating Kline. It's dinner. We work together. We're friends. Why do you make everything such a big deal?" I shot a hard look at Travis.

"Well, lucky for me, I've got Hugh looking out for you, so I don't need to worry."

Coach Lewis smiled. "Hugh's as good as they come. I'd say you're in good hands. How about you come by the house next week and we can catch up?"

"I'd love that."

He leaned forward and hugged me. "It's good to see you, girl. Travis, you can probably tone it down a little with this one. She's always been able to take care of herself. And I heard Shay's pregnant, so you've got plenty on your own plate."

"That's for fucking sure." Travis ran a hand through his hair before clapping the older man on the shoulder. "It was good to see you, Coach."

"You, too. Hugh, I'll shoot you an email with all the details, and I'll count on seeing both of you at the event?"

"We'll be there," I said, before he turned and walked out the door.

"Why are you such an asshole?" I hissed at my brother, and Hugh barked out a laugh.

"What? You're not going to be a coach at a small-town high school, Lila. You've got a job offer at one of the largest Fortune 500 companies in the country. I didn't want him to get his hopes up."

"I love you, Trav. But sometimes you just—" I looked away.

"What?"

"Never mind. I wanted to let you know that I'm going to tour Havenwood, that rehab place I told you about on the outskirts of town, on Saturday for Dad. I wanted to see if you'd go with me?"

"You're serious?"

I felt Hugh's finger stroke the outside of my hand. It was the slightest movement, but it comforted me. My brother could be a stubborn ass, and it helped to know I had Hugh's support.

"I'm very serious. Dad is open to it. He needs help, and this place has a great success rate. We've never tried anything outside of you getting angry and Dad repeating the same patterns over and over."

"That's on him, not me. And who the fuck is paying for it? Come on, Lila. How many times can this man let you down?" he hissed.

"Apparently, one more, because I'm not giving up on him."

"No. We're not doing this. I'm not spending a penny to help a man who won't help himself."

"I'm not asking you to pay for it. They have financing. I have a few ideas for how to cover the cost. I'm just asking you to come with me."

He scrubbed a hand down his face. "I have to work Saturday. Let's do it another time."

I knew what he was doing. He was hoping I'd give up. But he was betting on the wrong horse because that wasn't going to happen. I didn't give up on people.

That was Travis's MO. I didn't fault him for it, but I didn't appreciate him faulting me for wanting to try.

For caring.

"What if I go with her?" Hugh said, catching us both off guard.

Travis studied him and then nodded. "Fine. Hugh can talk some sense into you. Thanks, brother."

"Of course," he said, just as Danielle came over to hand Travis his bag of to-go food. He thanked her as she hurried back to the kitchen, and he turned back to me.

"Don't be pissed at me. I just don't want to see you get hurt." My brother kissed the top of my head before fist-bumping Hugh. "Thanks, dude. I'll call you later."

He walked out of the restaurant, and I shook my head.

"Why is he such a jerk sometimes?" I asked as Hugh's gaze searched mine.

"He's only this way with you, and you know why, Snow. It doesn't make it right, but he obviously has his reasons."

"I got sick as a kid and ended up in the hospital. Dad checked out as a parent for far too long. I get it. People make mistakes. Can you imagine being judged your entire life by your worst moment? The man lost his wife. He spiraled. If I can forgive him, why can't Travis?" We were standing near the bar, and I glanced around to make sure no one was listening.

"It's more than that. It was the neglect that led to you getting so sick and then you two being separated for a few weeks after all of that went down. He changed after that, you know? He swore he'd protect you, and he's held himself to it." Hugh ran a hand down his face as if he was torn between defending his best friend and being rational.

I understood Travis wanting to protect me, but he was punishing me now, too. Pushing me away from my home and the people I loved. The home I loved. A father that I loved.

"Trust me. I lived it. I remember. But I've moved on. And I think he's pushing me away because it's easier for him when I'm not here." I looked away and shook my head. "Yet, I live in one of the most dangerous cities in the US, and he's fine with it. He's only got a problem with me being here. He can't stand the idea that I still love our father."

"Hey, I'll talk to him, all right? I'm having lunch with him and Brax tomorrow."

I glanced down at my phone and noticed the time. "Thanks, Bear. I've got to go meet Kline for dinner now."

"He's not picking you up?"

"No. I said I preferred to walk. We're just going to Anders Steakhouse, and then I'll be home after. You got a hot date tonight?" I asked, all while holding my breath as I waited for him to respond. We were spending a lot of time together, and the thought of him out with a woman bothered me. I knew it shouldn't. Hell, I was going on a date, even if I didn't feel like going.

"I'm having dinner with my dad, Cage, and Finn tonight. It's our monthly Reynolds boys' night out." He chuckled. "Call me if you need a ride, all right?"

There was something in his gaze that I couldn't place. Was he upset that I was going out with Kline? Or was I reading into it because a part of me wanted him to be bothered by it?

"Thanks. I'll be fine." I held up my hand and waved before heading out the door. I was in a foul mood after my conversation with Travis. I needed to shake it off.

Anders Steakhouse was only a block away, and the breeze from the water moved around me as I breathed in the ocean air. I loved it here. Sure, there were some hard memories, but Cottonwood Cove was home.

Kline was standing outside the restaurant when I came around the corner, and his face lit up when he saw me. "I wish you would have let me pick you up. I feel like a douchebag meeting you here."

I chuckled as he wrapped his arms around me for a quick hug. "I came from work, and it was a block away. I do have my own car, by the way, but I like walking."

He nodded and held the door open for me as we stepped inside. I didn't recognize the hostess, but she greeted us with a warm hello and led us to our table in the back.

"Lila James? Is that you?" It was Marilee Compton, Drew's mother, waving me over like we were old friends. We weren't. She'd been one of the people who had spread a lot of rumors about my father around town, and I'd never liked her. And the apple didn't fall far from the tree with her daughter. Her husband smiled and held up his hand.

"Hi, Mr. and Mrs. Compton. It's nice to see you."

"I didn't know you were back in town. Drew didn't mention it," she said on a gasp, like it was shocking news. Me and Drew weren't friends, so I wasn't sure why she thought her daughter would know I was home or why she'd care.

"Yep. I'm back for a few months and working at Reynolds', helping out Hugh."

"Congratulations. I heard you won nationals. That's an amazing accomplishment," Mr. Compton said, seeming genuinely happy for me.

"Thank you." I smiled and then shrugged awkwardly. "And now, I've graduated and I'm back home for the summer to spend some time with my family."

"You know... good for you," Marilee said as she shook her head. Her eyes traveled all over my face as if she were memorizing every detail. "No one ever thought you'd turn out this well. What a nice surprise."

A pit in my stomach wrenched, and I felt the blood drain from my face at her words. She'd said what I always imagined people were thinking. I hated that people decided who I'd be based on the events that happened in my childhood. This was what Travis was always trying to protect me from. Maybe I was being too harsh with him.

"Yep. Even with all she went through as a kid, she ended up being a rockstar." Kline winked at me, and I wanted to throat-punch him for jumping on the bandwagon.

For not being appalled by what she'd just said.

I wanted to tell them all to fuck off.

To tell them that those comments have a way of making a person feel small.

To remind them that those same comments were swirling around when I was a kid, and I heard every last one of them.

The pity they felt for me and Travis.

They only made me push myself harder.

But I wouldn't give them the satisfaction of knowing that.

I'd just hold my head up high and be very careful who I allowed in my circle.

Just like I always had.

nine

. . .

Hugh

"WELL, THAT WAS GOOD," my father said as he finished off the last of the peach cobbler we'd ordered for the table.

"I'm glad we stopped going to Reynolds' or Garrity's, because it's nice to see Hugh actually remain at the table while we eat." Cage smirked. My father had insisted we go somewhere else starting this month, because the last few times we'd gone out, I'd ended up in the kitchen or dealing with some sort of work drama.

"Agreed. Good idea on that one, Pops," Finn said. "You seem a lot more relaxed now that you've brought Lila on board."

"She's already helped me a ton," I said, checking my phone for the hundredth time to see if she'd texted me, and she hadn't. I didn't want to be overbearing like Travis, so I didn't text her, even though I wanted to. But I wanted to make sure she got home safely.

"You've sure been checking that phone a lot more than usual. You waiting for a booty call?" Cage asked with a laugh, and my father smiled and shook his head. He'd raised three boys; he was not clueless about what went on. None of us were currently in relationships, and we all enjoyed women as much as the next guy—so he knew what we were up to. Although Cage was in a different boat these days as he was busy raising his daughter on his own.

"I'll have you know I haven't gotten laid in quite a while. It may even be a record," I said, and my father rolled his eyes.

"You might just be growing up, son."

"I'm a moody fucker when I go too long," Finn said with a shrug, and we all laughed.

"So then, why are you checking your phone like a fucking teenage girl?" Cage asked.

"I was just checking to see if Lila needed a ride home."

They all three started laughing like they were in on some inside joke that I wasn't aware of.

"Let me ask you something," Finn said, leaning in close to me. "Did this newfound celibacy start when Lila James moved into your casita and started working for you?"

"What? No. It started before that. There is nothing going on there. Are you fucking kidding me? Trav would lose his mind. She's just here for a little while. We're friends, nothing more."

"She looks good, though," Cage said, waggling his brows, knowing he was getting under my skin.

"That makes you a dirty old man. She's too young for you. And you couldn't survive the wrath of Trav." I laughed.

"So protective, brother. I see the way you look at her," Finn said. "You may be able to hide it from your best friend, but you know the Reynolds brothers have a gift. We can see through the bullshit."

"Oh, yeah? Where was that gift when this one shaved off your eyebrow in college?" I laughed. Finn could turn on the dramatics whenever he wanted to. It was the actor in him. But he'd lost his shit when Cage pulled that stunt.

"Don't go there." He pointed his finger at me and then at our oldest brother, and my father sat back watching with a big, goofy smile on his face. "You know my face is my money-maker, so that was a low blow."

"Then you shouldn't have told Elaine Bridges that I was into her." Cage shook his head with disgust.

"She told me she had made an entire bulletin board that was covered in photos of you. What was I supposed to do?"

"Um, nothing? She's a stage-five clinger. We never even dated. She's also much older than me. I'm just fucking thankful she moved away because that was a rough couple of weeks."

"And I see our dear baby brother did a wonderful job of deflecting the conversation. Just admit you want her. Own it, dick licker." Finn smirked.

"Never going to happen. I, unlike you two, am a man in control of both my emotions and my dick. Sorry you have to sit through this tonight, Pops," I said, winking at my dad.

"You know I love some good Reynolds brother banter." He smirked. "But I'm just going to say this, and we'll drop it."

"Ahhhh… I love when Pops gives his words of wisdom." Finn clapped his hands together.

"Let's hear it, old wise one." Cage chuckled.

"Watch yourself, buddy. I'm not that old." My father turned his attention to me. "The heart wants what the heart wants."

I grunted. "That's your advice? You've been watching too many sappy movies with Mom."

"That was a little cheesy, dude. Even for you," Finn said as he shook his head.

"Hey, it may be cheesy, but it's true. I wasn't looking for anything when I met your mom. She was way too good for me, and I knew it, but look at us. Five kids later, and we've built this great life together. You know why?" He raised a brow and took his time looking at each of us.

"Because the heart wants what the fucking heart wants," I said, and the table erupted in laughter.

"Take it or leave it, boys. I don't worry about this one," he said, slapping me on the back. "He's got a good head on his shoulders, and like I've always said, *you know when you know.*"

"Wow. This is really riveting advice, Pops. *The heart wants what the heart wants*, and *you know when you know*," Cage said after we paid the check and all pushed to our feet. "It's a good thing Mom's the therapist."

"You losing it, old man?" Finn teased.

More laughter erupted as we made our way outside.

"Hey, I'm a simple man, but I speak the truth. Always trust this." My father clasped a hand over his heart. "It's gotten me everything that matters in my life."

"You're a wise man," I said, pulling my dad in for a hug because he happened to be one of my favorite people on the planet. I went to him every time I needed guidance, and he'd never failed me.

We all said our goodbyes, and I knew they were just razzing me. But I also knew I needed to be careful where Lila was concerned.

I liked hanging out with her all the time, but it concerned me that I thought about her when we weren't together.

I knew better, yet I struggled with doing the right thing when it came to her.

I pulled in the garage, and when I stepped inside the house, the door to the casita flew open. "You're finally home?" she gasped.

I raised a brow because she looked angry. "I am. Am I not supposed to be?"

"No. Of course not. I just—I was waiting for you." She shrugged and then waved me toward her room. I followed her inside as she slipped on her flip-flops. "I'm going to Cottonwood Cove to skinny dip. Are you coming with me?"

Ain't that the million-dollar question.

"Did something happen with Kline?" My hands fisted at

my sides. She was off, and Lila wasn't a hothead, so something had obviously happened.

"Kline's fine, but he's not worth my time anymore. It's time to focus on the list."

I cleared my throat. I didn't completely trust myself around her.

She was wearing a pair of cutoff jean shorts and a white tank top. Definitely not what she'd left Reynolds' in when she'd gone to meet Kline for dinner. Her long, dark hair was pulled up in a ponytail, and she quickly stalked past me, heading for the door.

"You seem a little upset. Why don't we talk about it here? There's no rush to check things off the list. The water will still be there tomorrow."

She whipped around. "I'm tired of waiting until tomorrow. My whole life has been about tomorrow. I'm doing this right now, with or without you."

I groaned and followed her out the door. I sure as shit wasn't going to let her go down to the cove and strip naked alone.

At least, that was what I was telling myself.

We walked in silence for about half a block, side by side.

"You going to tell me what happened?"

She came to a stop and shook her head. "That's the thing. Nothing happened, per se. It's the same old shit, different day, Bear. It's my brother and his irrational behavior. It's the way everyone gossips about my father. And tonight, we were at the restaurant, and that damn Mrs. Compton was running her mouth."

She turned around and started storming toward the water again. Her ponytail swayed from side to side down her back. Her long, lean legs moved briskly, and her perfect ass was impossible to look away from. There was a path at the end of my street that led through the trees and down to the water. She maneuvered around the branches in the dark like she knew this place well, so I assumed she must be running over here in the mornings.

"What did she say? She's always been an asshole, just like her daughter."

She stopped again, my chest slamming into hers as she'd caught me off guard when she'd halted. The light from the moon peeked down through the tall evergreens and shone down on her pretty face. "She made a comment, and it pissed me off. Because it's what everyone thinks about me, you know?"

"Tell me," I said, moving closer as I shoved a branch away from my head.

"She said that I turned out better than anyone expected, as if I should have been a train wreck and it's such a pleasant surprise that I actually made something of myself." A tear rolled down her cheek, and I swiped it away with the pad of my thumb.

"Fuck her. What did Kline say?"

"He agreed with her!" she shouted. She turned and marched toward the little beach entry beside the water. The tide was coming in, and the waves lapped against the shore. "As if he knew what a shitshow my childhood was and couldn't jump on the bandwagon fast enough."

I followed her down the path, my voice calm and even. "Hey."

She came to an abrupt stop and whipped around. "What?"

"The way they're saying it sounds like a backhanded compliment, but the truth is, they're right, Snow."

She placed her hands on her hips, her mouth hanging open. "So, you expected me to be a failure, too?"

I chuckled. "No. Don't put words in my mouth. Someone's being a little dramatic now, yeah?"

"Dramatic? How? Do you know how it feels to know that everyone expected you to fail? How exhausting it is to prove that you're worthy? And then when you finally prove your-self, everyone tells you how shocking it is?"

"Stop overthinking it. It has nothing to do with what happened in your childhood. The shit you've accomplished is fucking badass. You're a national champion, Lila. The best collegiate female distance runner out there. That's fucking amazing. And I don't give a shit if your dad was drunk or sober or if your childhood was messed up or perfect. You've accomplished shit most people couldn't dream of. Not to mention, being a straight A student at one of the most competitive universities in the country. Own that shit. You've got nothing more to prove. Just hold your head up, look them in the eyes, and say, *Damn straight, asshole.*"

Her eyes widened, and she shrugged. "Never thought about it like that."

"You're always going to have people who aren't happy for your success, but only you control how you respond to it."

"Fair point. But Kline jumped on that train so fast like he knew my whole story. No one knows my whole story outside of you and Travis and maybe Brax. Just the stuff they've heard. They don't know what a good man my father is or all that he's been through."

"It's no one's fucking business. And I told you Kline wasn't the guy for you. So, if you kick his ass to the curb, I'll be fine with it." I smirked.

"I bet you will, Bear. Fine. I've got to get into my birthday suit and march into the tide. The least I can do is check some-thing off the damn list today."

I chuckled. "Why is this so important to you?"

"Because I just want to feel normal for once in my life. I've been so busy trying to prove I have it together that I stopped living somewhere along the way. And fear has been driving me for a long time. I just got drunk for the first time in my life recently; I haven't had sex yet or showered with a man. I've been so focused on achieving things that I've been missing out. I haven't had a ton of fun in my life." She shrugged. "So, I'm changing that now."

"You sure are." I smirked.

"So, are you just going to watch me or join me?" she asked as she unzipped her jean shorts and started sliding them down her legs as a little white lace peeked out.

Good Christ.

I let out a long sigh before turning around so I had my back to her. "You do know your brother will cut off my fucking balls and disown me for skinny dipping with you, right?"

She broke out in hysterical laughter. "Come on, Bear. Aren't you the one who just told me not to listen to what other people think? Why don't you just look him in the eyes and say, *Damn straight, asshole.*" She chuckled, throwing my words back at me. "And it's not like I haven't seen a naked man before. I just haven't had sex with one. Don't be a baby."

"I'm not being a baby. I'm trying to be respectful, for fuck's sake." I'd seen more naked women than the average man. But this was Lila.

"Well, stop. We're friends. Come on. I'll go in first so you don't have to see me if it's that horrifying for you," she said over a fit of giggles, and I knew she was moving toward the water because the leaves rustled beneath her feet, so I turned around.

To make sure she was safe, of course.

The moonlight caught her back side as it hovered above us. I was definitely being tested because the woman had the most beautiful body I'd ever seen. Like a work of fucking art.

Petite.

Lean.

Feminine.

She walked into the water and yelped. "It's so cold. Remind me why doing this naked is better than wearing a bathing suit? Because my lady parts seem to be the most sensitive to this temperature."

Did she really just say that?

I tugged my tee over my head and set it on the ground beside her clothing. Her bra and panties were on top, and I tried like hell to keep my dick from responding to the knowledge that she was wearing nothing only a few feet away, but clearly, he had a mind of his own because he throbbed against my zipper. I kicked off my boots before shoving my pants and briefs down my legs. I'd dove into the water naked more times than I could count. But doing this with Travis's little sister definitely felt like I was crossing a line.

She whistled from the water and taunted me a little more. "This actually feels so good. Are you coming?"

Jesus. She had no idea how the things she said affected me.

Am I coming? I'd like to.

I had a one-track mind most of the time, and sex had always been at the forefront of my thoughts until recently.

But ever since Lila came back to town, that had definitely changed.

I had my back to her before I turned around and strode toward the water. I made no attempt to hide my erection other than it being dark, but I was fairly certain she could see everything because she went completely quiet, her mouth gaping open as she watched me.

"It's always better in the water without clothes on, Snow," I said, as I walked a few steps into the cove and then dove under where I knew the ground dropped off. When I came up, I shoved the hair away from my face and moved to stand in front of her. She was treading water as she was a good foot shorter than me, whereas I was able to just stand with my chest above the water line.

"I agree. This might be my favorite thing I've checked off

the list so far," she said, her breaths coming fast as she continued to tread water.

"Yeah, this is hard to beat." There was only one thing on her list better than skinny dipping, and that was sex. But I wasn't about to say that. I offered my hand so she could take a break from moving her arms and legs to stay above water, and she took it. But then she lunged forward, and her hands landed on my shoulders.

Her chest brushed mine as her hard nipples grazed my skin. Without warning, my dick must have doubled in size and darted in her direction because she jumped and laughed when the tip of my cock grazed her. I reached beneath her armpits and held her a few inches away from me.

"Jesus, Snow. You can't be rubbing up against me like that," I growled, because I was on edge having her this close to me without any clothes on.

Her hands reached back out for my shoulders, and she pulled herself closer again, and I didn't fight her. Her legs wrapped around my waist, and I didn't move. Her hands found each side of my face. A halo of light from the moon illuminated around her as her gaze locked with mine.

"Why not, Bear?" she whispered.

"Because you're playing with fire." I kept my tone even, though I felt anything but. Her breasts were pressed against my chest, and her pussy sat on my lower belly, taunting my eager dick, who was standing at attention, even in the freezing cold water. I couldn't fucking think straight. I wanted her more than I'd ever wanted anyone or anything—but I knew better.

I would not be Lila James's first anything.

I wouldn't take her virginity or her heart.

She was leaving in a few months, and this couldn't go anywhere.

Not to mention the fact that her brother would fucking kill me.

He'd always been a good friend to me, and he deserved the same in return.

"Maybe I should put playing with fire on the list." She smiled so wide it made my chest hurt. My hands were hanging down at my sides because I was afraid to touch her.

"Lila, you need to get down. You can check this one off the list. Let's get out of here and head home." I leaned forward to urge her down, but instead, she slid herself down my body, rubbing all that sweetness along my throbbing cock, and I nearly came undone right there. Her eyes closed, and she moved back up ever so slowly and moaned.

Motherfucker.

Who'd have thought the most erotic thing I'd ever experience would be my best friend's little sister rubbing herself against my dick while we stood in the water under the moon, naked as a bear's ass.

Why the fuck did I think this was a good idea?

"Snow," I whispered. "We can't do this."

"Do you not want me?" she asked, and her eyes opened and locked with mine.

"It's not that, and you know it."

She rocked herself down and up again, taking her sweet time and grinding against all of my hardness. "That feels so good, Bear. Why can't we just let ourselves feel good?"

My hands grasped her hips to hold her still as I hissed. "Fuck."

I took a minute to catch my breath because the urge to push into her, take her right here, right now, was fucking strong.

"You know why," I growled, once I got myself under control.

"Because you're afraid of my brother? Or afraid of your feelings? Which one is it, because I know that you want me, and I obviously want you."

"I'm not afraid of your brother. I'm afraid of what crossing this line would do to all of us. You're fucking leaving at the end of the summer, Lila. You've never had sex, and you want me to just casually take that from you? Not fucking happening." I was angry, but I couldn't seem to push her away or walk out of the water. I just stood there, completely still.

"I'm not suggesting we have sex," she said, as she slid her hot little body down and up my cock once again. I didn't stop her this time. Instead, I hissed out a breath at the feel of her against me.

"What are you suggesting?" I asked, and this time, I helped slide her up and down again two more times as she rubbed up against me, and she groaned.

"I'm just suggesting we explore this, because I've never felt—*this*, whatever is happening right now; it hasn't happened to me before," she said, and her voice was all breathy and laced with need.

"You've never been turned on like this?" I moved my hand to the side of her neck, forcing her head up so she could look at me. "Open your eyes right now."

Her eyes flew open, and her breaths were coming faster as she continued to grind up against me over and over, her fingers digging into my shoulders as her gaze locked with mine.

"Never, Bear. And I don't want to stop right now," she said, her tone frantic.

I didn't want to do anything to take advantage of her, but I didn't want to stop her from feeling good either. It was fucking sexy as hell to see her chasing her pleasure while grinding all that sweetness against me.

"One time, Snow. We never talk about this, and it never happens again. You got it?" I asked, as I gripped her hips harder and helped her move faster, pressing myself into her where I knew she wanted me. We weren't having sex—we were just getting off by rubbing up against one another naked.

Was I actually trying to fucking justify this?

"I pinky promise," she said, and her lips were so close, I couldn't help myself. I'd be damned if the first time Lila James got off would be grinding up against me without my mouth on hers. My tongue snaked out and ran across her bottom lip, and she gasped. I nipped and licked and teased her before my mouth covered hers. Her lips parted, and my tongue found hers. Her hands tugged at my hair, and I lost all control. I slid her up and down, faster and faster. My dick was so hard, I knew I couldn't hold on much longer with her bare pussy grinding against me rapidly. Her head fell back, our mouths losing contact, as her entire body shook and trembled.

And fuck me if I didn't go right over the edge with her.

We continued moving, riding out our pleasure, both of us gasping for air as I processed the fact that I'd just gotten off while humping my best friend's little sister, who also happened to be a virgin.

And it somehow managed to be the best fucking sex of my life, and we hadn't even had sex.

Lila's head moved, and she tucked it between my collarbone and jaw, and her arms wrapped around my neck as she stayed completely still, waiting for her breathing to settle. It wasn't lost on me that she felt completely weightless, like she belonged there.

Somewhere she could never stay.

"Are you mad?" she whispered, and her lips kissed my shoulder before she pulled her head back to look at me.

"Not at you."

"I'm sorry. I know you didn't want that to happen. But it just felt so good, and I couldn't stop myself," she said, and my dick hardened again at her words.

"Don't apologize. But we need to stop talking about it and get out of the water right now, all right?"

She started to slide down my body, and then she paused

as her head fell back in a chuckle. "Ohhhhh. We've got a situation."

"We sure as fuck do," I grunted, as I held her a few inches from me and walked toward shore, setting her on her feet once we were in shallow enough water that she could stand.

"Don't be mad, Bear. This was on me, not you. I'm sorry for pushing it. I got lost in the moment. We don't need to make it a big deal." She tugged her long ponytail over one shoulder and wrung out the water. She wouldn't look at me, and I could hear the shame in her voice as we walked toward shore.

We stopped in front of the pile of clothes, and I reached for her panties and bra, holding them out to her, before tugging on my briefs and jeans.

She slipped into her shorts as I pulled the T-shirt over my head, even though everything was wet and sticking to us. I wasn't going to speak until we were dressed.

We started walking toward my house, and I turned to look at her. "There's nothing to be ashamed of. And that was not just on you. We both wanted it to happen, and it felt fucking amazing, so don't go beating yourself up. I'm just not the guy you're looking for, Snow. I may not get to be the first man who gets to have sex with you, but I'm not mad that I get to be the first man to give you pleasure."

She laughed. "Well, don't go getting a big head about it."

Did everything she said have to sound so sexual?

She had to be the sexiest virgin on the planet.

I felt like some sort of deviant around her.

I needed to shake it off because this ended now.

This was a one and done, and we wouldn't speak of it again after tonight.

ten

. . .

Lila

WHEN WE GOT BACK to the house, I was still floating on air. I'd just had my first orgasm, and it was with Hugh Reynolds. The man was a walking fantasy. Big and strong and commanding—and I was here for it. But he'd made it clear that it couldn't happen again.

The way his mouth had claimed mine.

The way his body felt against mine.

The way his hands gripped my hips.

"You all right?" he asked, snapping me from my stupor. His shirt was soaked and clinging to his muscular chest that had a peppering of dark hair.

"Yeah. I'm just going to go take a shower." I leaned against the door and smiled at him. Why did the first guy that I actually felt something for physically have to be the one who was completely off limits?

For so many reasons, it just wasn't possible for anything to come of this.

But that didn't stop me from wanting him.

"Hey," he called out, just as I turned to step into my room.

"Yeah?"

"What if we each grab a shower and you go pour us those

hot teas you made last night, and I'll find us a movie?" His tongue swiped out to wet his bottom lip, and I clasped my hands together, intertwining my fingers to keep from reaching for him.

"That would be amazing. Thank you. I'll see you in a little bit."

"Sounds good, Snow."

He walked toward his bedroom, and I ran to my room and turned on the shower. I rinsed my body, dried off, and grabbed my pj's. I glanced in the mirror and studied my face.

This must be the face of a woman who'd just gotten herself some.

I mean, I didn't really get me some, but I sure as hell got me *something*.

I brushed out my wet hair and pulled it into a bun on top of my head. I stopped in the kitchen and turned on the kettle before pouring us each a chai tea with some almond milk and carried the mugs over to the couch and set them on the coffee table.

Hugh walked out, his hair wet and tucked behind his ears. His chiseled jaw worked back and forth as he took me in before we both sat down on the brown, leather, L-shaped couch, and he placed a throw pillow between us, which made me chuckle.

"This house is so cozy." I reached for my mug and motioned to the other cup sitting beside it. "That one is for you."

"Thanks. Your brother and his guys helped me with every renovation I did here." He reached for his tea and grabbed the remote with his free hand before turning to look at me. "Are you okay with everything that just happened?"

He looked so tortured, the way his eyebrows pinched together with concern.

"I'm actually great." The strap on my tank top slipped down my arm, and his eyes widened. "Why are you being so weird? It's not like you didn't already see the goods." I waggled my brows.

He barked out a laugh. "I didn't really see the goods. I felt them rubbing up against me, though, didn't I?"

I shook my head and set my tea on the coffee table. I found it hilarious that he was uncomfortable about seeing me in pajamas, yet I'd dry-humped the man into oblivion. Well, can you really dry-hump someone in the water? I guess I'd wet-humped him? Either way, it was on me, and I had no regrets as long as he wasn't upset.

"You sure did." I waggled my brows.

"Are we going to be okay after what just happened?"

"I mean, I can only speak for myself. But I'm feeling pretty damn good. If sex is anything like that, I am so ready for it." I glanced over at him just as his lips twitched in the corners.

"I don't know, Snow. What just happened is going to be really hard to beat."

I leaned closer to him and whispered. "Really? Was that as good as sex for you?"

He was quiet for a minute. "Sex is different, but I've never gotten off by just having a woman rub up against me. At least not as a grown man. So, yeah, this is up there."

"I think I'm going to be a really great lover," I said over my laughter, and his head tipped back with a chuckle. "Seriously. I'm an overachiever in most things in my life, so why should this be any different? And I've had all these years to think about it, right? So, I think I'm going to kill it."

"I think you're going to kill it, too." He smiled. "Just don't rush it. Find the right guy."

What if I'd already found the right guy?

I wasn't about to tell him that, but my attraction to Hugh was the strongest I'd ever experienced. I felt safe with him.

Loved.

Worshipped.

What more could you ask for?

"Can I ask you something?"

"Sure." His gaze locked with mine.

"When was your last serious relationship?"

He shrugged. "Probably my freshman year of college. It's been a while."

"How come?"

His tongue slipped out and moved back and forth against his bottom lip as he thought about it. "Well, I guess having two parents who set the bar extremely high can work against you, too. I'm not settling for anything less than what they have, and I just haven't found that. Maybe it's not in the cards for everyone."

I nodded. I would love to have what his parents shared with one another someday myself. "I'm guessing that's what we're all striving for. How'd they meet?"

Hugh's whole face lit up, and I reached for my tea and took a sip. "They met in college. My dad went to this party with a friend of his, who happened to be dating my mom at the time. But when my father laid eyes on her, apparently, all the hair on his arms stood on edge, and he said he was hit so hard, he could barely see straight. When they got in the car to leave, he told his friend that she was the girl he was going to marry."

My mouth gaped open. "That's so sweet. What did the friend say?"

"I think he was a little shocked, and he said he'd step away because he'd just met my mom himself, and it wasn't serious."

"I love that. Did your mom feel the same way?"

Hugh barked out a laugh. "The way she tells it is hilarious. You know my dad is a jokester, and apparently, he teased her and gave her a hard time, so she never thought in a million years he was interested that first night. But here they are, five kids and a lifetime together later, and they're still crazy about one another."

I sighed. "I love that. I think you'll find it someday, Bear."

"We'll see. I'm not in any hurry, and I'm sure as shit not forcing it. Life is good right now." He yawned, and I wanted to move onto his lap so badly it was almost painful. I wanted to breathe him in and feel his arms wrapped around me.

"It is. We're going to be just fine. I should let you get some sleep. We can skip the movie." It was way too late to watch a movie, and I knew he'd just asked me to watch so that he could make sure I wasn't upset about what happened between us.

But a part of me wished he'd ask me not to leave.

Beg me to stay.

But, of course, he wouldn't. There was nothing going on between us. Why would he?

His eyebrows pinched together, and I wanted to rub my finger over the little line forming between his eyes. He was stressed about what had happened, and my stomach churned at the thought that I was the cause of that. He'd always been good to me. He'd offered me a free place to live and a job. He'd gone down to the cove because I'd pushed him to come with me. And then I'd practically violated the poor man by begging him to let me rub myself all over him.

Jesus.

I was the worst.

A horny, virgin monster.

"Hey," I whispered, and he looked up. His brows were pinched together, and it was impossible to miss the torment on his face. "I'm heading to bed, but thank you for talking things out."

"Of course." He wasn't looking at me; he was somewhere faraway. I pushed to my feet and reached for my mug.

"Hugh," I said as I looked down at him.

"Yeah." His green gaze met mine.

"It was a one and done. I give you my word. I would never do anything to hurt you and Travis. I know how close you are. It will be our secret, and it won't happen again, okay?"

He studied me for the longest time before his lips turned up a little in the corners. "We're good, Snow."

Yikes. He really does want to forget this ever happened. I've tortured the poor man.

"All right. Good night, Bear."

He forced a smile and reached for his mug on the coffee table and drank the last bit in the cup. "See you in the morning."

I leaned down and reached for his mug. "I'll take that for you. You've done enough."

The hard body.

The orgasm.

What more could a girl ask for?

He nodded. "Thanks. I never cared for tea, and now you've got me drinking it every night."

I held both mugs in my hands and went to walk past him, but his hand clasped around my thigh, and I sucked in a breath. He lowered his head and pressed it against my belly as he stroked my leg. I had both hands filled with these damn mugs, and I wasn't sure what to do. So... in my typical uncool fashion, I just leaned down and kissed the back of his head, and he chuckled.

"Get some sleep," he said, his voice gruff as his hand moved away.

"Yeah, you, too." I made my way to the sink, rinsed the mugs, and loaded them in the dishwasher before I looked back one more time to find Hugh watching me.

What was this? Damn it. I couldn't even ask Del or the girls because I couldn't tell anyone. It was our secret. It's the least I could do for him.

I smiled before walking toward my room, stepping inside, and closing the door behind me. My phone rang, and it was Del FaceTiming me. I plopped down on the bed, my back resting against the headboard, as her face came into focus.

"How was the date?"

The date? Oh, yes, I'd completely forgotten about my date with Kline. That was before the X-rated, skinny-dipping, porn-worthy make-out session with my brother's best friend.

"It was good," I said, chewing on the back of my thumbnail. I hated keeping anything from her, especially something as great as what happened tonight.

"You're all flushed. Oh my god. You did the deed?" she shouted over a fit of giggles.

"No. What? Of course not."

"Lila Mae James, I know when you're lying. Spill it, girl."

I shook my head, and I could feel sweat gathering at the nape of my neck. "There was a hot make-out session. That's it."

It was the truth.

She just didn't know who I made out with.

"Shut up!" she shouted. "Like a heated make out where you wanted more to happen?"

I covered my face with my free hand.

Oh, I wanted more to happen, no doubt about it.

"Let's just say that it ended with quite the fireworks." I chuckled over my words. We'd always shared everything, and this was no different, aside from trying to be respectful to Hugh and protect his friendship with my brother. I could share the details without getting into the specifics.

"Noooooooo."

"Yeeeees," I said, shaking my head. "It's not that big of a deal."

"Um, speaking from someone who has had several boyfriends and her fair share of sex... orgasms don't happen from making out all that often. He didn't, er, have the fireworks, did he?"

"I'm fairly sure that he did." I shrugged.

"Damn. That's not common. He got off on you getting off."

"Okay. I think we're good on the talk for now." I chuckled.

"Are you going to see him again?"

"I think we're just going to be friends. It was fun, but I'm not staying here forever, so what's the point?"

"The point is, you orgasmed from kissing the man. That's hot. Why not keep doing it? And you can lose that damn V-card to a man who actually turns you on."

"I don't think he wants that pressure, so I think that's a no."

"A *hard* no?" Her voice was all tease, and we both burst out in a fit of giggles.

"Something like that. All right, I'm going to bed. I love you, Delilah Bernadette McCallister."

"Love you more, you little horn dog. I can't wait for this weekend. Get ready to flirt with all the bikers, baby."

I shook my head. "Goodnight."

She waved, and I ended the call. I reached for my notebook and studied my list. I checked off skinny dipping and bit down on my bottom lip as I thought about the night.

So much had happened.

I just wished it wasn't with the one man that I couldn't have.

———

The next morning, we acted completely normal, and I was relieved. I'd gone for my run, and I'd just returned home to find Hugh mowing the lawn wearing nothing but some basketball shorts and a baseball cap turned backward on his head. His chest was on full display, and it was hard not to stare. I'd hurried inside and made us pancakes and juice as he and Travis both walked through the door, talking and laughing at the same time.

My brother sure showed up at the worst times, didn't he?

"You still pissed at me?" Travis asked.

"We're fine. But maybe you could shoot me a text to let me know when you're going to just show up for breakfast?"

"Sorry. Shay hasn't felt like cooking, and she doesn't like the smell of food when I cook, so, there you go." He kissed me on the cheek and dropped down to sit.

"Well, lucky for you, I made plenty of pancakes today," I said, as Hugh came up beside me to wash his hands at the sink. His hip brushed mine, and I swear that little bit of contact had my body blazing.

"You need any help?" he asked, as my brother typed into his phone and completely ignored us.

"Nope. I've got it."

His tongue swiped out and moved along his bottom lip as his beautiful green eyes locked with mine, and he nodded. His muscled chest had the name Reynolds tattooed in script across his heart. I wanted to trace the ink with my fingers.

With my tongue.

Oh. My. God.

What was happening to me?

I focused on the damn pancakes before piling them onto a plate and pulling myself together. We all sat down and started eating when Hugh's phone vibrated, and he looked down to read the screen. "My mom wants you to know she'd love you to come to Sunday dinner. Not everyone will be there this week since Brinkley is back in the city, and so is Georgia. Not sure about Finn. But I'm guessing Cage and Gracie will be there."

"Oh, I'd love that. Tell her thank you for the invite."

"Yeah." My brother held up his fork and pointed it at me. "That's who you want to be spending your time with. Hugh and his family. That fucking Kline is a player."

It took all I had not to laugh in his face. Kline hadn't even made a move. But I'd been the one to make the move on the big, beautiful man sitting beside me.

"Stop judging everyone, Trav. We've never liked being judged, but you do it to everyone, and it's not a good thing."

"Because it's my job to look out for you. I make no apologies," he said. "You're still going with her to check out that hippy treatment center on Saturday, right?" He looked at Hugh, and I pushed to my feet, taking my plate to the sink to rinse it off because my brother was ruining my mood.

"It's not a hippy place. It's an actual treatment center with a pretty damn impressive track record of helping people. I emailed you the website, so the least you could do is read up on it." Hugh's eyes locked with mine when I turned to look at him. My brother was too busy typing into his phone to notice. Hugh's green gaze was filled with empathy.

Thank you.

I didn't speak the words, but he heard them just the same.

He winked at me before turning his attention back to my brother as Travis completely changed the subject and started talking about football.

And I made my way to my room to get showered and cleaned up.

I picked up my notebook and stared at the list.

This was supposed to be my list.

For my eyes only.

So, I added something new to the bottom of my Snow Day list that I'd be keeping to myself moving forward.

Make out with my hot boss one more time.

eleven

. . .

Hugh

I'D PLANNED on putting distance between Lila and me after what happened out at Cottonwood Cove, but between living together, working together, and her brother pushing us together, that had not been the case over the last week. We hadn't talked about what happened again, but I couldn't stop fucking thinking about it.

Thinking about *her.*

We'd watched movies last night after she got back from spending some time with her dad and having dinner with her girlfriends. I knew that Kline was still flirting his ass off with her, but she didn't seem interested in him. Brax had shown up at Reynolds' last night with two women tourists, who were in town checking out some property. He was all jazzed about them, and they were both attractive and nice enough, but I just wasn't feeling it. I'd tried. I'd flirted and had a few drinks.

But I kept checking my phone to see if Lila was on her way home yet, and I couldn't get into it. Hell, common sense told me to go out and get laid. That would be the surefire fastest way to get her out of my system.

But I didn't want to do it.

I couldn't have her, but I didn't want anyone else, either.

Brax was all over my ass this morning, asking what was up after I'd ducked out early.

> **BRAX**
>
> What the fuck is your deal, jackass? They were both hot.

> You should have taken Jaqueline home. I don't have to hook up with her friend for you to close the deal.

I chuckled because I knew he was pissed. The dude always liked to have a wingman.

> **BRAX**
>
> She wasn't going to leave her friend. Unlike you, she's not a dick.

> You can't close the deal without me?

> **BRAX**
>
> Apparently not. Because you've bailed the last two times, and I've gone home with a bad case of blueballs, dickhead.

> <laughing emoji> <shrugging emoji>

> **BRAX**
>
> Don't use emojis to avoid the fucking question. What is your deal, and how much does it have to do with the hot little roommate you're shacking up with?

> Fuck. Off.

BRAX

> Dude. No judgment. I know you. You're
> fighting it. And I get it. Our boy is a crazy
> motherfucker, especially when it comes to
> Lila. If something is going on, you can tell
> me. I've got you.

I knew he did. But this was done, and there was nothing to
tell. It was no one's business.

> Nothing going on, brother.

BRAX

> When did the most honest dude I know
> become a liar?

> No idea what you're talking about. You want
> to come to Sunday dinner tomorrow? My
> mom is making your favorite.

BRAX

> Nice deflection. And you know I will never
> turn down Alana's fried chicken. Hells to the
> yes. And I'm here for you when you want to
> tell me what the fuck is going on.

> Thanks for that. You're being ridiculous,
> though. Nothing to tell.

BRAX

> Fine. What are you doing today?

> Going with Lila to check out that treatment
> center for her dad.

BRAX

Of course, you are. What a wonderful friend you are to her, you douche sack. You leave me high and dry with a raging boner, and you're going to skip around a treatment center with your best friend's little sister. Dude. This is madness.

STFU, dick weasel. Trav asked me to go with her. You can ask her yourself. She'll be at Sunday dinner.

BRAX

Of course, she will. You two are practically inseparable.

Well, your theory is fucked because Trav and Shay will be there, as well. And Georgia, my cousin Dylan, and her fiancé, Wolf, are driving in for dinner, too.

BRAX

Damn. Dylan's so hot. You don't think she'll tell the Navy SEAL that she kicked me in the balls in high school when I hit on her, do you? I'm a lover, not a fighter.

I doubt she remembers. She's kicked a lot of dudes in the balls. I think you're safe.

BRAX

<praying hands emoji>

I laughed when I read his message. Lila walked into the kitchen, and I tucked my phone into my back pocket.

"You ready?" I asked her. She was wearing a white sundress, and her long waves were falling down her shoulders and back. Her tan skin stood out against the dress, and she looked fucking gorgeous. It didn't matter what she wore:

a dress, jean shorts, running shorts and tee, or a fucking canvas sack. She looked good in all of it.

And don't even get me started about her birthday suit.

I'd never get the vision out of my head of Lila walking down to the water with her tight little ass on full display under the light of the moon.

I'd tattoo her ass on my arm if I didn't think her brother would kill me.

"Yes. You sure you don't mind going with me?"

"Nope. Will you be taking a tour?" I asked.

"It's not really like that. They are all about the privacy of their clients. I'm just going to meet with the lady who works there and check out the layout of the facility and pick up some paperwork to take to my dad."

"All right. Sounds like a plan. You seem a little nervous," I said with a chuckle as we walked to the car.

"I'm not nervous. Not at all." I opened her door, and she climbed into the truck. I reached for her seat belt and pulled it across her body.

She groaned. "How many times do I have to tell you that I don't need to be buckled in?"

"Oh, yeah, that's right. You keep telling me that. What can I say? It's a habit from buckling in Gracie when I have her, I guess." It wasn't. I did it to be close to her and because I knew it annoyed her. I liked seeing her all riled up. It had become part of our daily shtick.

"Whatever." She yanked at my hair and laughed. "You're full of it, Bear."

"Yeah?" I asked. My nose grazed hers, and I fought the urge to nip at her sweet mouth. "Well, whatever it is, you seem more relaxed now, so it worked."

I closed her door and got in the truck. We drove to the outskirts of town to Havenwood, the treatment facility she'd found for her dad. We talked all the way there. She told me she and the girls were still going to that biker bar tonight, and I wasn't thrilled about it.

"I don't think that's such a good idea," I said, as we coasted down the highway, the ocean on one side of us and the most beautiful mountains and tree line on the other. I loved growing up here. The mountains, the water, all of it.

"Well, you don't have to worry about it. Kline's coming with us," she said, and my head whipped in her direction, and she raised a brow. "Do you have a problem with that?"

I cleared my throat. "Of course not. I just thought you weren't that into the dude."

"Well, unfortunately, Del knew something was up the other night, and she's sort of the master at knowing when I'm lying. So, long story short, she thinks I had an epic make-out session with Kline, and she invited him to join us."

"You let her think that you got off to making out with that little fucker? I don't know how I feel about that," I hissed.

"Well, I certainly couldn't tell her the truth. So, there you go. He and I are friends anyway, and he was down to go, so it'll be fine."

I didn't like it.

The dude was getting credit for my magic schlong.

My lips.

My hands.

Fuck me, this is ridiculous.

We pulled up to the facility, and I did my best to shake it off.

Lila pulled out her phone and dialed a number before holding it to her ear. "Hi, this is Lila James."

She was quiet as she listened.

"Perfect. We'll meet you out front."

She ended the call and let out a few quick breaths before turning to me, her eyes wet with emotion.

"What's wrong?" I asked, my hand grazing hers on the seat between us.

"This could be the beginning of something new. A fresh start, you know? I feel really good about it."

Fuck. I knew she was putting all her eggs in one basket, and that worried me for her. Her father had been to the restaurant a few times, and Lila stopped by his house every day after work to check on him. She loved him, and I understood her need to help the man.

But I also knew you couldn't help someone who didn't want to be helped. I knew he said he did, but I wasn't certain it was true or if he was just saying what she wanted to hear.

He was completely unpredictable.

"One step at a time, Snow. Let's go check it out."

We both got out of the truck, and a woman walked out the front door of the large ranch house set on a couple of acres of property. The trees surrounding the place offered a lot of privacy, and I imagined this was a peaceful place to try to figure out your shit. I glanced over in the distance and saw a man walking near the tree line.

"Lila?" the woman called out and held up her hand.

"Yes, hi. You must be Lauren. It's so nice to meet you. This is my friend, Hugh."

I offered her my hand when we got closer. She was probably in her early forties, wearing a T-shirt and jeans, so they clearly kept things casual here.

She shook my hand. "It's great to meet you both. I'm glad you brought a friend because the process can be overwhelming and—" She paused and guided us to a bench a few feet away. "It's just good to have support."

We all sat down on the metal and wood bench, with Lila in the middle. "Yes. I mean, I want support for my father, first and foremost. I'm not worried about myself. And I feel like you could really help him, you know?"

Lauren's eyes softened, and she nodded. "You'd be surprised, Lila. This can be just as hard on the families as it is on the addict. So, I know you aren't worried about yourself, but I am. And I have a hunch Hugh is, as well, or he wouldn't be here."

I smiled the slightest bit because she was right, and Lila was so used to being stoic and strong that she'd forgotten that she needed support sometimes, too. Maybe she should add that to her fucking list.

"I get that. And yes, I'm lucky to have Hugh's support. I told you via email that my brother is not on the same page as I am with all of this."

"You did. And I know how that goes. Everyone deals with this in their own way. There is no right or wrong way to do it. Loving an addict is not an easy journey."

Lila swiped at the single tear rolling down her cheek, and I moved my hand closer to where hers rested between us, my pinky finger wrapping around hers. I wanted her to know I was here.

Lauren spent the next hour going over the paperwork and telling us how the program worked. Lila listened intently, and I spent most of my time watching her. Making sure she was okay. I knew the percentage of success stories with addiction was not as high as she wanted to believe. But I also believed people were capable of change, and everyone deserved a second chance.

If Tate was willing to do the work, then I'd support her on this. And I'd talk to my stubborn ass of a best friend about getting on board for his sister's sake. She needed him whether he believed in his father or not. He needed to be there for her.

"So that's everything in a nutshell. You've got all the pricing there, and I discussed the deposit that I'd need before I could admit him."

"Yep. Working on that right now. I should have the money here pretty quickly for you. And then the balance we can finance?"

"Yes. We'll set up a payment plan. Are you handling the

financial responsibility all on your own?" Lauren asked.

"Um, well," Lila said as she looked away and gathered her thoughts. "Probably, yes. And I'm fine with that."

"Are you going to be fine with it regardless of the outcome?"

"Of course."

"What I mean is…" Lauren reached for Lila's hand like they were old friends. They'd just met, but there was a comfort there. "I told you that I've been through this, Lila. That's why I work here. But my outcome with my brother was not what I'd hoped for. And that can get tricky when you're financially obligated to a program that might not work for your loved one."

"I understand the risks. I'd spend every penny I have trying—otherwise, what is all the hard work for? I mean, my father is the only parent I have. I can't bring my mother back. He's here. He's hurting. I won't turn my back on him, ever. That's not what you do when you love someone."

Her tone was serious, and it was clear that she meant every word she said. She would never give up on her father. I used to be in the same camp as Travis, where I worried she'd lose herself trying to save him. But today, I got it.

She wasn't going to lose herself. She was just a woman who loved hard. And she didn't give up on the people she cared about. It wasn't something to pity. It was something I admired. The blind faith that Tate would figure it out, even after all he'd done.

Hell, I was cheering for the dude now, too.

"I get that, I really do. We're very similar in our convictions." Lauren paused and smiled as she squeezed Lila's hand still in hers. "Would you consider doing something as a personal favor to me?"

"Yes. Name it."

"I'll get your father in as soon as you have the deposit money. We'll move him to the top of the list. But I want you to go talk to someone. It's important. This is not easy, and I want you to be okay, as well."

"Okay. Like a therapist?" Lila asked.

"Yep. Will you promise me you'll do that?"

"Um, er, I can try."

"I can promise you she'll do it. I know a great therapist who will do it pro bono," I said with a wink. My mother was well known in Cottonwood Cove as the best listener in town, but it was also her profession. She was amazing at her job, and I knew she'd be thrilled to work with Lila. She'd always worried about her and Travis when they were kids after all they'd gone through.

"Oh, you think she'd be willing to see me?" Lila looked at me before glancing back at Lauren. "Hugh's mom is a family therapist."

Lauren smiled. "Oh, that's amazing."

"She would for sure be willing to see you, as often as you needed. She loves you; you know that."

"Okay, then. I promise. And I'll get you that money very soon."

"All right. And your father seems ready to do this?" Lauren asked as we all pushed to our feet.

"Yes. He's on board. I feel really good about this. Thank you so much for agreeing to meet with me and for all that you're doing for my father."

"I'm happy to help any way I can. And you'll follow through on that therapy appointment, right?" Lauren's voice was teasing, but her gaze landed on me, and I nodded. She was counting on me to make sure it happened.

"You can count on it," I said. And I would make sure it happened, even if it meant I had to carry her to my mother's office myself.

Lila hugged her goodbye, and I held up my hand and waved as we made our way back to the truck. She didn't fight me when I helped her in the truck and reached over to fasten her seat belt. She was quiet. Deep in thought. Probably trying to figure out how the fuck she was going to come up with this deposit money.

Once I got in the driver's seat and we pulled down the long driveway, I glanced over at her. "You okay?"

"Yes. Yeah, of course. Just trying to figure out how it's all going to work."

"How much is the deposit?"

She cleared her throat. "The initial deposit is eight thousand dollars. And then the rest is paid over time."

I nodded. "And you have that kind of money?"

She'd just graduated from college, and she'd told me that her internship with the company who was holding a job for her had been unpaid. I couldn't fathom where she'd saved eight thousand bucks. She hadn't been working for me long enough to have made that much.

"My car is for sale. That's why I've been walking everywhere. I don't need one while I'm home, and I truly don't need one in Chicago. I can take public transportation everywhere. It's actually easier that way."

Jesus.

She'd really do just about anything to save the man.

She owned one thing, and she was so quick to give it up.

I remember her saving up for two summers back when she was in high school, working at the bakery in town to save up for that car.

"I haven't seen it at the house," I said, turning to look at her when I stopped at the light.

"It's at Brax's office. He's got that empty lot, and people sell their cars there all the time. He said he'd help me out. It gets a ton of exposure on that corner."

I rolled my eyes. Of course, the fucker was helping her and hadn't said a word.

"I'm guessing Travis doesn't know about this?"

"Of course not. Why would I tell him when he's dead set

against it? I don't need his permission or his money, Hugh. I can do this on my own."

"Why didn't you come to me for the money? You know I'd give it to you in a heartbeat. Take your car back, and I'll loan you the money. You can pay it back over time, all right?"

"What? No. I'm already living at your house and working at your restaurant. You've done enough for me."

The light turned green, and we started moving. "Listen to me. You've probably saved me more than eight grand just in the tweaks you've made to the books and all the areas you've found that we could cut back and places where we could increase revenue. And you cook breakfast and dinner for me every day. I owe you."

She chuckled. "You're exaggerating. But thank you for the offer. If my car doesn't sell, I may have to come to you for a loan, but I'd rather do this on my own."

I'd definitely have to talk to Brax about making sure that car didn't sell. The fucker was so sneaky.

"Well, I guess we know that Travis isn't the only stubborn one in the James family," I said, and my lips twitched when I felt her eyes on me.

"I do have a favor to ask."

"Shoot."

"Do you think your parents would be okay with me bringing my dad to Sunday dinner tomorrow night? I think it would be good for him to be around your family. And for Travis to see that he's trying."

"Of course. You know my mom. Everyone is welcome. And we will be talking to her about getting you on her schedule and starting therapy. Otherwise, I will throw your ass under the bus so fast with Lauren, your head will spin."

"You play dirty, Hugh Reynolds."

"Always," I said. As I glanced at her, her heated gaze locked with mine.

She didn't know the half of it.

twelve

. . .

Lila

WE PULLED INTO THE DRIVEWAY, and I looked over my shoulder to see Brax pull in behind us. Today had been a lot, and I needed to get ready before we went out tonight. Girls' night out had somehow turned into bringing boyfriends. Boomer and Parker were both joining us, and Del had arranged for Quincy and Kline to meet us. I hadn't realized those two were good friends, so I just had to hope that Del wouldn't make things awkward and blow my cover. Kline and I were just friends, and it made me nervous that she thought it was something more. I didn't mind him going out with us, especially now that he'd told me he and Danielle had hooked up. That took the pressure off.

Unfortunately, I'd come to the realization that the only man I was interested in happened to be the one I lived with.

Who I also worked for.

Who also happened to be my brother's best friend.

And he'd made it clear that nothing could happen between us again.

Maybe I was meant to die a virgin.

It wasn't supposed to be this hard, right?

"Well, look who's here. Mr. Fucking Secret Keeper," Hugh grumped beside me as he turned off the car.

"Don't make him feel bad for helping me."

"He should have stopped you from doing it." He pushed out of the car. He wasn't going to let this go. And this man had the nerve to call me stubborn?

"Hey. I was just showing a house on your street and thought you might be back. You want to go grab pizza with those girls from last night? They just texted me that they want to meet up," Brax said as he strolled up the driveway.

I knew Hugh'd gone out last night, but he hadn't said much about it, and he'd gotten home early, so I figured it didn't go well. But maybe that was just wishful thinking.

Hugh crossed his arms over his chest and stared at Brax before speaking. "Something you want to tell me?"

"Um, let's see. I'd like to get laid, and it can't seem to happen without my wingman, so let's get some pizza and go out tonight. Is that what you're waiting for?" he asked. Brax was a few inches shorter than Hugh but still stood about six feet tall. He had his hair cut close to his head and was always dressed like he was going to a meeting. Even if he was at a barbecue, the man was wearing a dress shirt and dress pants. He didn't do the casual thing like his two best friends. "And hello, lovely Lila. How are you doing today?"

He hugged me, and I could feel him doing something over my shoulder to Hugh because his body shook a little like he was trying to hold in his laughter.

"Fuck off. That is not what I'm talking about. You're helping Lila sell her car, and you didn't think you should mention that?"

Brax pulled away, and we all walked up the driveway toward the house. "I didn't think it needed to be mentioned. Might I remind you and the ever-overbearing Travis that Lila is an adult. She can sell her car if she wants to. And I understand that Travis is an asshole, and there's nothing we can do about it. But this attitude from you, Hugh…" Brax said with a smirk, as we made our way inside to the kitchen, and he leaned over the large island. "I'm not understanding why you're feeling so… protective?"

Hugh narrowed his gaze, and when he leaned on the counter across from Brax, I couldn't help but notice the veins in his forearms bulging. And why did I find that so ridiculously sexy? Was this just some sort of out-of-control, hormonal crush now? Even his forearms turned me on.

"Listen, fucker. She's family, and you know it. And you should have told me because I would have loaned her the money. So, get her damn car off the lot, and we'll forget you made that mistake."

I rolled my eyes. "Uhhhh, hello? I'm standing right here, and this is not your decision. It's mine."

"Yeah, I totally agree," Brax said, reaching for the plate of cookies I'd picked up at the bakery yesterday, taking one off the top and biting it in half.

"Oh, shut the fuck up, you ass kisser." Hugh railed at his friend before turning to me. "Listen, I've got the money, and I'm offering it to you. Stop being a stubborn ass about it," he growled when his gaze locked with mine.

I shook my head. "You're no different than Travis. I don't need your money. You've done enough for me. I don't care about the car, and I'm selling it."

He hissed out a breath and ran a hand down his face. "I did go with you today, so I think I'm slightly different than Travis, yeah?"

He was pissed. But this was not his decision to make.

"Listen. I need to go get ready to go out. Sloane's picking me up in an hour."

"Ohhhh, where are we going tonight?" Brax purred, and Hugh just stared at me like I'd slapped him in the face by not giving him his way.

I'm sorry that I don't casually ask someone for eight thousand dollars. Maybe that wasn't a lot of money to Hugh Reynolds, but it was a lot of money to me.

And Travis would never let me live it down if I borrowed the money from his best friend, and our father didn't succeed.

Because Hugh was Travis's best friend, not mine, right?

I mean, the reason he wouldn't act on his feelings for me, which I knew he had, was all because of his loyalty to Travis. How stupid was that?

Hugh wasn't the only one who was pissed now.

"I'm going to that biker bar on Front Street with the girls and their guys, and Kline is also coming with us." I forced a fake smile and looked directly at Hugh. I'd intentionally not mentioned that Kline and Danielle had something going on now because I enjoyed seeing him get all worked up.

It was childish, but when it came to Hugh Reynolds, I had no shame, apparently.

"Ahhh... we've been there a few times. I can't believe Travis isn't having a fucking meltdown that you're going there. That's not a tame place, but I personally love it. There's always a good fight and hot biker chicks," Brax said.

"Are you done?" Hugh grumped.

"I guess I must be." Brax smirked as he reached for another cookie, and Hugh slapped it right out of his hand. It took everything in me not to laugh.

"So, are you going to run to my brother and tattle on me?" I glanced at the large man scowling at me from across the kitchen island.

"No. You're right, Snow. You're a grownup. You can make your own decisions." He raised a brow, his mood completely shifting.

"Well, thank you. I appreciate that." I turned to make my way to my bedroom door.

"But now that you've got me thinking about it, Brax. I think we should grab the girls from last night and head over to that biker bar ourselves tonight. I'm in the mood for some hot biker chicks," Hugh said, his voice completely void of any emotion and loud enough to make sure I heard him. He was definitely doing this to irritate me. The thought of seeing him with a woman made my blood boil.

"Welcome back, buddy. I've missed you." Brax barked out a laugh, and I groaned as I whipped my door open and slammed it behind me.

I would not let him ruin my night just because I didn't give him his way.

If he wanted to flaunt another woman in my face, I wasn't above doing the same damn thing to him. After all, he was the one who insisted we couldn't cross the line again. That was his decision, not mine.

I glanced at my closet and pulled out my silk white tank top and then dug through my drawers to find my black cutoffs that I hadn't worn in forever because they were ridiculously short and usually garnered me more attention than I wanted.

But tonight, I wanted to make sure a certain set of green eyes were on me.

I spent the next hour curling my hair and putting on makeup. I went for a smoky eye, some bronzer, and then dabbed on my favorite pink lipstick.

This was more makeup than I normally wore, so I grabbed my notebook and added a new one to the list.

Embrace your inner sex appeal and flirt your ass off.

Hugh and Brax were already gone when Sloane got to the house.

"Holy mother of all sex goddesses—who are you, and what have you done with the virgin Lila?" Sloane said over her laughter as her eyes widened, and she walked in a circle around me.

I'd toned things down when I slipped on my tan cowboy boots, but the rest of me was definitely out to get noticed tonight.

"Can we drop the virgin talk for one night, please? I'm over it."

She wrapped her arms around me and kissed my cheek. "Well, I don't think anyone is going to be talking about your virginity tonight. Not when you're looking this smoking hot."

The door burst open just as I reached for my purse, and Del and Rina both gaped at me.

"Holy hotness. Girl, look at you," Del purred. "Kline isn't going to know what to do with himself when he sees you."

I groaned internally because the last thing I needed was her pushing things with Kline.

"I'm actually going to just have fun tonight. I'm not dating Kline. I just want to see where the night takes me." I grabbed my keys and phone and dropped them into my purse as we made our way out the door.

"Well, the night will take you wherever you want it to, looking like that. Damn, Lila. I always knew you were gorgeous, but wow." Rina slipped into the back seat of Sloane's car with me, while Del took the front seat.

"You're being ridiculous," I said. "But thank you. Where are the guys? I thought they were coming."

"I told them to come with Quincy and Kline so we could have a little fun first. You know, before the wet blankets get there," Del said, and the car filled with laughter.

"Yep. And I'm drinking tonight. Boomer is going to Uber there with the guys, and then he'll drive my car home. He agreed to be the DD tonight. So, get ready for some fun. We only have you here for the summer, Lila, and we sort of have this plan to make you love it so much that you never want to leave," Sloane said as she turned up the volume in the car, and we all started singing to our girl, Taylor Swift.

Did I even want to leave?

I'd been really happy since I'd been home. I'd never thought about staying, not with the way Travis carried on about the new job. But the thought of sitting behind a desk ten hours a day and living in the city didn't sound as exciting now as it did when I'd first graduated with a dual degree in business and finance.

But then I thought of Hugh, and what a jerk he'd been about me selling my car. About how horrified he'd been that we'd shared that moment out at the cove. And Travis was an overbearing asshole most of the time, and he'd never let it go.

This was temporary. I needed to stay focused on the goal.

Get Dad into treatment, and then I'd go back to my real life.

We all continued shouting out the lyrics to "Shake It Off" and laughing our asses off as we got out of the car.

Once we were inside, we settled at a high-top table, and the place was booming. A few guys were looking over at us, and one even sent over a tray of drinks. I was sticking to beer tonight, as I'd learned my lesson about being hungover, and I had no desire to do it again anytime soon. The girls were drinking shots, and Del asked the bartender for an empty shot glass for me, and I filled it with beer so I could join in.

Rock music was booming, and a very sexy man in a leather coat walked over to our table.

"Ladies, you're looking lovely tonight," he said, his voice deep. His blue eyes were locked on mine, and I quickly looked away. The man had to be in his early forties, but he rocked the silver fox look rather well.

"Thanks," we said in unison over a fit of giggles.

"Are you Tate James's daughter?" he asked.

I straightened my shoulders. "Yes. Do you know my dad?"

"I do. He's a good man. He did some work for me at my auto shop. I thought I recognized you from a few years back." He winked. "Was it Lily?"

"Lila," I said, feeling my cheeks turn bright red at the way he took me in.

"Not going to hit on you, darling. Not now that I know

you're Tate's daughter. But damn, you're easy on the eyes. I'll be watching out for you tonight. You ask for Roddy if anyone gives you trouble, all right?"

I just waved as he backed away from the table and made his way to the group of friends he was sitting with.

"Hot daddy. I could be so down for an older man," Sloane said, and we all gaped at her.

"If you weren't in a relationship?" Rina shook her head with disbelief.

"Well, of course. But a girl can look, right? And that man right there is every woman's wet dream. He looks like an older version of Jax Teller from *Sons of Anarchy*." Sloane held up her glass for another round, and I asked for a water.

I thought over her wet dream comment. I'd found my wet dream, in the form of a six-foot-three, long-haired, stubborn, beautiful man, who happened to be my roommate at the moment.

I understood the concept of a wet dream more than ever now.

I'd actually been awake for it.

"Oh my gosh, what are you thinking about? You look very guilty," Del teased, just as Parker, Boomer, Kline, and Quincy walked in.

A few people we'd gone to high school with came in behind them, and I realized this was a local hangout as much as a biker bar.

I liked the vibe. The music was great, and everyone was having a good time.

We ordered appetizers, and the girls continued drinking pretty heavily. I had a beer shot with them every now and then, but I'd switched over to water. My eyes kept scanning the door because there was only one person that I wanted to see tonight.

The one I lived and worked with.

The one who was probably coming here with a date.

"So, Del thinks we're together, huh?" Kline asked, leaning close to me so only I could hear. The girls were too busy singing to the music and having a good time to pay us any attention.

"Yeah. It's a long story. Thanks for playing along. That won't mess anything up with Danielle, will it?" I asked, glancing over my shoulder to make sure no one was listening.

"Nah. That's very new. She's cool. We aren't exclusive or anything, so if you have a change of heart with me, I'm still available." He raised a brow, and I chuckled.

"I think we've got a good thing going just how it is right now, don't you?"

"Sure," he said, his words slurring a little bit.

"What are you two talking about?" Del sidled up to me, standing between our bar stools.

"Just catching up a little," I said, anxious to get this conversation over with. When Del wanted to know something, she never backed down.

"I'm not interrupting anything, then?" she teased, eyeing us suspiciously. "From what I hear, you're good at more than making the drinks, huh, Kline?"

I spewed water all over the table and started coughing before reaching for a napkin and wiping up my mess.

"I don't know, but I think so." Kline winked at me.

"Be good to my girl. Ooooookay?" she slurred.

Oh my god. Please make her stop.

"Ooooookay, Del. I'll try." Kline looked at her like she had three heads before Quincy called her away when their drinks arrived.

"Sorry about that," I said, just as the door swung open, and Hugh and Brax stepped inside with two women I'd never seen before. The one standing really close to Hugh was pretty. She looked older than me, for sure, and she was very curvy. Her boobs were spilling out of her red tube top, and she was wearing dark jeans that fit her like a second skin.

Damn, I'd never seen a butt like that. It almost looked fake.

Her blonde hair fell in loose waves over her shoulders, and her red lips were overfilled but managed to look sexy as hell.

She was a total bombshell.

And I instantly hated her.

I'd never had that kind of reaction to someone.

But her hand trailed along his upper arm, and she moved it to his hair, and my hands fisted at my sides. I was grateful that I hadn't had much to drink because I wouldn't want to do anything to embarrass myself, and at least I could control my reaction because I was completely sober.

He was laughing with Brax, and a few guys walked over to him because everyone knew Hugh.

And his head turned slowly as if he knew I was watching. His sage-green eyes locked with mine, and everything else stopped moving.

I smiled. I felt bad for the way we'd left things earlier.

I couldn't stay mad at the man for caring and trying to help me.

After all, he'd been the one to go with me today.

I should have been thanking him, not getting angry at him.

His tongue swiped out and slid across his bottom lip, and he tipped his chin up just a little bit. Someone handed him a shot. He pulled his gaze from mine, and his head fell back as he downed the liquid. Hugh didn't drink often because the man worked so much. So maybe he was blowing off some steam tonight.

"So how long has that been going on?" Kline pulled me from my daze.

"What?"

He smirked. "Don't worry about me, Lila. I know what a crazy ass your brother is. I'm not going to say a word."

"I think you're misreading things," I said, glancing back over to see that annoying woman squeezing herself into the space beside Hugh at the bar.

Kline chuckled. "Well, I may not know you well enough to read you, but I have been working with Hugh for a while now, and he doesn't look at anyone the way he looks at you."

My chest squeezed at his words. "How does he look at me?"

"Like you're the only girl in the room," he said, before taking the last pull from his beer. "And also, like he's going to kill anyone who looks at you wrong. I'd been on the receiving end of that look a few times before I figured it out."

"I think you're probably confused. He's Travis's best friend, and he's always been protective."

He set his bottle down and chuckled. "I see how Travis is with you. And even though that bastard is crazy, there is no question that he's your brother. But that's not the way Hugh looks at you, Lila."

"There's nothing going on." I shrugged.

"Well, if you're telling the truth, and nothing's happened between you, then that dude is fighting it hard. I know when a dude is struggling, and he's definitely struggling."

I watched as Hugh accepted another shot and downed it quickly.

Was he struggling?

I thought I was the only one who was having a hard time.

A part of me had wondered if what we'd shared was just a pity make-out session, and he'd wished it had never happened, and not only because of Travis.

But maybe I'd been wrong.

I felt bad because I cared much less about what my brother thought than Hugh did. Crossing the line would be an issue in their friendship, but it wouldn't affect my relationship with my brother any more than Travis having a meltdown, which was nothing new for me.

Hugh had more to lose.

I hadn't thought that through because I didn't think it was any of Travis's business.

I knew I'd be doing us both a favor to just leave it alone and focus on my father these next few months and then head back to Chicago.

But for whatever reason, I couldn't stop thinking about that kiss.

And I wanted him more than I'd ever wanted anyone or anything.

But acting on that would only hurt the people that I cared about most.

And Hugh was at the top of that list.

thirteen

. . .

Hugh

I'D HAD my eyes on Lila all night. Following her every move like a goddamn stalker. I didn't like seeing Kline hang all over her.

This wasn't about me being protective. This was about me wanting her in a way I knew I shouldn't.

So here I was, hanging out at a bar that I didn't feel like being at, drinking far too much, with a woman who was working my last nerve.

"Hughey!" she shrieked and tugged on my arm for the millionth time tonight. She was hot, no doubt about it. I just wasn't interested. And the fact that she kept rubbing her gigantic tits against my back was irritating the fuck out of me because I had to keep turning around to put some space between us, which meant my eyes weren't on Lila.

I'd always been able to find Lila in a room full of people, but I needed to stop seeking her out.

But I couldn't stop looking.

So, I was going to get my drink on and try to forget about all this shit.

"Hughey! Why aren't you listening to me?" She tugged at my arm again, knocking the shot I'd just clinked with Brax right out of my hand, who fell over laughing because he thought everything was hilarious.

Including the fact that he'd helped Lila sell her car.

Not fucking funny.

But I had a solution for that. I just had to figure out how to pull it off.

"Jesus, Clara. Stop grabbing at my arm, and stop shrieking in my ear," I hissed, raising my hand to ask the bartender for some napkins.

Roddy was laughing his ass off from a table away. He and I had known each other for a few years, and I was hoping he could help me with Lila's car situation.

"It's Karmy, not Clara," the woman grumped, and then leaned down and licked the tequila off my hand.

Oh, for fuck's sake. She was not reading the room. I was obviously not interested.

"Dude." I looked at Brax after the bartender handed me some napkins, and I wiped the booze along with Karmy's saliva off of my hand. "You need to help me out here."

"Oh, like a threesome?" she asked, looking between us.

Jaqueline, her friend, was giggling as she basically wrapped herself around Brax. "Or a foursome."

"That's a hard no." My tone was harsher than I meant it to be, and I stepped away from Karmy. "There are a dozen dudes in this bar that would take you up on that offer. I'm just not one of them."

She pouted, her pufferfish lips looking odd when she tried to move them. "But you're the one I want. Do you have any idea how lucky you are? Everyone wants me."

"It's not personal. He's just got his eyes on someone else." Brax opened his arms for Karmy to walk into them.

My gaze moved to the restroom door where Lila and Del had gone a few minutes ago, but I'd gotten distracted by the shitshow currently invading my space. She wasn't back at her table yet, but maybe there was a line for the restroom.

Just as I was stepping back to look down the hallway, I heard shouting coming from that side of the bar. I was moving before I even knew why.

I charged past several tables and toward the hallway where the restrooms were. A guy had Lila trapped against the back wall, his arms caging her in as her legs struggled to kick him away. I couldn't see her face, but I knew it was her.

Del was shouting and punching him in the back.

And I saw red.

"Let her go!" Del shouted, and she continued to swing at him.

He was a big guy.

But I was bigger.

And it wouldn't matter if I wasn't. I was going to fucking ruin him.

I picked Del up and set her down a few feet away and wrapped my arm around the dude's neck and yanked him back before pinning him to the wall and pressing my elbow against his throat.

"You like to fucking hurt women?"

His eyes were wild, and he tried to swing, but I pressed harder against his throat, and he started gasping. I glanced over to see Lila's eyes wet with emotion, mixed with fear, as Del wrapped an arm around her.

"You okay?" I shouted, and the bastard took that moment to push me backward.

"She's at a fucking bar; that's what you get. Don't come here if you don't want to get laid."

What the fuck?

My arm rolled back before I could even think straight. I landed the first hit to his face, and I was fairly certain I broke his nose with one shot. He swung at me, but his drunk ass couldn't hit me if he tried. I slammed him against the wall, and my hand came over his throat.

I wanted to fucking kill him.

"Hugh!" Brax was grabbing at my arm and trying to pull me off.

"Let him go, Bear." Lila's voice pierced through all the noise. She was completely calm, and her tone remained even. "Please take me home."

I let him go, and he dropped to the floor, coughing and gasping like a little bitch.

A man who violates women is not a man I can feel any empathy for.

"Weren't you told not to come back here, asshole?" Roddy said, as he clapped me on the back. "Dugger, get him the fuck out of here. And make sure he knows he isn't welcome back."

I moved toward Lila, wrapping my arms around her and kissing the top of her head. "Are you all right?"

She didn't move, and when I pulled back to look at her, she nodded. "I really want to leave."

A few people had gathered around, including Lila's friends and Kline, whose eyes were panicked as he hurried over to check on her. Most of the patrons hadn't even noticed the fight, as this bar was known for this shit.

I didn't have my fucking car, and I was far too intoxicated to drive even if I did. Karmy was clawing at my back, and Brax pulled her off as I glanced over at Roddy.

I didn't have to say a word. The dude nodded.

"I've got you. Let's go," he said. I knew Roddy didn't drink, but I'd only ever seen him on a motorcycle, so I wasn't sure how he was getting us home.

"I'm out," I said to Brax, and I reached for Lila's hand as she said a quick goodbye to her friends, who were too drunk to completely comprehend what had just happened. Del looked visibly shaken as she kissed Lila's cheek, and we headed for the door.

Roddy paused at the bar, and the owner tossed him his keys. I pushed Lila in front of me, my hand still holding hers, but I needed my eyes on her as we made our way outside to the parking lot. He pointed at the red truck parked out front, and I held the door open as she climbed inside. I moved her onto my lap and pulled the seat belt across both of us, which made Roddy laugh as he started the engine.

"Damn, dude. I didn't know she was your girl." Roddy chuckled.

I didn't say anything in response, and neither did Lila, who had yet to say much of anything.

Because she was my girl, wasn't she? Maybe I couldn't have her, but she was mine.

"I realized she was Tate's daughter when she first walked in, so thankfully, I didn't make a move. I wouldn't want those fists on me." He chuckled as he headed toward my house. He'd picked up my truck a few times from my place when it wasn't working and had it towed to his shop.

"That dude wasn't making a move. He was forcing himself on her." My arms were wrapped around her so tightly, I looked down to make sure I wasn't hurting her. Her hand came over mine when my gaze locked with hers.

"Yeah. He's a bad guy. I didn't see him come in. The slimy fucker. He's been hauled into jail a few times for complaints about being too aggressive with women, and we had him banned from the place."

"Fuck," I hissed when he pulled down my street. "I should have beat his face in some more."

Lila's fingers were gently moving along my knuckles that I hadn't even noticed were bloody before now. Soothing and calming me the best she could.

I was still raging over what had just happened.

Seeing her struggle like that.

Seeing her eyes full of fear when I finally got him off her.

It did something to me.

"I think you did enough damage to his face. There was a shit ton of blood, and I'm fairly certain you broke his nose and jaw. Killing him wouldn't help your girl; it would hurt you. You stopped at the right time." He pulled into the driveway and glanced over at Lila.

"You all right, darlin'?"

She nodded. "Yeah. I'm fine. Just happy to be home."

Home.

I wish this was her home.

That was the booze talking.

Lila's home was in Chicago.

I unbuckled us and pushed the door open, lifting her out of the truck before turning and fist-bumping Roddy. "Thank you, man. I owe you. Come get dinner at Reynolds' this week on me."

"Damn straight, brother. Those are the best ribs I've ever had. Count on it."

I pushed out of the truck and waved as he backed away. I took her hand and typed the code into the garage keypad and led her inside.

As soon as I closed the door, her body started quaking.

The tears fell then.

I scooped her up into my arms and carried her toward my bedroom, and I set her down on my bed as I moved to the bathroom and started the tub.

I knew it would comfort her.

I didn't care if it was wrong to have her here. Right now, this was where she needed to be.

This was where I needed her to be.

I came back to the bedroom where she was swiping at her eyes. I bent down in front of her and placed my large hands on each side of her face. "Are you hurt?"

"No. He just scared me. I tried to kick. I tried to push him away, but he just kept pressing against me. He forced his mouth on mine, and I bit him as hard as I could," she said. Her words were coming fast, and I heard the fear there. "Del tried to help me, but we couldn't move him. He was too big."

I leaned forward and kissed her forehead and her cheeks

and her nose. I pulled back just a few inches from her face. "I'm sorry I didn't get there sooner. I saw you go to the bathroom, and I was just coming to look for you when I heard Del shouting. I'm so fucking sorry."

Her gaze searched mine. "Don't do that. You got there just in time. This isn't on you."

Her voice cracked a little bit, and I pushed to stand before picking her up again and carrying her to the bathroom. She chuckled when I set her down beside the tub. "You don't need to carry me everywhere, Bear. I'm fine. What am I doing in here?"

"I know you love taking baths, and I have a big tub, so I thought you might want to soak in it."

She nodded. Hell, I'd been naked with this woman in the cove. She needed comfort, and I was going to give it to her. I raised her arms, and her eyes grew wide, but she held them there. I tugged the tank top over her head and reached around her back and unsnapped her pink lace bra with one hand. She sucked in a breath, and I just stared at her perfect tits. I wanted to wrap my lips around her hard peaks, touch her, make her feel good.

But that was not what this was about. And maybe the booze was making me think irrationally, but I needed to keep her close.

I dropped to my knees and reached for the button on her jean shorts. I could tell she was holding her breath.

"I'm not going to touch you, Snow. I'm going to get you in the tub and sit here with you, okay?"

"Okay," she whispered, her fingers tangling in my hair.

I wanted her so fucking bad it was painful.

Physically painful.

My chest ached.

My hands itched to touch her.

I slid the denim down her legs and sighed when I took in the matching pink lace panties she was wearing.

So fucking perfect.

"I wore them for you," she whispered as her fingers continued stroking my hair. "I wanted you to see me in this."

I slid the lace down her legs, feeling every bit of her lean muscle beneath my fingertips. I leaned closer than I should have, my nose right at the apex of her thighs, and I breathed in all that sweetness. My restraint was slipping, and I struggled to stay in control. But I reached around her to test the water. I wasn't going to respond to what she'd said right now because she'd just been attacked. And I was drunk and turned on, so I sure as shit wasn't going to act on that right now.

I needed to get my head on straight and figure this shit out.

And that wasn't going to happen tonight.

But leaving her wasn't an option either.

I wouldn't let her out of my sight.

"Come on. Let's get you in the tub." I reached for her hand as she stepped into the water, and I dropped on the floor with my back against the tub.

"Thanks, Bear." Her voice was barely a whisper, and my gaze locked with hers when I looked over my shoulder.

"Always." I cleared my throat and looked away again.

We sat there in silence for a long time. Obviously we were processing what had happened tonight.

"I'm ready to get out of the tub," she whispered.

"Tell me what happened first," I finally said.

"Del and I went to the bathroom, and when we came out, he was standing there. Before I could process what was happening, he slammed me up against the wall. I should have reacted quicker. I was caught off guard."

My hands fisted at my sides, and I forced myself to remain calm and not react. She'd been through enough.

"This is not your fault in any way, shape, or form." I turned around to look at her. There were no bubbles in the bath, and I tried hard not to stare at her gorgeous body beneath the water.

"I know. And it's not yours either." She pushed to stand and reached for a towel, and I moved to my feet, keeping my back to her. "Sometimes shit just happens. Everyone is fine, okay?"

This was so Lila—trying to soothe me when she'd been the one who'd been attacked.

She tucked the corner of the towel at her chest and started walking toward her room, and I followed. She moved to her bathroom, and a few minutes later, she came out wearing those sexy little shorts and a tank top. Her hair was tied in a knot on top of her head.

She climbed beneath her covers and stared at me as I stood in the doorway with my hands gripping the top of the door frame.

"You care if I stay for a little while until you fall asleep?" I asked, not knowing what the fuck I was thinking by pushing this. But I didn't want to leave.

Hell, I couldn't leave her right now if I wanted to.

And I didn't want to.

"Yeah, of course."

I flipped off the light and moved to the bed, kicking off my shoes and staying above the covers. The last thing I needed to do was feel her body against mine. At least the comforter provided a barrier. The room was dark aside from the sliver of moonlight peeking through the gap in the curtains.

"Are you staying above the covers on purpose?" she asked, and her voice was all tease as she scooched closer to me. I put my arm around her and tucked her head beneath my chin.

"Abso-fucking-lutely."

She chuckled. "Thanks for staying with me."

"Always."

"I thought you might be going home with that woman who was hanging all over you."

"You jealous, Snow?"

"Yes," she said, her voice sleepy.

"I wasn't going home with her. I was there to check on you."

"She's pretty," she whispered.

"You're prettier."

I could feel her warm breath on my neck when she chuckled.

"So, nothing happened with her?"

"No."

"Why not?" she asked, making it clear that she wasn't going to drop it.

"I don't fucking know."

"Maybe you're interested in someone else?" she said, her voice just above a whisper.

"Maybe I am. But that doesn't make it right."

"Because of Travis?" she pressed, her fingers moving up and down my arm, and it was so soothing, I finally started to relax.

"He's my best friend. More like a brother. This would be a shitshow, and he'd be fucking pissed. And you aren't staying, Snow. So, starting this fucking storm when it can't go anywhere doesn't make a lot of sense. It's a friendship and an attraction; it'll pass."

"How do you know?" she asked.

"Because it has to. Get some sleep."

"Night, Bear," she whispered.

I didn't say a word. I just lay there listening to the sound of her breaths as they slowed.

And I dozed off right along with her.

fourteen

. . .

Lila

MY PHONE RANG for the fourth time in a row, and I groaned as my eyes opened, finding Hugh sound asleep beside me. Our hands were entwined, though he was above the comforter, and I was below. I wanted to laugh. I'd climbed on the man naked in the cove and rubbed myself all over him like a rabid animal, and he'd watched me bathe last night, yet he wouldn't come beneath the covers for fear of being too close?

I slipped my hand from his, and he groaned as I reached for the phone. His eyes sprung open when I pushed against the headboard and sat up. I held my finger up to him to let him know I was answering, and I put the phone on speaker.

"Hey, Trav."

"Are you fucking okay? I heard what happened last night. That piece of shit is lucky I wasn't there. Are you hurt?"

I let out a long breath. Everything was so intense with Travis. It always had been. His need to protect. To control all the things around him. Around me. I understood it. We didn't have a lot of control when we were young, but we weren't kids anymore. Things had changed. We were both okay.

"I'm fine. He didn't hurt me. Just scared me a little."

"I told you not to go to that fucking bar," he snapped, and Hugh sat forward, moving away from me a few feet and watching me intensely.

"It was actually fun. He's just an asshole, and that could have happened anywhere. How'd you hear about it already?"

"I called Brax a couple dozen times when you and Hugh didn't answer your phones. He filled me in. Said Hugh kicked the guy's ass, and he took you home. I guess he left some lady awfully disappointed, which meant Brax went home alone again because apparently, the dude can't close the deal without his wingman." He chuckled, his voice calming down a bit. "Hugh must be sleeping in. Thank fucking God he was there."

"Yeah," I said, and Hugh pushed to his feet and ran a hand through his long, wavy hair. The man looked too sexy for his own good this morning. His gray button up was wrinkled and unbuttoned a little lower than normal, with a little bit of chest hair peeking out. He was still wearing his jeans, and I wanted to ask him to come back and stay with me, but I could tell by the look on his face that was not going to happen.

The moment had passed.

Again.

"You want me to come get you? You can hang out with me and Shay today before we all head to the Reynolds' for dinner. Damn, you know Alana is the best fucking cook, and I could use a good home-cooked meal."

I heard Shay shout something at him in the background, and he laughed. "Sorry, baby. Cooking isn't really your thing, though. But you're damn good at making babies."

"Oh my gosh." I fell back in a fit of giggles, knowing he'd just gotten himself in trouble, and Hugh covered his mouth to keep from laughing. "I'm hanging up now. And no, I've got plans today. I'll meet you at dinner. I'm fine. I promise."

I ended the call and looked up to see Hugh watching me from the doorway. "What are you up to today?"

"I was going to go for a run and then head down to the cove to lay out with the girls. And then I wanted to make cookies for your mom tonight."

He nodded. "Sounds like a full day."

"What about you?"

"I'm going to head to the restaurant and do some paperwork. I've got some shipments coming in that I need to unpack. I'll see you later, all right?"

And just like that, he was distant again.

It's like every time we made some progress, he'd pull back.

I nodded and watched as he walked out the door.

I reached for my laptop and checked my emails, and there was one from Joseph Schneider, the man I'd interned for in Chicago, who'd offered me a permanent position at the end of summer. He was checking in to make sure we were still set for the September 1 start date and to let me know that they were offering me a slightly different position where I'd have a team working with me, and I'd be the lead. He wanted fresh eyes, someone who had a new perspective right out of school. The thought made my stomach twist. I would basically be a financial manager, which meant producing reports and making forecasts, recommending investment opportunities, analyzing market trends, and being involved in financial decisions for the company. Originally, I thought I was going to be more of an analyst. This was definitely a higher-level position with more responsibility, and it would look amazing on my résumé.

The pay left my mouth gaping open, and it would make it very possible for me to pay off my father's program quickly. I responded that I was thrilled for the opportunity and looking forward to it. It wasn't totally true because I wasn't ready to go back and start grinding again. I was enjoying being home and not being so exhausted and stressed all the time. Going back to Chicago meant picking up where I left off. This was a job where I'd be working twelve to thirteen hours a day, and corporate America could be cutthroat and most definitely highly competitive. Once again, I'd be proving myself every single day, and I was glad for the time I had here to catch my breath.

Joseph was a graduate of Northwestern University, and he'd also run cross-country there back in the day, so he'd been very supportive of me when I'd come to work at True Solutions. I was honored that he thought I was ready for a position like that.

I closed my laptop and reached for my notebook and added another line.

Catch your breath. Enjoy the little things.

That was what today was about. Going for a run. Going to the cove to hang out with friends. Baking cookies in the middle of the afternoon because you had time to do it. And going to a family dinner at the Reynolds'. I wouldn't take these kinds of days for granted because they wouldn't last long.

———

I was sun-kissed and relaxed when Hugh came through the door. I'd just finished putting the cookies I'd baked into a large Tupperware container.

"Damn. It smells good in here." He moseyed over and reached for an oatmeal chocolate chip cookie out of the container before I snapped the lid on.

He moaned after he popped the last bit into his mouth. I squeezed my thighs in response. How did he manage to make eating a cookie look sexy?

"Best cookies ever, Snow. Come on. Let's go."

"You didn't have to come back and pick me up."

"You don't have a car, right?" He raised a brow, clearly still irritated about that.

"I was going to walk."

"With a tub of cookies? Not after what went down last night. And sure as shit not while you're wearing that dress." He raised a brow and grabbed the Tupperware.

I glanced down at my yellow baby doll sundress. The front did dip a little low, but it was hardly sexy. I'd paired it with my white sneakers, and my hair was in a ponytail. This was totally appropriate for a family dinner. I followed him out to the truck and slapped his hand away when he reached for my buckle.

"This dress is not sexy. And you do not need to buckle me in. I'm a grown-ass woman. I'd think you'd remember that, seeing as I rubbed my naked body all over yours. I don't think you would have enjoyed it so much if I was just a kid," I hissed. I was tired of the games.

His eyes widened, and he slammed the door and climbed into the driver's seat. We didn't say a word as we drove to his parents' house, and I was fine with it. The mixed signals were giving me whiplash.

I jumped out of the truck before he could come around and open my door. I didn't need his help. As both he and my brother had forgotten, I'd been living on my own for the past four years. I walked up the path toward the front door and checked my phone to see a text from my father saying he was on his way.

"Hey," Hugh huffed from behind me, and I whipped around.

"Yes?"

"I'm sorry. I don't do things for you because I think you can't do them yourself." He shrugged, and he looked a little wounded, which, of course, made my chest squeeze.

"So why do you keep doing it, then?"

He glanced around to make sure we were alone. "Because

I like being close to you."

"I like it, too, Bear. But I'm not afraid of it like you are. So, you'll have to decide if you want to act on it or not. Otherwise, stop helping me so much because it's sending me mixed signals."

I turned on my heels and walked toward the door.

It needed to be said. We couldn't keep this up. Spending our days together, and last night he'd sat by the bathtub while I bathed and then slept in my bed.

No. This wasn't normal.

Hugh moved beside me and pushed open the door, and Gracie came charging at us.

"Uncle Hughey. Daddy got to catch puppies today from their mama!"

Hugh scooped her into his arms after he set the Tupperware on the entry table and chuckled. "Puppies, huh? That's exciting."

She reached for me. "Hugs, Lila."

I pulled her into my arms and spun her around. "Hey there, sweet Gracie. I'm happy to see you."

Hugh reached for the cookies, and I followed him into the kitchen where the conversation was already flowing.

Hugh's cousin, Dylan, and Georgia both hurried toward us, and I set Gracie on her feet as they both took turns giving Hugh and me a hug.

"You remember my fiancé, Wolf, right?" Dylan said, as he extended his hand to me.

"Yes, it's so great to see you both." He had one arm around her waist, and the way he was looking at her, had me longing for that.

That kind of love where it's clear they can't live without one another.

I made my way around the kitchen and said hello to everyone. Brinkley and Finn weren't here today, but it was still a lively group.

"Thank you for the cookies," Alana said, as she pulled me in for a hug. She glanced around the kitchen before leaning close to me. "Text me tomorrow, and I'll get you on my calendar this week. I'm looking forward to some one-on-one time with you."

I'd forgotten that I'd promised to make an appointment, but clearly, Hugh had remembered.

"Thank you so much for doing this."

"Are you kidding? I never get any time alone with you, so we can finally catch up. I'm so happy you're here," she said, and my chest squeezed. I'd always loved and respected her, and the thought of pouring out all the issues regarding my father made me very anxious. But if I had to tell someone, I think Alana Reynolds would be my pick. She was easy to speak to and probably the most nonjudgmental person I knew.

"I'm still pissed off about what happened last night," Travis said from a few feet away, and I turned to see him and Shay and Brax all standing with Hugh. They must have just come in.

And speaking of judgmental—my brother was the king of judgment.

He was still ranting about what happened last night, even after I'd told him everything was fine.

The Reynolds family didn't need to know all the gory details.

I saw my dad enter the kitchen as he stood off to the side, and his gaze locked with mine across the kitchen.

"Oh, my dad's here. I'm going to go say hi. He looks a little nervous standing over there alone," I said, and Alana squeezed my hand.

"You got it, sweetheart. I'm going to get this chicken out before these boys start eating the dessert first."

I chuckled and hurried over to my father and hugged him. "Hey, Dad. I'm so glad you're here."

"Of course. Thanks for the invite."

Hugh, Cage, and Bradford all walked over and welcomed him. Shay wrapped her arms around me from behind as my brother approached my father.

"I'm so happy you're home right now, Lila," Shay whispered and kissed my cheek. "I know he's been tough to deal with, but he just loves you so much."

Shay and I had always been close. She was good for Travis. She evened him out, where I seemed to cause him nothing but stress.

"I'm really happy to be home," I said, my gaze never leaving my father and my brother.

"Hey," Travis said, and I could feel his discomfort.

"Hi, son. It's good to see you."

They stood there, making small talk, and I stepped a few feet away to give them some privacy. Hugh walked over to me and Shay, with Dylan and Georgia right behind him.

"Don't run away from me, Hubert," Dylan said, over a fit of laughter.

"My name is not Hubert. Why do you insist on calling me that?"

"I just want to know who your plus one is for the wedding. Brax and Travis said you were out with some hotty last night," Dylan said, as Wolf walked over and wrapped his arms around her, resting his chin on her head.

"Yeah, Hubert. Who are you bringing to the wedding?"

"Georgia is bringing her mystery boyfriend that anyone has yet to meet." Dylan laughed.

"He's just not into meeting family. He likes to keep things cool, you know? But I'm not going to this wedding solo, and unless he wants me to take another dude, he best get on board." Georgia waggled her brows at me, and I chuckled.

"I am not bringing Karmy to the wedding. I don't even know her."

"That's not what I heard." Travis and Brax walked over,

and Hugh rolled his eyes. "I mean, I feel bad that Lila buzz-killed your night with you having to step in and handle things, seeing as Kline was apparently useless. Aren't you seeing that guy? Yet he lets you fend for yourself at a bar?"

Dylan and Georgia looked at me sympathetically. So, obviously, they'd all heard the torrid details of last night, thanks to my brother, who couldn't seem to stop talking about it. I glanced over to see my father deep in conversation with Cage, who was holding his daughter in his arms, and she'd reached over to pat my father on the cheek. It brought back memories to the happy times we'd had when I was a kid, because there were some, even if my brother was quick to forget.

"Kline didn't even see it happen," I finally said. "It's not his job to get into a bar fight because some guy was acting like a lunatic."

"Well, Hugh did." Travis raised a brow before fist-bumping his best friend.

"Hey, why don't you bring Lila as your plus one? I'd love for you to be at the wedding," Dylan said, looking between me and Hugh. "It's going to be so fun, and you're not going to be comfortable bringing some random woman."

"Yes!" Georgia shouted. "Brinkley is bringing that guy she's been dating for a few months, and he's a real snooze fest. And trust me, my date will be a nervous wreck being around the family, so me and Lila can dance and have some fun." She turned to her brother and put her hands together like she was praying.

"I think that's actually a great idea," Travis said, with a big smile on his face. "Put some distance between you and Kline. No sense getting attached to that dude when you're leaving in two months."

I wanted to tell him how completely clueless he was, but I was too busy staring at Hugh, waiting for him to insist that this wasn't a good idea.

"All right. I don't know if there are any rooms left at the hotel, but I can call and see," Hugh said, glancing at me before looking back at my brother.

"You don't need to get her a room. I'm sure you can get two queen beds in the room you have. You're probably the only dude on the planet that I'd trust to sleep in a hotel room with my sister." He barked out a laugh, and I looked up to see Brax watching me with a mischievous grin on his face.

He clearly knew something was up.

"So, you'll come?" Dylan asked, reaching for my hand.

"Of course. I'd love to see you walk down the aisle."

Was it terrible that I was hoping there weren't any rooms available with two beds? I wouldn't mind sleeping beside Hugh Reynolds one more time.

Clothed or naked.

Well, preferably naked.

Stooooop.

I was doing it again.

"We're going to have so much fun. It's going to be the wedding of the century. I'm so excited!" Georgia clapped her hands together.

"I can't wait," I said.

My phone vibrated, and I looked down to see a notification from the app where I was selling my car. There was a full-price offer. Relief flooded. I glanced over at my dad, and his gaze locked with mine.

I smiled.

We were going to be okay.

I sent a text back to the phone number and let them know we could meet tomorrow.

"Okay, everyone. Dinner is ready. Let's head to the table," Alana called out.

I made a face at Brax, and he held back for a minute while everyone hurried to find a seat.

"So, you're going to the wedding as the big guy's plus

one, huh?" He waggled his brows, and I tried not to laugh, but it was impossible not to.

"Stop. We're friends. Listen, I got a text, and someone just made a full-price offer on the car." I looked over my shoulder to make sure no one was listening just as my phone vibrated with a new text. "They want to meet tomorrow morning at nine a.m. He said he'll bring a cashier's check."

"All right. Travis is going to lose his shit that I helped you sell your car, and Casanova over there..." He motioned to Hugh, who was watching us from the table, his gaze narrowed and questioning. "He's not happy about this. But, I'll meet you at my office, and we'll do it together."

"Don't worry about them. Thanks, Brax. I'm so happy it sold so quickly."

"Me, too. But I'm getting daggers from your roommate, so let's get over there."

Brax sat between Georgia and Cage, and there was a seat for me between Hugh and my father, with Travis on the other side of Dad.

Alana was asking Travis all about the baby, and Hugh leaned down close to my ear. "What was that about with Brax?"

I looked around to see everyone in their own conversations and kept my voice low. "My car sold. That means my dad is in."

Butterflies swirled in my belly at the thought.

"Looks like you made it happen, Snow."

"I'm about to check number one off the list. And you know what comes next."

His heated gaze locked with mine.

"Number two," he whispered, as his tongue swiped out to wet his lips.

I just smiled and waggled my brows.

Things were looking up for me.

And I was enjoying every minute.

fifteen

. . .

Hugh

I'D GOTTEN TO REYNOLDS' early because I hadn't slept much and was on edge. This pull I felt toward Lila was fucking with my head. We'd dropped Lila at the house, and I'd gone out with Brax after Sunday dinner last night to grab a few beers just because I didn't trust myself to be home with her alone.

I couldn't stay away.

And now she was coming to Dylan's wedding?

Spending a weekend with me in the same hotel room?

I'd always prided myself on my ability to stay in control, but this was testing every bit of restraint that I had.

Every. Fucking. Bit.

So, I'd come in late last night after being razzed by Brax about Lila going to the wedding with me, which I'd waved off as ridiculous.

But he knew I was lying.

He was going with her this morning to meet the guy about the car sale. That wasn't a concern for me for reasons I wasn't willing to tell either one of them just yet. So, I'd left the house while she was out on a run because not seeing her was the only way I could try to figure this shit out.

I was behind the bar, going through some of the deliveries I hadn't unloaded this weekend, when the door swung open. Travis walked in, carrying two cups of coffee from Cottonwood Café. Even though it was owned by an overaged, sexually inappropriate woman, they made damn good coffee.

"Thought you might need this. I heard you and Brax were out late last night," he said, handing me the cup of coffee.

"Does that dude go five minutes without oversharing?" I laughed as I took a long pull and groaned.

He barked out a laugh as he slipped onto the bar stool across from me and set his cup down. "He didn't tell me. I called Lila last night, and she said you were out with Brax."

"Well, it's good to know the town gossip wasn't the one who told you." I shrugged.

"I was checking on her after what went down at the bar. I'm glad she's going with you to the wedding. I think she needs to get away for a few days. It'll do her some good."

"Yeah. It'll be a fun wedding, too. You know Dilly doesn't do anything simple. But I think Lila's doing really well, Trav. You worry too much. That girl has got her shit together."

"I don't doubt that. Hell, I'm so fucking proud of her. They're building a whole fucking team around her at True Solutions. She just graduated from college. That's how much faith they have in her. That's not what I worry about. I know she's amazing."

"What *are* you worried about?" I cleared my throat, guilt sinking in that he knew how I felt about her. Knew I was struggling.

"Kline fucking Barley. I guess Shay told her about a coworker she wanted to set her up with, and Lila shut her down. Said she was into someone else. That's not good, dude. I've already got to worry about my father guilting her into staying. I don't need her falling for some weak fucker who will derail her." He scrubbed a hand down his face. "I'm so stressed out about this baby. About being a new dad and fucking things up. I just need Lila to be okay, you know? And now, she's all hung up on getting Dad into this program. You and I both know it'll be a waste of money. I just don't know how to protect her anymore."

I came around the bar and pulled up the stool next to him. "Maybe you don't need to. Lila's got a good head on her shoulders. If she likes Kline, you need to trust her." Obviously, I knew it wasn't Kline she was talking about, but I sure as shit wasn't about to go there right now. "If she wants to help your father, let her do it. If he fails, she'll stop trying at some point. You can't control the whole world, brother. Life doesn't work that way."

"It's worked pretty well for me for a long time." He chuckled. "And what happens if she really falls for this dude? She stays here with a guy who isn't good enough for her and spends her life trying to fix our father? No. She thrived in Chicago because she wasn't burdened by the drama of our family. By our past. She got her fresh start far away from here, and I want that for her. That's why I'm so grateful that she has you. I'm so distracted with work and Shay and the baby, and I'm slipping, dude. So, thank you for stepping up for Lila. You are my brother in every way."

He clapped me on the shoulder, and guilt coursed my veins.

"Always. But I'm telling you, you're overthinking this shit. Maybe you should go with her to check out that facility. She's getting him in soon, and it might be nice for her to have your support."

His face hardened. "No. I won't get behind that. He's going to fail, just like he always does. I'm not buying into Lila's fantasy about saving a man who's beyond saving. I can't do it, Hugh."

I nodded. I knew I wasn't going to change his mind on this one. He had his reasons. "I get it. Don't worry about it. I'll be there for her. You focus on Shay and the baby. I convinced her to go see my mom at her office. Maybe that'll help her through all this, regardless the outcome with your dad."

"That's fucking amazing. Yeah, that'll be great. She's got a lot of shit buried in there, and she clearly doesn't want to deal with it, because if she did, I don't think she'd be so quick to help him. Thanks for pushing her to do that. I owe you."

"You owe me nothing. My mom was thrilled, and she's damn good at her job, so that'll be a good support."

"Yeah. I totally agree. Do you know how she's paying for this program? I assume they must do loans at this place?"

I wasn't going to tell him about the car. He'd lose his shit. This wasn't my story to tell, and I'd taken care of the situation anyway. "I don't know. She hasn't said anything about it, just that she has it covered."

"I can't let her go into debt over this, man." Anger and stress radiated from his shoulders.

"Trav, listen. Have you ever considered the idea that Lila could be right? He's never had treatment. What if this program actually works? Wouldn't it be worth it then?"

His gaze searched mine, and he shook his head. "No. My father died in the accident that took my mother's life. That's the day he gave up on his family. That's the day my childhood ended."

"I understand your anger. I really do. But Lila did her research. She came home with a plan, and she's probably the smartest person I know. So just have a little faith in her."

"It makes me crazy that she's doing this, but I also hate that every time I see her, I'm an asshole." He shrugged. "I guess I could support her without supporting the idea of getting him help. I should stop busting her balls and enjoy this time with her being home."

"That's a good plan. She's not changing her mind on this, so you may as well get on board as best you can. Spend some time with her without riding her ass so much."

"Yep. I can do that. Damn, dude. You're like your mom with this therapy shit," he said, as the door swung open, and Kline made his way inside and glanced over at us. His shoulders stiffened a little when he saw Travis, but he played it off well.

"Hey, guys. How's everyone doing?" Kline made his way around the bar. "I stopped by to do that inventory you asked me to do. I never got to it last night because we were packed from open to close."

He was a good guy. A reliable employee. Just not good enough for Lila. And the poor bastard wasn't even with her, but he was going to get the wrath of Travis.

"Thanks for doing that." I nodded.

"It's good you're here. We were just talking about Lila," Travis said, his voice hard.

"Oh, yeah? What about?"

"About the fact that she's leaving at the beginning of September. This is temporary."

Kline nodded as he reached for the clipboard behind the bar and glanced over at me before his eyes moved back to Travis. He could just tell him right now that nothing was going on, and why the hell wouldn't he?

"I know. She's been very clear about that."

"Good. So don't get any ideas about changing that. You got it?" Travis pushed to his feet and squared his shoulders. It was hard not to laugh because he was such a fucking brute sometimes, but beneath it all was a really good man.

A man who loved his sister fiercely.

"Yeah. I got it. This is temporary between us, too." Kline shrugged, and a part of me wondered why he didn't just say it and get Travis off his back.

"Then we'll get along just fine. But if you hurt her, I will hunt you down. And your boss here, he'll probably beat me to the punch."

"Okay, Rambo. I think he gets it." I chuckled, and Kline

shook his head with disbelief before turning back to his clipboard.

"I'll see you later." Travis held his hand over his head and waved as he pushed out the door.

I turned to look at Kline. I couldn't get a read on the guy. There was no reason for him to act like he was with her if he wasn't. Was I missing something?

He looked up at me and raised a brow. "You owe me one. That dude is crazy."

I shoved my hands in my pockets. "So, why'd you go along with it?"

"Because she's a great girl; she deserves to do whatever she wants to do right now. So, if me going along with it takes some heat off her, I can live with that. As long as Danielle doesn't get wind of it and think something's really going on. Plus, I've got a pretty cool boss, and I think he'd appreciate me playing along. Unless I'm totally misreading things?"

Fuck. Was it that obvious?

"I don't know what you're talking about." I smirked. Because nothing was going on. We hadn't acted on it outside of that one night down at the cove.

Unless you counted me sitting in the bathroom while she bathed, which I suppose could be considered inappropriate.

And the night I slept in her bed.

And the millions of times I've fantasized about her…

"Sure, you don't. And don't worry about it. Your secret is safe with me!" he yelled, and he was still laughing as I made my way down to my office.

My secret sure as shit wouldn't be safe if he kept shouting like that.

Not that there even was a secret at this point.

My cell vibrated, and I looked down to see my sibling group text that was constant, and I'd missed a shit ton of messages while I'd been talking to Travis, so I took a minute to get caught up on the Reynolds family drama of the day.

> **BRINKLEY**
>
> When is everyone heading to the city for the wedding? Kaeran doesn't want to go too early because you guys make him so damn nervous.

Kaeran was her boyfriend, and none of us were big fans of the guy.

> **CAGE**
>
> That's a stupid reason, which is very fitting for his stupid name.

I barked out a laugh because my brother was a grumpy dude, but no one made me laugh as much as Cage did.

> **BRINKLEY**
>
> Glass freaking houses. Your name is Cage. It's hardly common.

> **FINN**
>
> I see we're all cheery this morning. Tell KAREN to relax. His panties seem to be wound tight.

> **CAGE**
>
> <Preach emoji>

> **BRINKLEY**
>
> Why isn't there a middle finger emoji?

> **FINN**
>
> There is. Update your phone. <middle finger emoji>

> **BRINKLEY**
>
> Learn something new every day. <eye roll emoji>

GEORGIA

Happy Monday, guys. I just got to class, but it hasn't started yet. We get to paint some naked dude today, and I can't think of a better way to start my day. <eggplant emoji>

FINN

Atta girl. Way to live up your last few months of college. What I wouldn't give to go back.

CAGE

I see you're taking your classes very seriously, Georgie. Life isn't all paintings and penises, you know. And, Finn, you took six years to graduate, so stop whining.

BRINKLEY

I think Hugh's next restaurant should be named Paintings and Penises. I'd totally go there.

GEORGIA

I see the moral police is out in force today. Thanks, big brother. Brinks, I am totally here for the restaurant name, but let's lose the painting part. I like the idea of it just being called PENISES! And where is Hugh, anyway?

FINN

Probably having his gourmet breakfast served to him by Lila. The dude has found a way to get freaking meals included in her living in the casita. I don't see Georgia doing this after she moves in.

GEORGIA

You'd be correct unless he wants ramen noodles or gummy bears for breakfast. Lila's coming to the wedding as Hugh's plus one, and I couldn't be happier about it. Dikota also isn't looking forward to coming or meeting you guys.

CAGE

What is with all the weird spellings of names with the guys you two date? I mean, he must have received endless dick jokes his entire life. What were his parents thinking? And why the fuck isn't he looking forward to meeting us?

GEORGIA

Gee. I wonder why?

BRINKLEY

I'm glad Lila's coming as Hugh's plus one so we won't have to deal with him freaking out that some woman thinks he's going to want to walk down the aisle. #commitmentphobe

You assholes don't miss a beat. I'm sorry that I don't jump into relationships as quickly as you two, Brinks and Georgie. I'd never date anyone who wasn't excited to be around our family. We're the fucking best. So, tell those dudes to fuck off.

FINN

Fuck, yeah. The voice of reason is here. Welcome, brother.

CAGE

Agreed. What the fuck is their problem with us? I'm offended, but seeing as the last guy Georgie brought home was a vegan mute, DICKOSAURUS is an upgrade.

They purposely spelled their names wrong just to fuck with them. Because we were Reynolds, and that was just what we did.

GEORGIA

HE WAS MAKING A STATEMENT ABOUT THE WORLD BEING A SHITSHOW!

FINN

By not speaking? I don't think people heard the message, Georgie. Glad you kicked that dude's ass to the curb. I don't trust a person who chooses not to speak.

CAGE

Or eat a goddamn steak.

Or wears a pinky ring.

GEORGIA

Okay, okay, I get it. But Dikota is different, I promise. My nude just showed up, and oh my. <fire emoji> <eyes bulging emoji>

BRINKLEY

Stop being so judgy. I liked the vegan mute. What was his name?

GEORGIA

His name was Legend.

Yet he's barely memorable? Tough name for a vegan mute. Don't be staring at penises too long, Georgie. Diktok might get jealous.

GEORGIA

<Eye roll emoji>

BRINKLEY

I have to get back to work. Thanks for the riveting conversation. And none of you answered my question. Love you.

I was still laughing. My siblings were the best people I knew. Even when they drove me crazy, I loved the hell out of them. Everyone finally responded to Brink's question, and we were all heading to the hotel on Friday, which was close to Wolf's parents' home, where they were getting married.

Danielle and Kline were going to be in charge of Reynolds', and my manager at the other bar, Marcy Stevens, would be overseeing things at Garrity's and Burgers and Brews for me while I was gone. I wasn't anxious about leaving because I wouldn't miss this wedding for the world.

"Hey," Lila said, standing in the doorway, holding a plate. "I missed you this morning and thought you might be hungry. I brought you some banana pancakes and bacon."

My dick twitched at the sight of her in the white sundress with skinny straps on her tan shoulders. I could see myself pushing those straps down and kissing my way down her neck to her perfect tits that I ached to touch.

To taste.

Fuck me.

This was why I was staying away.

Every fucking time I saw her, this was what happened.

"That sounds great. Thank you."

She stepped in and set the plate down, along with a napkin and some utensils before dropping to sit in the chair across from me. "Are you avoiding me?"

I could hear the hurt in her voice. I was avoiding her because we needed some distance. I was doing it for her.

For Travis.

I pulled the foil from the plate and looked up at her. "Yeah. I am."

Her gaze narrowed. "Well, at least you're honest."

"You know I'll never lie to you. And I'm doing it for you, so don't look so hurt."

She rolled her pretty eyes. "Don't take the moral high road and then claim it's for me. You're not doing it for me or for yourself. You're doing it for my brother, who isn't involved at all." She pushed to her feet and moved to the doorway. "You know what... I take that back. You're doing it a little bit for yourself because I think you're terrified of the way you feel, Bear. I just never would have pegged you for a coward. I've got to get to work."

Shots fired.

What the fuck was that about?

A coward? I'd been called a lot of things in my life.

A player. An asshole. Noncommittal. Cocky.

A coward? Never.

I was not afraid of Lila James.

I wasn't afraid of anything.

sixteen

. . .

Lila

HUGH and I spent the rest of the week completely avoiding one another. I was fine with it. If he wasn't grown up enough to own up to his feelings, then that was on him. It wasn't like I was pressuring him to have a serious relationship. I was here for two more months, and weren't flings his specialty? I tried not to be offended by the fact that he wouldn't go there with me, but it definitely stung.

And we'd be going to the wedding tomorrow together.

Obviously, I wanted to be prepared just in case something was to happen. So, I'd asked my best friends for some tips, and somehow, I'd been wrangled into going to the place where Sloane gets waxed. She'd picked me up from Reynolds', and I glanced over as I said goodbye to Brandy and found Hugh's eyes on me.

His eyes were always on me.

He was just too much of a baby to do anything about it.

"Rina and Del are meeting us there," she said after I jumped into her vintage Volkswagen bug and buckled up.

I laughed. "Is it normally a group event?"

"No. But Del and Rina are in the mood for some mac 'n cheese with a side of awkward sexual questioning at Cotton-

wood Café, so I told them to meet us at the wax place first."
She pulled out onto the road and glanced over at me. "So, you
think Kline's the guy? He's perfect fling material."

I felt guilty not telling them the truth, but it was just easier
this way. The humorous part was that nothing was happening
anyway, but if there was a chance that I ended up in a room
with Hugh Reynolds this weekend, and he stopped worrying
about my brother and made a move, I wanted to be prepared.
The girls had all shared horror stories about being embarrassed that they hadn't groomed anything *down there,* and I'd
always liked being prepared for things. I'd been preparing to
lose my virginity for far longer than necessary. It was almost
ridiculous at this point.

"I don't know. Time will tell," I said, as she pulled into the
parking lot, and I looked up to see a large sign that read *The
Pretty Kitty.*

"We're here." She turned off the car and giggled.

"Really? I couldn't tell by the gigantic sign."

"Meow," she said over a fit of laughter. "Let's go, girl.
Del's car is here, so they must be inside."

Del and Rina both hugged us when we stepped inside.

"I saw Kline yesterday at the grocery store, and he actually blushed when I brought you up. He said things are going
great," Rina said with a wide grin spread clear across her face.

I didn't know why Kline was playing along, or why I was,
either. Nothing was even happening with Hugh, and nothing
was happening with Kline. And I certainly didn't want to do
anything to hurt him and Danielle. But he claimed Danielle
wanted to keep things casual, so he had no problem with it.

"It's nothing serious."

"Yet, here we are?" Rina giggled. "The first time I did this,
it was not pleasant. It gets easier every time."

"Great. I feel a little awkward about her seeing everything," I whispered.

"Please. This woman has seen more pussies than most of

the men here in Cottonwood Cove." Sloane waggled her brows. "And I'm guessing yours is gorgeous, just like you."

We all laughed at how ridiculous she was, when a woman with bright pink hair came out of the room. "Hey, ladies, good to see you."

She hugged each of my friends before turning to me. "Hey, I'm Veronica. You must be Lila. You're the virgin, right?"

I gasped and turned to glare at Sloane. "You told her?"

"Um… no," Sloane said over hysterical laughter. "That would be on you. She just meant a virgin waxer."

"Ahhh… okay. I'll pretend I didn't hear that. None of my business. Let's go, my little virgin waxer." She led me into a room, and they each took a seat in the tiny waiting area outside of the room.

The next forty minutes were not very pleasant. And remember, I had a pretty high suffering rate with all the training I'd done over the years. But, hot waxing your vajazzle—it was up there in the misery department.

"Damn. Something is off with this wax today," Veronica said for maybe the fourteenth time after ripping off the bandages.

"But it's okay, right? It's working?"

"Um, yes. It's definitely working. It just seems hotter than usual."

"It's normal that it hurts, right?"

"Oh, yes," she said, placing cold rags all over my lady parts while I lay there spread eagle. Normally, this would be mortifying, but it was burning so badly that I didn't care. The cold rags were soothing. "It always hurts, but it's just doing an extra good job today, I guess."

I surged forward, sitting up on my elbows. "What does that mean?"

"I think the heater thing is on the fritz, so the temperature may have been a little off." She cleared her throat. "Luckily, you kept that little landing strip, so I didn't pull your entire vagina off with wax." She barked out a laugh like the whole thing was hilarious.

I glanced down at the cloths covering me up. "Yeah. I'd sort of like to keep my vagina."

"For sure. It's still there. I just checked." Her laugh was ridiculously high-pitched. "Let's have you lie back, and I'm going to put some salve on it. I get this from a special healer, and it works wonders," she sang out. "But, maybe you can have your boyfriend blow on the sensitive area later if it still hurts."

I groaned. What the hell was she even talking about? "I don't have a boyfriend. I need to have someone blow on it?"

She pulled off the towels, and I tried to sit back up, but the woman nearly karate chopped me in the throat. "Lie down. Oh, what a shame that you don't have a man. You've got yourself a pretty kitty there, girl. But you could just fan it yourself with a notebook."

I had to fan myself now?

And did she seriously just say I had a pretty kitty?

I flinched when she started applying what felt like a mix of Vaseline and superglue on my bikini area.

"Does everyone have to fan themselves after they get waxed?"

"Well, I think we all like to be fanned downstairs, am I right?"

I laughed and shrugged awkwardly. "Oh, yeah, sure."

"You might be a little irritated. The first time is always the worst, and like I said, the wax was a bit hotter than usual, but at least it did the job. You should be fine by tomorrow, or for sure in a few days."

"A few days?" I squeaked.

"I highly doubt that long. The healer said this stuff works miracles."

I glanced down to see myself slathered in some sort of

ointment, but I couldn't really see what was beneath it. I sat forward and pulled up my panties, wincing a little when I pulled on my shorts. I followed her out to the lobby and handed her my debit card, and she quickly rang me up.

"Our girl is looking very chic downstairs," Veronica said to the girls, and everyone laughed.

What was this? Hot wax banter? Is that a thing?

"Of course, she does. And I knew you'd work your magic," Sloane said.

"How'd it go?" Del asked me.

"It was fine. Not the most pleasant experience, but I survived."

"There were some issues with the wax, and it was definitely hotter than usual. But Lila took it like a champ." Veronica shrugged.

"Let's hope Lila takes everything like a champ," Sloane said, and everyone burst out in laughter. I rolled my eyes because the virgin jokes were exhausting, and my bikini area was currently on fire.

"You okay?" Del said, leading me out the door.

"Yes. I'll live. She gave me some salve from a healer, so she said I should be fine in a few hours or a few days," I said as we walked. I kept my legs apart to prevent my clothes from rubbing because I was feeling super raw down there, and I was starting to get concerned.

"What? Salve from a healer? Sloane, what kind of witch doctor did you send her to?"

"I don't know. She's never given me any special salves. I've never had any issues with her," Sloane said as we walked toward the cars.

"Wait, didn't she take off one of your eyebrows once?" Rina asked, as we paused in front of the two cars.

"Oh, well, yeah. That did happen the one time. Faulty wax, or something. But, you're waxed and cleaned up, and that's what matters."

"True. At least it's over," I said, shifting my legs to try to cool the fire between my thighs. What the hell was in that salve?

"Lila's driving with me," Del said. "We'll meet you guys there."

We all got in the cars and headed to dinner.

"Well, at least you'll have this weekend to recover before you see Kline next week." Del pulled out of the parking lot and drove the short block to Cottonwood Café.

I was quiet. "Yep. That's a relief."

I'd gone through all of this to make sure I looked good for *this* weekend. But she didn't know that.

Del put the car into park. "Lila Mae James. Cut the shit."

"What?"

"Sloane and Rina may have been born under a log, but I was not. You did not get waxed for Kline Barley, and we both know it. I've given you enough time to come clean, even pouring on all the chatter about Kline that we both know isn't true, but now I'm forcing you to spill it."

"How do you know nothing's going on with Kline?"

"They don't call me the world's most observant human being for nothing," she said, as we watched Sloane and Rina walk into the restaurant.

"Nobody calls you the most observant human being." I laughed.

"Well, they should start. Because I saw the way you were with Kline at that biker bar. I saw the way Hugh lost his shit on that asshole who grabbed you and the way he looked at you. We've never lied to one another, so why are you starting now?"

I sighed. "I'm sorry. I just—there really is nothing going on with him, but I do wish there was. But we did share a few moments."

I quickly told her everything. About the night at the cove, the night he slept in my room, even though nothing happened, and the way he'd run me a bath after what happened at the bar and sat there with me.

"Holy hotness," she whispered. "What did he look like naked?"

I chuckled. "It was dark, but from what I did see—and felt —he's everything you would imagine he is. I mean, I humped the man into oblivion, Del. It's kind of mortifying."

She leaned forward and hugged me. "He's just scared because he and Travis are so close. And I guess I get it. You're not staying, and it's not like you're someone he could have just a fling with."

"Why?" I asked.

"You're not that girl, Lila. And you have a history with him. It could fuck up everything." She looked away, and I followed her gaze to Sloane standing in the doorway with her hands up in the air, annoyed that we hadn't come inside.

"Shit. We'll talk more later."

"Del, no one can know anything ever happened, okay?"

"Girl, you know I will take it to the grave. But I want all the details this weekend when you go to that wedding. And you're sharing a room?" She fanned her face before turning off the car.

"Well, between him avoiding me like the plague, and my vagina being set on fire, I think it's safe to say nothing is going to happen. Just another boring day in the life of Lila James."

"You got to grind up against a naked Hugh Reynolds in the cove. You're the horniest virgin I've ever met," she said over her laughter. "You never get to call yourself boring again."

I pushed the door open, still laughing, and looked up to see Sloane with her brows raised.

"Are you talking shit about Veronica?" she hissed.

"Nope. We're talking shit about you," Del said over a fit of laughter.

And just like that, we had dinner, got questioned by Mrs. Runither, and laughed our asses off, just like we always did.

I'd gone to Del's after we'd eaten to borrow a black backless gown for the wedding as it was a black-tie event, and I didn't have anything to wear. Her sister loaned me some strappy black heels, and I'd been relieved that the dress fit perfectly, minus the fact that my boobs were a bit smaller than Del's. But the low dip in the front was fine with or without tatas falling out of it.

When I made it home, I forced myself to shower, and I cringed when I saw how red and irritated it was between my legs. I reapplied the salve that Veronica had given me, and to say I was uncomfortable would be an understatement.

I barely slept a wink because Hugh hadn't come in until well after midnight, and my mind kept wandering to Karmy and wondering if he was with her.

Or someone else.

I had no right to be jealous. We weren't... anything. Yet I tossed and turned all night and got angrier with each passing hour.

———

"You're awfully quiet," Hugh said, as we merged onto the freeway to head toward the city.

"Am I?"

He chuckled. "Are you mad at me?"

"No. I have no right to be mad at you, do I?" I looked out the window.

"I mean, you're the one who called me a coward. I think I should be mad."

"But you aren't mad, are you? Because you know it's true."

"I don't believe that me thinking with my head for once in my life makes me a coward. You're leaving, Lila. So what

181

happens if we cross the line for the next, what—two months? That's only eight fucking weeks. And then what? There's this weirdness every time we see one another? Your brother fucking hates me forever? Why even go there?"

Wow. He'd really put a lot of thought into the timeline. The man rarely had relationships that lasted longer than a weekend, and now he was concerned eight weeks wasn't enough time? This was definitely interesting, and it supported my coward theory even more.

"Wow. You act like I'm asking you to marry me. Do you put this much thought into the other women you like?"

"No. Because they aren't you. You're different, and you know it."

"And so are you. That's why it makes sense to me," I said, watching the trees fly by as we moved down the highway.

"What makes sense to you?"

"I've known you most of my life, Bear. I know what a good man you are. I'm obviously very attracted to you, and I think you're attracted to me. So, why fight it? We both know I'm leaving; there's no secret there. I'm not looking for forever. For the first time in my life, I want to just have some fun. Why not allow ourselves to act on it? And I like the idea of you being my first."

He stared straight ahead at the highway. "And Travis? You think he'll just be fine with it?"

"I don't really care what he thinks. I'm a grown-up, and it's none of his business," I hissed. "I mean, did he ask you permission before he hooked up with Shay?"

"Well, that would be weird. Shay's not my fucking sister. It makes a difference, Snow."

"It doesn't have to. This isn't for him or for anyone else. We're already friends. This could be something that is just for us. He doesn't need to know. I'm certainly not going to tell him. Nor did I call and inform him any time I hooked up with someone when I was away at school. Because it's. None. Of. His. Business."

He was quiet, and I let that sit there between us. I was feeling more confident lately, and I was done just going along with whatever Travis wanted, just for the sake of keeping the peace. I loved my brother very much, but that had nothing to do with my personal life.

"Brax said the car sold, and the guy picked it up? You haven't filled me in on that," he said, completely changing the subject.

"Well, you haven't exactly been around. God knows what you've been doing. But yes, the car deal went through."

He looked over at me, his lips turning up just the slightest bit in the corners. "You jealous, Snow?"

"Yeah, I guess I am. I'm not the one pretending I don't care."

"I'm not either. If I didn't care, this would be easy." He cleared his throat. "And Finn was in town last night, so he came to Reynolds', and we stayed up late, talking and drinking beers. I wish I could tell you I've been hooking up with random women because that would have you running for the hills. But for whatever fucking reason, that hasn't happened since you've come home."

I tucked my lips beneath my teeth to keep from blatantly smiling, because that was a relief.

"Good to know."

He chuckled. "So, did you call Havenwood? What's the plan?"

"Yep. She sent over a bunch of paperwork, which Dad and I filled out together two nights ago, and I emailed it all back to her. We should be getting a call next week. He's ready to go. We've talked about it. He said he's sick of being a slave to his addiction. So, giving him this chance is the best we can do, right?"

"I agree. And you did it. You came home with a plan, and you made it happen."

"Well, the real work starts now. That's why I asked for the amount of time off that I did before starting the new job. It's already July in a few days. I'm guessing he's going to need at least thirty days in a program, probably longer. I'd like to be here the first few days that he gets out, if possible. So, that's where the whole timeline came from, but that was all pending he'd agree to go, that we found a place that would take him, that the car would sell, and everything would fall into place. Now he just has to do the work." I sighed. It was all happening.

"That's great. Did you tell Travis?"

"Yep. I asked him if he'd drive us there next week to check him in. I told him my car was in the shop because I don't need to deal with his wrath or have him tell Dad that I sold my car and make him feel guilty."

"What did he say?"

"He said that he was busy, and he wouldn't be going out there." I shrugged. I'd ask Del if I could borrow her car. Travis could do what he wanted to get in the way of this happening, but it wouldn't stop anything.

"I'll take you, all right?"

I nodded. "Thank you."

"My mom said you guys met this week."

"Yeah. She's the best. The first meeting was just talking about me coming home and getting Dad into a program. Apparently, next week we're diving into the juicy stuff," I said with a laugh and then winced when I shifted, and the discomfort between my legs reminded me not to move.

"What's wrong? You okay?"

"I'm fine." This was not something I was about to share with him.

He nodded, but when he gazed over at me, I didn't miss

the concern I saw there. "All right. If you need anything, just say the word."

Would asking him to blow on my vajazzle be too much?

Because my *pretty kitty* was on fire.

seventeen

. . .

Hugh

WE'D TALKED ALL the way to the city, and that was the thing with Lila. It was easy. The conversation, the laughter, the attraction.

"So, did you get us two rooms?" Lila raised a brow when I pulled into the valet at the hotel and put the truck into park.

"Nope. They didn't have any other rooms available," I said, which was not true, but I'd never actually called to ask.

Like I said, I was all over the fucking place with this girl.

I climbed out of the truck and came around to help her out as I pulled our suitcases out of the truck bed, and the valet greeted us and handed me a little card to call when I needed my truck. Another guy walked over and took our luggage, and we followed him inside.

We paused in the grand foyer.

"Wow," Lila said, spinning around in her yellow sundress, long, dark waves falling down her back. "This is so pretty. Look at the chandeliers."

I glanced up at the light fixtures overhead and chuckled. "Swanky, huh?"

I moved to the front desk and told them my name as the older woman typed on her keyboard. "Yes, one king suite on the top floor with city views. We have all the wedding guests staying on one floor, per the Wayburns' request."

"Sounds great. Thank you." I took the cardboard portfolio with the keys tucked inside and slipped it into the back pocket of my jeans as we walked toward the elevators. The guy who took our luggage said he'd meet us upstairs.

Once we stepped on, I looked up to see Lila eyeing me as she stood against the opposite wall from me. "Did you try to get two queen beds?"

"I've always preferred a king over a queen. I'm a tall guy. I need to stretch out." I smirked.

"Did you ever call the hotel and ask for two rooms?" she pressed. It made sense. I'd been avoiding her for days, yet here I was, sharing a room with her. Trust me, I didn't understand it myself.

The doors opened, and I motioned for her to step off without answering her question, just as the guy who'd taken our suitcases came walking out of our room and held the door open. I had no idea how he beat us there, but I slipped him some cash and thanked him for taking care of that.

Lila walked inside first, and I closed the door behind us. Floor-to-ceiling windows with views of the city spread across the far wall. A large king canopy bed sat in the middle of the room, reminding me that I'd made no attempt to change the sleeping arrangements.

And instead of feeling panicked, I felt anything but.

Lila hurried over to the windows and stared outside. "Wow, this is gorgeous."

I was looking at a much better view as I watched her. As if she knew it, she slowly turned around. "So, we're sharing a bed?"

"It won't be the first time, right?" I said, my voice gruff.

"Yeah. You're right." She moved to the bed and sat down, but she winced a little, which caught me off guard. I'd thought she'd winced in the truck, as well, but she'd insisted she was fine.

"You okay?"

"Oh, yeah. I'm fine. Just sore from my run yesterday." I was surprised she hadn't gone for a run before we left today, but she'd been in her room all morning.

"All right. So, we've got a few hours before the rehearsal dinner. Is there anything you want to do in the city while we're here?"

"I'm easy," she purred. "What would you like to do?"

Oh, you can't begin to comprehend what I'd like to do.

"We could grab something to eat. Are you hungry?"

"Sure. I could eat," she said, her dark eyes searching mine.

I moved closer, my legs bumping hers as she sat on the edge of the bed. My hand reached for her fingers as I looked down at her.

"I heard what you said in the car. I want you to know that, okay?"

"Okay. So, are you going to stop avoiding me?"

"Yeah. I don't think I can keep it up anyway," I said, moving to sit beside her, but our hands remained intertwined.

"Why?"

"Because I can't stop thinking about you. And I'm fucking trying, Snow. I'm trying to do the right thing. But it's killing me." There. I said it. It was the truth.

"The right thing for who? For Travis? For someone who isn't even involved in this? It's ridiculous, you know that, right? We're both adults."

"He's my best friend. He's your brother. So, he's involved no matter how you look at it. And you being—" I ran my free hand through my hair and let out a long, tortured breath. "I don't want to take anything I don't deserve from you, Lila. So, this is complicated for a million reasons. Plus, you're not staying, so we're playing with fire."

"First of all, me being a virgin is not an issue. You're not taking something from me; you're giving me something. I would much rather my first time be with someone I feel safe with and care about. I've had lots of opportunities, Bear. They just never felt right. But this does." She moved to climb on my lap. "And since when do you worry so much about the future? Do you normally ask a woman how long she'll be sticking around? Why is that playing with fire?"

"Because it's you," I said, tucking her hair behind her ear and breathing her in. I itched to kiss her. To taste her.

"I'm a grown woman. And I want you. We've always been good friends, and that won't change. We'll just be sharing something special while I'm home, and it's no one's business but ours. *Nothing will change.* We're together all the time at work and home, anyway. So, to the outside world, nothing will be different. This is just for us."

Fuck. She was saying all the right things.

"Just for us," I said, my lips grazing her ear. "You sure about this? Because once we start, Snow, I won't be able to stop. I've been fighting this for weeks."

"I've never been surer about anything."

That was all it took. My mouth covered hers. My hand tangled in her hair, while the other shifted her onto my lap so she was straddling me. But I felt the way her body flinched when she ground against me, and I pulled her back. Her lips were plump, eyes filled with desire, and dark waves falling all around her. So sexy and gorgeous I nearly came undone at just the sight of her.

"Why'd you stop?" she asked. Her breaths were coming hard and fast, and her eyebrows pinched together with concern.

"You flinched. I felt it. We're not doing this unless you're certain, Lila."

She groaned and covered her face with her hands. "I did not flinch because I'm hesitant."

I tugged her hands away from her face. "Look at me. Tell

189

me what's going on. Are you nervous? We can take things slow."

My hands moved down her sides and settled on her hips.

"No. Nothing like that. I did something stupid," she whispered.

"Tell me. What did you do?"

"I wanted this to happen," she said with a shrug, and her cheeks pinked. She was so fucking sweet sometimes, and her vulnerability and honesty was something I was drawn to. "And I hoped it would happen, you know? So, I went to this place yesterday with the girls. It's called The Pretty Kitty."

My eyes widened. "What the fuck is The Pretty Kitty?"

"It's a waxing place. And I got my bikini area waxed just in case you were to see me."

"I have seen you, and you're fucking perfect," I said, searching her gaze and trying to figure out where this was going.

"You saw me in the dark, in the water. I just wanted to be ready." She shrugged.

"So, you went to a waxing place and got waxed?" I asked.

"I did. But the wax was having some issues and was maybe hotter than normal, and I don't know. Oh my god, this is so embarrassing." She shook her head and covered her face again with her hands.

"Hey," I said, wrapping my fingers around her wrists and pulling her hands down. "If we're going to do this, you have to be able to talk to me. There's nothing to be embarrassed about. So, the wax was hot? Isn't it supposed to be hot?"

She chuckled. "Yeah, I guess so. But it was hotter than usual, and then she used this healing salve that I think I possibly had a reaction to, and so it's a little irritated on the sides of my—er, vajazzle."

I barked out a laugh. "Your vajazzle? Do you mean your pussy is irritated, Snow?"

Her mouth gaped open, and it was fucking adorable. She

was sexy and innocent at the same time, and it turned me the fuck on.

"You've got a dirty mouth, Bear. But I like it. She did say that I should have my boyfriend blow on it." A smile spread across her face, and a pink hue covered her cheeks. "Of course, I told her I didn't have a boyfriend. And yes. That's the situation. So, I didn't flinch because I'm hesitant. I'm just a little uncomfortable in my bikini area."

"You want me to blow on your pussy, Snow?" I chuckled at how awkward she was when it came to talking about this shit. Hell, I was a sexual man. Nothing about this bothered me—her being a virgin. Her being my best friend's little sister?

That bothered me.

A bad wax job. I didn't give a shit, but I didn't like the idea of her being in pain.

I pushed to my feet, holding her in my arms, and gently set her down on the bed as I hovered above her.

"What are you doing?" she whispered, her eyes wide and wild with need.

"Let me see what's going on."

She shook her head and squeezed her eyes closed. "I can't believe this is happening."

"Open your eyes, and look at me," I demanded, and I waited for her dark brown gaze to lock with mine. "You don't need to be shy with me. I think you're the most beautiful fucking woman I've ever seen. Let me just check it out, and maybe I can help."

She slowly nodded. "Okay."

I reached for the hem of her dress and pushed it up, and she lifted her ass a few inches off the bed so I could pull the fabric all the way up and rest it on her stomach. She wore a pair of white lace panties, and I sucked in a breath at the sight of her. Lean, tan legs. White lace. And the way she was lying there, looking like an angel as she let her guard down so I could see what was going on, it had my dick throbbing against my zipper. My fingers trailed up her thighs, and I pushed them apart enough that I could stand between them.

"Right here? Is this where it's bothering you?" The area on the outside of her panties was definitely red and irritated.

She nodded, her chest rising and falling rapidly. I ran my fingers gently over each side as her legs fell open even more. Back and forth, I soothed her heated skin with the tips of my fingers. She moaned a little bit as I continued soothing her for several minutes before moving to the band of her lace panties and waiting for her eyes to meet mine. "Can I take these off and see if it's irritated there, as well?"

She didn't speak. She just nodded and bit down on her juicy bottom lip. I slipped her panties down her legs and dropped them on the floor. It was only red on the sides, and I licked my lips.

"So fucking beautiful, Snow." I continued moving my fingers up and down along the irritated skin as I dropped to my knees at the foot of the bed. She pushed up on her elbows to look at me.

"What are you doing?"

"I'm going to make you feel good. Has anyone ever tasted you before?" My hands continued moving along her sensitive skin as she looked down at me.

"Once. But I didn't like it."

"Yeah? What didn't you like?"

"It just felt too personal, I guess. I wasn't comfortable, so we didn't do it for very long." Her voice was just above a whisper.

"Does this feel too personal now?"

"No," she said, without hesitation.

"Okay, I want you to tell me if you're uncomfortable or if you don't like it, okay? But I think you're going to like it. Do you trust me?"

"One hundred percent."

Those words fueled me. She trusted me. She was comfortable with me. And I felt the same about her. I'd always been a man who liked to please the woman I was with, but this was different.

Next level.

Almost a feral need to please her. To make her feel good.

My hands moved down her thighs and beneath her knees, and I pulled her down gently to the edge of the bed. I looked up at her to see her watching me intently.

"I want you to lie back on the bed and just relax, okay? I'll be careful with the area that's hurting, but I think this is going to feel good." I waited for her to nod before she fell back. "Do you know how many times I've thought about tasting you?"

"How many?" she asked, her words breathy and laced with need.

"Every fucking day since the day you came home. Multiple times a day if I'm being honest." I leaned forward and blew just a little between her legs, and she nearly came off the bed. "You like that. Maybe the lady was right, and that's just what you needed."

"Yes," she whispered. "More."

I chuckled as I did it again several times before I buried my head between her legs. Careful not to let my scruff irritate the outside area as I spread her legs wider, my hands moved along the sides again to soothe her as my tongue swiped out along her slit.

So fucking sweet.

She writhed beneath me, and I continued licking and sucking every inch of her. She tangled her fingers in my hair and tugged my head harder against her center. I smiled against her because I loved that she knew what she wanted. What she needed. I sucked hard on her clit, and her back nearly came off the bed. I moved one finger to her center, stroking her there while I continued sucking, before slipping the tip of my finger inside slowly, and she groaned. She was so fucking wet and so fucking tight, I didn't know if it would even fit. She tensed at first, but then she pressed my head back down to her core, and I continued. I nibbled and licked and sucked as I slipped my finger in all the way and then out, slowly at first and then quicker as she began to relax. Her hips started moving, setting the pace. She was soaked, and I knew she was chasing her release. I swear nothing had ever been hotter in my life. My free hand moved around the outside of her thigh and gripped her ass as I moved faster.

I pulled out my finger and slipped my tongue inside. In and out.

"Bear," she cried. "More."

I moved my thumb to her clit; my tongue continued to slide in and out of her as her entire body began to shake, and she tugged at my hair as she came apart beneath me.

Her frantic breaths filled the air around us.

I held her there as she rode out every last bit of pleasure.

Once her body relaxed and her breathing slowed, I released her legs and pulled back to look at her. My tongue swiped out to lick my lips, which were covered in all her sweetness.

Her gaze searched mine, her chest still rising and falling, eyes wild.

"Wow," she said, and I chuckled.

"You're so fucking sexy. How did that feel?" I pushed the hair behind her ears and stroked her cheek.

"Amazing. I hope we can do it again very soon," she said as her teeth sank into her bottom lip.

"Baby, I'm just getting started." I pushed to my feet and stood as she sat forward and pulled her dress down. I moved to the phone and called the front desk.

"How can I help you, Mr. Reynolds?" a woman asked on the other end.

"Hi. Can you send up some Benadryl, Neosporin, and Tylenol and just charge it to my room?"

"Absolutely. Anything else?"

"That'll do it. Thank you." I ended the call and reached for the room service menu before sitting back down beside her on the bed. I leaned my back against the headboard and opened my arms, knowing she'd climb right in, which was exactly what she did. She settled her cheek against my chest.

"What's the Benadryl, Neosporin, and Tylenol for?"

"That shit salve she gave you didn't help. I think you were having an allergic reaction to the ointment. The Benadryl and Neosporin will help, and you'll have the Tylenol if it continues to cause you discomfort." I kissed the top of her head. "What are you hungry for?"

"You," she said with a chuckle.

"Oh, you can have as much of me as you want. But let's feed you first and pace ourselves."

I perused the menu, and she glanced up at me.

"What are you going to get?" she asked.

"After your sweet pussy, nothing looks nearly as appealing."

Her eyes widened, and her cheeks pinked, and I barked out a laugh.

I fucking loved it.

eighteen

. . .

Lila

WE'D BOTH GOTTEN BURGERS, and Hugh had insisted I take a bath before he wrapped me in the hotel robe and applied the Neosporin to the irritated skin. I didn't know that anything had ever felt more intimate than this man sitting beside my tub once again, even though it was a large enough bathtub for both of us, and then drying me off and applying ointment to my irritated bikini area.

That was not something I ever expected a man to do for me.

Hugh was this big, rugged guy, but he was so attentive and caring at the same time.

I'd offered to return the favor and attempted to drop to my knees, but he'd tugged me back up and pulled me onto the bed, where we'd both fallen asleep for two hours.

Apparently, orgasms really wiped me out because I rarely napped, but I'd had no problem dozing off.

We'd gotten up and dressed for the rehearsal dinner, which was here at the hotel restaurant. It was going to be a small group, and just family, and I was thankful that I had my black cocktail dress from the awards banquet I'd attended after winning nationals.

"Damn, you look gorgeous," he purred as he tugged me close to him.

He wore a white button up, which was wrinkled, per usual. But he wore black fitted dress slacks and dress shoes. His hair was wavy and thick. After watching the little he had to do to make it look sinfully sexy, I envied him. I'd had to add waves to my hair after the bath and the nap, as my hair obviously took a bit more effort.

"You look beautiful," I said, pushing up on my toes to kiss him.

We hadn't kissed enough. I wanted to spend hours kissing this man.

He must have felt the same way because the next thing I knew, his hands were beneath my butt, and he lifted me up, causing my dress to bunch at my waist, and my legs wrapped around him. He turned so my back was against the wall, and his tongue tangled with mine. My fingers were in his hair, and I'd never wanted someone so badly in my life.

We stood there kissing for what felt like forever, when his phone buzzed in his back pocket. He groaned and pulled back.

"What are you doing to me, Snow?"

"I could ask you the same thing."

"Yeah? Do you know how much I want you?" he asked, his voice gruff and his lips just a breath away.

"You did stop me from returning the favor." I looked up at him and studied his gaze. That little voice in the back of my head had wondered why he didn't let me unzip his pants and pleasure him the way he'd pleasured me.

His sage-green eyes searched mine. "And you think that's because I don't want you?"

I shrugged. "I don't know, but the thought did cross my mind."

He gripped my hips and lowered me over his engorged

erection. My eyes widened as he slid me down and then slowly lifted me back up. "It's definitely not that."

"What is it, then?"

"I'm not ready to take anything from you. Right now, I fucking love pleasing you. But it's not because I don't want you. I've never wanted anyone more."

I let out a long, strained breath and placed a hand on each of his cheeks. "Pleasing you would be giving me something."

He smiled this big, wide grin. "You're too fucking sweet for your own good, Snow. Come on. Everyone's downstairs waiting for us. You can tell me all the ways you want to please me after dinner."

He slid me down his body until my feet hit the floor. The man was so tall. His hands were large. His shoulders broad. Yet, we somehow fit together, no matter what position we were in. Standing. Hugging. Sitting. Me grinding against him. I didn't know how it worked so well, but it did. "Sounds like a deal."

He adjusted himself and groaned before pulling the door open, and I couldn't help but laugh.

We stood next to one another on the elevator, the backs of our hands touching, as his finger looped around mine until the doors opened. Then we both stepped off and made our way to the restaurant.

His hands slipped into his pockets, and we were just two friends attending a wedding together again.

"Hugh! Lila!" Georgia came running toward us with a mopey-looking guy behind her. He had surfer vibes, but he looked uncomfortable as he stood there.

Hugh wrapped his arms around his sister before she turned to me and gave me a big hug. "Damn, Lila. This dress is gorgeous."

"Thank you. I love yours," I said, taking in her black slip dress.

"Thanks. This is Dikota," she said as she introduced us.

"Nice to meet you." I smiled, and Hugh grunted something, but the way he stood hovering over the smaller man had me biting back a laugh. He could be so big and growly when he wanted to be.

Gracie came running up and held her arms up for Hugh, and he scooped her right up. Cage gave me a hug and glanced over at Hugh and then at Dikota, and the two brothers appeared to be communicating without using words.

"There they are. Lila, I want to introduce you to Kaeran." Brinkley paused to hug Hugh, and then he extended his arm to her boyfriend, who nodded and shook his hand.

"How's the restaurant business, Hugh?" Kaeran asked.

"It's going really well. I found me a secret weapon," he said, winking at me, and I swear my belly did little flips and I felt my face heat. "Lila has things running smooth enough to let me sneak away for a weekend."

Georgia studied her brother before turning to me with a big smile on her face. "Come on, let's get a drink."

The next hour was spent greeting family and seeing all Dylan's sisters, who I hadn't seen in years. They were all pregnant, aside from Dylan, and everyone was joking that there must be something in the Honey Mountain water. I met their husbands, and everyone was having a good time.

Wolf's family was making their rounds, as well.

We were waiting for Dylan and Wolf, who hadn't shown up just yet.

"Of course, those two are late to their own rehearsal dinner," Everly said with a laugh as she typed out a text on her phone and let us know she was texting Dylan now.

"Hey, they're the only ones allowed to be late," Vivian said.

"They're here," Charlotte and Ashlan said at the same time. The Thomas sisters were as close as the Reynolds siblings.

It was refreshing.

"And who do we have here?" a very attractive man said, reaching for my hand as we stood in the private room and were just getting ready to head to the table.

"Oh, hi. I'm Lila."

"I'm Sebastian, the big, bad Wolf's brother." He chuckled and raised the back of my hand to his lips, slowly, and kissed it.

Hugh was watching from a few feet away as we'd intentionally kept our distance. We were just friends, after all, at least for appearances. His green gaze locked with mine, and I didn't miss the heat there. Nor the anger.

Or was it jealousy?

"It's nice to meet you," I said, pulling my hand away as politely as possible.

"Oh, for God's sake, it's my rehearsal dinner. Keep your paws off the guests. Sorry about that, Lila," Wolf said, before giving me a brisk hug. Dylan swooped right in and did the same.

"I'm so glad you're here. I see you've met my brother-in-law-to-be. Charming, isn't he? He's all bite and no bark, so be careful with that one," she whispered close to my ear and then glanced over to see her cousin brooding as he watched us. "Ohhhh, someone does not look happy. Such a protective *friend*, huh?" She chuckled and then winked at me.

Hugh appeared at my side after hugging his cousin and her soon-to-be husband, then glaring at Sebastian.

"Hugh, my man. I didn't realize you two were together." Sebastian extended a hand, and Hugh took it with a scowl on his face and gave him an equally grumpy greeting.

He didn't respond to the comment; he just placed his hand on the small of my back and led me toward the table where Georgia was waving us over to sit beside her.

I hugged Hugh's parents and their grandparents, who I hadn't seen in a long time. There were maybe forty people attending the dinner, and it managed to feel very intimate as they were all family.

I'd never had a family unit like this, and I definitely admired it.

Or like the Sunday dinners I'd been attending at the Reynolds'.

It was something I think I'd always craved.

A hand found mine beneath the table, and I glanced up to see Hugh watching me before he leaned close to my ear. "You okay?"

I nodded. "Yes. Of course."

I reached for my wine glass to take a sip, and he leaned close again. "How's your *vajazzle* feeling?"

I chuckled and squeezed his hand. "Very good. Thanks for asking."

"It's something, Snow. One of a kind."

I shook my head and tried hard not to laugh. Finn was sitting on the other side of Hugh and asked him something that he and Cage were clearly arguing about.

Georgia tapped my arm, and I turned to look at her. She leaned close enough so only I could hear her. "So, what do you think of Dikota?"

"He seems really nice," I said, as I glanced around her to see him awkwardly talking to Charlotte's husband, Ledger. Dikota did not seem comfortable being here at all, nor did he seem to be making any effort to hide his discomfort.

"He's not as outgoing as I am. He's sort of this broody guy. But, girl, he's got this possessive streak that I've never experienced. Some guy said hello to me at a restaurant the other day, and he punched him in the face. I was so startled because I didn't think he even liked me that much. But wowsers, right?"

I tried not to react because red flags were going off in my head. Being jealous is one thing, but getting physical at a

201

restaurant because someone said hello? That didn't seem right.

"That's an intense reaction. How long have you guys been together?" I tried to move the conversation to a safe subject.

"Three months. He's a total wild card. I never know what I'm going to get. But it's kind of fun, you know?"

"Yeah. I'm sure it is. And he goes to school with you?"

"Nope. He's in a band downtown. I met him through a mutual friend. He's not into school because he feels like it sort of puts people in a box. And, of course, I get it, because, hello, I'm graduating with a degree in art. You can't put artists in a box, you know?"

"I get that. So, what do you want to do when you graduate?"

"Well, thanks to my dad and Cage, who both enjoy life inside the box," she said with a chuckle. "I minored in business. That's why it's taking me the extra semester to graduate. They were so terrified I wouldn't be able to find a job as an artist. But I don't know what I want to do yet. I'm open. How about you? Are you excited to go back to Chicago and start your career there?"

I thought about it.

The thought of leaving did not excite me.

Maybe that was because I'd come home to help my father, and even though things were happening, we still had a long road ahead of us.

"You know, I'm happy to be home right now. That job in Chicago is going to be a lot. Sort of like school was. Long hours. Not much of a life outside of work. The city is so busy, you know? It's been nice being home and being back in nature and not being rushed every second of the day. And I love working at the restaurant. It's been a great couple of weeks so far."

"Well, Hugh seems like a different person since you started working there, so thank you. He'd been stretched too thin. You're helping more than you know. And he doesn't seem to be out man-whoring anymore," she said with a laugh. "I think he likes having you at the house."

My chest squeezed at her words. Because I liked being there, too, at the house and the restaurant.

But my mind kept wandering back to what had happened in our hotel room a few hours ago.

What I was hoping would happen later tonight.

Butterflies swarmed my belly, and I glanced over to see Hugh laughing with his brothers.

"Thank you. It's been really nice being home."

The dinner was filled with laughter and several toasts to the happy couple, and I had a great time.

Each of Dylan's sisters got up and said their favorite *Rocky Balboa* quote but geared it toward her wedding day.

"I stopped thinking the way other people think a long time ago. You gotta think like you think... on your wedding day," Charlotte said.

One after the other had stood and read one to her over a room full of laughter, as apparently, they were big fans of the movies.

I happened to be a huge Rocky fan, too, so I thoroughly enjoyed myself.

"Okay, I need to get my beauty sleep, and all of my sisters are carrying tiny humans in their bellies, so we're going to call it a night," Dylan said as she pushed to stand.

Wolf pouted that they weren't spending the night together, causing more laughter.

We made our rounds, hugging everyone goodbye, and we all piled into the elevator up to our floor, agreeing to meet the following day to head to the wedding.

Once we got inside the room, I wasn't sure what would happen. I didn't know what he'd meant when he'd said that he didn't want to take anything from me.

He unbuttoned the top two buttons on his dress shirt and

leaned against the bar area and watched me. "Do you want a drink?"

I shook my head. "No, thank you. I don't want a drink."

The corners of his lips twitched, and he gave me a half nod. "What do you want, Snow?"

"I've made it clear. I want you."

"You sure about that?"

"Very."

He raised a brow. "We can't go back once we cross the line."

"I'm not someone who does things spontaneously. I'm not looking to go back. I'm looking to go forward."

"And you're sure you want to do that with me? Even if I can't give you what you deserve?"

"What is it that I deserve, Bear?" I asked, closing the distance between us.

"Everything. *Every. Fucking. Thing.*" His hand found my cheek, and he studied me. "You don't want your first time to be with some guy who lives in Chicago? A guy you can date and end up with? I mean, you've waited all this time. There must be a reason."

I reached up for the button on his shirt and slowly undid it. "I never knew what I was waiting for until that night out at the cove. And that's when it hit me."

"What hit you?"

"I think I've been waiting for you," I said, moving my fingers down to the next button. "I wasn't thinking about the future for the first time in my life. I was living in the moment, just like I'm doing right now. I went to school in Chicago for four years. I dated. I had plenty of opportunities, but none of them ever felt right."

"And this feels right? Even with it being completely fucked-up in a million ways?"

"I know what this is. We're good friends. We're attracted to one another. I feel safe with you. I know it's not forever.

And I'm okay with that. We'll do this for as long as we feel like doing it, and then when I leave, we'll go back to being just friends. No one ever has to know. This is just for us."

He nodded as I unbuttoned the final button on his shirt and ran my hands up his muscled abdomen and where his last name is written in script across his chest.

Reynolds.

"You know how much I care about you, don't you?" he asked, as his thumb stroked my bottom lip.

"I've never questioned that. So, will you stop fighting me? Stop fighting this?"

His green gaze locked with mine, and he nodded slowly. "Yes."

My fingers moved down to the waistband of his dress pants, and I lowered the zipper as his eyes stayed locked with mine. His tongue snaked out to wet his lips, and I'd never wanted anyone as badly as I wanted him. I slowly dropped to my knees and looked up at him one last time before tugging his pants down first and then his briefs.

His enormous cock sprung free, and I nearly gasped at the sight of it. A chuckle escaped his lips, and he lifted his legs a bit off the floor and freed himself of his clothing.

I hadn't seen a lot of penises, but I'd seen a few.

And this one did not look like the rest.

This looked like the alpha penis. It was large and thick and magnificent.

"You ever done this before?" His voice was gruff and sexy, and I squeezed my thighs together.

I nodded. "Yes. Once."

And I'd hated it. But I wanted to do this with him in a way I'd never imagined I would.

I wanted to make him feel good the way he'd made me feel good.

My hand found his shaft, and I gripped it as his head fell back and he groaned. "Fuck, Lila. I've thought about this so many times. About fucking that sweet mouth of yours."

Moisture pooled between my legs, and I licked the tip of his erection, swirling my tongue around it slowly. His fingers tangled in my hair, and I wrapped my lips around him, taking him in a little bit at first. I took my time, and he didn't rush me.

His fingers gently stroked my hair, and he moaned as I took him in deeper.

It turned me on that I was affecting this big, strong, sexy man this way.

I knew Hugh was experienced—and I obviously wasn't. But it didn't seem to bother him at all.

I went deeper, and he started to move faster.

I loved it.

The sounds he was making were feral. His grip on my hair tightened, and I continued moving him in and out, swirling my tongue and enjoying the feel of him against my lips.

I never knew it could be like this.

I tilted my head back just enough to look up at him and see his hooded eyes on me.

"Slip your hand beneath your dress and tell me if you're wet," he commanded.

I did as he said, and he continued to rock in and out of my mouth. I groaned when I found myself soaked, and his fingers continued grinding against my scalp in the most erotic way as he helped set the pace. "Keep touching yourself. I want you to come with me."

I hadn't even known that was a thing.

Hadn't even known that I could ever touch myself in front of a man.

But I wanted to do it.

Wanted to chase my pleasure right alongside him.

My entire body buzzed with need. His breathing grew

erratic, and little pants escaped my lips, which were wrapped around him.

"So fucking sexy, Snow. Seeing you on your knees with my cock in your mouth."

I whimpered because I was ready to detonate.

I took him deeper.

Faster.

His groans filled the space around us.

Deep and husky and sexy.

He attempted to pull my head away, but I refused to move. I wanted to stay right here.

"Come for me, right now," he demanded, his voice deep and laced with desire.

Warm, thick liquid filled my mouth, and I squeezed my eyes closed as my entire body started to shake.

Hugh growled my name, and I went right over the edge with him.

Quaking and gasping as sensation flooded every inch of my body.

It was the most erotic moment of my life.

And I only wanted more.

nineteen

. . .

Hugh

HOLY. Fucking. Shit.

I'd never experienced anything like this before.

This need. This desire. This want.

Lila fucking James was inexperienced, yet she managed to give me the best blow job of my life, all while getting herself off at the same time.

I'd never seen anything or anyone sexier.

I looked down at her as she pulled away and wiped her mouth with the back of her hand. She looked up at me with big, dark, trusting eyes. "Wow. Is it always like that? Or is this just a Hugh Reynolds thing?"

I reached down and pulled her to her feet, brushing the hair away from her beautiful face with my hands. "It's never like that. It's definitely a Lila James thing."

I couldn't believe all that had happened today, and I'd yet to really touch her. Or kiss her. Sure, we'd pleasured one another. But I wanted to kiss every inch of her sweet body. We'd crossed a line, and there was no going back now. And even with the guilt that I felt about betraying my best friend, I only wanted more.

I only wanted her.

I was a greedy bastard. Especially when it came to Lila.

"I hope the sex is just as good as everything else has been," she whispered, and I barked out a laugh before reaching for my briefs and pulling them on before my dick started thinking about going for round two.

"We're not having sex tonight, Snow." I pulled her back into my arms and kissed the top of her head.

"Why not?"

"Because today has been a lot, and this is all pretty new to you, so we're not fucking rushing it. You've come twice, and I haven't even been inside you yet. Nor have I kissed you nearly enough or explored your gorgeous body. There's no rush. We've got two months, right?" I asked her casually, but for whatever reason, those words stung. Hell, normally two months with someone would be a really long time.

But with Lila, it felt like it would never be enough.

We'd decided to do this, so I wasn't going to run anymore.

But I also wasn't going to rush anything.

"I thought you were a player," she said, her voice teasing.

I pulled back to look at her. "Are you shaming me for trying to be a good guy?"

"Maybe. But you can't call all the shots, or this won't work. We've got two months, so you need to play fair. I feel like you hold all the power." She moved to sit on the bed and crossed her arms over her chest.

"Oh, yeah? How do I hold all the power?" I moved closer, pushing to stand between her knees.

"Because you have what I want," she purred.

My dick shot up in response.

She knew what she was doing.

I placed my hand beneath her chin and lifted so her gaze would meet mine.

"Trust me. You have what I want. But we don't need to rush. I'll never deny you, Lila. But I won't do anything that I think will hurt you."

"You think you're going to hurt me, Bear?" She raised a brow.

"I think the way I want you right now—I might lose control, not be as patient as I need to be. And being your first time—it's probably going to hurt a little, and you're already hurting from that bullshit wax job, so we need to slow things down."

"Remember, I was a college athlete. I have a pretty high suffering rate." She waggled her brows.

"Tell me something else you want, and I'll do it. And then I'm taking you to bed and I'm going to kiss every inch of your body until you cry out my name over and over."

She sucked in a breath, and her teeth sunk into her juicy bottom lip. "Anything I want outside of sex?"

"Yep."

She smiled. "There's a huge tub in there. Take a bath with me. No sitting on the side lines. I want you naked in the water again, just like at the cove." She chuckled.

I moved fast, startling her as I tossed her over my shoulder and slapped her ass. I jogged to the bathroom as she laughed hysterically. "I can do that. I mean, soaking in warm, dirty water is obviously sexy to you. So, I'll give it a try."

I set her on the bathroom counter and moved to the over-sized bathtub and turned it on. Lila reached over to her makeup bag sitting beside the sink and pulled out a hair tie before gathering all her hair on top of her head and fastening it in place.

She chuckled. "The water is not dirty. And you in the tub is always sexy."

"I want to see you naked." I leaned against the wall beside the shower and crossed my arms over my chest.

Waiting.

"You've seen me naked." Her tongue came out to glide along her lips.

"The first time it was dark. The second time I felt like

some creeper checking you out after all you'd been through that night. So, now I want to take my time looking at you."

Her breaths came faster, and a slight pink hue spread across her cheeks, beneath the little spackle of freckles. She hopped off the counter and walked over to me, turning around and giving me her back.

"Can you unzip me please?"

My fingers grazed down her silky skin as I moved the zipper down to her waist. She stepped away from me and turned around, her gaze locking with mine as her hands fell from her chest, and she let the dress drop into a puddle at her feet.

"Fuck," I hissed, as I took her in.

Golden skin. Lean and sexy and slight curves in all the right places. My mouth watered, my eyes landing on her perfect tits, covered in black lace. She reached behind her and unsnapped her bra and then slowly let it slide down her shoulders before she tossed it on the floor beside her dress.

I now knew the definition for perfect tits.

These should be sculpted in gold.

A perfect handful. A perfect mouthful. Gorgeous pink nipples that were pebbled and dying to be tasted.

She watched me and then looked down. "They aren't all that dazzling. They're pretty small, right?"

"They're the best tits I've ever seen, Snow. Don't sell yourself short."

She chuckled and reached for the band of her panties and slid them down her legs and then twirled for me, as if she were enjoying the way I was watching her.

"You're beautiful," I said, my voice gruff.

"You know you don't have to say that. I'm kind of a sure thing." She chuckled.

Did she really think I was just blowing smoke up her ass?

"And you're not too bad yourself. So how about you strip down and let me peruse that body of yours."

"No fucking problem." I shoved my shirt off my shoulders, as the buttons were already undone. And my briefs followed. We stood there gawking at one another like two teenage kids who'd never seen the opposite sex naked.

I'd seen lots of women bare themselves for me over the years.

But nothing had compared to this.

Because none of them had been Lila.

I moved toward the tub as the water was dangerously close to the top, and I turned off the faucet. "I suppose I need to get in first, seeing as I'm the big one."

"Yep." She smiled and moved closer. I stepped in and yelped at the water temperature.

"You're not getting out of this, Bear," she teased. Once I was settled in the unusually hot water, she climbed in with ease and settled between my legs. Her head leaned back and fit perfectly in the nook of my neck.

My hand moved up and down her arm before trailing over to her breasts. I traced my fingers over each one like I'd been dying to do. Two hard peaks responded to my touch, and she sighed.

"Thanks for bringing me with you this weekend." Her eyes closed, and I loved the feel of her body against mine.

"Thanks for coming with me."

"Do you think you'll ever get married?" she asked. "Have a family?"

"I don't know. I'm not against it, but I've never felt the need to get serious with anyone."

Never felt anything close to what I feel for you.

"I think you'd make someone a great husband, and you'd be a really good dad, Bear." Her voice was soft and sleepy and sweet.

Normally, this conversation would have me running for the door. But it was different with Lila. We were sitting in a tub naked, yet having a conversation like this with her was completely natural.

"How about you?" I asked. I wanted to know what she wanted out of life. She'd always been so focused on school and running, and I had no idea what Lila's dreams were.

"I honestly never thought about it much until now—being home again. I've been so determined these last few years to achieve certain things." My hands settled on her stomach, and her fingers rested on top of them. "I think I've spent so much time trying to prove to everyone, but probably mostly to myself, that I could be successful in spite of my circumstances. That's one of the hard parts about living in a small town. Everyone knows your story, and when it's a sad one, there are a whole lot of judgments about you out there. It's easy to believe they're right, you know?"

"You've got nothing to prove," I said, wrapping my arms a little tighter around her.

"I know that now. And I see your family, and your cousin's family, and I actually love it. I don't think I ever used to believe that was something that I could have because I didn't have it growing up. After my mom was killed in that accident, our family was never the same. But I would love to have a partner to grow old with and a bunch of little kids to raise and love on." She chuckled.

So honest and genuine.

"I think you can have anything you want, Snow."

"Yeah. I know my brother wants me to have this big career and this grand life, like it will somehow make up for the things we went through. The things we lacked in a way," she said, letting out a sigh. "Sometimes, you just go through things. You lose people you love, and you experience hard times, but it's what you do with that that counts. You can either stay down, or you can get up and fight. Sort of like the Rocky quotes your cousins were referencing tonight. And I feel like Travis is stuck in this really angry place, and it's time to get up and fight. He's going to have a child and be a father. And he needs to let it go and start living *his* life."

"I think when you were in the hospital for those few weeks when you were sick, and then you and he got split up by social services for a while…" I said, clearing my throat because it was still hard to talk about. "It did something to him. He decided you were his to protect from that day on. He shut down with your father, and he couldn't forgive him because he loves you so damn much. That's what makes this so hard. Because I fucking know that, Lila."

"And I love him, too. But I don't tell him who he can talk to or go out with. I don't tell him where he needs to live or what to do with his life. He's not my father. And I've allowed him to play that role because it's always been me and him against the world, in a way. But we're not fighting anyone anymore. We're both okay." She glanced over her shoulder and smiled, and her dark eyes welled with emotion. "My father neglected us because he was drowning in grief and using his addiction to numb himself. And that's what addiction does. It robs you of your logic. He's been addicted to painkillers and alcohol for so long that he doesn't know how to exist without them anymore. And Travis never lets him forget long enough to try to get clean. If someone told you over and over that you didn't deserve to breathe the same air as them, wouldn't you want to numb your-self? My father needs to deal with all that's happened in the past and move forward, and my brother needs to let him do that."

I nodded. "How do you always see the good in people?"

"I don't think you have to look that hard if you want to see it. I see the good in you, Hugh Reynolds. I always have."

My fucking chest tightened at her words.

"Thank you. Give your brother time, okay? I'll help you get your dad settled, and Travis can focus on the baby and Shay, and maybe if he sees that Tate is taking this seriously, he'll get on board at some point."

My best friend was a stubborn man. A good man, but a stubborn one.

Lila was right. The world was very black and white for Travis.

The few weeks they'd been separated when they were young had been brutal for him. My parents had gone to bat for both of them, and tried to get temporary custody, but the system is flawed in a lot of ways, and the red tape and paperwork kept them apart for several weeks. My father had helped Tate by hiring him at Burgers and Brews so that he could prove he was holding down a job and getting his life in order. He'd agreed to be drug tested daily until social services returned both Travis and Lila to their home. But Travis had never been the same. For a twelve-year-old kid, it had been traumatic, to say the least. He never forgave Tate, who continued his vicious battle with addiction. Travis had always been one step ahead, not letting Lila get in the car with their father most of the time. Making sure she ate well and was cared for. My best friend had become a parent to his sister at a very young age.

"I will. I love him so much. You know that. I'm just done doing whatever he says, just because he thinks he's right. I'm actually quite capable of taking care of myself."

I nodded because Lila James had grown into a strong woman.

A capable woman.

And the most beautiful fucking woman I'd ever laid eyes on.

"You are." I ran my thumb down her cheek.

"Okay, the water's getting cold. Should we get out?" she asked.

"Yep." I wasn't in any hurry to get her naked body off of mine.

She climbed out and wrapped a towel around her and

held one out to me as I stepped out of the water and drained the bathtub.

She moved to her suitcase and dug through it, pulling out her pajamas.

I raised a brow. "You aren't going to need those. I told you I planned to kiss every inch of you until you fall asleep."

And I was a man of my word.

twenty

. . .

Lila

HUGH HAD KEPT HIS PROMISE, and I'd finally given into sleep late into the night after he'd literally worshipped every inch of my body—and yes, I'd cried his name out more times than I thought possible. I remember a friend telling me orgasms were rare.

But not when you were with Hugh Reynolds.

They were as common as clearing your throat or blinking.

Just when you thought you were done, he was serving you up a big plate of pleasure.

My body was on a high, and it hadn't come down.

And—I was still a freaking virgin.

I was giving the Virgin Mary a run for her money on this one.

I'd been naked in front of this man so many times, had endless orgasms, yet my V-card was still firmly intact.

"How the fuck am I supposed to keep my hands to myself with you wearing that dress?" Hugh said, as I reached for my purse. We were getting ready to head to the wedding.

"You like it, huh?" I twirled so he could see that it was backless. My hair was in a chignon at the nape of my neck.

Hugh was wearing a fitted black tuxedo, and to say the man took my breath away, would be a massive understatement. Tall and lean and gorgeous. His thick hair stopped at his shoulders, and he pushed it behind his ears, showing off those sage-green eyes.

"I do." He trailed his fingers down my back and then moved beneath the waistband, which had some stretch to the fabric, and he palmed my butt cheek. "And that fucking Sebastian better keep his eyes off of you."

"You better tone down that jealousy. This is temporary, remember?" I teased, patting him on the cheek.

"I was protective of you before—" He paused to think about his next words. "So no one will be the wiser."

I liked that he was jealous. Because I felt the same about him. I couldn't stand the thought of Hugh with another woman. I knew it was just because we were playing house and having fun. Once I went back to my real life, he'd return to his, and all of this would be a faint memory. But that didn't mean I didn't want to scratch out the eyes of any woman who looked at him right now.

Cage, Gracie, Finn, and his date, Sonia, met us by the elevators. Hugh had filled me in that Finn had only gone out a couple of times with Sonia, and it wasn't anything serious.

"Good timing," Cage said, and Gracie charged her Uncle Hugh, and he scooped her right up. She was wearing an adorable white flower girl dress, as she was going to be part of the wedding party today. "How'd you guys sleep?" Cage asked with a brow raised, as if he were questioning the arrangements.

"The best I've slept in years," Hugh said, blowing a strawberry on his niece's neck, and her head fell back in laughter, and I felt my cheeks heat at his words.

"Interesting for a man who never sleeps all that well. How about you?" Finn directed the question at me as we stepped onto the elevator.

I cleared my throat, wondering if they could all see through me. If they knew that I could have won an Olympic gold medal for the most orgasms collected in one night. "I slept well, thank you. How about you?"

"Not so well for me," Finn groaned. "Sonia's wave machine had me on edge. There is nothing relaxing about the noises coming out of that thing. I was preparing for a shark attack all night. Or it might have been the strong incense she burned in our room, which had my stomach rumbling, thinking it was time for breakfast every hour."

Sonia rolled her eyes. "Finny, you know you loved it."

Finn glanced over his shoulder at me and Hugh with wide eyes and gave us the slightest shake, making it clear that he did not enjoy it.

"Yeah, Finny. Stop whining. Try sleeping in a room with a four-year-old who sings in her sleep," Cage said, winking at his daughter.

"Daddy..." Her head fell back in a fit of giggles against Hugh's shoulder. "I was singing in my sleeps again?"

"Hey, that's a sign of happiness. A kid who sings in her sleep. That's a good life, man," Hugh said, nodding at his brother and kissing Gracie's cheek.

When the doors opened, Cage reached for Gracie and set her on the floor before taking her hand in his. "All right, remember what I told you about attending a wedding."

"Don't be a baby?" she asked her father, and we all laughed as we walked behind them.

"I didn't say that. I said you were a big girl," Cage corrected her as he led us through the lobby toward the bus that was shuttling us all to the Wayburns' house for the ceremony and reception. "I said that big girls can walk down the aisle without stopping to chat with everyone in each row."

She giggled, but it was drowned out by the fact that Sonia was talking a mile a minute to Finn, who looked like he was feigning interest, and Hugh leaned down so only I could hear.

"I didn't want to throw you under the bus, Snow, but Gracie wasn't the only one singing in her sleep last night." His lips grazed my ear.

"Oh, yeah?" I asked, as we stepped outside.

"You like my head buried between your legs, don't you?" His voice was all tease, and I squeezed my thighs together to stop the ache that was building.

"It wasn't a terrible way to fall asleep," I said as we walked toward the bus.

Hugh's hand moved to my lower back as he guided me up the steps. The pad of his thumb grazed the exposed skin just above the waistband of my bare back, and chill bumps covered my skin. I'd never been like this before. I'd even wondered for years if something was wrong with me. I'd wondered if maybe I was dead inside or missing something, as I'd never been that girl who was boy crazy or thought about sex all the time.

But, times had changed, and I was officially boy crazy—at least about this one in particular. I thought about having sex with him all the time.

And I hadn't even had it yet.

But the way I wanted this man—it was indescribable.

Georgia and Brinkley were waving us over, and we all gawked at one another's dresses.

"Where's your date?" Hugh asked, as we took the seat in front of Georgia on the bus.

"He has a migraine." She shrugged. "It's fine. I can dance my ass off and have fun on my own, and I won't have to worry about him."

"Well, there's a red flag," Brinkley said, leaning in to speak as she sat in her seat beside Kaeran, who gave us a curt nod.

"You know I love me some red flags. I've yet to date a man who didn't come with a whole slew of them." Georgia smirked.

"I think Mom would call that emotional baggage. And you've always liked fixing broken things, Georgie," Cage said from the seat beside her.

"I guess the apple doesn't fall far from the tree." She shrugged, referring to their mom being a therapist.

Hugh bumped me with his shoulder, and I shifted my attention back to him. He was holding his phone in his lap and turned it for me to see a text from Finn in their family group chat.

FINN

> This isn't going to work out with Sonia. Her sleep contraptions alone kept me up all night. But I think the thing that put me over the edge was the fact that she traveled with a tripod and wanted to film us last night when we were getting busy. That's a hard no for me. It's going to be a long day. Feel free to interrupt as much as possible.

My mouth gaped open, and I chuckled before Hugh responded quickly and tucked his phone back into his pocket. I loved this about them. This family fiercely loved one another.

It was a short bus ride to the Wayburns' house. The estate was like something out of a magazine. When we stepped off the bus, we were led through a gorgeous garden overflowing with the most beautiful peonies and hydrangeas I'd ever seen. Lush trees offered shade, and white lanterns hung from every branch around the large, beautiful estate. There were men in black tuxedos with tails sitting in three chairs, playing the violin. I'd never experienced anything more elegant in my life.

We were each greeted with a glass of champagne before making our way to the rows of chairs on the expansive grass area. Hugh introduced me to several family members that hadn't been in attendance last night at the rehearsal dinner, and we took our seats in the third row back on the bride's side. Hugh and I sat beside his siblings, taking the two end seats beside the aisle. Hugh said that Dylan had requested that he sit near an aisle so if she got nervous, she could find him easily. I knew they'd always been close when we were young, and that bond had only deepened with time.

The sun was out, but there was a breeze swirling around us, making it the perfect temperature for an outdoor wedding. People flooded in, filling the chairs quickly, and there must have been a good two hundred and fifty people in attendance.

I looked up to see Sebastian escorting his mother to her seat beside her husband. She wore a gorgeous champagne-colored gown, and everyone was dressed to the nines. When Sebastian turned around to head back down the aisle, he spotted us and hurried over.

"Ah… I love seeing all of Dylan's cousins," he purred, as he smiled at each of them, and everyone stopped to say hello before Hugh's siblings returned to their individual conversations that they'd had going on. And then his gaze locked with mine. "Hello, Lila. Might I say that you are looking striking in that gown."

A loud enough growl left Hugh's lips that had Cage and Finn turning to see what was going on. Sebastian barked out a laugh.

"And hello to you, Hugh," Sebastian said, his voice teasing. "I do enjoy seeing you all worked up. I'll see you two at the reception. Save me a dance, Lila."

He held up a hand before moving back down the aisle and out of view.

"Real smooth, brother." Finn leaned in and chuckled.

"That dude has a way of getting under my skin." Hugh ran a hand down the front of his face, and Cage studied him for a long minute before the music started to play.

Wolf entered first and stood beneath the large arched gazebo covered in pink and white florals surrounded by greens that matched the rest of the garden. He didn't look nervous at all as he stared down at the end of the aisle as if everything that mattered in the world was at the other end of the grassy path. It was impossible to miss the love between these two, and it restored my faith in just how magical it all could be. I wondered what it would feel like to be loved like that.

I thought about the photos I'd seen from my parents' wedding day. How happy they'd been. How different my father looked when he was standing beside the woman he loved.

Hawk escorted Wolf's sister, Sabine, down the aisle first, and then Ashlan, Vivian, and Charlotte walked down the aisle with their husbands, taking their spots up front. Everly, being the maid of honor, walked in with Sebastian, him standing beside his brother and Everly standing beside the spot that Dylan would soon be residing in.

The wedding song began to play, and everyone rose to their feet. Hugh caught me off guard when his hand came back behind him, as he stood in front of me. His fingers reached for mine, and his thumb stroked the outside of my hand.

Dylan was a vision in a white, fitted satin gown, dipping low in the front, with a train that ran behind her. Her arm was wrapped around her father's, and a few of the guys in the back of the audience whistled. Hugh leaned down to let me know they were all from the Honey Mountain Fire Department where Jack Thomas was the captain.

A lump formed in my throat when I noticed Dylan and her father's eyes were welled with emotion, and I could visibly see that she was trying to keep it together. Completely overcome. She paused when she stood in front of us for just long enough to reach out and squeeze Hugh's free hand and smile as a tear broke free, running down her gorgeous face. Hugh reached up and swiped it away, kissing her cheek, and she whispered something in his ear before she and her father began walking toward Wolf once again.

Toward her future.

Her long train ran a few feet behind her as she moved with grace and ease down the aisle. Her hair was pulled back in a French twist at the nape of her neck. She was the most elegant bride I'd ever seen. Wolf was clearly losing his patience as he started taking steps toward her, which made everyone chuckle.

"Don't you dare rush this. I'll be right there, big, bad Wolf," Dylan called out, and everyone erupted in laughter.

"You're walking too slow, Minx. I'm done waiting."

More laughter.

Dylan and her father stopped in front of Wolf, who'd stepped a good five or six feet forward from where he originally stood. He reached down to swipe away the tears she was trying to control. Jack shook his new son-in-law's hand and kissed his daughter's cheek and then took his seat up front.

"Can I have you both finish walking back to the gazebo, since Wolfgang has you in the aisle?" the minister said, and the chuckles surrounded us once again.

"What did she say to you?" I whispered close to Hugh's ear once we were seated.

He looked down at me, his eyes blazing with something I couldn't read. He leaned close and whispered, "She said she wanted me to find the happiness that she'd found. We'd always joked in college that we'd be single forever, so I guess she's just feeling all the things today."

I nodded and turned my attention back to the front. The ceremony was gorgeous. They each read their own vows, which were both hilarious and sweet. You couldn't miss how much these two loved one another. I knew that Dylan Thomas was strong from all the times I'd met her and the stories I'd heard over the years, but Dylan Wayburn was a woman who felt everything, and she wasn't hiding it today.

We watched as they were announced husband and wife, and we jumped to our feet as they headed back down the aisle, along with the wedding party. We followed them out and made our way to the reception, which was gorgeous. The tented area had crystal chandeliers hanging throughout the space, and the tables were covered in white linen with black velvet napkins.

Elegant and modern and beautiful.

There was a live band performing throughout dinner, and the DJ had arrived after we'd finished eating to get the party started.

I met more people than I could possibly remember, but I was having a fabulous time. We were seated at a table with all Hugh's siblings and his parents. Georgia and I had gotten to spend some time talking to Charlotte, Ashlan, Vivian, and Everly, which had been really nice. And every single time I looked up, Hugh's eyes were on me. Somehow, we'd find one another no matter where we were in the crowded room, and it comforted me.

"I'm glad you're here," Cage said, as he dropped into the chair beside me after dancing with an older aunt who had been relentless about him taking her out on the dance floor.

"Me, too. This is such a lovely wedding." I reached for my glass of wine while Georgia left to go use the restroom and call and check on Dikota.

"I don't just mean the wedding, Lila. I mean, back in Cottonwood Cove. Working with Hugh. He's been pretty stressed out, and I can see you've helped take a lot of that weight off his shoulders."

I smiled. "Well, I've really enjoyed being home. And I love

working at the restaurant. I'm going to be spending more time at Burgers and Brews and Garrity's when we get back, now that we have things running smoothly at Reynolds'. He just needed more staff. He was taking on too much."

"Yeah. That's Hugh. He's found himself in this business, and he's never stopped for a minute since he changed course right after college. Did you know that he was actually going to school to be a sports agent originally?" he said, his cheeks a little rosy, most likely from the cocktails he'd indulged in tonight. Everyone was having a really good time.

"No. I didn't know that."

"Yeah. But then my father got colon cancer when Hugh was in college, so he decided to get the business degree and take over the family business to help out Dad." He glanced out on the dance floor and chuckled when he saw Hugh spinning Gracie around.

"I'd heard about your father's cancer, but I didn't know Hugh changed his plans during that time," I said, leaning forward, my eyes wide.

"Yes. It was a really rough couple of years. But Dad's been in remission for a while now. Hugh being Hugh jumped into gear and did what he needed to do for our family. I was in vet school at the time and not living close. And, well, you know how family dynamics work. Everyone knew Hugh would take care of things, just as he always does. It's who he is. He comes off like a selfish playboy, but he's actually the dude who takes care of everyone. Just not always himself," he said, glancing back at his brother and his daughter.

"Well, people aren't always as they seem, are they?" I said, keeping my voice steady and trying to make light of the situation while still processing what he'd just shared.

"You promised me a dance, Lila." Sebastian startled me as he stopped at our table.

Cage chuckled as if he knew this was not going to go over

well. But I nodded and turned back to Hugh's older brother. "Excuse me. I'll be back after this dance."

"I don't think it'll take that long, but we'll see," Cage teased, and I wasn't sure what he meant by that.

Sebastian led me out to the dance floor as "Perfect" by Ed Sheeran started playing. He placed one hand on my lower back and one on my upper arm, but he didn't pull me close. We kept a distance between our bodies, which I was grateful for. He looked down at me. "You look gorgeous. Tell me what's going on with you and the grumpy cousin."

I chuckled as he swayed us from side to side, and my gaze moved past his shoulder, looking for Hugh. "He and my brother are best friends. We're good friends. Always have been."

"I see. Does he always growl any time a man speaks to one of his friend's sisters?"

I smiled, feeling my cheeks heat. "He's always been protective."

"Well, I have a gift for helping people along. So, you're welcome," he said, his voice low.

My body tingled, feeling him before he made his presence known.

Bear.

"I'll be cutting in now," Hugh demanded, his voice deep, and he made no attempt to hide his irritation.

"Ah, we've been waiting for you." Sebastian stepped back and winked at me before stepping away.

Hugh pulled me against his body. His arm wrapped snugly around my waist, and the other moved behind my neck.

Possessive and protective at the same time.

"What the hell is that dude's deal?" he hissed against my ear, his breath tickling my neck.

I chuckled. "I was going to ask you the same thing."

"It's killing me to keep my distance. They're about to cut

the cake. What do you say we sneak out of here as soon as that's done?" He pulled back. His hand moved beneath my chin, and he tipped my face up to meet his gaze. His green eyes blazed with pops of amber and gold.

I nodded, and he turned and led me off the dance floor.

And I had a feeling our night was just getting started.

twenty-one

. . .

Hugh

WE WERE FINALLY BACK at the hotel, and I'd just slipped the key into the door of our room, and we stepped inside. The wedding had been great, but I was ready to be alone with Lila. It had been torture keeping my hands off her all night.

And that fucking Sebastian. Don't even get me started.

I was done waiting. Hell, we'd crossed the line so many times, I didn't know where it was anymore.

As soon as the door closed, I pressed her back against the wood, and she gasped with surprise.

"Are you sure you want this, Snow? All of it?" I asked, reaching for her hands and pinning them above her head. I was losing control with this woman. I'd never wanted anyone more.

Not even close.

"Yes," she said, no hesitation. Her gaze locked with mine, looking at me like she could see straight into my soul. "I've wanted you for so long, I can barely see straight."

I released her wrists, running my hands down her arms, over her gorgeous breasts, down to her waist where I slipped them behind her and cupped her perfect, tight ass. I lifted her off her feet, and her legs wrapped around my waist as her head fell back in a fit of laughter.

"You know you don't need to carry me everywhere," she said, as I dropped her onto the center of the mattress and hovered above her.

"I like carrying you," I said, as I nipped at her sweet mouth and pulled back to take off her shoes. I unbuckled the straps and slipped them off one at a time before hovering over her once again. "This dress is driving me fucking crazy."

I slid both straps off her shoulders, pleased to see that she wasn't wearing a bra. My hands moved down to trace along the outside of her tits as the fabric pooled at her waist. My mouth was next, covering one breast at a time and teasing her nipples with my tongue, flicking and licking as she writhed and panted beneath me. I needed her naked now.

I pulled back, and with one swift move, I flipped her over onto her stomach so I could find the zipper, and she gasped.

Her breaths were coming hard and fast, and her cheek rested on the mattress as she lay perfectly still. I could see a smile on her gorgeous lips as I slipped the zipper down. The black fabric easily fell from her body, and I dropped it onto the floor before staring at her perfect ass in a black lace thong. My fingers traced across her skin and up her back as I leaned down and kissed her neck. I reached for the pins that were holding her hair in place and slipped them out, letting her loose waves fall around her. I tossed them onto the nightstand beside the bed and took her in.

"Bear, please," she whispered, and I knew what she needed. What she wanted. I pulled back and rolled her over so I could look at her.

She pushed up on her elbows and watched as I tossed my jacket onto the chair behind me and then tried to unbutton my dress shirt before losing my patience and tearing the son of a bitch open. The buttons flew all around the room as her eyes widened, and she laughed.

"I'm so fucking done holding back," I said, shoving the shirt off my shoulders and reaching for my pants. I stood there stark naked in front of her, my dick pointing at her so eagerly you'd think the bastard had been inside her before.

"So don't," she said, her voice all breathy and sexy. "I want you."

I closed the distance between us, almost predatory in the way I moved.

"I'm all yours, Lila." I leaned down and kissed her, her mouth parting as my tongue slipped inside.

My dick throbbed with need, but I didn't want to rush things. My hand slid between her legs, knowing that sex was not going to be comfortable because it was her first time, and —I happened to be hung like a racehorse. I wasn't being cocky; it was the reality. I was a big dude, and I assumed it might be painful for her. And the thought of hurting Lila did crazy shit to me.

I stroked my hand between her legs, and she was already soaked. I slid one finger inside, and a little gasp escaped her sweet mouth, and then she found her rhythm as I slid in and out of her. She tugged on my hair as she ground against my hand, and I slowly moved a second finger inside. She halted her movements for a minute, and I pulled back to look at her, pushing her wild, long hair out of her face.

"My dick is a lot bigger than this, Snow. So, we're going to take our time until you're ready. There's no rush, and I want you to tell me if anything hurts."

Her hand came up and rested on my cheek. "The only thing that hurts is when you deny me."

Fuck me. This woman owned me.

I pushed all the way in, her eyes closed, and she arched her back and started moving her hips once again.

My mouth covered hers, and she found her rhythm. Faster. Needier. Our kiss grew more desperate each time I slid my fingers in and out. Over and over. Her breaths were labored, and my dick throbbed, but I didn't let up. We kissed until my lips were raw. She groaned against my mouth, and I could feel her tense as she gripped my shoulders hard. I knew she was close, and I wanted to watch this beautiful woman come apart beneath me. I pulled back as her sweet body moved in perfect rhythm. Back arched, tits bouncing ever so slightly, lips plump from where I'd just kissed them, and she went right over the edge. She gasped before crying out my name with a need I understood, because I felt it, too. She quaked and shook, and her gaze never left mine as she rode out every last bit of pleasure. A layer of sweat covered her forehead, and I leaned down and kissed her softly before pulling my hand from between her legs.

She hadn't said anything, but she reached for my hand and placed it on her heart, which was still beating rapidly.

"This is what you do to me," she whispered. "No one has ever made my heart race."

I reached for her hand and placed it over my heart. "Watching you come apart like that did the same thing to mine. The most beautiful fucking thing I've ever seen."

Her lips turned up in the corners, and her eyes welled with emotion. "No more waiting, Bear. I'm more than ready."

I pushed to stand and found my pants on the floor. I dug out my wallet, finding a condom that I had tucked away. I walked back over to the side of the bed and tore off the top of the foil wrapper, and she sat up and placed her fingers around my palm. "Show me how to do it."

I handed it to her, and I guided my hands over hers as she slid the latex over my erection.

And I'd be dammed if it wasn't the most intimate thing I'd ever experienced with a woman. Her desire to learn how to please me was so sexy, I nearly lost it right there.

"The easiest way is not the most exciting," I said, tucking her hair behind her ear. "But it's the only way I can control how slow I go, with me on top, so I can see if it's too much for you."

She nodded. "It won't be."

I leaned her back, and she spread her legs apart, making room for me to settle between her thighs, and I kissed her for the longest time, wanting to get her worked up again so it would be easier for her. I rocked against her, and we found a rhythm. Her hand reached down between us, and she gripped my cock. I hissed out a breath because it was taking all the restraint I had not to take her right here and now. And the slightest touch from her had my body buzzing with need. She spread her legs further, and my hand slipped down to find her wet and ready once again.

Damn, this girl just kept shocking the shit out of me.

I pulled my mouth from hers because I wanted to see her.

Needed to see her.

Make sure she was okay.

I guided my dick to her entrance, teasing her a little bit as our breathing grew erratic.

I pushed in just a little, and her hands moved to my shoulders. She lifted up, encouraging me for more.

I moved slowly, inch by glorious fucking inch, and nothing had ever felt better.

"More," she whispered, pulling my head down and kissing me.

I was lost in the moment.

Lost in this girl.

The best fucking feeling I'd ever experienced. I kissed her and rocked forward, holding myself up on my elbows as I slid deeper.

Further.

She bucked up against me, letting me know she was okay, and her tongue tangled with mine. I thrust forward, feeling her tense at first, but her hands traveled down my back to my ass as she urged me for more.

Once I was all the way in, I struggled to breathe as I tried hard not to move. I wanted to give her time to adjust to my size. I pulled my mouth from hers, needing to see those eyes on me.

"Open your eyes," I said, when I found them squeezed shut. They flew open, and she smiled the tiniest bit. "Are you okay? Do you want me to stop?"

Her mouth fell open. "No. I'm good. It was a little uncomfortable, but not anymore. I want your mouth on mine."

Damn. That turned me the hell on.

My mouth crashed into hers as I slowly pulled out and slid back in at the same pace. We did that over and over again until she responded by bucking up against me to set the pace.

We found our rhythm.

Slow at first.

And then faster.

Meeting one another thrust for thrust as I pulled out and drove back in.

We were both covered in a layer of sweat as we did this again and again for what felt like forever. If I died right here, right now, buried deep inside Lila James, I would leave this earth a happy man.

"I'm close," she whispered, and my head reared back.

I'd never expected her to enjoy the first time, but fuck me if that wasn't the sexiest thing I'd ever heard.

My hand came between us, knowing just where she wanted to be touched. Her back arched off the bed again, and my lips found her nipple. Moving from one hard peak to the next.

I sucked and licked as I drove in and out of her.

Nothing had ever felt better.

I could feel her tightening around me, and I knew she was close.

Her nails dug into my back, and she gasped as she clenched around me like a motherfucking vise, and I couldn't hold on any longer. She cried out my name as her entire body started to shake. I thrust once, twice—and I roared out my release, going right over the edge with her, both of us shaking and panting and riding out every last bit of pleasure.

Fucking ecstasy.

I'd had my fair share of sex in my lifetime—but nothing had ever compared to this.

I continued to prop myself above her. My arms burned, and I rolled onto my side, taking her with me, as I wrapped my arms around her.

My breathing was still labored, and the sliver of light from the moon coming through the curtains offered enough light for me to see her gorgeous face.

Our breathing slowed, and I pulled back to look down at her.

She bit down on her bottom lip and smiled. "Do I look different?"

I barked out a laugh. "You look fucking beautiful."

"Do I look like a woman who just had her world rocked by her sexy lover?"

Damn. This girl turned me on in a way no one ever had, and she could make me laugh without even trying.

When I was with Lila, it was easy and honest and real.

Those were not words I would use to describe most of my past relationships with women.

It had never gone very deep.

But right now, it felt like I was in so deep, I'd never be able to come up for air.

I slowly pulled out of her, watching her face as I did so. "Sexy lover, huh?"

"You are that, Hugh Reynolds. The sexiest man I've ever met." She chuckled as her fingers moved through my hair, stroking it away from my face.

I kissed the tip of her nose before pushing to my feet and walking to the bathroom to dispose of the condom before pulling on a pair of briefs. I reached for a washcloth and let the water heat up before holding it beneath the hot water and wringing it out.

I found her lying there sleepily, and I slowly moved her legs apart, holding the warm cloth between her thighs, and she sighed.

"You're so fucking gorgeous, Snow. How do you feel?"

"Thank you," she said, as I continued cleaning her up. "You know how you hear about something for so long, and then it's this built-up thing, and you just want to get it over with, and you know it won't live up to all the hype?"

"Yes," I said, raising a brow at her and preparing to get sucker-punched in the gut about not living up to her expectations.

"That was so far beyond what I thought it would be. I think I'm a big fan of sex now." She laughed, and I set the cloth on the nightstand and dove on top of her, tickling her and running my beard over her neck.

"Good. We can have lots of it over the next two months." I paused to look down at her.

"Thanks for making my first time so special, Bear. I'll remember it forever." She ran her fingers over the stubble of my jaw. "Another one bites the dust on my list."

"Guess we're going to have to keep filling that list with new things to try. We're knocking them off too fast."

"Yeah, it's been really great being home this summer. There aren't going to be a lot of days to knock things off the list once I start the new job. All work and no play." She shrugged, and the mention of her leaving had my chest squeezing.

I wasn't that guy.

I didn't get attached.

I needed to be careful because this was temporary.

I'd always been good with temporary.

"We'll have to remedy that while you're home, yeah?"

She nodded, tucking her lips beneath her teeth and looking away before her gaze returned to mine.

"Can I ask you something?"

"Of course."

"Cage told me that when you found out your dad had cancer, you changed your whole plan about what you wanted to do with your life. I didn't know you wanted to be a sports agent."

My shoulders stiffened at the mention of it. It was a terrible time in my life—in my family's life. My father tried hard not to make it a big deal, but he'd gone to hell and back, and his battle with cancer was not an easy one. He was a very proud man, and asking for help was not in his nature. "Yeah, it wasn't something I was dead set on. I didn't mind changing the plan to keep the restaurants going. And we all rallied around him during that time, and thankfully he's cancer-free today."

"Cage said that you rallied the most." Her eyes were welled with emotion.

"Cage has a big mouth."

"Looks like we have a few things in common, Bear."

"What's that?" I asked.

"We'd both do just about anything for our family." Her tongue slipped out to wet her lips, and I hardened at the sight.

"What else?"

"We both love sex, right?" She chuckled, and I leaned down and kissed her.

Because I couldn't get enough of this woman.

But I had two months with her, and I planned to take advantage of every last minute of that.

twenty-two

...

Lila

"YOU KNOW this makes you kind of clingy, right?" I teased. Hugh and I had been back for over two weeks since returning from the wedding, and he'd started cycling with me when I ran in the mornings because he said he didn't like the idea of me being out here alone.

"I don't give a shit what it makes me. It's still dark some mornings when you leave for your runs, and it's not safe. Plus, you're so warm and toasty that when you leave my bed, I can feel it."

Yes, we spent our nights tangled up in his bed together. Travis had only been over a few times since we'd returned, and it was easy to just act like we always did.

Because nothing had changed outside of the fact that we couldn't keep our hands off one another now.

The day we'd come home, I'd gotten the call from Lauren that they were ready for Dad to be admitted. Travis had stuck to his guns about not going with us, and Hugh had stepped up and driven my father there with me once again.

The man just kept showing up for me, time and time again.

Dad was hopeful and grateful and willing to try, and I

couldn't ask for more than that. He had two weeks under his belt as of today. I'd gotten a few emails, but we weren't allowed to visit in person the first two weeks, which meant they were focusing on him. It was exactly what he needed. He'd never delved into the reasons that he'd spent most of my life numbing himself. We'd always just been trying to clean up the messes that followed his addiction. And maybe Travis was right, and it wouldn't make a difference, but what if it did? Wasn't it worth a try?

I would be visiting him for the first time next week, and I was looking forward to it.

I turned down the final stretch of my run and glanced over my shoulder at the sexy man on a black beach cruiser pedaling along, and I started pumping my arms because we always raced the last two hundred meters before his house. I could hear him laughing from behind me, and I knew he was closing in.

"I'm coming for you, Snow!" he shouted as he pulled up alongside me, and I pressed on, the driveway sitting just a few feet away.

I came to a halt at the bottom of his driveway, with him right next to me as I bent over my knees, gasping for air and blinking at the sight in front of me.

My little piece of crap Honda Civic was parked in his driveway. Once I caught my breath, I looked up at him.

"I think I beat you today," he said, as if there wasn't a big elephant in the room.

He could beat me every day on that bike if he wanted to, but he never did. He just stayed beside me no matter what speed I went; he was always right there.

"We tied," I said, wiping the sweat from my forehead. "Do you know why my car is in your driveway?"

"Oh, that thing? Is that yours?"

I crossed my arms over my chest and raised a brow. "I'm fairly certain it is."

"Hmmm." He nodded. "Well, I bought it a while back. Would have given it to you sooner, but it needed some work. Roddy's had it in his shop, and he said he'd be dropping it by this morning. The keys are under the mat. You can't drive an old car into the ground, Lila. You need to get the oil checked regularly and make sure the brakes are working."

"You bought my car?"

"Yes."

"Why?"

"Because I could." He shrugged. "You shouldn't be without a car. You shouldn't be dealing with all of this with your father on your own. I can afford to help you out, and I wanted to do it."

I wanted to be pissed off.

He'd gone behind my back, after all.

But instead, I felt overwhelmed with emotion. Hugh had been so good to me in so many ways, and I didn't know how I'd ever repay him.

I nodded, but no words left my mouth, and a tear streamed down my cheek.

"Hey," he said, getting off the bike and pushing down the kickstand before moving toward me. He used the pad of his thumb to swipe away the tear. "None of that. It's just money. It's not a big deal. I'm not planning to take it with me." He smirked.

"Thank you. I will pay you back. You know that, right?"

"I don't want you to."

I sighed. "We can discuss it in the shower. How does that sound?"

"You want to have your way with me, huh?"

"Always," I said, as we walked up the driveway and checked out the car. There was a set of new tires on it, and he'd clearly had it washed because it looked like a brand-new car.

We locked the door, a habit we'd started when we'd

returned from the wedding, because Travis had been known at times to drop by unexpectedly, and it was a drama neither of us wanted to deal with. We were just having fun.

Probably the most fun I'd ever had in my life.

And, of course, it was a damn secret.

Del was the only one who knew what was going on. I felt horrible lying to Sloane and Rina, so I'd told them the breaking news that I'd lost the big V-card, but I'd said it was with a tourist that I'd met at the restaurant. I'd had to think quickly as Kline and Danielle had made their relationship public when I got back from the wedding. Kline had come to me all sheepish, like he'd done something wrong. But they'd been seen out by the staff, so the jig was up. I thanked him for playing along for as long as he had, and I was happy that he'd found someone he really seemed to like. I'd then had to make up a story to the girls and Travis that things had fizzled out with Kline.

Del was enjoying being in on the secret, and I knew that she would take it to her grave.

She was so happy for me, and it was nice to have someone to share it with because I was exactly where I wanted to be right now.

And I'd never felt that way before.

But the whole thing was aggravating because it didn't need to be a secret. I shouldn't have to lie to my friends or have Kline cover for me. Hell, it was none of Travis's business who I spent time with. I wasn't doing it for Travis, at this point. I was doing it for Hugh because their friendship was important to him, and Travis wouldn't take out his anger on me; he would take it out on Hugh. I would never want to come between their friendship, no matter how stupid I thought the whole thing was. So, it really didn't matter if no one knew what was going on. It was temporary, and I was happy. That was enough for me right now.

We'd made it to the bathroom and stripped down before

we both moved under the hot spray of water. It was crazy that just a few weeks ago, I'd never had sex or showered with a man or talked about what felt good and what didn't, and now, I did all of those things every day with Hugh.

He squeezed some shampoo into his hands and motioned for me to turn around. The man loved doing sweet things for me, and I was here for it. I loved every minute.

When we were at work, we acted like we were just friends. Well, aside from last week, when he'd bent me over his desk in his office and had his way with me after we'd locked up. Or two days ago when everyone had gone home, and we were getting ready to leave, he'd dropped to his knees behind the bar and buried his head between my thighs until I cried out his name over and over.

Life was good right now.

"You're off today, right?" he asked against my ear.

"Yeah. I'll come in later this afternoon to do some paper-work. I'm meeting my brother for coffee, and then I'm having lunch with the girls," I said, turning around after he rinsed out my hair.

I reached for the soap and lathered up my hands before running them over his chest and down his stomach. His muscles rippled beneath my fingertips, and he sucked in a breath when I traced over the deep V leading down to the light trail of dark hair. He instantly hardened beneath my touch, and I loved that I affected him the way that he affected me. The water poured down on his beautiful body, and he looked like every woman's fantasy. I wrapped my fingers around his erection, sliding my hand up and down as his eyes fell closed. Without a word, I dropped to my knees. I wasn't nervous with Hugh. He encouraged me to take what I wanted and not to be afraid to use my voice.

Or my mouth, apparently.

He groaned as I wrapped my lips around him.

Starting my day in the shower with Hugh Reynolds was my favorite thing to check off of my Snow Day list.

———

I loved how quaint downtown Cottonwood Cove was. I walked, even though Hugh had gotten my car back for me. So, he'd basically paid for the deposit for my father's rehab, along with fixing my car up, and I still couldn't get over the fact that he'd done that.

Red brick ran down all of Main Street. There were tons of little boutiques, along with the post office, the library, and several restaurants, including Reynolds', where I worked. Light posts were on every corner, and the floral hanging baskets were always overflowing with seasonal flowers.

I was looking forward to seeing Travis as I hadn't spent much time with my brother since I'd been home. It didn't surprise me, but he seemed to feel guilty about it. He was a workaholic and a newlywed expecting his first child. He had a lot on his plate. I understood it, and I wasn't offended at all.

I opened the door of the cute coffee house, Cup of Cove, which had opened when I was in high school. It was small and charming, and they sold coffee, tea, donuts, and coffee. And no one here was going to grill you about your sexual escapades, thank goodness, because I was terrified of seeing Mrs. Runither for fear the woman would know something was going on with me.

When I pulled the door open, the smell of cinnamon flooded my senses. The walls were a pale pink, the flooring a rustic, white-washed, wide-plank wood floor, and three antique wood chandeliers hung overhead.

I stepped inside and found my brother sitting in the back on a pink velvet love seat, and he looked completely out of place with his work boots, baseball cap, and his chronic frown. But his lips turned up in the corners when he saw me, and my chest squeezed a little.

Travis James was the most protective, loyal brother on the planet. There had never been a day in my life where I didn't know that I was deeply loved by at least one person—and that was my brother. But he was also stubborn and close-minded, and even though I loved him fiercely, I was not going to just do whatever he wanted me to, just for the sake of keeping the peace.

Times had changed, and I'd grown up.

"I got you a chai latte with almond milk," he said, as he pushed to his feet and wrapped his arms around me.

"Thank you." I sat on the love seat across from him. "How's Shay feeling? She said she's been pretty sick in the mornings."

"Yep. It's been rough. And she's all over my ass because I work too much." He chuckled. "I'm sorry I haven't spent much time with you. But I saw that little shithead Kline hanging all over Danielle when Shay and I were at dinner the other night. I guess he moved on quickly."

I rolled my eyes. "Yes. It was never anything more than a friendship. He's a good guy. We're friends."

He nodded. "How was the wedding? Hugh said you guys had a good time. I'm glad you've got him looking out for you."

"I don't need anyone to look out for me, Travis. I wish you'd get that through your thick skull."

He leaned forward and set his mug down. "I don't like you going down this rabbit hole with Dad, Lila. This is why I didn't want you coming home. You're running down a dead-end street. And who the hell is paying for this?"

I groaned because he was like a dog with a bone when he had a point to make. He never let anything go. "Dad is two weeks into the program, and he's doing well. Why can't you consider the fact that he is capable of change? He's the only family we have, Trav."

His hands fisted on the table, and the veins on his neck bulged. I could see he was trying to control his voice from going to a full shout. "Let me see… He wasn't there for us at all after our mother was killed in a car accident. He checked the fuck out. He completely neglected us, and you got so sick, you ended up in the hospital for a few weeks. You could have died. And where was he? Oh, that's right, he was fucked-up on God knows what prescription meds the man was taking. He was so neglectful that the hospital called CPS, Lila. He is the reason that you wound up in some shitty stranger's house in fucking foster care after getting out of the hospital. Is that not enough?"

I reached across the table and covered his hand with mine. "I'm not questioning your reasons for being angry. But he was injured after he fell off that ladder, and he got hooked on pain meds. He's human, and he's an addict. Instead of hating him, why not try to help him?"

"How about the next decade after that, Lila? Huh? You ran every fucking day of your life to escape what was going on in that house. The short spurts of sobriety followed by the endless fuckups. He hardly attended any of your races, even though the whole town came out to cheer you on because you were kicking so much ass. Where was he?"

Travis had never missed one of my races before I left for college. He'd turned down a scholarship to go away to school, and he stayed home to attend a small community college here in Cottonwood Cove so he could look after me. My brother had sacrificed a lot for me, and I loved him for it. But holding on to all this anger was not good for him.

"He was suffering, Trav." I squeezed his hand. "I love you, and I know that you lost your childhood because you were stuck raising me. And that wasn't fair, and you have every right to be angry. But carrying all that baggage and hate—it's not healthy. You're going to be a father, and this should be the happiest time of your life, but you seem more stressed out than ever. Talk to me."

He pulled his hand away and ran it down his face. "I need you to know that I have never regretted one day of being your brother. I would do it all over again to keep you safe. But I'm struggling with you being home, knowing that this man can derail you. He's selfish, and he let his children flounder after losing their mother, and I don't respect that. And you're here to help him? You have this amazing job waiting for you in Chicago, and you finally have a break from running and all the pressure you've been dealing with, and you come back home? To help a man who never helped himself nor stepped up for you? So, yeah, I'm fucking worried. I'm worried you'll fall for some douchedick like Kline Barley and then give it all up to stay here and spend the rest of your life trying to help our father, a man who doesn't deserve your time. And then what was it all for—all our hard work to let you have a chance at a good life, only to throw it all away?"

My mouth gaped open. Holy shit balls. I had no idea how deep this all ran with him.

"A chance at a good life? I have a good life, Travis. And it doesn't matter whether I'm in Chicago or home. That doesn't change things. I have my degree. This is a summer break after graduating because I've never had one in all my years in college because I was always training. And I'm really freaking happy being home and seeing my friends and the people that I've missed. It's the most relaxed I've been in a long time. There's no pressure to accomplish anything, no intense schedule, nothing to prove." I swiped at the tears running down my cheeks. "The only person that I can't seem to please is you, Travis. It's never enough. And I can't feel guilty for loving our father just because you don't. That's not fair."

"Because you're all good, Lila. You always have been. And

that man has been threatening to take you down with him since you were a little girl. You just can't see it because you want to fix everyone. And you're wrong about not pleasing me. There is no one in this world that I am prouder of than you. But that's why I don't like you being home. Look what happened when you first got here. You got hit in the face by some asshole that our father runs with. If Hugh hadn't been there, who knows what would have happened," he hissed, and then looked away and shook his head. "The sooner you get back to your real life, the better."

I didn't even know what my real life was anymore, because in all honesty, I didn't think I'd ever really stopped long enough to think about what I wanted out of life. What would make me happy.

I shrugged. "And I'll just see my niece or nephew once or twice a year because you don't like having me around?"

"Lila," he said, leaning forward again, his eyes full of empathy now. "If I could move Shay and me to Chicago to live near you, I would do it today. But I started this business years ago, and now there are a lot of people who rely on me. But I'm thinking maybe we'll get a condo in the city near you so we can spend a few weeks a year there. I've seen how much you've helped Hugh with his business, so Shay and I are talking about hiring someone to do the same for me so we can leave more often, and I won't have to work so much."

He'd started his construction company after he graduated from college while I was in high school. Most kids his age were out having fun, but Travis had grown up fast, and that had all been for me.

I nodded. "I think that's a great idea."

"So, have you talked to your new boss? Did you find out anything more about the corporate housing they're offering you the first year?"

"Yep. I'll be heading up a new department, which is insane and exciting and also super scary." I chuckled, even though this conversation had my chest feeling like there was a heavy weight sitting there. "And they sent me some photos of the housing, and it looks really nice. There's plenty of room for you and Shay and the baby to come stay with me. It's walking distance to work, so it'll be really good, Trav. I don't want you to worry about me. I'll go back and bury myself in work, and I'll barely have time to come home for visits." A sarcastic chuckle left my lips, and I didn't care. It stung that he wanted me to leave so badly.

He sighed. "Just don't put all your eggs in one basket with Dad, okay? That's all I ask. And you haven't answered me about paying for this program. Where is the money coming from?"

"They gave him a break on the price, and they are going to finance the payments," I said, reaching for my tea. It wasn't a complete lie, just an extension of the truth.

"I'll take care of those. I don't want you bogged down with that."

"This was my choice, and I have no regrets. Can you just do one thing for me, please?"

"What?" He crossed his arms over his chest.

"Come to one of the family meetings to see how Dad's doing."

"He won't make it that long, so sure. I'll agree to come at the end of the program if he's still there. And will you do one thing for me?"

I raised a brow. "What?"

"Just don't get too attached to being home, because your life is back in Chicago, Lila. Promise me you will stick with the plan."

"Yes, Travis. I will stick to *your plan*, just like I always have." I rolled my eyes because this was ridiculous. He may have good reason to be angry and to want to protect me, but being an overbearing asshole was not necessary.

"That's all I needed to hear. And how is working for Hugh?"

Spending my nights in his bed. Showering with the man every day. The endless orgasms. The laughter and the fun. The Sunday night family dinners with the Reynolds. Which thing specifically was he talking about?

"It's been great. I like working there, and I've been spending a lot of time with his family. I love them. You know that."

He smiled. "There's no one better than Hugh and his family. Although, if you asked the female population of Cottonwood Cove, they may not agree. Hugh's left a wake of broken hearts behind him." He barked out a laugh, and I didn't like it.

"I haven't seen him with any woman since I've been home, but obviously, I'm staying in the casita, so I don't know what he does at night." I kept my voice even.

"I think he's been working a lot, and he's too busy to be Cottonwood Cove's biggest playboy these days." He chuckled. "Brax has been going out solo without his wingman, and it's not going so well. Will he hire someone in your place after you leave, seeing as you've helped him so much?"

The thought of leaving and not seeing Hugh every day made a lump form in my throat.

"I'm sure Brax will survive. I don't know what Hugh will do when I leave. He's hired more staff these last few weeks, and that has taken a lot of pressure off him. So, if we get things set up right, I don't think he'll need someone like me anymore, unless he continues to expand to the city. Then he'd definitely need more help."

He nodded. "You've been good for him. Exactly what he needed."

And he'd been exactly what I needed.

twenty-three

. . .

Hugh

THE WEEKS HAD NEVER MOVED AS FAST as they were now. Probably because, for the first time in my life, I wanted time to stand still. But here we were, the first of August, which meant I had one month left with Lila. I'd never spent this much time with a woman before, hell, with anyone—including my siblings.

We worked together.

We lived together.

We played together.

And goddamn, did we play well together.

I couldn't get enough. What are the fucking chances that the one time I don't tire of someone, the one time I'm not feeling itchy and running for the hills because it's too much togetherness, it's with the one woman I can't have.

I mean, I have her, but not really. She's not staying, and we both know it. Not to mention the hurdle of her brother, which would be a big one, and could cost me the best friend I've ever had. But I'd risk it all for her. That was the sick, twisted thing—she was worth the risk, and that was why I was where I was now.

I wondered if there'd been some truth to her words when

she'd called me a coward when I'd tried like hell to keep my distance. I wasn't a man who gave a shit what others thought normally. Yes, Travis was different, but I'd take whatever wrath he wanted to throw at me when it came to Lila. He wasn't the reason I was holding back.

Not anymore.

There was a lot more to consider, like her happiness. She had a huge job waiting for her, and she was excited about it. If I wasn't tethered to this town with three restaurants, I'd talk about making the move with her. That was how all-in I was. But that wasn't a possibility, and I'd never hold her back from pursuing her dreams.

And they weren't here.

So, I'd just enjoy the time I had with her, and I'd get over it when she left, because that was the deal.

Who the hell knew if I was even capable of being the kind of man she deserved. I'd never done it before, so why the hell would I think I could do it now?

I'd gone with Lila to visit her father this morning, and I'd been surprised when she asked me to come inside. He'd made it for thirty days and was one month into the program, which Lila was very proud of. I'd gone with her to support her. I hadn't planned on being part of the family therapy session. I'd been raised by a therapist, so I wasn't completely clueless as to what all took place in a session. But holy shit—it had been really heavy, and I was fucking glad that I'd gone with her. And now we were sitting in my bathtub, soaking in hot water, because this was what I did now. I took baths with Lila almost daily, and I fucking liked it. She'd been quiet since we'd gotten home.

"You all right?"

"Yeah. That was a lot, huh? I'm sorry I dragged you into that. I didn't know he was going to open up so much," she said, her voice soft and sleepy.

"I didn't mind. But I'm sure it was a lot to process." My

arms were wrapped around her, my hands resting on her stomach. She traced along my forearm with her fingers.

"I didn't know he blamed himself for my mother's death, Bear. That's a heavy weight for someone to carry, you know?" she whispered.

Tate James had opened up that he and his wife had fought the night of her accident because he'd gotten drunk, and they'd needed some groceries so she could make dinner for the kids. So, she'd gone to the store after shouting at him about being too drunk to help her. And she'd been at the wrong place at the wrong time. A teenager had run a red light and hit her while making a left turn into the grocery store.

Tate had broken down and sobbed as he relived that night, and I held Lila's hand and sat beside her. He'd talked about how he'd gone into a dark place after that, more drinking, which led to him falling off a ladder at work and hurting his back. That started the cycle of his addiction with painkillers and alcohol and the destruction that followed.

"He'd never told you that before?" I asked, her head tipping back and settling in the crook of my neck like it always did. Like she was made for me the way her curves fit along all my hard edges so easily.

"No. We've never talked about my mama's accident. And I know it doesn't fix all the mistakes that he's made, but at least it explains how and why he lost himself."

"It does. And maybe talking about it will help him to heal."

"He looks a lot better, doesn't he?" she asked.

"He does." It was the truth. There was color back in his cheeks, and he'd put on some much-needed weight.

"I think no matter what happens to my dad, this was a good decision. I'm not clueless like Travis thinks I am. I know the percentage of success in these programs isn't off the charts. But not doing anything means you have zero chance of getting better. I think it's worth a try, and it's the first time he's ever opened up, so that feels like progress."

"It does," I said as I turned my hands over and intertwined my fingers with hers. "You have such a fucking good heart, Snow."

"Says the man who drove me there and sat through that painful session holding my hand. The man who secretly bought my car to pay the deposit for my father's program. The man who treats his employees like gold and gives up his own dreams to take care of his family."

"You don't want me to get a big head now, do you?" I teased, but her words did something to me. I liked that she knew me better than most. I wasn't a man who shared a lot. I was a good time, and I liked to have fun, but I'd always held my feelings close to my chest.

"I think your head is already big, so there's no risk." She chuckled, and I nipped at her ear.

"That's true. So, we've got the fair all day tomorrow. Are you up for it?"

"Of course. I'm looking forward to it. God, I used to barely sleep the night before the Cottonwood Cove fair. Plus, it'll be fun to meet all the kids on the cross-country team and talk to them, too. And, I'm on the schedule, though I've heard my boss is a bit of a softy for some of his employees."

I leaned down, and my tongue snaked out and trailed down her neck, and she shivered. "Oh, yeah? Do you know which employees in particular he's soft for? Because I can think of one that he's really hard for."

She laughed, and her head tipped back, giving me better access to her mouth as she wiggled her ass against my erection. "Have you ever done it in a bathtub?"

"Well, seeing as you're the first woman I've taken a bath with, that's a no. It's kind of challenging to move in here." My hands traveled up her stomach and covered her two perfect breasts. "And we don't have a condom."

"I told you I got on the pill last month. I've obviously never been with anyone before, and you said you've never been with a woman without a condom. How about you let me be your first?"

The thought of being inside Lila without something between us was not one I hadn't thought about a million times over the last few weeks.

"You sure about this?" I asked, my voice gruff.

"As sure as I am about you, Bear," she said, her voice all breathy and sexy as hell. She pushed up and positioned herself right over the tip of my dick and slowly moved down, taking me in one inch at a time. She felt fucking amazing. "And I can do all the moving for both of us."

I didn't know when it happened—when I'd fallen completely in love with this woman, but it had happened. I'd finally experienced what my father had always talked about. What my brothers and I had teased him about for years. It wasn't that the hair on my arms stood on edge like what had happened to my father, or that I knew I would marry Lila James.

It was a repeated clarity that I experienced day after day with this woman. My heart no longer belonged to me. It was hers. No one else would ever have it—that I was certain of.

But I didn't know what the fuck that even meant.

I was not a relationship guy. I knew it. She knew it. Her brother knew it.

This felt like the most intense relationship I'd ever had, and it had only been a few weeks. Longer if you counted the time that we weren't having sex, but still, what did that say about me? Chances that I'd fuck it up were strong.

We were good friends who were attracted to one another. She'd said it herself.

Of course, I loved her. Hell, I probably always had. I'd just never gotten to spend so much time with her.

She had an amazing opportunity waiting for her in

Chicago, and I would die before I'd ever hold her back. So, I'd enjoy this time with her. It was more than I deserved, and I was grateful for it.

She gripped the sides of the tub and moved her body, controlling the pace as she rode me slowly at first, sliding up and down my cock over and over and bringing me just to the edge before she'd start it all again.

I gripped her hip with one hand, and the other settled on her clit. I took control, and she chuckled.

Faster.

Harder.

The water splashed out of the tub and spilled onto the floor.

Little gasps escaped her sweet mouth, and she turned her head, waiting for me to kiss her as her nails dug into my arms. She never fell apart now until my mouth was on hers. Like she needed that connection before she let herself go, and I fucking loved it.

I kissed her hard, and she cried out my name against my lips.

And I thrust into her one more time before following her right over the edge.

Because I'd follow this girl anywhere she wanted to take me.

―――

Cottonwood Cove fair was clearly Lila's favorite thing in the world, but it sure as fuck wasn't mine. Everyone in town was here. Kids were all sugared up and shouting, and I'd witnessed one epic meltdown from Donny Welby's five-year-old son when he didn't give him the buck to go let him try to win a goldfish. I was glad the kid made a scene because Donny had stiffed one of my servers last week, and it wasn't the first time. The cheap bastard could stand to eat a little humble fucking pie.

We'd been hustling for the last few hours, trying to keep up with the rapid food orders coming in. Kline and three of our employees were running our booth and getting out plates of the best ribs in town to as many people as possible. Danielle and Brandy were holding down the fort at the restaurant, but with almost everyone in town here, we wouldn't get much traffic there.

"Go," Kline said, as he elbowed me in the side. "Things have slowed down enough. We've got this."

I gave him a questioning gaze and cleared my throat. "Not sure what you're talking about."

"Dude, you don't always have to be such a cool cat. You're dying to go see how it's going over there for Lila. We're good."

I glanced around to see that things had drastically slowed, and our line was under control, as everyone had their food now, and they were playing games and standing in line to go on rides.

I nodded. "Thanks."

On my way to see Lila, I found my mother standing with little Gracie, laughing her ass off at my father, who was shooting basketball after basketball from the furthest distance, and he didn't seem to be getting even close to the net. I came up behind them and scooped up my niece and kissed her on the cheek. I'd already seen them at my booth several times, but Gracie always got excited no matter how often she saw me. She reached for the bill of my baseball cap and tipped it up before rubbing her nose against mine. I'd worn a hat today because it was hot as hell out, and at least it kept my face shaded. "Hey, sweet girl. I see the old man's a little rusty."

"I'm trying to win the damn giraffe for Gracie." My father

turned to me and handed me a ball. "For the love of God, please just get one in so we can go get some ice cream."

I set Gracie down, took the ball, and bounced it twice before pulling back and taking my shot.

It swooshed in the net, and Gracie squealed.

My dad fist-bumped me. "I owe you one."

"Where's Cage?"

"On a date," my mother whispered with a raised brow. Cage didn't go out often, and I highly doubted that this was more than a hookup because he didn't want to complicate Gracie's life, even though we'd all told him repeatedly that he still deserved to have a life of his own. But every once in a while, he asked my mom to watch her and claimed he was going on a date, which I guessed was more of a booty call.

"Good for him."

"We saw Lila. Everyone was gathered around listening to her talk about her journey. Those kids are all in awe of her. They want her to come out and run with them. She really should think about coaching. She's such a natural with the kids," my mother said, and my father agreed.

"She's got a huge job she's leaving for soon. I don't see coaching in her future." I watched as Mandy Slater handed Gracie the gigantic stuffed animal and then batted her lashes at me.

"Hey, Hugh," she purred, and it was hard not to laugh. The girl was maybe fifteen years old, but every time she came to the restaurant with her parents, she went out of her way to say hi to me.

"Hello, Mandy," I said, my voice firm, making it clear I wasn't interested in a fucking teenager.

It only made her giggle more before she waved and ran off to the next customer.

"Growling at them doesn't seem to make them like you any less," my mother said with a laugh.

"He's always been a lady magnet," my father chirped, and I rolled my eyes.

"What's a lady magnet?" Gracie asked, and I shook my head as I started walking backward toward the cross-country booth.

"Good luck explaining that one to Cage. I'm going to check on Lila." I held my hand over my head before turning and jogging off to find her.

Like I couldn't wait another fucking minute.

When I approached the booth that Coach Lewis had reserved for his team, I saw Lila standing beside him in front of the group as kids fired off questions for her. Travis was standing there, leaning against a white wooden fence beside their booth. There were probably a good forty people there, sitting at the tables and eating cake while most of the kids were sitting on the grass in front of Lila and their coach.

Del, Sloane, and Rina were sitting at a table sipping on their red Solo cups and watching their best friend.

"Hey," I said as I clapped him on the back. "How's she doing?"

"Man, sometimes I forget that she's a grown-up." He chuckled as he turned to give me one of those half-bro hugs. "Listening to her talk about the work she put in to get where she did, the struggle while trying to balance her classwork, and most of all, the amount of pressure she dealt with leading up to nationals. She never complained, you know?"

"Yeah, that's not really her shtick, right? She's tough. That's what I keep telling you. You don't need to worry so much." I watched as her head tipped back in laughter when one of the high school dudes asked if she was single. He was looking at her like she was the most beautiful woman he'd ever seen—and he'd be fucking right.

Mine.

The possessiveness I felt over this woman startled me at

times. I'd never been that guy. Never needed to claim anyone as my own.

Until now.

And I wanted to fucking claim her.

I needed to figure this shit out.

She glanced over just then, her gaze locking with mine before it moved to her brother and then back to the people sitting in front of her. "I'm just here for the summer before I head back to Chicago, so I'm single and plan to stay that way."

Ouch. Why did that sting? We'd kept everything a secret, which had been my choice. What the fuck did I expect her to say?

And we hadn't put a label on what we had.

Also, my choice.

"Did she tell you that the guy who hired her, Joseph Schneider, called her again? Dude, they're building a whole team around her. Can you imagine that? Being that smart that a big company is making a department that you're going to run? Fuck, I'm proud of her."

I knew she had a big job. I didn't know they were building a whole team around her, but it didn't surprise me. She'd completely turned my business around in the few months she'd been home.

She'd completely turned my entire life around, too.

"That's amazing. She's fucking brilliant," I said, my eyes not leaving her.

If you put me in the middle of Times Square on New Year's Eve and told me that she was there, I swear to fucking God, I'd find her within seconds. I always found her. Like she was calling to me from wherever she was.

"Yeah. Aside from her being so invested in the rehab program." He shook his head, and I pushed to stand and turned to him.

"She's here for one more month. You should get your ass

down there and support him," I said, putting my hands up when his mouth gaped open to stop him from interrupting. "It would mean a fucking lot to your sister. He's doing well, dude. I've been there. I've seen it. And Lila wants you to sit in on one of those family meetings. How about you put your pride aside and do it for your fucking sister, because she puts everyone first, including you."

His eyes widened with surprise, but it needed to be said. Instead of fighting me like I thought he would, he stared for a long minute before nodding. "You're right. I should do it for her. And, I've got to admit, I never thought he'd stay in there this long. I imagined him sneaking away and her being devastated."

"Maybe you've underestimated both of them," I said, turning back to watch her as someone inquired about her plans after she goes back to Chicago. Travis shifted to hear her answer, as well.

"I'm actually sad to be leaving if I'm being honest. It's been really nice being home. And for those of you who haven't been to Reynolds', which I'm sure is no one," she said with a chuckle, and they all laughed. "It's the best food in town, and I've loved working there and spending time with family and friends."

Her three best friends howled from the back, and there was more laughter.

"So, we'll see how it goes. I love the city, but it's not really home." She shrugged. "But work will keep me so busy that I won't have time to get homesick."

She left it at that, and I glanced over to see Travis listening intently, his eyes narrowed as he ran a hand down the back of his neck. Shay walked up just then with two giant churros, and she paused and gave me a hug.

"Look at you. You're starting to show a little," I said, reaching over for the churro she'd just handed her husband

and tearing the top off and taking a bite. He didn't even flinch.

"Yeah. I literally just woke up two days ago with a belly." She smiled.

A hand clapped me hard on the shoulder, and I turned to see Brax standing there. "What's up, boys? Oh, I see we're watching the lovely Lila, aren't we?"

"Put your eyes back in your head, dick licker," Travis snarled before Shay's sister walked over, and he and Shay turned to talk to her.

"Yeah. What he said." I smirked as I continued watching Lila.

"Well, then... I guess it's too late for you to put your eyes back in your head," he said, leaning in close so no one could hear.

I didn't fight him or have a witty comeback.

Because he was right.

It was too late for me.

twenty-four

. . .

Lila

THE LAST TWO weeks had flown by. I'd always been one of those people who looked forward to the next thing. Putting big red X marks on my calendar days to mark another day passed. Another day closer to a goal.

A certain race.

A certain test.

A certain hurdle to get over.

Hell, I'd even made a list to check off during my summer home. Which, by the way, I'd attacked said list and never even looked at it much anymore. Because, for the first time in my life, I wasn't checking off days or goals because I was actually living. And having the best time doing it. I reached into my nightstand drawer and pulled out my notebook, staring at all the things I'd checked off since the beginning of summer. I hadn't really told off Drew Compton, but I'd ignored her when she pretended that we were friends when she'd run into me and Hugh having dinner at the bar at Reynolds' one night. And not giving her the time of day felt just as good as telling her off, so Del agreed we could check that one off the list. I stared at each thing, realizing there wasn't anything more I wanted at this point.

Well, aside from one thing.

The one thing I knew I shouldn't put on the list because accomplishing it wouldn't help anyone, including me.

But I couldn't stop myself.

#13. Tell Hugh Reynolds that I love him. Not a friendship kind of love. That I-can't-live-without-you, people-write-poetry-about kind of love. The real deal.

Because when I wasn't with Hugh, I missed him.

When we were at Reynolds' together, and he was down in his office and I was upstairs, I missed him.

And thinking about leaving him made me feel like I couldn't breathe.

I wrote it down and tucked my notebook back into my nightstand. I wasn't going to act on it. Hell, he'd probably freak out. Our relationship was a secret because he cared more about what my brother thought than he cared about what was happening between us.

And that was the great reminder to keep my head on straight and just enjoy it while it lasted, because we were just having fun.

Falling in love with him was what he'd feared would happen, right? He didn't want any of this, and I'd pushed for it. I knew he enjoyed spending his summer with me because he always wanted me with him, texting and calling when I'd leave the restaurant to do an errand. But maybe this was me reading into things. Hugh was my first love and the first man I'd had sex with. I was probably feeling all these things because I was mixing up sex and love. They weren't the same. Hugh enjoyed having sex with me. And sure, he loved me like a friend, but that was not how I loved him.

I shook it off because I was just thinking too much lately. Time was closing in on me, and it was forcing all these feelings to the surface. I grabbed my keys and headed to my car. Hugh was already at the restaurant this morning, but I had a therapy session with his mother, and then I was driving out to pick up my father from rehab. He'd completed the in-house portion of the program in six weeks and seemed like a new man. Today was a big day for him. He'd be coming home. He'd continue to attend meetings and follow the program, but he would be doing it from his own home.

I parked in the lot beside Alana's office and popped in next door at Cup of Cove to get us each an iced tea and a pastry, like I did each time I met with her. It was the least I could do as she'd insisted I keep coming back while I was home, not to mention the endless Sunday night dinners I'd attended every week since I'd been in Cottonwood.

"Ah… thank you for this. I was craving a scone this morning, and you somehow read my mind," Alana said, taking the drink and the little white bag from me after I walked in.

I sat down in the chair across from her and set my iced tea and scone on the little side table.

"Of course. Thanks for always making time for me."

"Honey, I will always make time for you." She smiled and pulled out her notebook. "Talking to you has been so refreshing for me. The way you're so open to trying things and delving into your feelings. You're a therapist's dream." She chuckled.

I laughed. We talked about everything, outside of my feelings for her son. She knew I was seeing someone, and she said she didn't need to know who it was. I'd just said that I was happy. That we were having a lot of fun. But mostly, we talked about my dad and my brother and all the tension that lived between them.

"Well, it's been so amazing getting to spend this time with you."

She smiled, staring at me for a long moment and nodding. "So, today is a big day. But first, I want to talk about what happened this past weekend. Travis went to the final family session, right?" she asked.

I'd seen Alana on Sunday night at dinner, and she never

brought up anything outside of this office that we talked about here. She'd made it known that I could call her night or day if I needed to talk, but that she would never put me in an uncomfortable position and ask anything when we weren't in a session.

"Yep. It was pretty amazing," I said with a long sigh as I clasped my hands together. "My father talked about the guilt he carried around my mother's accident. About his years of numbing himself anyway he could. And Travis didn't blow up. He just listened."

"Wow. That's progress. Did he tell your father how he felt? About all that bottled-up anger?"

"Yes. And it was painful. Reliving that time when we were separated for those few weeks, the anger he felt about having to grow up way too fast, about taking on a paternal role with me and how my father allowed it." I swiped at the single tear coming down my cheek. I'd learned this summer that you can't bury things that you don't want to think about. And even though it's painful to unpack it all, it's necessary. It's the only way to get past it.

"That couldn't have been easy to hear for either of you," she said.

"I was actually relieved to have him finally say it because he's so damn angry all the time. And I don't want that for him. He has a new baby coming in a few months; he should be focusing on the joy in his life. So, letting it all out seemed like it helped. I could physically see his shoulders relax after he'd said it. And Dad listened, and he cried, and he apologized. He said he'd lost his wife, and he'd been broken. He made it clear that it wasn't an excuse, but it was the truth." I sniffed a few times, and she handed me some tissue, and I didn't miss the way she dabbed at her own eyes with a tissue of her own.

"Grief is nobody's friend," she said with a shrug. "And everyone handles it differently. But your father is trying, and that has to count for something with Travis. Six weeks your father stayed in there and faced all these things he'd been running from. How do you feel about him getting out today? When will he start working at Roddy's Auto Shop?"

Hugh had called in a favor and gotten him a job because that was just who Hugh was. Roddy liked my father, so he was happy to help out. Things were falling into place.

"Yeah, thanks to Hugh, he's got a job to go to. Something to focus on. He starts work tomorrow, actually. I'm ready to see how he does. I considered moving back in with him, but he and his doctors think it will be good for him to get into a routine, and seeing as I won't be here in two weeks, it's easier to let him get adjusted to things on his own." I felt guilty that I was relieved that no one thought I needed to move back into Dad's house. I was ashamed to say that I wanted to savor every last day that I had with Hugh.

"And how do you feel about leaving? It's getting close. And you've gotten quite attached to the guy you've been spending time with, right?"

Did she know it was her son? She'd never pushed. And I hadn't said much about how I met him, just that I had someone special I was casually seeing.

"I'm not feeling the way I thought I would, to be honest." I shrugged.

"Meaning?"

"I thought I'd be ready. Maybe even excited. I mean, Joseph has literally built this team around me, and that's thrilling in a million ways. But it also feels like a part of my life that I left behind when I came home. The part that I don't miss much. The stress and the pressure. I'm going to be under a microscope there, and I'll have a lot to prove. And being here, I just get to be... me. No one cares what I accomplish every day. I mean, Hugh is so encouraging and so impressed every time I come up with an idea to increase revenue," I said with a chuckle. "And we've been talking so much about him expanding to the city and all the ways to make that work. But it's not pressure; it's exciting and inspiring. I don't know, I sort of like building something and not sitting behind a desk all day, staring at a computer screen. The restaurant is fun. I jump in wherever I'm needed, and friends come by, and it just sort of feels like… I'm living, which probably sounds crazy."

"It doesn't sound crazy. Your life here is very different from what it will be there. Hugh told me you guys took the boat out last night. It's probably slower and more peaceful for you here, and I get that."

I felt my face heat at her words, wondering if she could read my mind as I thought back to what Hugh and I had done on his boat last night. That we'd grabbed takeout from the restaurant and eaten out on the water. And I'd ended up climbing on his lap and having sex with him right there under the moon. Did it get any hotter than that?

"Yes, we did. Life is just so different here, you know? I run in the mornings out in nature and not on a treadmill. I have a fairly flexible schedule at work, but we work hard, and I feel good about what I've accomplished at the end of the day. And I look forward to dinner with my—er, guy friend," I said awkwardly. "And I think my feelings have grown stronger for him than I'd planned, but I'll be okay when I get back to my real life. I guess, the bottom line is that my life is pretty full here. It's not just about my job or how much money I'm making or chasing anything, I've just been really happy, and I don't know that I've ever really experienced that before now."

"Well, I think you hit the nail on the head when you said it. You're just *living* now. And it feels good. But if you aren't happy when you get back to Chicago, and if you find that you enjoy working to live more than living to work, well, you can change what you're doing. And if your feelings have grown with the guy you're seeing, it's okay to tell him that. That's the thing about life—there really aren't any rules aside from trying to be a good human." She chuckled. "But everyone is allowed to find their own path. And you've just been on the same one for so long that I think jumping off for a little bit has been really good for you."

"I never thought about it like that. But I like the sound of it. The new me could stand to be a little more flexible," I said with a laugh.

"So, do you think you'll talk to this guy about your feelings?"

"It's a little tricky because we sort of had a deal, you know? This was just a temporary thing. We'd have fun. I don't think he's feeling the same way as I am, and I don't want to pressure him. He stuck to his end of the agreement. I'm probably romanticizing things because we have a lot of fun together. I mean, I don't see him all that much," I said, quickly trying to cover my tracks so she didn't know that I was talking about Hugh because everyone knew we spent a lot of time together. "But the time I do get to see him is pretty special."

She studied me for a moment as she tapped her finger to her lips a few times. It was something she always did when she pondered my words. "I see. Why don't you think he feels the same way about you?"

Because he's the one who wanted to keep it a secret from my brother. And if he felt about me the way that I feel about him, he would just tell Travis. Consequences be damned.

"He's not really a relationship guy." I shrugged.

She chuckled. "Neither was my husband when we met. But he sure changed his mind quickly."

I loved how easy it was to talk to Alana. "He sure did. I'm so grateful for all the time you've made for me. I'm going to miss our talks."

"Well, I plan to see you a few more times here before you leave. I want to be a safe place for you to talk about how it is with your father post rehab. How things are going with

Travis once your dad is back home. And how things go saying goodbye to everyone." She smiled at me, her eyes a little wet with emotion. I wondered if this was what it felt like to have a mother. Someone who just cared so much about your feelings. I felt such a connection to this woman. "But, the good thing about modern technology is that our sessions don't need to end. I have a few clients that I talk to via Zoom every week. How about you and I don't say goodbye? Would you be okay with that?"

I pushed to my feet and walked toward her just as she stood. I held up my arms and hugged her tight. "I'd like that so much."

Her arms wrapped around me, and she held me there for a little longer than usual. "I would, too, sweetheart."

When I pulled away, we both laughed at how weepy we were. "I'm not even leaving for two weeks."

"I know." She chuckled as she swiped at her cheeks. "I've just really enjoyed getting to spend so much time with you this summer. I know that Hugh is going to miss you terribly."

I sucked in a little breath, caught off guard by the mention of him. I was always so cautious of how much I spoke of him when I was here so she wouldn't know what was going on between us. But I never held back about gushing about the man that I was seeing.

"Oh, I think Hugh will be just fine," I said, as I cleared my throat.

She just nodded and smiled. "I've never seen him so happy as he's been this summer. I mean, obviously, you've helped him a ton at work. But I think he's enjoyed having you stay at the house with him."

"Yeah. He's been a really good friend to me." And I was in freaking love with the man. Ridiculously in love.

"You've been a really good friend to one another." She squeezed my hand.

"Thank you. I'll see you in a few days. I'm going to go pick up my father now." I walked backward toward the door.

"Good luck, and let me know if you need to talk."

I waved as I pulled the door open.

"Oh, and, Lila," she called out, and I turned around to look at her.

"Yes?"

"Be proud of yourself. Your father has battled with addiction most of his adult life. And you came home, did your research, and found him a place that could help him. And the man has stayed clean and sober for six weeks. Probably the longest he's ever gone. So, take that in, sweetheart."

A lump formed in my throat, and I nodded before letting the door close and making my way to the elevator. I thought about what she'd said as I moved down to the ground floor. Regardless of what happened now, he'd taken the first step. This was something to be celebrated. And I knew in my heart that he could take the next step, too.

When the doors opened, I walked off the elevator and made my way outside. My car was parked in the lot, but next to it was Hugh's red truck. He stood there, leaning against the front end, wearing a pair of jeans and a white button up— wrinkled, as always. He had on a baseball cap, and he pulled off his aviators, his sage-green eyes finding mine.

"What are you doing here?" I asked, my stomach flipping around at just the sight of him.

"Kline's going to cover me. And seeing as you have the place running so smoothly, they can survive a few hours without me. I thought you might not want to do this alone today."

"Oh, yeah?" I asked, stepping closer, desperate for his mouth to be on mine.

He reached up and flipped his cap around, knowing that it always did something to me. His tongue swiped out to wet his plump lips, and I squeezed my thighs together. How in the hell was I going to survive without this man?

"I've got you, Snow." He leaned down and hugged me. "Come on. We'll pick up your car later."

When he pulled back, his hand found the small of my back as he led me to the passenger side of his truck, and he helped me inside. I didn't stop him when he pulled my seat belt across my body. Instead, I leaned forward, my lips grazing his ear. "Are you playing dirty today, Bear?"

"Always." He moved closer, his mouth just a breath from mine. "I like seeing you get all worked up. Plus, I thought you could use the distraction today."

He was sexy and thoughtful at the same time, which always surprised me because most guys I knew were one or the other.

But Hugh Reynolds was the whole package.

twenty-five

. . .

Hugh

LILA WAS HAVING dinner with her dad tonight, as he'd just gotten home from rehab, and she wanted to spend some time with him and get him settled. I'd given them their space after riding out to Havenwood with her and dropping them both at her car, and she drove them to his house.

My brother, Cage, was coming to Reynolds' to meet me for a quick bite in thirty minutes, as Gracie was hanging out with my parents tonight. So, I was down in my office, finishing up the schedule for next week. My phone buzzed, and I looked down to see a message from Brinkley in the sibling group text.

> **BRINKLEY**
>
> Kaeran and I broke up. I thought you'd all be thrilled to hear that.

> **FINN**
>
> Do we need to have Hugh kick his ass, or did you dump him?

BRINKLEY

No dumping. He wanted to take the next step, and I wasn't feeling it. The wedding was an eye opener. We spent the whole weekend together, and I was just...

Bored out of your mind?

CAGE

Exhausted from having to hold the conversation?

FINN

Desperate to get away?

GEORGIA

Ready for a change?

BRINKLEY

Stooop. He's a great guy. We just didn't have much in common.

CAGE

Because he's a major snooze fest. You'd have more in common with a rock than that dude. Good riddance, KAREN!

BRINKLEY

Not nice. Can we go back to focusing our attention on Georgie's boyfriend, who didn't attend the wedding?

Oh, you mean, Mr. It's Not About Me, so I've suddenly got a migraine, Diktok?

FINN

Or, Mr. He Should Be Extinct, Dikosaurus?

CAGE

How about, See You Later, Dikonater?

BRINKLEY

You Dik not go there, did you?

GEORGIA

You are all complete dickheads. Not dik-heads. Real dickheads. He gets migraines because his IQ is abnormally high, and he can't turn his brain off.

Wait. Did Dr. Dik diagnose himself?

CAGE

I'm going to need to see something in writing. Who possibly diagnosed him with too high an IQ? The dude has a limited vocabulary and can barely form a complete sentence.

FINN

Maybe we should get him a dik-tionary to help him out.

GEORGIA

I get it. He's not your favorite. Subject change, please.

BRINKLEY

What else is going on?

GEORGIA

Hughey, when does Lila leave? Are you sad?

FINN

I think our Hughey is going to be a bit down in the dumps. I know this because he's never around to hang out. Didn't invite me on the boat last night when he took his "roommate" out for a ride.

I didn't know you were in town. I thought you were in the city.

I did know he was in town, but I wasn't going to admit that I purposely didn't invite him, and I was fucking happy about it because Lila had rocked my world when she'd climbed onto my lap. When we were together, nothing else mattered.

CAGE

I call bullshit.

BRINKLEY

I'm kind of on their side on this one, Hughey. Seems a little suspicious.

GEORGIA

I get it. I love her, too.

No one loves anyone. Take it down a notch, assholes.

FINN

Ohhh... we hit a nerve. There's definitely something going on.

CAGE

I'll get it out of him. I'm here. Sitting at a table alone in your restaurant, looking like a sad sack of shit, and Mrs. Runither is making crazy eyes at me. Get your ass up here.

Coming now.

FINN

That's what she said!

I barked out a laugh and slipped my phone into my back pocket, making my way upstairs and finding my brother quickly. Unfortunately, the old horndog, Mrs. Runither, hurried over to intercept me before I made it there.

"Hello, Hugh. This place is packed, as usual."

"Yep." I shoved my hands into my pockets because I was irritated that I had to stand here and talk to her. I glanced over to see Cage watching me with a hand over his mouth, trying not to laugh.

"Have you found yourself a lady yet? A big, strapping man like you shouldn't be alone," she purred, making every attempt to be sexy, but appearing desperate. And considering her age, it was awkward as fuck when she grabbed my hand and studied the size of it.

I leaned in close to whisper in her ear. "I've taken a vow of celibacy, you know, since the Irritable Bowel Syndrome started. There's nothing quite like getting the shits in the throes of passion."

Her eyes doubled in size, and she pulled her hand away.

That oughta do it.

She waved at me before hurrying back to her table.

"What the hell did you say to her?" Cage asked when I sat in the seat across from him as he took a sip of his beer.

"It's amazing how quickly someone will run when you tell them that you've got a bad case of the shits." I laughed.

Danielle came to our table and took our order before we were alone again. The restaurant was going off, and it still caught me by surprise sometimes as a little part of me was waiting for the other shoe to drop, and it just never had.

"Only you would have to come up with ways to get women to back off." He smirked.

"Please. You've got plenty of women after you," I said. "You need to get out more, brother."

Danielle set my beer down, and I thanked her before taking a long pull.

"I do fine. I've got Gracie, and the office is busier than all fuck lately because everyone and their mother has some sort of odd animal these days that needs special care."

I chuckled. "More Botox for their four-legged friends?"

He glanced around and leaned forward. "Get this. Mrs. Lapper came in with a chick. A fucking chick, dude. And she's asking about veneers because she thinks the other chicks have better teeth. I feel like I'm being punk'd half the time, and then I realize they're just completely insane."

I tried to control my laughter when Danielle set our plates down, and Cage and I both dove into our rack of ribs.

"I guess your job is as interesting as mine. You should hear the bullshit excuses that I get when employees can't come to work. Brandy, the hostess, called in yesterday and said she needed a *me*-day. What the fuck is a me-day? She said her anxiety was high because she'd gotten a haircut and didn't recognize herself."

Cage glanced up front, where Brandy stood behind the hostess stand. "Isn't that her?"

"Yes. She has recovered after taking the me-day yesterday."

"Her hair is long. What did it look like before?"

"Exactly the same. She informed me that taking off a half an inch of hair that has belonged to her for a long time is an emotional experience." I dropped the bone onto my plate and sucked the sauce off my thumb.

Now my brother was laughing, and I loved to see it. Cage had a ton of responsibility, and he didn't relax all that often.

"Fucking people, man. I don't get most of them."

He wasn't kidding. Most people annoyed my brother, including his siblings half the time.

"It's fine. Lila picked up the slack, of course. She moved people around, and we didn't even notice Brandy's absence."

He stared at me for a long moment while he chewed before reaching for his napkin and wiping his mouth. "She's been a big help to you. How do you feel about her leaving?"

"She has been. But I knew this day was coming. There's no surprise there."

"How about the way you feel about her? Has that surprised you?" he asked.

I could play it off with most people, but never with Cage. The dude could tell when you were bullshitting him without even trying. He'd just always been good at reading people.

"Sure. I wasn't expecting it."

"What are you going to do about it?"

"Nothing. She's leaving. She's got a great job to go back to. Plus, who the fuck knows where it would even go? I'm not a relationship guy. You know that. And Travis would lose his shit." I shook my head and reached for my beer.

"I call bullshit."

"Shocker," I said, rolling my eyes.

"First off, everyone sees it, dude. The only reason Travis hasn't called you out on it is because he's too fucking preoccupied with his own shit."

"Everyone sees what?" I ran a hand down the back of my neck.

"The way you look at her. The way she looks at you. You aren't fooling anyone if that's the goal. And Travis wouldn't give a fuck if it was the real deal. You're his best fucking friend. And it kills me to say this to you because I know that you've already got the whole long-hair, Grecian-god look going for yourself, and your ego does not need stroking—but you're the best fucking guy I know. Don't tell Finn. I've given him the same pep talk, so I'd prefer you don't compare notes."

I barked out a laugh. "Was that an actual compliment?"

"Don't deflect. What's your fucking story? Why are you using Travis as an excuse? What's holding you back?"

I leaned back in my chair. I was still trying to figure out shit myself, and I didn't come here for a therapy session. But Cage was a straight shooter, and I trusted him with my life.

"Lila is—she's amazing. She's gorgeous and smart and kind. She's driven and determined and loyal. I mean, what the fuck isn't there to love about her?"

His eyebrows rose at my words. "You're in love with her."

It wasn't a question; it was a statement. I dropped the rib back onto my plate and wiped my hands.

"I don't know what it is. But it's something."

"You know what it is. Since when are you a coward?" I'd been called a coward twice in my life—both times in the last few months.

"I'm not a coward. I'm a realist. I know who I am. Come on, Cage. When was my last relationship? Why do you think Travis would lose his shit? Because he knows I will most likely fuck it up. And it's not even an option. She's leaving in two weeks. They built a whole fucking program for her to run. I live here, with three restaurants to run. There are a million reasons why it can't work."

He nodded, his arms folded over his chest like the broody bastard he was. "You only need one reason for it to work."

I shook my head and ran a hand down my face. The closer it got to her leaving, the more panicked I was. "Yeah? What's that? Because I live in the real world. Where guys like me stay single because they're damn good at it. A world where you need to keep your job so you can pay your bills. I don't live in a fairy tale, man."

He chuckled, but it was sarcastic in a Cage kind of way. "I sure as shit don't live in a fairy tale, brother. I'm raising a fucking toddler on my own, and somehow, she's turned out to be a little angel. I haven't ruined her yet. I have to pencil in sex, which is my favorite thing to do outside of spending time with Gracie, and I have to coordinate my sex life around our mother's social calendar. So don't talk to me about fairy tales. You've got a shot at the real deal. I see it in your eyes, whether you want to admit it or not. And you're not going to screw it up. You're the most reliable guy I know."

"Look at my track record. I wouldn't have the first clue how to make this work."

He sighed and reached for his beer, taking his sweet-ass time to respond. He set the glass down. "News flash. No one has a fucking clue how to make it work, brother. When Dad met Mom, he'd never been in a relationship. They figured it out because they loved each other. No one knows what they're doing until they find someone worth doing it with."

"Awfully wise for a guy who hasn't had anything serious in years."

"Right. And I have a four-year-old daughter who came from a woman I spent one night with. So, you aren't talking to the poster child for relationships. But I've been in love, and I know what it looks like."

Presley Duncan.

The name we never spoke of anymore. Hell, I was surprised he'd brought it up.

"And what does it look like, ole wise one?"

"Take a look in the fucking mirror, smartass."

I chuckled. "I don't even know what this is or how she feels. We made a deal. We'd have a little fun for a while. Hell, she's never been with anyone else. This could just be her testing out the waters before she finds the right guy. I hardly think anyone looks at me and sees forever. Because I sure as fuck never have."

"Until now." He smirked. "Listen, I'm here to tell you that you're lucky to feel it once in your life. We all love to give

Dad shit, but he's right. It's a one-and-done situation most of the time. I know that it happened to me at the wrong time, so I blew my shot. But you've got nothing to lose."

"I've got everything to lose. If I fuck it up, I lose her. If she doesn't feel the same way as I do, I lose her. If she wants this job in Chicago the way I think she does, I lose her. There are very few scenarios where it works out. So why risk making it awkward and pissing off Travis, putting Lila in an uncomfortable situation to tell me she cares more about her job than me? Or that she was just having some fun this summer and wants to go back to being friends?"

"Do you think there's some sort of class that dudes take that suddenly makes them ready to take a shot?" A cocky laugh escaped, and seeing as I was fluent in Cage's sarcasm, I knew it was his way of telling me that I was being a dumbass. "I got news for you, brother: Nobody knows what the fuck they're doing."

"That's your advice?" I downed the rest of my beer.

"You don't need advice. You'll either let her go without taking a risk and spend the rest of your life regretting it, or you'll just wake up and realize that you're being a dumb fuck, and you'll go for it."

"That was riveting. It's amazing you aren't a therapist." I smirked.

"Well, I hope like hell that you come to your senses and do something about it."

"Why is that?"

"Because I can't wait to see the infamous Hugh Reynolds running around town like a pussy-whipped motherfucker who can't live without his girl," he said with a chuckle.

"Never going to happen. I'm going to stick to the plan. Let her go chase her dreams while I go back to my unfulfilling life of meaningless sex and mind-numbing conversations with people I don't give two fucks about. And Lila can go take over corporate America and marry some preppy intellectual asshole who wouldn't know good sex if it slapped him in the face."

Cage looked down, searching for something on the floor beside his feet before he snapped back up and raised a brow. "Sorry. I must have lost my tiny violin, you dramatic motherfucker. Stop being a coward and man up."

I sucked in a breath because that insult struck a fucking nerve with me. "If one more person calls me a coward, I swear to God, I'll snap."

"I wouldn't mind seeing you snap and doing something about it." He shrugged. "Listen, I need to say this to you. I know that you gave up your dream to be a big, fancy sports agent in the city to come back here and help out Dad. It was stand-up of you. But if this isn't what you want, we can sell it all. I'll help you. You deserve to be happy, brother."

I squeezed the back of my neck with my hand because this conversation was wearing on me. "I love what I do. It wasn't the plan, but I'm not complaining. I needed to do it, and I made it work. I'm fine with that. But asking me to ask Lila to do the same thing for me—never going to fucking happen. She's not some big fish in a little pond."

"Neither the fuck are you. So that's it, isn't it? You don't want to ask her to stay. And with how insane Travis has been about her leaving here, I get it. I know she has a big opportunity back there. But why not ask her? Let her make that decision for herself."

"Because she'll feel bad. It's who she is. She wants to take care of the people she loves, and I won't be an obligation. What, so she can resent me in twenty years? No. If she wanted to be here, she'd tell Travis to fuck off, and she'd be here. She's excited for this opportunity, and she deserves that."

"Do you remember how I said I'd be staying in Los Angeles after vet school? I'd enjoyed city living, and I had no intention of coming home."

"I remember." I nodded.

"But things change, Hugh. You came back to help Dad, and you don't regret it. And I found myself deep in diaper duty and not doing exactly what I thought I'd be doing. And guess what?" he asked.

"What?"

"I wouldn't change a fucking thing. I may have lost Presley all those years ago and managed to fuck that up. But I got a second chance the day Gracie was born. And I'd move to a deserted island if it meant she'd be happy. So, I changed course. I came home, and I don't regret it. It's okay to change your mind. You did. Maybe she will, too."

I looked away as I thought it over.

She wouldn't.

Lila James had always known what she wanted, and she went after it.

"All right, I appreciate you talking this through with me. I'm going to enjoy these last two weeks with her, and I'll move on once I know she's settled and happy."

"That's the plan?" he asked, looking completely disgusted.

"That's the plan. Don't judge it, brother."

"Fine. I'll be here when you realize you fucked up." He shrugged as we both pushed to our feet.

"And this stays between us? I don't need Georgie and Brinks in my business."

"Of course. I'm a vault," he said.

"Thanks. All right, I'm going to head home. How about you?"

"Gracie is sleeping at Mom and Dad's tonight. I'm going to meet a friend for a drink at the bar."

"I'll bet you are. I'll call you tomorrow," I said.

"Yep. Thanks for dinner."

I gave him one of those half-bro hugs and clapped him on

the back before heading out the back door. I'd left my truck at the house, and it was a nice night to walk home.

My phone buzzed in my pocket, and I saw a text from Lila.

SNOW

Hey. Just left my dad's and got back to the house. You want to meet me at the cove for a little skinny dipping and a trip down memory lane? <winky face emoji>

I chuckled.

Hell, yeah. On my way now. And this time, you won't be grinding on my dick. You'll be riding it.

LILA

Promises. Promises. I'm almost there. <eggplant emoji>

Just as I slipped my phone into my back pocket, it buzzed again. I continued walking toward the cove and looked down, surprised that this text wasn't from Lila.

CAGE

Hugh's in love, and he's too much of a <cat emoji> to do anything about it.

GEORGIA

Awww… Did Hughey finally admit his feelings?

FINN

Is he in love with Mrs. Runither or Lila?

BRINKLEY

I'm guessing Mrs. Runither, right? <laughing emoji>

What happened to you being a vault, dickhead?

CAGE

There are no secrets between the Reynolds siblings, right? And if I can't get through to you over the next two weeks, then hopefully one of these fools will be able to make you see the light.

FINN

There are no secrets between said fools? Should I tell Hugh that you're the one who told Mom that he wanted a journal last Christmas so he could document his feelings every night?

CAGE

No. That one was actually supposed to stay in the vault, you loose-lipped bastard. And it made Mom happy. I swear Hugh got hives when she pulled him aside and told him how proud of him she was that he was getting in touch with "all those feelings." #winningthesiblinggame

I thought it was Brinks who pulled that one. You're just scoring all the points tonight, brother. #onceadickheadalwaysadickhead

BRINKLEY

Hey, Cage, since we're confessing... Georgie was the one who scraped all the paint off your fancy, black Lexus last year, and we let you think it was one of the Wilson teens.

GEORGIA

Why are we confessing? It was better to let him be disgusted by "some loser, stoner teenager" than to know his sister doesn't like to look over her right shoulder when she backs out of the driveway.

I turned down the path toward the cove and had to stop walking for a minute because I was laughing so hard.

FINN

Why can't you look over your right shoulder?

GEORGIA

I have a permanent kink in my neck. I think it's genetic.

CAGE

I think you're being lazy. Who the hell doesn't look over their right shoulder? You scraped all the paint off my new car. That was expensive to fix, Georgie! This is the shit I'm talking about.

GEORGIA

It was an accident. Humans make them sometimes, or didn't your alien leaders teach you that?

BRINKLEY

You could just do one extra Botox appointment for a hamster, or put a nice set of hair extensions on a sloth, and that would totally cover the expense for the paint job. #lifeofasmalltownanimaldoctor

GEORGIA

Yeess. Good idea. I'm here for that, Dr. Judgment.

CAGE

I'm with a woman, and I'm putting my phone away because you're all aggravating me.

FINN

Is she real or a blow-up woman?

FINN

Before you insult me, you had it coming for calling us fools.

GEORGIA

He actually called you a loose-lipped bastard. Gotta go. Dikota wants to watch a silent film, so I'm putting my phone away.

Fucking Dikwich was on my last nerve. I didn't know what she was doing with that dude. I pushed a shrub out of the way, and when I came around the corner, the water just a few feet away, Lila James stood there wearing a white sundress.

"You wanted to come back to where it all started, huh?"

She slipped both of the skinny straps off of her shoulders, and her dress pooled at her feet. She wore nothing beneath it.

My mouth watered at the sight of her.

Standing there stark naked, looking like the goddess she was.

"I still think about that night all the time, Bear." She chuckled. "But this time, I intend to do what I wanted to do that first time."

I moved toward her, almost predatory, and reached behind my neck for the collar of my tee, tearing it off as I closed the distance between us.

I couldn't get to her quick enough.

twenty-six

. . .

Lila

"SO, you literally checked everything off the list, and you still have a little over a week to go," Del said, as we sat at a table in the back of Cup of Cove while Sloane and Rina went up to the counter to grab our drinks and pastries. I'd transitioned most of the responsibility I'd had at the restaurants to a few of the new staff members, as I was leaving in a week. So, I popped in and out all day, just because I loved being there. But I was getting in some quality time with my girls today.

"Yes." All but the one thing I'd added to the list. But you can't win them all. I'd thought about telling him how I felt that night when I'd waited for him down by the cove. I'd worked up the nerve to do it, to tell him that I loved him, but he'd seemed so off. He'd fired off relentless questions about the new job. If I was excited to lead the new team. How honored I must be by all that responsibility. How I'd be taking corporate America by storm.

The truth was, I wasn't that excited. But admitting that I loved being home and playing house with a man who hadn't even admitted to anyone that we were together—it felt a little pathetic and lame.

"And your dad is doing so amazing. Working for Roddy,

and he's got another week under his belt. You must be so proud." She smiled and reached for my hand.

"I am."

Hugh had even left a standing offer for Roddy to come to Reynolds' and eat anytime on him. Roddy usually came once a week, and they'd grown to be good friends.

Del studied me for a long moment. "You still haven't told him?"

"No. He's been asking so much about the new job. Almost like he can't wait for me to leave, you know? I read this article in a magazine when I was getting my hair done yesterday about how women tend to romanticize the man that they have their first sexual experience with. Did you know that?" I whispered, looking around to make sure no one was listening. "I think that's probably what I'm doing, while he's ready to go back to his old ways and ship me off to Chicago. And we all know my brother can't wait for me to leave."

"Your brother is such an asshole sometimes." She shook her head. "I love having you here. And maybe you're misreading Hugh."

I widened my eyes when I saw the girls behind her, and she'd just said Hugh's name.

"Misreading Hugh about what?" Sloane asked.

Del cleared her throat. "I said I'm misreading *you*."

"Me or Rina?"

"Both."

It took everything I had not to burst into laughter at the turn in conversation. My phone vibrated on the table, and I glanced down to see Joseph Schneider's name light up across my screen. I pushed to my feet and told them I needed to step outside.

"Hi, Mr. Schneider. How are you?" I asked, walking around the side of the building where it was quiet.

"I'm doing well, Lila. Boy, are we ready for you. Our cross-country superstar who's going to lead this company's younger new hires and show them how we do it. You model the work ethic you had here before, and we'll have this place running like a fine-tuned machine."

I forced a chuckle because honestly, nothing about that sounded appealing to me.

"Sure," I said.

"So, the reason I'm calling. I know you have a summer job out there, and you aren't scheduled to come back until next week." He paused, and I heard him asking someone for a coffee with no sugar and extra cream. "But Mr. Hopkins, the president of True Solutions, is coming into town in two days. He was really hoping to meet you in person, and he's leaving the country next week for two months."

"Oh," I said, my stomach twisting in knots.

"I know we had your ticket booked, but I wondered if you could move that date up? We'd fly you back here tomorrow, late afternoon, give you time to get settled in your new place tomorrow night, and then meet with him the following day. We'll even fly you first class, and then we'll obviously pay to have your car shipped back along with your things, which we already had scheduled. We'd just move it all up."

Tomorrow.

"I, um, I could probably make that work." What was I supposed to say? The thought of leaving tomorrow had me breaking out in a sweat. I'd need to say goodbye to the girls. Go see my dad, my brother and Shay. Everyone at Reynolds'. Roddy, who'd been so good to my father. Alana and Bradford and Cage and Gracie. I'd text Georgia, Brinkley, and Finn as they were back in the city. We were supposed to all have Sunday dinner together the night before I left.

But that wasn't the reason my heart was pounding.

Hugh.

A lump formed in my throat. I'd known I was leaving, but I wasn't prepared for it to happen so soon. I wasn't ready.

"Listen, we can fly you home in a couple months to see

your family again, since we're rushing you out here. But it would be an effort that would not go unnoticed by Mr. Hopkins and myself."

"I understand. Just text me the info, and I'll be on that plane tomorrow." Look at me, already back to being robotic and getting into work mode. Desperate to please whoever I needed to impress.

"We'll send a car to pick you up at your address, so just send that to me, and we'll also have a car waiting for you when you land in Chicago." Wow. He had it all figured out. My head was reeling with all I had to do.

And all I wanted to do was run straight to Reynolds' and beg Hugh to tell me not to go.

To ask me to stay.

"Okay, I will see you tomorrow," I said, but he'd already hung up the other line.

I walked back inside, and all three girls stopped talking when they saw my face.

"Who died?" Sloane asked.

"My summer." I shrugged. I should have said my freedom. My joy. It had all just vanished with one phone call.

A text came through with the flight info. The man wasted no time. I sent him my address so he could send a car, and he'd already changed the plan, because my flight was leaving first thing in the morning.

I filled the girls in, and everyone sat there looking like we'd just lost out on Taylor Swift concert tickets.

"I'm not ready for you to leave," Rina whispered.

"Yeah. That was too short. Your pubes have probably not even grown back in your bikini area," Sloane huffed, and I couldn't even laugh because I was overcome with emotion.

Del didn't speak. Her eyes welled with emotion, and she shook her head. "Well, you came, and you conquered."

Now tears were streaming down my face just as they started running down her cheeks.

"I love you all so much. Thanks for making this the best summer of my life."

"Look at you. You came here a boring virgin who never had any fun—and now you're all sexed up from your out-of-town lover, who we oddly have yet to see," Sloane said, raising a brow as she looked between me and Del. "You've skinny-dipped, taken shots, had sex, rehabbed your father, and you even have Hugh Reynolds smiling and relaxed because you've got his restaurant running so smooth—if that's really the reason that hunk of a man is smiling all the time." She smirked.

I didn't question her. Maybe they suspected something was going on. We were together all the time. But I didn't really care at this moment because I would have to say goodbye to him now, and I'd be gone by this time tomorrow.

The door opened, and Travis walked in. He paused at the counter and placed an order before turning and seeing us there.

I flung myself into his arms, and he wrapped me up, just like he used to do when I was young.

"Hey, what's going on?" His voice was soft and kind. This is the side of my brother that I'd missed.

I pulled back and filled him in on the call that I'd just received.

There was a weird mix of sadness and relief in his gaze. I swiped at my tears as my friends pushed to their feet.

"Hey, why don't I call Shay and tell her you and me and her are going to sleep at Dad's tonight? Wouldn't that be a perfect last night for you?" he asked. Travis had actually seemed impressed with my father's sobriety, as he was going on two months between his six weeks in the program and his first week home.

I'd always wanted my brother to come home and have a relationship with our father. But that would mean that I wouldn't be in Hugh's bed tonight. Probably never again.

My heart ached.

It ached for something that was never really mine.

"Sure," I whispered, catching Del's eye when I looked away. I saw all the empathy there because my best friend knew that I was hurting. Hurting for a million different reasons, but only one mattered at the moment.

"I love you, guys. I'll be back in a few months, okay?" I took turns hugging them, anxious to get to Reynolds' to find Hugh.

We hugged, and we cried, and Travis hurried me to his car, as he said he was heading over to Reynolds', as well, which meant I wouldn't get to talk to Hugh alone.

Del mouthed the words, "*Tell him*," before turning and walking to her car with Rina and Sloane. But what would be the point of saying anything now? I was leaving in less than twenty-four hours.

If Hugh didn't want me to leave, I'd need him to tell me that.

Travis was on the phone with Shay, telling her to pack a bag because they'd be staying at my dad's tonight. He ended the call just as we pulled out of the parking lot.

"I'm so damn proud of you, Lila," he said, catching me off guard.

"Thank you." My voice was quiet as the reality of what was happening was setting in. I was leaving in the morning. I was sleeping at my father's. I'd have no time alone with Hugh. No more showers or boat rides or skinny dips in the cove. No more cuddles in bed or morning runs with him biking beside me. No more Sunday dinners or long conversations about what we wanted out of life.

I'd come home to help my father, and I'd done it.

I didn't know how long it would last, but it was a start, and I felt hopeful.

I'd wanted to lose my virginity, and I'd done that, too.

With the kind of man women dream of spending a night with. And he'd been all mine all summer.

But time was up, and we were both going to return to our normal lives.

But I'd found my new normal, and I'd loved it.

"I was wrong, you know?"

"How so?" I asked, as he pulled into the lot behind Reynolds'.

"About Dad. He's different, and I never thought I'd say those words. You were right not to give up on him. I'm not holding my breath that this will last forever, but it's lasted longer than it ever has in my lifetime, so I'm going to enjoy it."

A tear slipped down my cheek. "Will you keep your eye on him?"

"I will."

I nodded. "Thanks for staying at the house tonight. I can get us some takeout, and we can all have dinner together, okay?"

"I'll get dinner. You get your stuff packed up. I know you love Sunday dinners at the Reynolds', so if I can give you a Monday night dinner at the Jameses', I'd like to do it."

I chuckled and wiped at my cheek before pushing the door open. Travis followed me inside, and I felt guilty that I'd wished he wouldn't have. Hugh was standing behind the bar, talking with Brax, who was sitting on a bar stool across from him. They looked like they were having a pretty intense conversation.

"Lila, thank God you're here. I need to talk to you." Brandy smiled at me as we approached the hostess stand and then raised her brows at my brother, letting him know she didn't want an audience.

"I'll be at the bar." Travis stepped away, and I hated that he was going to be the one to tell Hugh that I was leaving sooner than expected. Maybe this was for the best. There'd be no drawn-out goodbye. No sad ending to something that was supposed to be a summer fling.

"What's going on?" I turned my attention to Brandy, but my gaze kept moving to the bar, where my brother was definitely filling in Hugh and Brax on my news. Hugh's eyes found mine, just like they always did. His smile looked forced, or maybe I was reading into it. Maybe he was relieved that this was over.

"Lionel asked me out," Brandy all but squealed, as she leaned so far over the hostess stand that I had to reach for her shoulders to make sure she didn't fall over.

"Yes. I knew he liked you. It just takes some boys a little longer to figure it out," I said. My voice was all tease, but my heart was shattering in my chest, my mind reeling that my time with Hugh was over. And I couldn't let anyone know how sad I was because the whole thing had been a secret.

Brandy gave me all the details about how he'd asked her out, and I gave her some suggestions for what to wear before my brother called for me.

"I'll come say goodbye before I leave, but I wanted to let you know that I'm leaving a few days early, and I'm heading back to Chicago tomorrow."

"What? No! Hugh had a whole surprise party planned for you next week," she said, before slapping a hand over her mouth. "Don't tell him I told you. But I think he's going to take it the hardest of all."

"He'll be fine," I said, shaking my head and processing the fact that he was going to throw me a party. "This place is running so well now you won't even know I'm gone."

"Are you kidding? You light up every room you enter, Lila James." Brandy came around the hostess stand and hugged me so tight I had to fight back the tears threatening to fall. I was going to miss this place so much.

"I'll be back soon, and I'll definitely come and see you all." I swiped at the single tear running down my cheek when I pulled away. Brandy had full-on streams of tears running down her face.

"Well, we can still text every day. I'll send you a picture of my date outfit, okay?"

"I'm counting on it." I held up my hand in a wave and made my way to the bar.

"Hugh said he can pack your things up, and I'll get them shipped to you in Chicago. We'll just run by the house so you can pack the bags that you want to take with you tomorrow," Travis said.

Hugh wasn't looking at me. He wiped down the bar top, his baseball cap tugged down a bit so I couldn't see his eyes. Brax was looking at me with the saddest expression on his face.

"Okay. Well, the car is picking me up at Hugh's house in the morning. That's the address I gave them." I shrugged.

"Just text them and give them Dad's address. I was just telling the guys that I never thought I'd willingly agree to sleep at that house ever again." Travis chuckled.

"I can take you to the airport if you want." Hugh looked up at me, and my chest squeezed. His lips turned up a little bit in the corners, but those sage-green eyes told a different story.

He looked... upset.

Sad.

Wounded.

That couldn't be right. He'd known I was leaving this whole time. I was probably making something out of nothing.

"Thank you," I said, my voice just above a whisper because I was fighting back the big lump that had lodged in my throat.

"Dude. She's got this big, fancy company sending a car for her. She'll probably get champagne on the drive over." Travis waggled his brows.

"Ahhh, that's hard to compete with. Well, I've got your

check downstairs. You want to come down with me and grab it?" he asked, his voice calm and steady as his eyes locked with mine.

"Sure, yeah."

"Hurry it up. Then I'll run you over to Hugh's to pack what you need for now," Travis said, and I nodded before following Hugh to the back room and down the stairs to his office.

I stepped inside, and he closed the door behind me. I wanted him to pin me to the door and kiss me senseless, but he didn't do that. He walked around the other side of his desk and sat down. I moved to the leather chair across from him and did the same.

He fiddled with some paperwork before looking up at me. "I'm happy for you, Snow. It sounds like they're excited for you to get there, huh?"

My bottom lip quivered, and I bit down hard to stop it from shaking. "I didn't know Travis was going to offer to sleep at my dad's house. That wasn't my idea."

"Hey, you have nothing to explain. This was what you always wanted, right? And it's all because you didn't give up on your father." His eyes softened, and he smiled.

"But I didn't plan on saying goodbye to you like this," I said.

"It's all right. We always knew this was going to end, didn't we?"

My vision was blurry as my eyes overflowed with tears and trailed down my cheeks. Hugh was up on his feet and bending down in front of me. He used the pads of his thumbs to swipe away my tears and then scooped me up and settled me on his lap, his arms wrapped around me.

"I wasn't ready to say goodbye," I said, my voice cracking as I couldn't hold back all that emotion any longer.

"But this is what you want, right? This job? Chicago?" he asked, and he pulled back to look at me, his eyes searching mine. I didn't know what he meant. Why he was asking that.

"It's a good job." I shrugged.

"Well, then, you go out there, and you kill it. They're lucky to have you. And you accomplished everything you set out to do here, so you should be fucking proud of yourself. I'll keep an eye on your dad for you, okay? You've got my word on that. Don't worry about a thing." His mouth was so close to mine, and now his eyes were welling with emotion, too.

I love you.

I wanted to say it. Needed to say it.

"Hey, hey, Trav, wait up!" Brax's voice startled me, coming from the other side of the door out in the hallway, and Hugh reluctantly moved to his feet, setting me down in front of him before we heard Brax's loud voice again. "Are you sure they're down here?"

"Why the fuck are you shouting?" Travis asked, and Hugh stepped to the other side of his desk, and I sat back down in the chair.

Brax was giving us a warning that my brother was coming. He definitely knew something was going on between us.

But now, none of that mattered, did it?

I was leaving, and he was going to let me.

"It's open!" Hugh yelled, as we heard them approaching the door.

Travis pushed the door open and was still laughing at something Brax said before turning his attention to me. "We need to get going. Shay's craving ice cream, and we need to go get your bags."

"Yeah, of course." I pushed to stand.

Hugh grabbed an envelope off his desk and handed it to me. "Here's your last check. Thanks for everything you did for me this summer, Snow."

"It was the best summer I've ever had." I wanted him to

know that it was all because of him. But I couldn't say it. Not now. Not here.

I reached for the envelope as he came around the desk and wrapped his arms around me.

"We're all going to miss you," he said, before leaning down against my ear. "So fucking much."

My brother and Brax were already out the door, and I shook my head frantically, keeping my voice low. "I'm sorry. This isn't how I wanted to say goodbye."

"It's all right. You go enjoy this time with your family, okay?" He leaned down and kissed me hard before pulling away quickly.

It felt final.

It felt like goodbye.

And my heart shattered into a million little pieces.

twenty-seven

· · ·

Hugh

IT HAD BEEN six days since Lila James had left Cottonwood Cove. She'd spent that final night with her father and her brother and Shay. Cage had somehow heard that she'd left, and he and Finn had come over with a bottle of tequila in typical Reynolds brother fashion, and I'd drunk away my blues. Or at least tried to.

I'd spent the next few days moping around and checking my phone every five minutes to see if she'd texted or called. We'd sent a few messages, her letting me know she'd made it there safely. I'd told her that I'd packed her things up that she'd left behind and dropped them at the post office because we both knew Travis would put it off for weeks if not months.

There was this big, gaping hole in my chest, and I'd never experienced anything like it before. It didn't help that it had been raining since she'd left. It was gray and dreary outside— exactly how I felt.

I was heading to my room to grab a shower as I'd just worked out, and I passed by the casita.

Her casita.

Hell, she'd spent every night in my bed, so this room didn't feel like Lila's more than any other room here. Hell, every inch of this house felt like Lila's. I dropped onto the bed and glanced around. I looked over at the nightstand and noticed a pair of earrings there that I must have missed when I'd gotten her things together. I picked them up and looked at the little pink studs before reaching for my phone.

> Hey. How are you doing?

Our texts had been awkward since she'd left. Distant and nothing like the way we'd texted when she was here. Because we'd been together then. We'd never really said goodbye as everything had happened so fast. I'd been talking to Brax that day at the bar when Travis had dropped the bomb on me that Lila was leaving. I'd asked Brax to run some comps on Reynolds', Garrity's, and Burgers and Brews for me. I just wanted to know if there was an exit strategy if I were to leave all this behind and follow her to Chicago.

But before I could even make that happen, she was gone.

SNOW
It's busy. Long days. Kind of exhausting.

Before I could respond, my phone buzzed again.

SNOW
I miss you, Bear.

> I miss you, too. But you're doing okay?

SNOW
Sure.

I didn't like the way she sounded. It matched the way I felt.

> I found your earrings. I'll drop them in the mail tomorrow, all right?

SNOW

Okay. Thanks.

Sure. Talk soon.

She didn't respond, and I groaned at how stupid I sounded. I didn't know why the fuck I wasn't just telling her that I was going out of my mind since she'd left.

I didn't want to make her feel bad. Hell, she looked so guilt-ridden about spending her last night with her family and not with me.

I didn't need pity. This was the deal, and I'd signed up for it.

We'd agreed that we'd go back to being friends after she left, and we'd never discussed any other option as she'd left before either of us had prepared for it.

I set her earrings back down, noticing the drawer of the nightstand cracked open the slightest bit. I leaned forward and pulled the drawer all the way open, seeing her Snow Day notebook in there.

I took it out and kicked off my shoes, pressing my back to the headboard. I chuckled as I read her list, seeing each thing checked off with little notes beside them.

#1. Get Dad into a program.

There was a note beside it that said: Six weeks and counting. He did it.

#2. Lose my V-Card.

There was a note beside it that said: My first time is worthy of a gold medal. Holding out for the right guy was definitely worth the wait.

My chest squeezed as I read her words.

I continued reading the list and flipped the page, my eyes zeroing in on number thirteen. The one I hadn't seen.

#13. Tell Hugh Reynolds that I love him. Not a friendship kind

of love. That I-can't-live-without-you, people-write-poetry-about kind of love. The real deal.

She hadn't told me, but I knew she loved me. Didn't I?

Why was I being such a fucking pussy about this?

She loved me. I loved her. Life was fucking short. What the fuck was I waiting for? I picked up my phone and shot a text to Wolf, Dylan's husband. He'd told me he was interested in investing if I opened a restaurant in the city. I gave him the short version about what was going on and said that I needed his help.

He responded within seconds.

WOLF

> Done. Can you come to the city today to discuss?

> On my way.

I grabbed my keys, and when I made my way outside, Brax was walking up my driveway.

"Hey, I came to check on you. I went by the restaurant, and they said you hadn't been in the last few days," he said.

"Yeah. I've got bigger things on my mind. You want to ride with me to the city? I'm going to talk to Wolf about possibly buying me out of the restaurants."

Brax's eyes widened. "You're really fucking doing it. What about Travis? Does he know?"

Brax climbed into the passenger seat as I settled in the driver's seat. "He's next."

Brax and I talked through every possible solution on the drive to the city.

"Are you sure she won't want to leave Chicago? Should you talk to her before you do anything rash?" he said, as I pulled into the parking garage where the Lions' headquarters were located. Dylan and Wolf both worked here.

"I'm not going there until I have a solution that isn't just about her giving up her dreams. I need to have something to offer her on my end. I won't do anything or make any decisions until I speak to her, but I need to know my options."

He nodded. "I like seeing you all pussy whipped. It looks good on you."

We climbed out of the truck, and I flipped him the bird. We both laughed. After taking the elevator up to Wolf's office, Dylan was there as soon as the doors opened.

"Hey," I said, wrapping her up in a hug. "How'd you know I'd be here right now?"

"I have your location." My cousin held up her phone and smirked. "Of course, I know. I'm Dylan Thomas-Wayburn... I know all things. And I knew you loved Lila before you even knew it, so there you go."

Brax chuckled, and I shot him a warning look. "I knew. I was just being a—"

"Coward? Baby?" Dylan asked.

"Pussy? Weak motherfucker?" Brax added, and even I had to laugh along with them.

We followed Dylan down to Wolf's office, and she closed the door while Brax and I each took a seat in the leather chairs across from his desk. Dylan settled onto her husband's lap, and he wrapped a hand around her and pulled her down for a kiss. I loved seeing her happy. She deserved it.

So did Lila. And if that was something that I could give her, I was damn well going to try.

We spent the next two hours going over every option. Dylan left to go grab us all sandwiches, while Wolf, Brax, and I crunched the numbers.

"So, the bottom line is this," Wolf said. "I can buy you out, or I can flip them. But I know these are family-run businesses, and I think you should keep them if possible. I believe your best option is to let me take over the financial piece, you and I partner up, and we get people that you trust to manage all three places. But they remain yours. So if, for any reason, Lila wants to come back, now or later, it's all yours once again."

I nodded. I couldn't ask for more than that. "Thank you. I really appreciate you stepping up for me."

"You're one of the most important people in my wife's life, and that makes you one of the most important people in mine. I have the resources to help you, and I'd like to see you keep all three places. Selling them is very final. Let's just give you a way out without selling them off."

"I don't think it gets any better than that. And who knows? You could fly there, and she could reject your ass." Brax laughed with this dopey smile on his face, and I rolled my eyes.

But the thought had crossed my mind.

But deep down, I knew she loved me as much as I loved her.

"I don't see that happening," Wolf said, as he shook his head. "But regardless of the outcome, you have options. If she wants to come back to Cottonwood Cove, everything stays as is. If she wants you to stay in Chicago, you can open something up out there, and I'll invest in that one, too. But these will remain in your name. Leave here knowing that you're covered, all right?"

I was overwhelmed by his generosity. I nodded, letting out a long breath that I hadn't even realized I'd been holding. "I don't even know how to begin to thank you."

"You don't need to thank me. I'm happy for you, man. I know how it is to feel that way about someone and not know how the fuck it's going to work out. But there's always a fucking way. And if it's the real deal, you'll move fucking mountains to make it happen. Or you'll ski down them in your underwear if that's what it takes." He laughed, and I filled Brax in on the crazy-ass stunt he'd pulled to win Dylan back. The dude was a Navy SEAL for a decade, so skiing down Honey Mountain in his underwear in frigid temperatures was just another day at the office for Wolf.

The door flew open, and in walked Dylan, with both of my sisters right behind her. Georgia and Brinkley were holding bags with sandwiches in them, and Dylan had a tray of drinks she was balancing.

We all pushed to our feet to help them, taking the bags and the drinks and setting them on Wolf's desk.

"What are you two doing here?" I asked, as I raised a brow at Dylan, knowing she'd called them to tell them what was going on.

"It's about damn time you admitted how you felt. And we were hungry, so here we are," Georgia said, making her rounds and hugging everyone.

"You need to talk to Travis before you leave for Chicago. You should go there with a clear conscience." Brinkley slapped me on the chest and looked up at me.

I nodded. "I will. I needed to get this all figured out so I could let him know the plan. And then book a flight to Chicago."

"That's already done. Georgie and I booked you on a flight out tomorrow morning. We used Finn's points." She chuckled. "I emailed you the confirmation. So, you best get your ass back to Cottonwood Cove and talk to your best friend and make things right."

"Can we please eat first? I'm starving," Brax groaned. "And we'll need to fuel up before you tell Travis that you're in love with his sister. We may even need the Navy SEAL for backup."

The girls chuckled, but Wolf raised a brow. "Do you want me there?"

I shook my head. "No. But thank you. I've got this. Travis and I have gone to blows before, and I probably have this one coming for not telling him sooner. I'll take it on the chin if that's what he needs to do."

Brax shivered dramatically. "I'm a lover, not a fighter. That shit terrifies me."

"Hugh's going to be just fine." Dylan smiled up at me. "I'm happy for you. You deserve this. Now let's take the food down to the conference room so you can get back home and deal with the broody brother and then go get your girl."

And that was exactly what I planned to do.

We all ate together, and then Brax and I were back on the road, pulling into Cottonwood Cove around dinner time. It had been a long day, but I finally felt like I was doing what I was supposed to be doing.

I hadn't felt that way in a long time.

Because Lila James had been the missing piece I hadn't even realized I was looking for.

"Are we really doing this?" Brax asked.

"You don't have to come with me. I'm ready to tell him, and I don't mind doing it on my own."

"Hell, no. I may not be a good backup, because you know that I bruise like a peach. But I'll make sure he doesn't kill you," he said with a chuckle.

I wasn't worried about Travis hurting me. Hell, I was bigger than him. I just wanted him to know that I loved her, and I hoped that he would believe me. He was my best friend, and he was important to me. But I wasn't walking away from Lila regardless of what Travis had to say about it. He could punch me as many times as he wanted to, and it wasn't going to change the outcome of this. I'd fucked up by lying to him, and I'd own that. But I wouldn't apologize for loving his sister.

We pulled in front of his house and got out of the truck.

"Are you nervous?" Brax whispered as we walked up the sidewalk leading to his front door.

I chuckled. "Not even a little bit."

"Thank God that one of us is okay. I feel like I'm going to shit my pants."

"Relax. It's fine." I knocked on the door, and Travis pulled it open right away.

"Hey. Did you get my text that Shay is at her sister's for dinner? I wanted to see if you wanted to meet at Reynolds' for a beer."

I hadn't seen the text. "Nah, we've been driving. Just came from the city. But I need to talk to you."

His brows cinched together. "Something happen with my dad?"

"Nope. I checked on him yesterday, and he's doing really well." I walked inside after he took a few steps back, inviting us in.

"What's wrong with him?" Travis flicked his thumb over his shoulder at Brax, who was unusually quiet.

"He's nervous," I said, when we reached the kitchen. "He thinks there's going to be a fight, and you know he's a delicate flower."

He and I both chuckled, and Brax crossed his arms over his chest and rolled his eyes.

"Why would there be a fight?" Travis walked to the fridge and pulled out three beer bottles.

"Oh, I don't think glass bottles are a good idea." Brax set his on the counter after Travis handed them to us.

I set mine down, as well, leaning over the kitchen island, across from Travis. "I'm in love with Lila. I should have told you sooner, but I didn't know it was going to turn into something serious."

He set his bottle down on the counter, his face turning bright red with each passing second as he processed my words. "What the fuck did you just say to me?"

"You heard me. And you getting mad isn't going to change anything."

"Look at me, Hugh," he said, his voice eerily calm. "Did you fuck my sister?"

"I'm not going to answer that because it's none of your fucking business. I love her, and that's what matters."

"Oh, yeah? So, you were just fucking her all this time and keeping it from me. And now it's turned into something serious? So, you were willing to cross that line when you didn't know?" he shouted, as he came around the corner and stopped right in front of me.

"If that's how you want to look at it, that's your choice. I'm in fucking love with your sister. Don't belittle it," I said, my voice coming out louder and harsher than I meant it to.

His fist came at me, just as I'd expected. A shot to the cheek, which nearly knocked me on my ass, but I didn't go down. And I didn't put my arms up because I'd let him take as many shots as he needed to take before we could move on. I felt Brax move closer, but my gaze stayed locked on Travis.

He didn't come at me again; he just stared for a long while before he spoke. "So, you love her?"

"I do."

"Does she know that?" he asked, reaching for his beer and popping off the lid before he took a long pull.

"Probably not. But I'm going there tomorrow to tell her."

Travis set his bottle back down, and Brax groaned as if he were preparing for the worst.

"And what? Drag her back here?"

"You know what, Travis. That's also none of your fucking business." I squared my shoulders and stepped forward, crowding him. I was done with him acting like he knew what was best for her. "That decision is up to her. I have someone willing to take over all three restaurants here. So, if your sister wants to stay in Chicago, that's where you'll find me. And if she wants to come home, that's also where you will find me. She's a grown-ass woman with a mind of her own. And you're a grown-ass man with a wife and kid on the way. Stay in your own fucking lane, brother."

I prepared for the hit. He'd never been one who could

handle hearing things that he didn't like. But I wasn't afraid of Travis. I respected how much he loved his sister, but his days of thinking he had a say over her life were over.

The hit never came. Instead, he reached for his beer bottle again and took another sip. "All right, then. It's serious enough that you're willing to walk away from everything here? Your family? Your business? Your parents' businesses?"

"Without a fucking doubt. I don't give a fuck where I am as long as I'm with Lila." Now it was my turn to reach for my bottle and pop off the cap and take a long pull.

"Holy shit. Never thought I'd see the day." Travis held up his bottle to clink it against mine.

"Wait," Brax whispered. "Are we good? Can I get my bottle, too, or might this turn ugly again?"

Travis barked out a laugh. "Nah. Shay's been all over my ass that I'm too overbearing with Lila and said she thought my sister wasn't excited about leaving at all. But I'd been too blind to see past what I thought was right for her. And on that last night with Lila, I could tell she was upset about leaving. And clearly, I ruined your fucking lovefest, or whatever the fuck you two have going on, which I prefer not knowing. I'm sorry, man. You're the best dude I know, and if you feel that strongly about her, I couldn't ask for better for my sister."

"Trying not to be offended over here," Brax said, his voice higher than normal, and I finally let out a laugh.

I turned my attention back to Travis. "I don't know what's going to happen, but I know that I'm not leaving as long as she wants me by her side."

We spent the next hour with Brax and Travis telling me how to handle things once I landed in Chicago. But I didn't need help with any of it. I was going right to her, face-to-face, and I'd tell her that I fucking loved her.

Something I should have said a long time ago.

I was exhausted by the time I got home. I'd gone over to

see my parents and tell them my plans, and, of course, they were both completely supportive because that's who they are.

They were fine with whatever I decided to do with the restaurants, and that took a lot of pressure off my shoulders.

I dropped down on my bed after taking a shower and saw a text from Lila, which had me sitting forward. It was two hours later in Chicago, so it was close to midnight there.

SNOW

I miss you, Bear.

That was all it said—yet it said so much more. She was sad, just like I was. But I'd be there tomorrow, and I'd tell her everything. Face-to-face. I wasn't going to pledge my love over a text or a phone call.

Miss you more.

I missed her in a way I'd never known possible. My body physically ached. She was the first thing I thought of when I woke up in the morning. The first thing I thought of when I stepped outside and saw the sun just coming up. The last thing I thought of before I went to sleep each night.

And I couldn't get to her soon enough.

twenty-eight

. . .

Lila

I'D BEEN HERE for a week, and I'd worked more hours than any human should ever have to work in a twenty-four day. And I didn't see that lightening up any time soon.

The five people that they'd hired to be on my team were all new college grads, as well, and the atmosphere reminded me of race days.

Like everyone was willing to do whatever it took for the win.

The way I'd left things with Hugh had haunted me, and then we'd both just sort of gone quiet after I left because we didn't really know what to do.

At least I didn't.

And to say I was miserable would be a massive understatement.

My body physically ached. I couldn't sleep. Couldn't eat.

So, I focused on work.

The corporate housing they'd given me was swanky and really nice, but it just felt cold and lonely to me. The furniture was velvet and way too fancy to curl up on. I slept in one of Hugh's T-shirts that I'd snagged when I'd packed up that last night before I left, and it was the only thing that comforted me now.

I'd never felt so alone in my life.

Sure, I had friends from college here, but everyone who lived in the city was working long hours, or they'd moved to the suburbs, which wasn't an easy trek, especially when you were working fourteen-hour days. Luckily, my apartment was close enough that I didn't need to even use public transportation because it was a short walk to and from work.

I'd left my car in Cottonwood Cove, dropping it off with Brax again, hoping he could sell it for me. I'd asked him to give the money to Hugh so I could pay him back for helping my father.

Thoughts of Hugh had my heart aching so severely that a permanent lump had lodged in my throat. And one thing that I'd learned from being home this past summer and spending all that time with Hugh, crossing things off my list that were important to me, is that life is what you make it. And you could spend your entire time on this earth working, if that was what was important to you. And for a long time, that had been important to me. But I'd realized that I actually liked living an awful lot. I'd spent the last few months loving and laughing and living every single day. And staring at a computer screen with rows of numbers was not living to me anymore.

I'd changed.

Hugh had brought a part of me to life without even knowing it.

Being at the restaurant and working on his books was completely different than being here and feeling more like a robot than a human.

I didn't know if Hugh felt the same way about me, but I thought he did.

But regardless of what he wanted or if there was a future for us, my life was not here.

I knocked on Mr. Schneider's office door, and he called out for me to come in.

"Lila, this is a pleasant surprise. You can't already have those reports done for me, can you? Although I guess being a collegiate national champion, anything is possible for you, huh?" He motioned for me to take a seat.

"I don't have those done yet, but Julia is making real progress. That's what I wanted to talk to you about."

His gaze narrowed, and he nodded. "Go ahead."

"I'm so grateful for the opportunity that you've given me. From the internship to the position that you offered me here to head up this new department. But I'm not the right person for the job," I said, feeling a weight lift off my shoulders as the words left my mouth.

"Oh, that's just exhaustion talking. We all go through it when we first start out and put in those grueling hours. You were made for this, Lila. I don't have any doubts that you can do it."

I smiled because he did mean well. "I know that I *can* do it. The problem is that I don't want to. You see, I found out that there is a lot more to life than I'd ever realized. And now that I've had a taste, it just doesn't matter how much money I can make, or what I can accomplish professionally, because it doesn't make me happy. And I've waited a really long time to be happy. So, I hope you won't be upset with me because I truly am grateful for the confidence that you have in me. But those are shoes that I just don't want to fill anymore."

He stared at me for a long while before he spoke, and I held his gaze, making it clear that I was not going to waver.

"I want to be upset, but I'd be lying if I didn't say I was happy for you. The rat race can be exhausting, and I'm probably not one to give advice about a happy life. I've been married three times and hardly have a relationship with any of my kids. So, you know what, Lila James?"

"What?" I asked.

"You follow your gut. Good for you. I think Julia would probably be thrilled to be promoted. Do you think she's up for the task?"

"One hundred percent. She's smart and driven, and she definitely wants it."

He chuckled. "And what about you? What do you want?"

"I want to go home." I shrugged. "I want to swim in the cove and have dinner with my father and get to see my niece or nephew as often as I want—and go convince the man that I love that he loves me, too."

"Well, that sounds a whole lot more fun than looking at a computer screen all day." He chuckled. "I am sorry that it didn't work out, but I'm glad that you know what you want."

He could have been angry. They'd invested in me coming on board, but I guess that was just part of the game when it came to corporate America. They'd win some, and they'd lose some, and they accounted for that financially. I thought about offering my two weeks' notice, but I'd only been here for a week, so I certainly wouldn't need to train anybody because I hadn't even figured out the position yet. I'd already spoken to Julia, and I knew she was ready to step up to the challenge.

"Thank you. I appreciate you being so supportive."

"Of course. I hope you find what you're looking for."

We both moved to our feet, and I shook his hand. "That means the world

to me. And I definitely will. I'll have my things out of the apartment in a few days."

"Take your time. Though I'm guessing you're in a hurry to get home."

"Something like that," I said, holding up my hand and waving at him before stepping out of his office.

When I turned down the long hallway toward the reception area, I heard my name being mentioned.

"You're here for Lila James?" Vi purred, and her voice sounded unusually flirty, and she giggled after she said it.

I guessed someone good-looking was most likely dropping off another pile of work for me. One that I wouldn't be taking with me on my way out the door.

I couldn't wipe the smile off my face when I came around the final corner.

My mouth fell open as I saw Hugh Reynolds standing there in all his glory. Tall and lean, a navy blue baseball cap on his head, a pair of dark jeans, and a white buttoned up that was even more wrinkled than usual.

"Hi," I said, the word coming out all breathy as I came to a stop a few feet from him.

My legs weren't moving, as I was literally stunned that he was standing here.

"Hey, Snow." He closed the distance between us as his tongue swiped out to wet his plump lips. I didn't miss the little gasp that escaped Vi as she watched him stride toward me.

"What are you doing here?" I whispered.

"You forgot this." He held out my Snow Day notebook, and I chuckled as I took it.

"Wow. You came all the way here to give me the notebook?" My voice was all tease because the way he was grinning at me made it clear that wasn't the reason he was here.

"Well, you left the last thing on the list unchecked. What kind of guy would I be if I didn't help you rectify that quickly?"

"You did help check quite a few of those off the list, didn't you?" I moved forward, my chest bumping into his as I tipped my head back to look at him. His hand looped around my waist, tugging me forward, and he turned his cap around and winked at me.

"I sure did. And it inspired me to make my own list. I did it on the plane ride here."

"Is that so?" I asked, my breaths coming hard and fast. I didn't even care that we were doing this in the middle of the reception area with Vi watching us like she was watching a movie.

He reached into his back pocket and pulled out a piece of paper.

"I only have one thing on the list, because only one thing matters."

I glanced down at the paper.

#1. *Go get your girl.*

I didn't need to speak another word. My arms reached up for him, and he lifted me off the floor, my legs coming around his waist. I buried my face in the crook of his neck, breathing him in.

He started walking and pushed through the doors until we were out of the waiting area near the elevators.

"I don't want to get you in trouble at work," he said against my ear. "But I needed to say something to you, and it couldn't wait another minute."

He set me down on the floor, and I swiped at the tears rolling down my face. I gasped as I took him in and noticed the bruise on his cheek.

"What happened?" I reached up and feathered my fingers across the discolored bump that was there.

"Your brother knows. He actually took it much better than I thought he would."

"My brother knows what?" I asked, shaking my head.

"That I'm in love with you. That I'm moving to Chicago if that's where you want to give this a try. Because I'm all-in, Snow. And I'll follow you wherever you want to go."

I couldn't speak. I'd waited so long to hear him say those words to me. I shook my head, trying to push down the lump lodged in my throat, robbing me of my words in this moment.

"Take your time," he said, smiling as his large hand rested on the side of my neck while his thumb stroked my cheek.

"I love you," I said, as I finally calmed my breathing and pulled myself together.

"I love you, too."

"You told Travis, and he hit you?"

"Yep. I thought he'd hit me a couple times, but he just needed to react, and I don't know, he just looked at me, and I think he saw it there."

"What did he see, Bear?"

"A man who's in love with his sister. A man who's losing his mind because the love of his life is gone, and he didn't get to tell her how he felt."

"I hated the way we left things, and then I didn't know what to do when I got here. I wasn't sure how you felt, and I've just been so miserable," I said, the last word breaking on a sob.

He wrapped his arms around me and pulled me close. "I'm sorry I didn't do something sooner. I knew how I felt for a long time, and I should have manned up. I was just so afraid of holding you back, and I didn't know how to make it work with me there and you here. But that's not an issue anymore. I realized that being with you is more important than anything else."

I pulled back and looked up at him. "What does that mean?"

"It means that I found a way to come here if you want me to."

"What about the restaurants? And your family? Your life is in Cottonwood Cove."

"My life doesn't work without you." His forehead came down to touch mine. "That's the truth. I go where you go."

I chuckled. "Well, I've got good news for you."

"I don't know, Snow. I think my news is going to be hard to beat."

"I think you're right." I pulled back, taking both of his hands in mine. "I just quit my job. I kind of hate it here. I want to go home. With you. I want to work at the restaurant every day and skinny dip in the cove every night."

"Damn. Your news just trumped mine." He waggled his brows. "But you don't have to decide anything today. How about we go back to your place and skinny dip in the tub? Or we can just get naked and get in bed."

"Now you're speaking my language," I said, as I bumped my shoulder against his side and tugged him over to the elevators and pressed the button to go down.

When the doors opened and we stepped onto the elevator, he rushed me, my back pressing into the corner, his chest pressed against mine. "I fucking missed you."

"I missed you, too. I'm so glad you're here."

The doors opened, and he led me outside. "Where do you live?"

"About a block down that way." I pointed to the right, and he moved so fast he caught me off guard. He scooped me up, and once again, my legs wrapped around his waist, and my head fell back in laughter as he started to jog in that direction.

"I need to get you there now," he said, as he continued to run down the street with people staring at us as we moved by them. And I didn't care one bit.

That was the thing about Hugh. He taught me how to have fun and how to do the things that make you happy.

And he made me happy.

"You do know that I'm a fairly fast runner, right?" I said over my laughter as we approached my building. "We're here."

"Are you really going to pull out the national title when I just sprinted all the way here with you in my arms?" he teased, as he set me down on the ground.

"I think you could give me a run for my money."

Another elevator ride up to my apartment before we finally pushed inside the door.

We were alone for the first time.

Hugh whistled. "Fancy. You sure you want to leave all this behind?"

"The only appealing thing to me in this apartment is the man standing in front of me with his cap on backward and that bathtub in the bathroom."

"Ahhhh… I can work with that," he said, as he stalked toward me and then threw me over his shoulder and smacked my ass. "Let me see the place."

"I could give you a tour if you'd put me down," I said, over a fit of laughter.

"I like looking around and having your sweet little ass right next to my face." His words were all tease, but I squeezed my thighs together because I knew that we would be naked within seconds.

He tossed me onto the bed, and I bounced, unable to stop smiling. "Did you miss my sweet little ass?"

"Damn straight, Snow. I missed everything about you. Your lips." He hovered over me, and his mouth covered mine. My lips parted, and his tongue slipped inside before he pulled away as I squirmed beneath him. "I missed your face. And your beautiful fucking body. And don't even get me started about your tits."

His hand slipped beneath my blouse and moved up my side until he cupped my breast, tweaking my nipple and making me gasp.

"Not my cooking, huh?" My breaths were coming hard and fast as he moved to my other breast.

"Oh, yeah. The pancakes and the bacon. I definitely missed those, too. But you know what else I missed?"

"What?" I whispered.

"The sound of you coming on my lips when I bury my face between your legs and lick you until you can't take any more."

"I missed that, too," I said, smiling up at him as he tugged my pencil skirt up, letting the fabric gather around my waist.

"Well, we can't have that, can we?"

And just like that, he tugged me down to the edge of the bed, dropped to his knees, and showed me exactly what I'd been missing.

twenty-nine

. . .

Hugh

WE'D SPENT a few days in Chicago figuring out what we wanted to do, and Lila felt strongly about heading back to Cottonwood Cove. She'd already started talking about us expanding the restaurant together, and it was the most excited that I'd been since I'd started this venture. Because doing it with her was a lot more fun than doing it on my own. And Wolf had been pleased that he wouldn't need to be in the restaurant business just yet, but he had reminded me of his offer to partner up if we did decide to open in the city.

We'd been home for two weeks, and Lila had officially moved in with me. She'd also started helping coach the cross-country team over at the high school a few days a week, and I could tell that it was something she felt really good about.

No one seemed surprised at all that we were together, and Travis had completely embraced the fact that I was dating his sister now. We'd even double-dated twice since we'd been back home.

Lila had spent some time with her brother and her father when we returned, making it known that she wasn't happy in Chicago, because if she were, we would both still be there.

No question about it.

She wanted to come back to Cottonwood Cove because she felt like it was home. She wanted to be near her father and her brother and Shay and to see the new baby often once he or she was born. Her friends, my family, all the people that loved her here were all the things that made this home.

But it was important they knew that she didn't need to come home or to give up her career for me. Because I would follow this girl anywhere she wanted to go.

Lila had been surprised to see her car in the driveway when we'd returned. I'd informed her that I wasn't going to buy the same damn car twice, and I demanded that Brax take it off the lot and bring it to my house. She'd laughed her ass off and thanked me by dropping to her knees as soon as we'd walked through the door.

Now that we'd admitted how we felt, and everything was out in the open, we couldn't seem to keep our hands to ourselves. I'd never been a guy who enjoyed PDA of any kind, but with Lila, I didn't fucking care. If she was in the room, my hands were on her.

I was down in my office, and Lila was upstairs doing some inventory while we got ready to close up. I'd come down here to turn off my computer before we went home for the day. My phone buzzed on my desk, and I leaned back in my chair when I saw it was a text from Cage in our sibling group chat.

CAGE

Mrs. Remington just brought her pug, Mr. Wigglestein, into the office and asked me if I knew of any single female pugs that were looking for love. Apparently, she wants to breed him. Does she think I'm running a fucking dating app for dogs?

It's not a bad idea. There's someone out there for everyone, brother. <heart eyes emoji>

Laura Pavlov

FINN

Yep. If Hugh Reynolds can settle down, I don't see why the pug can't.

BRINKLEY

I love sappy Hugh so much.

GEORGIA

I love Hughey being all gooey for his girl. So, while you're feeling so happy... if she breeds Mr. Wigglestein, can I get a baby Wigglestein and have it live with me in the casita?

CAGE

First off, it pisses me off when people use salutations on animals. He's not a congressman. He's a fucking dog, who happens to have major breathing problems, and she should focus on keeping him alive, not procreating. Secondly, you don't have a job yet, but you're already adopting an animal? Do you know how much work they are, Georgie?

GEORGIA

Oh, what was that? I fell asleep for a minute. It must have been the fact that you're giving me that same old broken-record speech that I've heard on repeat since I started college. <sleeping emoji>

As long as you take care of it, and it doesn't shit in my house, I'd be fine with it.

FINN

Cage, do you remember when Hugh pooped in the house when he was around five years old because he wanted to measure it, so he took a big shit behind Mom's fake Ficus tree?

CAGE

I do. Because he used my blue school ruler to measure his giant crap and got his shit all over it.

HUGH

Hey, big hands. Big feet... Big shit. That thing was a good eight inches. Not bad for a five-year-old.

BRINKLEY

Ewwww... No more shit talk. I'm currently stalking a football player who refuses to give me an exclusive interview. Remind me why I chose sports journalism. I could just be reporting on the local news, and life would be much easier.

GEORGIA

Because you had a crush on that football player, Johnny Walker, in high school.

Johnnie Walker is a brand of scotch. She had a crush on Willie Nelson.

FINN

Willie Nelson is a country singer. It was Johnny Nelson. Have you all been dipping in the sauce already?

BRINKLEY

Damn that Johnny Nelson for making me think this would be easy. That kid was putty in my hands.

GEORGIA

Well, Dad always says, nothing worth fighting for ever comes easy.

FINN

If I had a nickel for every time that I haven't gotten a part I auditioned for and Dad has said that...

> You'd have a fucking quarter? You've gotten almost everything you've ever auditioned for.

FINN

Look at you, pumping me up. I have to agree with the girls. I love soft Hugh.

> Nothing soft about me, fucker.

FINN

There he is. But I do like seeing you happy, brother.

CAGE

You going to just keep playing house, or are you going to put a ring on it?

> Did you seriously just quote Beyonce?

A dozen Beyonce memes came flying through our text chain, and I laughed my ass off.

"What's so funny down here?" Lila asked, as she appeared in the doorway.

I knew that I'd marry her, sooner rather than later.

But we weren't in a rush.

We were enjoying the moment.

"You know, the usual. Cage just quoted Beyonce." I pushed to my feet. "Is everyone gone?"

"Yep. Kline and Danielle just left. We just need to turn off the lights in the kitchen, and everything else is done."

"I love when you talk shop to me, Snow," I said, following

her up the stairs and watching her cute ass sway in the little skirt she was wearing.

"Well, your dad asked me to grab a bottle of wine he wanted to try, so let's just get that first before we head out. We can drop it by tomorrow on our way to work."

I followed her into the bar, and she reached up to get the bottle she wanted. I came up behind her and grabbed it easily, my chest to her back. I set the bottle down on the counter, and my hands moved to her thighs before sliding beneath her skirt. She sucked in a breath, and I fucking loved how responsive she was every single time I touched her.

My dick strained against my jeans, and my lips found her neck. "I think we should add fucking in the bar to the list."

"I'd be good with that. I already locked up," she whispered. My fingers moved beneath the lace of her panties to find her soaked.

"Always so wet and ready for me." I nibbled on her earlobe as I slipped a finger inside.

"Bear," she said, as I moved my finger in and out, teasing her the way I knew she liked to be teased.

"You like that, baby?" I asked, moving my lips to the other side of her neck.

I would never get enough of this woman.

"Yes," she said, letting her head fall back on my collarbone.

I pulled my hand away just long enough to unbutton my jeans and lower my zipper, freeing my throbbing cock. I lifted her skirt and slid her lace panties over.

She turned her head to the side, offering me her sweet mouth, just as I plunged into her. I kissed her as I moved inside her, our breaths the only audible sound in the room, my tongue and my dick moving at the same speed. Lila fell forward, and my hand wrapped around her, finding her sweet spot, knowing just what she needed.

"I fucking love you, Snow."

"I love you." She gasped as I moved faster, and she met me thrust for thrust.

"Come for me," I demanded.

She cried out my name as she went over the edge. And I was right there with her. I pumped into her one more time as she tightened around me, and I followed her into oblivion.

A guttural sound escaped my throat, and lights shot behind my eyelids as I continued riding out my pleasure while circling her clit as she bucked against me.

Nothing had ever felt as good as this woman.

Not even close.

I wrapped my arms around her as we both caught our breath.

"How does it get better every time?" she whispered.

"Because we were made for one another."

Ain't that the fucking truth.

———

Thanksgiving was here, and my mother lived for the holidays. My siblings were all in town, and the wine was flowing, the house smelled like turkey, and I had my girl by my side, which was all that mattered.

Travis and Shay were here, and she was ready to pop any day now. Tate had been sober for over four months and had started dating Camille McCallister, Del's mom, which Lila and Del were thrilled about. So that meant Del, her boyfriend, Quincy, and her sister, Jory, were all here, as well. My mom's favorite saying was *the more the merrier*, so she loved that our group was growing.

"Yeah, I'm not feeling this," Finn said, as he huddled in the corner with me and Cage, referring to his date, Cami, who'd gone straight to the tequila when she got here and was already three sheets to the wind and making quite a scene.

"Why do you bring women you barely know to family

events?" Cage asked, raising a brow and making it clear he didn't approve.

"I hooked up with her a few days ago, and she said she didn't have anywhere to go for Thanksgiving while we were in the middle of sex. What was I supposed to say?"

"How about, it's weird to talk about the holidays while I'm inside you? That would be a good fucking start." Our oldest brother did not hide his irritation.

"Why are you annoyed? She's *my* fucking date," Finn whisper-hissed.

"Because she belched in my face, and she smelled like tuna and soy sauce and tequila. Do you know what that does to a man's appetite? Yeah. It's not a good combo."

"You narcissistic bastard. She just shoved her tongue down my throat. I'm the victim." Finn threw his hands in the air, and I couldn't help but laugh.

I looked up to see Lila watching us with a big smile on her face. My gaze locked with hers, and she bit down on her bottom lip, and I swear it took everything in me not to haul her ass into the bathroom and take her right now.

I loved this woman like crazy, and I'd never get enough of her.

"Oh, for fuck's sake. Now we have this weepy sap to deal with every time we're in a stressful situation." Cage flicked me in the shoulder hard. "Hello? We're dealing with a crisis, and you're looking like a lovesick motherfucker."

"He's got a date who has bad breath. That's your crisis?" I raised a brow.

"Well, Dad's over there completely clueless that she's wasted, and he's showing her his record collection. She looks like she's going to topple over. *Be better, Finn*." Cage crossed his arms over his chest, and Finn barked out a laugh.

"Bite me, you arrogant prick," Finn hissed.

"You're an actor. Can't you do better than that?" Cage taunted him, and I turned to see Travis walk over.

He clapped me on the shoulder. "Well, remind me to keep my mouth shut until Shay gives birth."

"What happened?" I asked, and I looked up to see Lila with her hand on Shay's belly, smiling like something magical was happening.

"Hmmm... let's see. Shay said she was starving, so I made myself a plate of appetizers, which, by the way, your mother makes the best deviled eggs. Anyway, I made her a plate, too, because she says I'm not thoughtful. But when I hand her the plate, she glares at me and says I should know that she doesn't eat deviled eggs. How the fuck would I know that when she's never told me?"

Everyone laughed, and I shook my head. "She's really pregnant, dude. It'll pass. Did you get her something else?"

"Funny you should ask. I went back and got her some chips and dip." He paused and glanced at each one of us. "She proceeds to tell me that she hasn't been able to eat sour cream dip since her second trimester, and she's appalled that I don't know that. I can't fucking win."

"What's so funny over here?" Brinkley asked, as she sidled up beside me and leaned in where we were huddled together.

"Finn's date is a train wreck, and Travis has pissed off his pregnant wife." Cage shrugged.

"Well, here's some scoop for you," Brinkley whispered. "Georgie said she broke things off with that jerk of a boyfriend."

"Dikson?" Finn asked.

"Diktok," I corrected.

"It's Dikota, you wienershnitzels," she said, shaking her head. "He's old news. Done. Donezo."

"Yeah, we get it. They're done. Thank freaking God she kicked his ass to the curb. That guy was the worst. Well, Karen was the worst. Dikmunch was a close second." Cage smirked.

"You need a woman. You're far too cynical for a man your age." Brinkley raised a brow at our oldest brother, and I couldn't help but laugh.

"I do just fine. Don't you worry about me."

"Uh, Finn. Your date just vomited on Dad," I said, as Lila and Del ran toward him with towels.

"You sure can pick 'em, Finny." Brinkley laughed.

"Yeah. I'll be taking her home now."

Everyone was hurrying around my father, who, of course, was telling Cami that it was fine and not to worry because she was in complete hysterics now.

Cage got called away by Gracie, and Travis moved to Shay's side. She smiled up at him, and he shot me a crazy look over his shoulder, which meant that he had no idea why she was smiling at him. Brinkley slapped me on the shoulder and said she was going to get another cocktail.

My mother moved beside me. "Hey. Another eventful night, huh?"

"Something like that. You did a good job, Mama. It was perfect."

"Perfect is overrated. It was good food and a crazy group, with a side of vomit. Sounds like a good Thanksgiving to me." She chuckled. "But do you know what has made this holiday extra special?"

"What?" I asked, placing an arm around her shoulder.

She glanced over her shoulder to make sure no one was around. "You taking me with you yesterday to pick out the ring… It meant the world to me to get to be part of that with you. To see the thought that you put behind it, and the fact that you know you've found the person you want to spend the rest of your life with."

"There's no one else I would have wanted beside me when I chose it."

"You did really well, sweetie. And don't even get me

started about the way you look at one another; it's really something."

Normally, I would roll my eyes at a comment like that, but not this time.

Because she was right.

I guess our parents knew better than we did because they said we'd know when it was right, and they weren't fucking kidding around.

Because everything about Lila James was right.

And I'd wanted my mom with me when I picked out the ring that I would give her when I asked her to marry me.

"Thank you. I think she's going to love it."

She kissed my cheek, and my father called out to her to ask if we had any ginger ale. "Time to go put out Finn's latest fire."

I chuckled as she walked toward the kitchen, and Lila came over to me and stepped right into my arms, and I wrapped her up.

"Never a dull moment," I said, as I kissed the top of her head.

"That's what I love most about this." She tipped her head back to look up at me. "Look around, Bear. My dad's here, and he's actually dating for the first time in two decades. My brother and Shay are having a baby. Cage is teaching Gracie how to play Go Fish over there. Brinkley is giving Georgie dating advice, which is basically that all men suck, and she should stay away. Finn is cleaning up vomit because he didn't know his date was a bit of a lush." Her head fell back in laughter.

"Is there a point to this madness?"

"Everyone is living, and there's nothing better than that." She shrugged.

"And what about us?"

She turned in my arms and faced me. "I'm exactly where I

want to be, with the person I want to be with. I'd say we're living the best way possible."

I leaned down and kissed the tip of her nose. "I couldn't agree more. How about we live even better by sneaking out the back door and heading home, where I can get you naked in front of the fire?"

"I like the sound of that."

"Do you need to go say goodbye to your dad?" I asked.

She glanced over her shoulder and then looked back at me and smiled. "Nope. I think they're all going to be fine. Tonight, I'm only going to worry about you, Hugh Reynolds."

Well, you don't have to tell me twice. I grabbed her and flipped her over my shoulder, settling my hand over her ass as she burst out in a fit of giggles.

"So much for being inconspicuous!" she shouted. "Goodbye. Happy Thanksgiving. We're heading home."

I held one hand over my head and waved, and I heard the room erupt in laughter, but I didn't even turn around and say goodbye.

I ran right out the back door toward my house, with my hand slipped beneath her skirt and her laughter filling the air around me.

She was right—this was the best kind of living.

I wouldn't have it any other way.

epilogue

· · ·

Lila

HUGH and I were hosting a graduation dinner for Georgia, as we'd all been in the city for her ceremony this morning. She'd driven back to Cottonwood Cove with us because her car was in the shop, and we'd spent the rest of the day setting up for her party.

I hurried to our room to change into my dark skinny jeans, cream sweater, and tall brown boots that came past my knee. Georgia and I had gone shopping together in the city a few weeks ago, and I'd fallen in love with these boots. It was cold now as we were in mid-December, and we'd just gotten our first snow fall. There wasn't a lot on the ground, but it had definitely stuck, and with the floor-to-ceiling windows in the house, it looked like a winter wonderland outside. I had the fireplaces going in the family room and the living room, and we'd put up our Christmas tree the day after Thanksgiving. The house was festive, and I had candles burning, so the whole place smelled like pine.

Hugh had run to Reynolds' with his brothers to pick up the food, and I wasn't sure what was taking so long, but when those three got together, you never knew. Brinkley had just gotten here, and she was filling me in on this football player who was refusing to meet with her.

"Some of these guys are just so full of themselves," she said, reaching for her wine glass. "And it's so male dominated with reporters that you have to be pushy."

"Well, we know you're good at that." Georgia laughed. "You will not be pushed around by a bunch of cocky dudes."

I chuckled, and Brinkley nodded, turning her attention to her younger sister. "Damn straight. So, tell us about this interview you have next week."

"It's sort of embarrassing, considering I just graduated from college, but the art gallery pay is just so low that I couldn't afford to work there and live in the city. So, the school set me up with an interview with that publishing company, Lancaster Press. They moved here from the city not that long ago."

"Yes. Lots of companies are leaving the hustle and bustle of the city and moving their hubs to more residential areas. The cost of rent is much lower, and it helps the economy for these smaller towns because it offers lots of new jobs to the residents. The Lancasters bought the whole building downtown, so they have a ton of space, and I heard that some people still commute from the city, but they hired a lot of people that live here, as well," I said. I was obviously intrigued as I studied finance and watched the market closely. With Hugh wanting to open a new place in the city, there was a lot to consider financially.

"Oh, yeah. I heard the dude that runs it, Maddox Lancaster, is in his late-twenties and is a broody, hot playboy." Brinkley waggled her brows.

"How do you possibly know this?" Georgia asked.

"I'm a reporter. It's my job to know things. And I'd hear about him when he lived in the city. Super rich family and drop-dead gorgeous, so everybody wanted to get their claws in the guy. The Lancasters are like the first family of San Francisco. But he's always photographed with different socialites at events, and I've yet to see him in a relationship. But his private life has been kept very… private."

"Well, it is called a private life for a reason." I chuckled. "And my brother said he recently bought that big spec house that he built last year. That place is massive."

"Great. A rich, cocky playboy. This ought to be lots of fun." Georgia rolled her eyes.

"So, what does the job entail?" I asked.

"Apparently, the guy needs a full-time administrative assistant because he's so important." Georgia reached for her wine glass. "And I need a job because I'm pretty broke. I don't want to be shacking up with you and Hugh forever. You need your privacy."

Georgia was moving into the casita.

"Don't be silly. We're both looking forward to having you here."

"I just hope I get this job because everything else pays pretty crappy, and I don't need a lecture from Cage. He's trying to get me to come work at the front desk at his office. I do not need to be working for my brother."

"You're going to get the job. You just graduated from college; you're overqualified. And you'd be the perfect assistant," Brinkley said.

"You think so?"

"Yes," we said at the exact same time and laughed.

"Your calendar is color coordinated," I reminded her. "You're always bright and sunny, which makes for a perfect assistant, and you're upbeat and organized."

"You'll get this gig because you're brilliant and smart and talented. He should be so lucky," Brinkley said.

The door flew open, and just like that, everyone started pouring in all at once. I hurried to help Hugh get the food out on the kitchen island, and we all ate and laughed and talked. Gracie was trying to convince Hugh to get a puppy, and then she made her way over to me, knowing that I'd be the weaker link. I picked her up and walked over to my boyfriend, and we both started in on him.

"Why don't you get the dog?" Hugh asked his brother, and he didn't hide his annoyance. Saying no to Gracie was not easy for him.

I could see Hugh as a father when I watched him with his niece. I was surprised how easy it was for me to see our future. I'd always been looking toward the future in regard to what I needed to achieve, but not anymore. I'd arrived exactly where I was meant to be, and I knew that this man was my forever. I saw us with a houseful of kids and growing old together.

"Because I'm with animals all day, and Gracie is still too young to take on that much responsibility. But if you are going to let a four-year-old work you, and be a big marshmallow, that's on you."

Hugh barked out a laugh. "Says the man who dressed like a unicorn for Halloween."

Cage reached for his daughter and kissed her on the cheek. "Go ask Grandma if she likes dogs."

He set her down, and she ran off.

"I'm getting her the damn dog for Christmas. I'm just trying to keep it a surprise," Cage hissed, and Hugh wrapped an arm around my shoulder.

"So, who's the marshmallow now?"

"I'm the fucking marshmallow. Is that what you want to hear?" Cage moved toward the island to get a second plate of food.

Hugh leaned down close to my ear. "Hey. I have a little surprise for you after we get everyone out of here." His tongue dipped out to wet his lips, and I could feel my cheeks heat. Something about the way he looked at me got me every damn time.

"What are you up to? You didn't already get a dog, did

you?" I whispered, my hands moving beneath his hoody so I could feel his warm skin as I slid up the sides of his ribs.

"It's not a dog, but I think you'll like it." He nipped at my bottom lip just as Georgie barreled up beside us.

"I hate to ruin this steam fest going on over here in the middle of your kitchen during my graduation party," she said, with a goofy smile on her face. "Can we do cake now, because a bunch of my high school friends want to meet over at Garrity's to celebrate."

I pulled my hands away, already missing the feel of him beneath my fingertips. Brinkley and Alana met me at the island, and they started clearing off the platters as I pulled out the graduation cake. I heard Hugh giving his youngest sister advice about her interview next week, and he told her to just be herself. And then Cage walked up and told her it was all about selling yourself. Finn jumped in and told her that men in powerful positions like confident women, so go in there and act like you own the room. And then all three of them argued about whose advice was better.

Everyone gathered around the island, and we all congratulated Georgia before cutting the cute cake that was the shape of a giant graduation cap.

I'd pushed for Hugh to hire a pastry chef who I'd interviewed for the restaurant, and he'd agreed. People were so crazy about the desserts, we were considering opening a small bakery in the open space next to Reynolds'. I loved brainstorming with him about different ways that we could grow the business, but maybe that was just because I loved being with him so much.

We ate cake, and chatter filled the open space before Georgia said she needed to go. Everyone started the infamous Reynolds goodbye, making their rounds and heading out the door. Alana hugged Hugh a little longer than usual, patting his cheek and beaming up at him. They were such a loving family, and I was thrilled to feel like such a part of it.

Once everyone was gone, Hugh got my coat and helped me slip into it. "I want to show you something."

"Okay," I said, curious what this big surprise was. He zipped up his coat and then put a beanie over my head before grabbing his.

"Come on." He reached for my hand and led me out the door and down the street before cutting up the path to the cove. It was our favorite place to go late at night when the tide was coming in.

"Was your mom okay tonight? She gave you an awfully long hug."

"She's just really happy for us." He tugged me closer, pulling me in front of his big body and wrapping his arms around my shoulders.

"You aren't planning to skinny dip in that freezing water, are you?" I asked, as he held up a branch, and I ducked beneath it.

"Not tonight." He chuckled, and we continued walking toward the cove.

There were lights up ahead, and I gasped when we came around the final turn. There was a big blanket set out, with rose petals on the ground all around it. A metal fire pit sat a few feet away, with a roaring flame that I recognized from our backyard. Dozens of white candles—that were clearly battery operated or the whole place would have gone up in flames— lined a path down to the blanket. Even the surrounding trees were covered in little white twinkle lights. Two vases over- flowing with wildflowers sat on the blanket alongside a bottle of wine and a platter with what looked like cupcakes and chocolate-covered strawberries. My favorite. My hands covered my mouth as it nearly took my breath away. I whipped around when I realized Hugh no longer had his arms around me.

There he was. This big, sexy bear of a man, down on one knee. His hair was tucked beneath his beanie, and the twinkle lights allowed just enough light to let me see the depth of those sage-green eyes of his.

"What are you doing?" I gasped, dropping to my knees in front of him.

"I don't think you're supposed to get down on your knees." He chuckled, and I scooched forward.

"I go where you go," I said, my words breaking on a sob.

He smiled, and my stomach fluttered just like it always did around him. He reached up and swiped the single tear rolling down my cheek. "I love you, Lila Mae James. You make me want to be a better man."

A sob escaped my throat, and he leaned down, pressing his forehead to mine, knowing it would comfort me. "No crying, baby."

"Okay," I whispered, as I tried to muffle the sob that was slowly sneaking out.

"You make me want things I never knew I'd want. And I want them all with you. I knew the minute you came into the bar to talk about your schedule that I was a ruined man." He leaned down and kissed me.

"Will you marry me, Snow?"

"Yes! Yes! Yes!" I shouted, my hands on each side of his handsome face as I tugged him down for a kiss.

"You sure about that? You want to do forever with me?" he asked, when he pulled back.

"I'm positive."

He reached into his coat pocket and pulled out a little black box. When he opened it, I shook my head frantically, pushing back the tears because I'd never seen anything more beautiful.

It was a square diamond on a platinum band, with little diamonds surrounding it.

"Yeah?" He took the ring out of the box and slipped it onto my finger.

"It's absolutely stunning. I love it. I love you." I shook my head with disbelief, still processing that all of this was happening.

Hugh pushed to his feet and helped me to mine, leading me over to the blanket beside the fire.

"Thanks for saying yes," he said, one brow raised as we both dropped down to sit.

"Thanks for asking," I teased. "How did you pull all this off?"

"My brothers and my parents helped set it up while you hung out with Brinks and Georgie. And then Travis and Brax were down here getting the fire going when I texted to say we were on our way. So, it was a group effort." He chuckled. "And I went by to see your dad a few days ago and asked if he'd be okay with it, and he got all weepy and emotional."

"Thank you for including him. I can't believe you did all this." I glanced around, taking in all the little details. The fire danced in front of us, and the water splashed against the shore in the distance. I couldn't think of a more romantic setting. "It's perfectly us."

He leaned close to me, holding up a white-chocolate strawberry, and I wrapped my lips around it, taking a big bite and groaning.

I thought Hugh would grab one for himself, but instead, he tugged me forward, his mouth covering mine.

He kissed me like it was the first time.

He kissed me like it was the last time.

He kissed me like it was forever.

THE END

Thank you so much for reading Into the Tide!

Do you want to see Hugh's sweet gift to Lila to prepare for their wedding day? Click HERE:

INTO THE TIDE BONUS SCENE

. . .

Are you excited for Georgia to interview with Maddox Lancaster? Pre-Order Under the Stars, a Grumpy/Sunshine, Office Romance

HERE: UNDER THE STARS

While you're waiting for for Under the Stars...

Have you met the Thomas girls yet? The cousins of the Reynolds! Always Mine is a small town, friends-to-lovers with a hot hero and a fierce heroine! Head over to Honey Mountain now and start this series FREE in Kindle Unlimited today!

READ Always Mine FREE in Kindle Unlimited

acknowledgments

Greg, Chase & Hannah…thank you for being my inspiration for everything that I do and supporting me every, single day. I am forever thankful for YOU. I love you always!

Willow, I am endlessly thankful for the laughs, the love and your amazing friendship. There is no one I'd rather drink a vampire cocktail in the middle of the day with. Love you so much!

Catherine, thank you for being endlessly supportive and such an amazing friend. Love you always!

Nina, thank you for guiding, listening and supporting me through this journey! Cheers to many more years together! Love you!!

Valentine Grinstead, I absolutely adore you! So thankful for YOU! Love you!

Kim Cermak, Thank you for keeping me on track, helping me with endless questions and always being so kind and amazing. I am FOREVER grateful for you!!

Christine Miller, I can't begin to thank you for all that you do for me EVERY DAY!! I am SO THANKFUL for you!

Sarah Norris, thank you for the gorgeous graphics and always being willing to help even when I remember things at the last minute! LOL! l am incredibly grateful for YOU!

Debra Akins, thank you for the amazing reels and TikToks and for helping to get my books out there! Your support means the world to me!! Thank you so much!!

Kelley Beckham, thank you for setting up all the "lives" with people who have now become forever friends! Thank you so much for all that you do to help me get my books out there! I am truly so grateful!

Doo, Meagan, Annette, Jennifer, Abi, Pathi, Natalie, and Caroline, thank you for being the BEST beta readers EVER! Your feedback means the world to me. I am so thankful for you!!

Madison, Thank you for taking the gorgeous photos for the Cottonwood Cove Series. And this cover with you and Patrick is absolute perfection!! Thank you so much!! Xo

Emily, Thank you for designing these gorgeous special edition covers for this series! I am in love with this cover and I adore working with you! Xo

Sue Grimshaw (Edits by Sue), I would be completely lost without you and I am so grateful to be on this journey with you. Thank you for being the voice I rely on so much! Thank you for moving things around and doing what ever is needed to work. With the timeline. I am FOREVER grateful for YOU!

Ellie (My Brothers Editor), So thankful for your friendship! I am so happy to be on this journey with you! Thank you for always making time for me no matter how challenging the timeline is! Love you!

Julie Deaton, thank you for helping me to put the best books out there possible. I am so grateful for you!

Jamie Ryter, I am so thankful for your feedback! Your comments are endlessly entertaining and they give me life when I need it most!! I am so thankful for you!!

Christine Estevez, thank you for all that you do to support me! It truly means the world to me! Love you!

Crystal Eacker, I am so thankful for you! Thank you for doing whatever is needed! You are such an amazing support and I'm forever grateful!

Jennifer, thank you for always being willing to do whatever is needed with each release. Thank you for making sure we are on track in the group and for being such an amazing cheerleader! Your friendship means the world to me! Love you!

Paige, I am so incredibly thankful for YOU! You are such a bright light and I am so thankful that this book world brought me such a special friend! Thank you for being such an amazing cheerleader and such an amazing friend! Love you!

Rachel Parker and Sarah Sentz, my sweet good luck charms with every release, I am forever grateful for you both!! Xo

Mom, thank you for reading all of my words, and for the feedback and the love! I am so thankful that we share this love of books with one another! Ride or die!! Love you!

Dad, you really are the reason that I keep chasing my dreams!! Thank you for teaching me to never give up. Love you!

Sandy, thank you for reading and supporting me throughout this journey! Love you!

Pathi, I can't put into words how thankful I am for YOU! Thank you for believing in me and encouraging me to chase my dreams!! I love and appreciate you more than I can say!! Thank you for your friendship!! Love you FOREVER!

Natalie (Head in the Clouds, Nose in a Book), Thank you for all the support this year and always! I can't wait to see what the future holds, and I am so grateful to be on this journey with you! Love you!

Sammi, I am so thankful for your support and your friendship!! Love you!

Marni, I love you forever, my little Stormi, and I am endlessly thankful for your friendship!! Xo

To the JKL WILLOWS... I am forever grateful to you for your support and encouragement, my sweet friends!! I can't wait for us to all be together this year!! Love you!

To all the bloggers and bookstagrammers who have posted, shared, and supported me—I can't begin to tell you how much it means to me. I love seeing the graphics that you make and the gorgeous posts that you share. I am forever grateful for your support!

To all the readers who take the time to pick up my books and take a chance on my words...THANK YOU for helping to make my dreams come true!!

keep up on new releases

Linktree Laurapavlovauthor
Newsletter laurapavlov.com

other books by laura

Cottonwood Cove Series

Into the Tide

Under the Stars

On the Shore

Before the Sunset

After the Storm

Honey Mountain Series

Always Mine

Ever Mine

Make You Mine

Simply Mine

Only Mine

The Willow Springs Series

Frayed

Tangled

Charmed

Sealed

Claimed

Montgomery Brothers Series

Legacy

Peacekeeper

Rebel

A Love You More Rock Star Romance

More Jade

More of You

More of Us

The Shine Design Series

Beautifully Damaged

Beautifully Flawed

The G.D. Taylors Series with Willow Aster

Wanted Wed or Alive

The Bold and the Bullheaded

Another Motherfaker

Don't Cry Spilled MILF

Friends with Benefactors

follow me

Website laurapavlov.com
Goodreads @laurapavlov
Instagram @laurapavlovauthor
Facebook @laurapavlovauthor
Pav-Love's Readers @pav-love's readers
Amazon @laurapavlov
BookBub @laurapavlov
TikTok @laurapavlovauthor